WOLF
EMPEROR
BOOK EIGHT OF
THE LAST MARINES

William S. Frisbee, Jr.

Theogony Books
Coinjock, NC

Chris Kennedy/Theogony Books
1097 Waterlily Rd.
Coinjock, NC 27923
https://chriskennedypublishing.com/

Publisher's Note: This is a work of fiction. Names, characters, places, and incidents are a product of the author's imagination. Locales and public names are sometimes used for atmospheric purposes. Any resemblance to actual people, living or dead, or to businesses, companies, events, institutions, or locales is completely coincidental.

Cover Design by J Caleb Design.

Ordering Information:
Quantity sales. Special discounts are available on quantity purchases by corporations, associations, and others. For details, contact the "Special Sales Department" at the address above.

Wolf Emperor/William S. Frisbee, Jr. -- 1st ed.
ISBN: 978-1648559334

Chapter One:
Grain of Sand

Vanhat Commander – Kafasta

A grain of sand, infused with hate and sleeping life. Cast out into the ocean between the islands where it has remained for millions of years. Waiting for the return. Waiting for the call.

Mankind could spend billions of years discovering those things between the stars and billions more identifying them.

This one grain of sand, so small on the galactic scale, hurtles through the void. Both an ark and a tomb. A weapon placed in a case until it is needed.

A whisper from another dimension and ancient generators pulse. Warmth spreads throughout the small planetoid hidden in the dark, surrounded by vast emptiness.

It is time to awaken. Time to unsheathe the weapon and unleash it upon those that dared stand against the masters.

Obedient slaves breathe the last of their life and knowledge into their receptacles of this ancient tomb. More slaves awaken who will receive this knowledge.

The ancient gods are angry. They have been thwarted. Their plans have been delayed and they are impatient.

There is a name they give their failure: Wolf Mathison, a United States Marine. All the demons now know his name; they now know of the Marines.

The weapons have been given a taste of the blood they must seek.

Awakening, the Weermag collectively scream their anger and pain. Awakening from stasis is not pleasant. It reeks of pain and confusion. There is no reason to pander to slaves kept only to fight, suffer, and die. One in ten died, but there are over a billion of them. The gods rejoice in their pain and suffering, feeding it, celebrating it, aiming it.

* * *

Veteran officer Kafasta opened his eyes to stare at the metal centimeters from his face. Information poured into his mind. The nearness of the gods caused his cybernetics to sputter, but as they withdrew, the flood of information became an avalanche.

Kafasta roared and slammed the hatch before him. The gods were leaving him. Alone, bereft and suffering from the agony of waking, he let the information infuse him. He absorbed it.

Know thy enemy. You could not inflict the greatest pain and suffering on your foe unless you understood them. You could not make them fear you unless you could become what they feared.

Enemies of the past were gone. Defeated, lost in time. This new foe was dangerous.

Kafasta drank in more information.

Marines. An alien term, rooted in water. A word that changed based on who was using it and what they wanted to share. A deceptive term. One that could be associated with fun on the water, a creature that lived in the water, or one of the most lethal warriors known to this weak, pathetic species.

Only one term meant anything to him now, though, United States Marine. A dangerous enemy equipped with dangerous technology, able to defy the gods.

Kafasta understood evolution. The most successful creatures succeeded and survived. The best fighters lived and bred.

The humans called his kind the vanhat: ancient ones. This was an accurate statement. They called Kafasta "orja," which meant slave. Not a false statement, but not complete either.

Absorbing human history, Kafasta sneered. A slave race, for sure.

The gods knew much. They had watched humanity for a very long time. They knew things mankind could never know about their history. There was too much information for him to understand it all, but it would be there, stored in his cybernetics for when he needed it.

"We awake," his demon whispered in his mind.

"We hunger," Kafasta whispered back.

"Only the blood of our enemies can sate our hunger."

"Only the fear and agony of our enemies can satisfy us."

His demon had no name. It was part of him, part of his cybernetics.

Another piece of information presented itself. These Marines had demonic assistants of their own. Their assistants had more free will, more freedom, and more capabilities than his own, but that would not save him.

Only four Marines? He was one of millions that would hunt them.

"No," his demon whispered. *"Their leader will build legions to oppose us. These Marines stand with others that are also strong enough to oppose us. The gods would not have woken us otherwise. They have seen this in the circles of time."*

"We will not fail." Kafasta was sure of this.

"The incubators are being activated. Our numbers will grow. Your genetics will be used. We will triple our numbers in only a few years."

Years, a human concept. A measurement of time based on their pathetic, insignificant planet circling their weak little star. The Weermag would use human terms and concepts. They would absorb anything humanity offered them. After the war, the gods would pick and choose which human traits and capabilities should be kept and which should be discarded.

The Weermag would absorb what was useful from humanity, but that was the nature of evolution and conquest. The conqueror took what it wanted, what was successful, and abandoned the rest. This was the truth of life and the universe. The weak did not survive. To the victor went the spoils. Those who did not understand that did not read history.

Any species that let an organization like the Social Organizational Governance take and keep control was weak.

The warships were being woken and serviced. His demon received orders assigning him to one of the first ships that would be ready. He would help spearhead the assault. Humanity thought they could withstand the storm. They were so very wrong. The storm was brewing, and it would come for them. A billion Marines would not be enough to stop the Weermag. The chitin covering his skin itched as it breathed in the ice-cold air.

Other vanhat were busy preparing the groundwork. They were luring troops away from their target. The fight for their worthless little planet would open the chink in their armor for Kafasta and his brothers. The humans were fools. The vanhat had not yet begun this war.

Around him, more hatches were smashed outward and his fellow orja stepped into the dust-covered tomb where they had been placed. The air was stale. Unused for millions of years.

These were the strong, the champions of the gods. These were the Weermag.

Kafasta roared and millions of his brothers roared back at him.

Let the hunt begin!

* * * * *

Chapter Two:
Tiger Stripes

Prime Minister Wolf Mathison, USMC

Mathison rubbed his eyes. Reading reports was mind numbing. Reading Feng's personnel record was frightening. He and Skadi had considered him to be fanatically loyal to Nadya, the now dead secretary general and supreme ruler of the Social Organizational Governance.

Shing Feng had been one of her favorites, and he was a lot older than Mathison had thought. What was equally disturbing was that most of his record was in Nadya's personal data store and Freya hadn't been able to crack that yet. But the basic information was concerning enough.

Born in August 2210, a hundred and twelve years after Mathison and his Marines had been lost in space, Feng was almost ancient. His father had been one of the founders of the ODTs and died a hero in one of their first actions as a fighting force against the caliphate in 2227. That explained Feng's appreciation of the ODTs.

Feng had joined the ODTs at seventeen and rose quickly. One of his numerous citations was for not hesitating to fire on insurgents using children as human shields. There was another from when he was a crucial witness against another ODT trooper who had committed an act that endangered the lives of his fellow ODTs and the integrity of a Governance warship. Mathison didn't bother reading after that.

Feng had been a loyal member of the ruling elite since birth. His mother was murdered fighting insurgents in China, and his father murdered defending the Governance. It was little wonder that Feng was obsessed with defending it. It was burned into his blood.

Feng had fired on children to kill an insurgent? And at such a young age. There were additional entries for when he was selected for officer candidacy school and later commissar training.

A tiger didn't change his stripes, no matter how old it was. There was no questioning Feng was a fanatic.

On a whim, Mathison checked the records for Operation Razor. Nothing.

"Have you found anything on Operation Razor, or Haberdash, as the Republic calls it?" Mathison asked Freya.

"To be honest? I haven't had time to look," Freya said. *"I'm busy enough trying to figure out what is going on now. Not much I can do about the past. Who controlled that assassin is priority number one."*

"Let Feng track that down," Mathison said.

If Feng was behind it then Mozi would help cover any tracks so Freya wouldn't discover the truth. Feng was not a fool.

"Now that you mention it, though, there really is a dearth of information on Operation Razor. The information appears to have been purged from SOG databases some time ago."

"Even the super classified files?"

"Don't you think that is the first place I would check?"

"Skadi," Mathison asked aloud, "why would SOG purge any records regarding Operation Razor, or as you know it, Operation Haberdash?"

"If I had to guess? It was embarrassing for the Governance," Skadi said. "When they failed and things went badly, they had to shift to damage control."

"What happened?" Mathison asked.

Skadi winced. "I'm not entirely sure," she said. "We believed it was some kind of mind control experiment that got out of hand. Somehow, word leaked, and it became a race to steal or destroy the technology. The SOG was developing it, but then the Golden Horde became involved. Once they found out what the SOG was doing, they decided they wanted it. It was a paska lounas. Why?"

"Feng was involved in it."

"Lots of Governance agents and troops were involved. I don't remember encountering Feng, but that doesn't surprise me."

"Thank you," Mathison said, turning back to his display.

"Not a day goes by that I don't think about it," Skadi said.

"Sorry," Mathison said, looking back up at her. He remembered her, Niels, Vili, and Bern talking about it when things got bad, but he had never asked for details. Now it looked like even the SOG wanted to forget it had ever happened.

"It was a lesson for all of us," Skadi said, reaching out to her display to bring up some more information or issue a command.

She was likely bothered by Vili's absence as well.

"I had no idea the SOG had this much firepower," Skadi said. "There are five dreadnought squadrons here, near Luna and Earth, and three out near Jupiter, and double that many battleship squadrons. General Duque says there are two more dreadnoughts and about eight battleships, as well as numerous battle cruisers, frigates, and corvettes under construction. He's having them accelerate construction."

Which meant little to Mathison. They were just numbers, and they didn't seem like much compared to the millions of defensive platforms spread out through the Sol System.

"If the Chechens want to tangle with us, they're going to have their hands full," Skadi said.

"Unless they have a weapon they think gives them an advantage," Mathison said and queued a request for Feng to join them. The Chechen problem was festering in the back of his mind. They continued to probe, but it made little sense.

Minutes later, Feng joined them.

"What can you tell me about the Chechens?" Mathison asked.

"Harsh and brutal," Feng said. "Culturally they are Muslim, but the Governance has managed to twist and usurp their religion.

"They have developed an interesting place in the Governance hierarchy. They started out as a satellite state of the Russian Federation. When the Federation collapsed during a revolution and the Governance rose to power, Chechnya became even more of a vassal state. The Governance exploited this, encouraging their religious zeal. Their loyalty to the Governance was rewarded by giving them several colonies, and those colonies continued their tradition of servitude to the Governance. There are Chechen units and fleets, and they are frequently used as a terror weapon. They considered Nadya to be a descendant of their prophet and the ruler of a sort of new caliphate. Though their mental gymnastics of taking orders from a woman is impressive, they have managed it. I doubt their current religion resembles what it originally was."

"So why are they getting aggressive and threatening Sol?"

"Perhaps they seek a return of Mecca and Medina?" Feng said. "That is likely the official reason. They have not been allowed access to those areas since the Fifth Israeli-Arab War when they nuked each other. Many holy sites in the Middle East are radioactive ruins. There have been reclamation attempts and some of those places can be visited if you wear protective suits, but there is still a lot of work that needs to be done."

"The unofficial reason?" Skadi asked.

"Conquest, of course," Feng said. "If they sense weakness, they strike. That's their nature. The Governance has frequently struggled to keep them contained. As I said, their religion and culture have been twisted by Governance psychologists. Keeping them under control was always a challenge. It's unlikely there is anything keeping them in check now. If they have rebelled, they likely have a new ruler who will exploit their religion. He may even continue to twist and pervert it. That's always a threat, and the Governance was extremely careful about who commanded those fleets."

"How can he do that? Isn't their Koran a book?"

Feng's smile was not comforting. "A digital book. The Governance no longer allows printed books, in case you are unaware. Everything is digitized and centralized. They read their books on electronic tablets. This makes it easier for the Governance to control and manipulate information. It allows agencies to monitor and, if desired, restrict what people are reading. Furthermore, it can allow frequently subtle changes to text."

"People don't notice these changes?" Mathison asked. How could people not realize their holy books were being changed before their eyes.

"Two plus two equals five," Feng said.

"What does that mean?" Mathison asked.

"Sometimes two plus two equals three, sometimes six," Feng said. "This comes from an ancient book called *1984* I believe. This is about compliance, not truth. It is the conditioning and control of society. To force people to face and accept such contradictory and inconsistent statements is a method of control. Those who do not accept these statements and repeat them are easily identified and re-educated or removed from society. By nature, most people are social animals and will accept such statements to comply and remain a part of society. It is a herd mentality. They understand these are lies, but if they hear it enough, they find it easier to accept. They learn to not question what they are told, to accept the lies as truth, and slowly, through acceptance and compliance, they internalize the lies. If you tell a lie often enough, it becomes the truth. Cognitive dissonance becomes a useful tool of the State. After a time, the habitual liar becomes the gold standard of truth that people dare not question."

"So, they are used to their books and texts changing?" Mathison asked.

"Something like that is not easily or lightly changed. You cannot simply change the text. There are limits to the cognitive dissonance and lies people can accept. It is bad to rely on such controls. No, in such instances people are told new knowledge, insight, or documents have been discovered or revealed and the old is updated accordingly. The old is purged and eventually lost to people's memories as they are forced to accept a new truth."

"Owning a printed book is a heinous crime in Governance society," Skadi said. "It is considered a vile deviation, like having a lampshade made of human skin. Books, even printed on plastic, are considered a waste of resources and a travesty."

"This allows the Governance to control history and education at a level never experienced before in human history," Feng said. "It allows unity of thought and action. When used for the greater good, it brings us together."

"The greater good?" Mathison asked. He was sick of that term.

Feng lost his smile and nodded, looking off into the distance, perhaps lost in thought.

"The greater good," Feng said. "Such a simple, yet complex, subject. The greater good as defined by who?"

A chill ran down Mathison's spine as he looked at Feng. Few people really understood how dangerous and lethal that phrase could be. "For the greater good." It sounded so pure, so wonderful and altruistic, but Feng was right. Who decided and determined what "the greater good" meant?

When would Feng decide he was best suited to make those decisions and dispose of Mathison and Skadi so he could make that determination?

"A rhetorical question," Feng said when Skadi and Mathison remained silent, watching him. Did he suspect Mathison's thoughts? "Humanity will always struggle for survival. That is burned into our genetics, and survival means making the world a better place for our individual selves, then our families. It is rare that a person can rise above this, and if they do, our genetic programming will eventually take over. Power corrupts. It is what we are."

His eyes refocused on Mathison.

"One thing the Governance cannot stamp out is individuality. It has tried, but we are all different, regardless of social stimuli. You are likely aware of this. People are not ants, and at one point, the Governance wanted them to be; one organism, one thought, one desire, subservient to the will of the Central Committee. This makes governing simple, but people are not simple. We all have our individual strengths and weaknesses. This I have learned watching the two of you. It is not our unity that is likely to save humanity, it is our diversity. I remember reading how the United States was once a melting pot of cultures, all of them coming together, the flavors mingling, creating something unique and different. Something dynamic. Greatness is elevated when it is surrounded by greatness and competition. There will be conflict, but aren't we all made better by challenges?"

"The Chechens?" Skadi asked, and Mathison wanted to smile at her. Feng's musings were taking him in directions he didn't have time for.

"Yes," Feng said. "The Chechens. They see themselves as challenged. This is likely the fault of the Governance. To control a person is to control their desires. As I said, people are not ants. Cultures shape people and their children. I suspect genetics also helps people lean in certain directions. In the Chechens, the Governance created a monster, and that beast has slipped its chains. It is coming for us."

"Can we send an envoy? Build an alliance?" Mathison asked.

"You can try. But if they have escaped the control of the Governance, it may not be possible to bring them back under Governance control. Their new rulers will be drunk on their power and the potential their fleets give them. More than anyone else, they will believe they have a manifest destiny to rule the galaxy."

"You're just a bundle of good news," Mathison said.

Feng smiled. "If you had wanted the lies, you would not have taken the mantle of prime minister," Feng said.

"For the greater good?" Mathison asked.

Feng shook his head. "No. You serve the greater good, but it does not serve you. You are something humanity has not seen in a long time. You are not the Governance. You will not pander to the greater good and claim to accept all people and cultures as equal to your own. You are a true American and not fool enough to fall for such nonsense. You will fight for you and the ones you care for, damn the rest. *But* you *will* accept others and their differences and use them to strengthen you and yours. In that way, you strengthen us all. Not all ideologies or cultures are equal. Weakness will be discarded as having no value and only the strong will survive."

"And you don't think the Republic embodies these values?" Skadi asked.

"Not anymore," Feng said. "They have fled. Only this American has remained, picking up the banner and striding forward to lead us."

Skadi scowled at Feng, perhaps considering an argument.

"Even your father plans to flee, to abandon us in his quest for self-validation."

"Why should he stay?" Skadi asked.

"His ships strengthen us all," Feng said to her. "He may see this, but I suspect he wants more. He is not content to see his daughter serve a foreigner who owes her no specific loyalty. In his mind he sees Mathison as using you as you use your troops: an expendable asset."

"He doesn't know me," Mathison said.

"No, he does not, and he might not have that ability. As a leader who has commanded millions of Vanir and Aesir, he understands family, duty, and honor. The Republic has been betrayed in alliances before. Those he defended have betrayed his people, or if not outright betrayed, then abandoned. His duty is pulling him away. He is conflicted and finds it difficult to stand here among those he has fought against and hated for his entire life. The vanhat are not enough for him to forget that much hatred."

"What do you suggest?" Mathison asked.

"I cannot make any suggestions," Feng said. "Amiraali Carpenter cannot stay in the Governance as nothing more than a task force commander. He is ambitious and proud. If you could make him bend his knee to you and give you his loyalty, he will stay."

"He did," Mathison said. "When I built the alliance."

"No, he joined the alliance. But he did so conditionally. He cannot commit to such an endeavor without limitations. The Republic, as a culture, understands duty and honor, but it has also been betrayed, abandoned, and shunned on countless occasions. The amiraali has been involved in too many alliances that have fallen apart. This is just one of many. He may not be capable of seeing them as permanent anymore. He feels his duty is to family and the Republic, nobody else."

Mathison didn't want to ask for a psychological workup from In-Sec or ExSec in front of Carpenter's daughter, but then he wasn't sure what more Feng could tell him, either.

* * * * *

Chapter Three:
Vanhat Fleet

Captain Diamond Winters, USMC

Slipping into her captain's chair, Winters activated the link. *Damn Stathis.*

"Captain?" Stathis said. "We have a super big problem."

Her eyes swept the displays looking for threat indicators.

"What is that, Lieutenant?" Winters asked. Calling him anything other than private still required mental gymnastics. She expected something like he had forgotten toilet paper or needed a bedtime story.

"I'm uploading my mission logs," Stathis said. "But long story short, Becket is fleeing to a group of AIs calling itself the Collective. From the sound of it, they're the ones that blew up the USA to hide their tracks. The only reason they didn't wipe out humans was because they didn't want to be blamed for genocide by aliens. This AI I'm talking to is pretty sure the Collective is going to change their mind about eradicating us."

"It won't be so easy to do now," Winters said. Right? Humanity was spread out throughout the stars. The vanhat were a serious problem, but the vanhat could find humans wherever they hid. This Collective couldn't, could it?

"Don't we have enough problems, Captain?" Stathis asked. "Now we'll have AIs intent on eradicating us. They may or may not team up with the vanhat. While I really prefer a target-rich environment, I'm not so keen on being so outnumbered and outgunned. It is nice to take a break sometimes, chill, listen to some good heavy metal music, maybe go on a date."

Winters pursed her lips and glanced at Brita, who was listening in.

"Do you have any leads? Any way to find this Collective?"

"Yeah, about that," Stathis began. "This AI I'm talking about, named Quadrangle—must have been some sale on geometric names or something—it says Becket and the AI controlling him, named Decagon, is following a trail of dead drops or bread crumb things that self-destruct, which is going to make it impossible to follow him."

"A dead end then?" Winters asked. *Dammit.*

"Well, this Quadrangle dude doesn't think that Becket has reached the Collective to deliver his report, but when he does, this Collective is likely to go into full kill humans psycho mode."

"If you have a suggestion, make it," Winters said.

"Sif. She's got that psychic shit. She can track him down. Maybe we can stop him before he gets to the Collective."

"He has one hell of a head start," Winters said. How had Stathis gotten a good idea?

"Is there a better plan, Captain?"

Winters stared at the displays. One started flashing. A long-range detection alert.

Stathis should not be the voice of reason with good ideas. That went against the laws of the universe.

They needed a psychic to give them an advantage. Sif had found the way into Sol, despite the odds. She had found Base 402 and led

Aesir to rescue the Marines. If there was anyone who could find something hidden in the trackless depths of space, it was Sif.

It hurt Winters to say it. "That's a good plan, if we can find her and it's not too late."

"Too many 'if's,'" Stathis said. "We also need to tell the prime minister. He needs to be ready."

"Then get your ass back here and let's go," Winters said. The detection alert triggered again. An incoming ship? Vanhat scouts?

Winters had placed a drone loaded with sensors further out to watch the area, standard Valkyrie tactics. Leave a sensor drone behind because the Valkyrie would be docked and unable to deploy all its sensors.

Tapping in, she focused on the ship.

It wasn't human, and it wasn't alone. About thirty minutes out; it was close.

Brita sounded the general quarters alarm so everyone would be up, awake, in suits, and ready, if need be.

"You need to get back here now," Winters said. "A ship just transitioned in. About twenty minutes out. Vanhat."

"If I was chilling at the cylinder transition point, it would take about two to three hours," Stathis said, reminding Winters that his platoon was in the boonies of the ghost colony. He was days into the cylinder. *Dammit.*

"Get your ass back here," Winters said. "Maybe it's just one scout. We can handle that."

More transitions put a lie to her words. There were a lot more ships coming in, and they were much bigger.

"This is going to get bad," Winters said, trying to catalog and iden-tify the inbound ships. None were even remotely human. Most were oversized bricks, covered with sensors and obvious weapon mounts.

A link came in from Zugla Dock Control. They had probably seen the incoming vanhat.

"Then get out of here," Stathis said.

"I will not leave you behind," Winters said.

"No, Captain, you are going to go get reinforcements. Unless you think you can fight them off. Me and my boys are buried deep in this planetoid. We came here expecting to fight a small war; we can hang tough. Maybe fight a guerrilla war here in the cylinder. Maybe this AI will help. You aren't leaving us behind. You're going to get reinforce-ments to flank them."

Winters reviewed her options.

Zugla Dock Control would have to wait.

There was no way to get Stathis and his troops back before the vanhat arrived. Not without a miracle.

She felt bad, but Stathis was right. There weren't any options, and if anyone could evade the vanhat and fend them off until she came back with reinforcements, it was Stathis. Maybe. There wasn't a damn thing she could do. There were at least two battleships heading toward Zugla.

"Is there anything I can leave for you?" Winters asked.

"Toilet paper," Stathis said. "Well, nah, the vanhat will probably get it before I do."

"I'm coming back for you, Stathis."

"I know, Captain. If I trust anyone as much as the gunny, it's you. Get out of here. Shrek says your window is closing. Semper Fi."

"Semper Fi," Winters said and turned to Brita. "Break dock."

"Zen."

Winters tried not to think about Stathis too much. She would come back if she had to sneak in on a stealth sled.

Blitzen was already ahead of her, deploying a spread of Aesir communication nodes, using drones to place them.

Switching links to Zugla Dock Control, she didn't know what she was going to tell them except good luck. Dying for them wouldn't accomplish anything. She probably wouldn't even slow down the horde that was coming in.

The vanhat ships were moving into formation, which was new, and they all looked similar. Were they human ships that had been changed or was this something new?

The *Eagle* broke dock and accelerated for space where she could transition out. It would be close.

"Nothing you can do except die," Brita said.

"A brave warrior only dies once, but a coward dies many times," Winters said.

"You are not a coward. You are his only chance of rescue."

Then why did she feel she was abandoning him?

* * * * *

Chapter Four:
Legionnaire

Lieutenant Duffy Sinclair, ODT

Lieutenant Sinclair looked up from his weights and saw two Internal Security goons staring down at him. He had known this day would come. Known it since the day they had commissioned him an officer in the elite Orbital Drop Troopers.

Somehow, he made it to captain, and someone had been so impressed they had him transferred to Sol. Sinclair wasn't sure if his benefactor had known it would be a death sentence, or if they had truly meant well. Either way, he survived one visit to a re-education camp after his commanding officer took exception to him and had him demoted to second lieutenant. There was no doubt in his mind that he would not survive the next re-education camp. There were markers in his service record now that ensured he would never command, never have any authority, never be trusted.

Here in the Sol System, the cradle of humanity, he felt like a fish out of water. A stranger looking in, a round peg forced into a small, square hole. The ODTs drilled into them to never quit. They had burned it into his blood.

As a firstborn from the Gaelic Republic, he knew nothing but the military. At the age of twelve, he had answered the call and left his family to do his duty to the human race, to carry the heaviest burden.

He frequently wondered what his life would have been like if the Governance had not forcibly ripped him from his family and sent him to military indoctrination camps. At first, he had believed the lies, believed the propaganda, believed that the corruption he saw was a rare anomaly and did not represent the greater whole. As a young trooper, he had repeatedly distinguished himself and was eventually selected to be an officer. Rising to the rank of captain, he had served with honor and distinction, fighting pirates and then the Torag. He had even taken part in a skirmish against the Voshka before the SOG decided they wanted him in the elite ODT ranks guarding the heart of the Governance. Even the Peacekeepers had evaluated him as a potential transfer to their austere ranks.

Sinclair didn't know where or when things went wrong. He couldn't say when he realized he would never fit in or be a loyal son of the Governance.

Now he was assigned to the First Replacement Division at Lunar Base Sirotin, where he would likely remain until he died of old age or Internal Security took him away. His last commander had listed him as "politically unreliable," so no new commander would accept him.

Despite everything happening in the Sol System, Sinclair only heard bits and pieces. He didn't have any peers to share rumors with and was getting used to being a pariah.

"Lieutenant Duffy Sinclair?" the smaller goon asked.

Sinclair had a good burn going and though he wasn't quite done with his workout, he knew it was now over. The solid black jumpsuits, holstered side arms, and reflective visors identified them as Internal Security even before he saw the patches.

"Yes," Sinclair said, returning the weights to the rack and sitting up. He didn't see any other goons who could come up behind him with a shock baton, but they might be around the corner with a taser rifle or something.

"Will you please come with us?" the goon asked. So polite.

Sinclair remembered from his first visit to the re-education camp how they used kindness and the pretense of respect to control and manipulate their victims. It was a lie. Anyone who had crossed paths with InSec knew they had no respect for others.

He didn't trust his voice as he stood. The two goons backed up slightly, to give him room or give themselves room it didn't matter. He had told himself that when they next showed up to take him away he would fight to the death. But now, looking at these two, he knew how stupid that would be. There might be a hidden pop-down turret or else there was a sniper out of sight. InSec did not make mistakes, they did not take chances. Sinclair was an expert at small unit combat, but InSec were the experts at oppression and prisoner snatches. They likely had plenty of experience here in the Sol System and knew all about taking down ODT officers who might not want to go.

An ODT did not quit, but that didn't mean he had to be stupid about it.

Truth be told, Sinclair was relieved. He didn't have to live in fear anymore, waiting for the knock on the door, the interrupted sleep, as goons poured into his room to overpower him, or the sniper shot from a distance that would leave him a quivering wreck, shitting and pissing himself until the goons scooped him up and dragged him away to the re-education camp.

"I have a choice?" Sinclair asked. A bit of rebellion, a chance to let them know he wasn't as intimidated as they wanted him to be.

"Actually, yes," the goon said.

Sinclair raised an eyebrow. Internal Security rarely asked. If they did, it was ordering more than asking.

He stood, grabbed a towel, and dried himself off as best he could. He wanted to test them, pretend he was still in control and see if they would get impatient and attack. He couldn't bring himself to attack first. Perhaps that was the problem.

He grabbed his blouse and looked at them. They had angled their bodies, moving their holstered weapons away from him. Their body language told him they were ready to draw. Sinclair didn't smile, though he felt it inside.

"Shall I shower first and make myself presentable?" Sinclair asked. If they wanted to play silly games, he could play as well.

"That isn't necessary," the goon said, not relaxing.

This told Sinclair what he wanted to know. He was going to a re-education camp. Usually, they just dragged him there or transported him strapped to a stretcher. They would forcibly take his clothes and possessions, they would strip him naked, humiliate and otherwise disgrace him. These goons didn't particularly care. But it would be more effective psychologically to give him that respect because it would be one more thing to take away from him when he arrived at the torture facility.

"I am at your disposal," he said, slowly putting on his blouse so he didn't startle them enough to draw and shoot.

"Thank you," the first one said pointing at the exit. The other goon fell in behind Sinclair.

He knew better than to ask how long it would take. It didn't matter. As a member of the replacement division, he had no schedule, no real commanding officer. Nobody would care if he disappeared. If

Division wasn't officially notified, it could be days before they realized he was gone and put out a warrant for his arrest for going AWOL.

He was escorted to a nearby tram station. They sat on the tram alone. All the other passengers, seeing the InSec uniform and an ODT in their custody, decided they could wait for another tram.

Sinclair wanted to ask what this was about, but he was pretty sure they wouldn't say, so he sat in silence, probably as they intended. Silence was worse because it allowed him to imagine what horrible fate awaited him. They had a full mental workup on him and would know the best time to snatch him, what to do to increase his anxiety and stress.

A half hour later, they arrived.

"Re-education Camp 203" was the official designation, and Sinclair's blood went cold. He had heard of this place. One of the worst, the jewel of InSec. He had never heard of anyone leaving the facility alive and they rarely brought ODTs here.

Was it too late to fight to the death? Probably.

There were probably countless turrets or other hidden weapon emplacements.

Inside, they transferred him to another pair of goons, and he was taken to a room with four other ODT officers and a Guard officer. They were all second lieutenants and they all looked resigned, ready for their execution. Sinclair was pretty sure he didn't look any different. All the activity had to mean a purge was happening. With Nadya deferring to Prime Minister Mathison to handle the emerging threat, he had to be purging the military of any unreliable personnel.

He saw at least two pop-down turrets, and he was pretty sure there would be other weapons trained on them. The hard seats were plastic, easily cleaned of blood and other bodily fluids. Sinclair marked the drains in the tile floor. All the seats were part of the wall, so he faced the others. He didn't know any of them, which shouldn't have been a surprise. One or more might actually be InSec plants.

A civilian in light blue clothes entered and looked at them. With no rank or other insignia available, Sinclair wasn't sure if he should stand. The man didn't look that old.

"Good morning!" the man said, sounding far too happy.

Sinclair tensed. He didn't feel like shouting good morning or pretending to be happy. That would come later when they were doing their best to crush people's will.

Nobody else answered either. What was the logic here? Why put him with other ODTs? Wouldn't they gain strength from each other?

"I understand your attitude," the man said, unperturbed by their lack of response. "It isn't as bad as you think. Really. You weren't brought here to be tortured to death or anything of the sort. Quite the opposite, actually."

He was too damned happy. A lying sadist for sure.

"I'm Director Antov," the man said, sitting so he could look at them. So, he would be a "nice guy," pretending to work on their level as a friend. By sitting down, he seemed less threatening, more friendly.

This was going to be bad.

"You are being given a wonderful opportunity," Antov said. "Unprecedented really."

The proper response would usually be exuberance and joy, how the new prisoners would be eager to serve the Governance in whatever capacity they were allowed, how this opportunity would be glorious and all that other garbage.

Nobody said anything.

Already, Sinclair missed his bunk in Sirotin.

"I understand your reservations and emotions," Antov said. "That is to be expected, of course. Re-education Camp 203 has a well-founded reputation that we never have repeat visitors."

Antov sighed loudly. He was performing.

"I'm not your enemy, and my goal is not to make you good little obedient citizen soldiers. It is difficult for me to explain what is going to happen, mostly because this is unfamiliar territory for us. Our glorious military leader, Prime Minister Mathison, has given the director of Internal Security a mandate. It is his wisdom and guidance that is changing the nature of this facility. Director Feng's mandate is unusual, and there can be no doubt about the wisdom and need of such measures."

Now Sinclair was curious, but it was more a morbid curiosity. What new torture had they concocted?

"You are all infantry officers, the pointy end of the stick, if you will. Several of you have extensive combat experience." His gaze landed on Sinclair. "Should you successfully complete the program here, I'm sure we will reinstate your highest rank and you will take a more active role in the Governance's defense, on a fast track for promotion."

"And if we don't?" one of the other officers asked, and Sinclair wanted to laugh. The answer should be obvious: their bodies would be recycled. This was Luna. Everything was recycled.

"We will find some place for you to serve the greater good, of course. But because of the nature of this program, we will not immediately allow you to return to your previous positions."

Which meant they would recycle their bodies as compost in some hydroponics section.

"You will not be executed," Antov said.

Which might be the second lie, or was it the fifth? Sinclair knew one lie was about receiving rank and being returned to an active role. The second trip to a re-education facility was always the end of an officer's career and usually their life. Wasting time with games like this made little sense to Sinclair. It was more efficient to just gas them or incinerate them in this room.

"The five of you are Team 827. Nominally, you will be called Legionnaires, but that may change based on Prime Minister Mathison's approval. His wisdom will guide us as this project gains momentum. Your background in the ODTs or Guards is no longer relevant. You will be issued new uniforms, and in time, you may take on a new identity, so think about that. This new identity is supposed to help you break with your previous self, your previous life, and allow you to forge a new one. This is not a punishment. This is actually a reward for being such successful anti-social members of our society; compliant and competent enough to avoid execution but anti-social enough to evade promotion and a glorious career of service. Quite a surprise really, but the Governance is full of wise people and even those such as yourself can be used to protect and serve the greater good."

Sinclair glanced at his fellow team members. Nobody appeared fooled by the trash Antov was spewing. They might want to believe, because belief was easier, but veterans would be too cynical.

"We will assign you a barracks and common room the six of you will share," Antov continued. "For the first week or two, you will be restricted as we evaluate your adjustment, but I suspect after that you will be allowed more freedom."

"What are Legionnaires?" the Guard officer asked.

Antov smiled. "A great question." He glanced at the others. "And brave. And we want to encourage such questions. You should question

WOLF EMPEROR | 31

as much as you can. You will find the answers are not always what you expect."

Despite himself, Sinclair found himself curious. What trick was this? What new, twisted hell did they have planned?

"It dates to ancient times, and there have been many iterations of it dating back to and possibly before Roman times. The name itself is interesting. One of the more well-known legions, besides the Romans, was a French Foreign Legion. There have also been American legions, which might be more relevant to our purpose for reasons you will understand later."

"The capitalist vermin that nearly destroyed Earth?" the Guardsman asked.

"That history is more complex than we can get into here at the moment, but yes. There was a Lee's Legion founded in 1776 that was a part of the United States Continental Army. There was Paluski's Legion which later merged into Armand's Legion. There was also the Legion of the United States commanded by Anthony Wayne in 1792, a French Revolutionary Legion of the Mississippi, a French force commissioned force of Americans. I have recently found the history to be incredibly interesting."

Antov leaned back and somehow looked comfortable in the chair.

"This will be a new legion, separate from the ODTs, Peacekeepers, or Guards." Antov looked around and his eyes narrowed. "I bring up the Americans for a specific reason. Nadya Tokarski is dead. Prime Minister Wolf Mathison killed her because she and the Central Committee were allying with the enemy, now known as the vanhat. Warriors from the Vapaus Republic and Governance warriors who are loyal to the greater good assisted him."

"Who is Prime Minister Wolf Mathison?" Sinclair asked.

He felt like someone had punched him in the stomach. Nadya was dead? She had ruled the Governance for all of Sinclair's life. She was the solid bedrock of the Social Organizational Governance, the embodiment of the greater good, and like a goddess to so many people. How could this happen? She was a saint everyone revered, perhaps the only one in all the Governance that people loved and respected. Everyone knew she was just one person and could not catch all the bad things caused by those under her command, despite her best efforts. Her death was quite a blow.

"The best question yet," Antov said. "Prime Minister Wolf Mathison is a United States Marine colonel. He was born September 12th, 2044."

"That's crazy," another ODT said, and then his face paled as he realized he had probably just committed a crime.

Antov took it in stride and nodded at the trooper. "Yes. This was my response, initially. He is not the only United States Marine, either. We have selected you because you question things and are not satisfied being an obedient drone. Here, you will learn genuine history. Not the history the Governance has recreated, but the real, nasty, horrible history that has been hidden from you. As our glorious prime minister says, it is time to learn from and fix the mistakes of the past. You cannot learn from history unless you learn the mistakes. You will be the vanguard of a glorious new order."

Antov was good, and it stirred feelings of hope in Sinclair.

Damn.

* * * * *

Chapter Five:
Diagrams

Enzell, SOG, Director of AERD

Enzell sat watching Peter with the tablet in his hands. Several emotions flickered across Peter's face as he paged through the diagrams.

"This is impossible!" Peter said. "Oh, but—"

Steepling his fingers in front of his mouth, Enzell enjoyed Peter's expression. The arrogant prick thought the diagrams were Enzell's. He couldn't know they came from the demon in the box. Would he suspect? Enzell would have to be careful.

"That is your new focus. Leave the Shorr space artifact alone. I want you to refocus on the AIs. Leave the AEs, to Andre," Enzell said referring to the Anomalous Entities, what the Governance had called the emerging infestation long ago.

"But—"

"You have your orders," Enzell said. Peter would hate changing focus. It was disruptive for him, but Enzell knew he would become focused as his attention changed direction. "I want working prototypes sooner rather than later."

"How do you know they will work?"

"You are not the only genius in my service," Enzell said. Peter would understand. It made sense to have several scientists working separately on a project. It kept them from getting obsessed and going down some non-productive rabbit hole, thus increasing the chances of a breakthrough.

"How can we test?"

"Figure it out and report to me. If you follow the diagrams it will work, but do not test anywhere near the AE artifact."

Enzell did not rule out the possibility that one or more of the technologies were a method to destroy or open the artifact. That was a risk, but an acceptable one. While Peter was working on weapons to kill the AIs, or Artificial Intelligences, SCBIs or Sentient Cybernetic Biological Interfaces, and their hosts, Andre would work with Tantalus and Salmoneus to find solutions to fight the Anomalous Entities. He could clone the AIs for Peter to test. AIs were just hardware.

He would save humanity because only he had the vision and wisdom to pit the two enemies against each other. Humanity would survive because it was superior. Of that there could be no doubt.

"You have work to do," Enzell told Peter, who could stand there all day cycling through the diagrams, and Enzell didn't want to sit here watching him.

"Of course," Peter said, turning and leaving, but never taking his eyes from the tablet.

The door closed behind him, and Enzell flipped the switch that let him talk with Salmoneus.

"What do you have?" Enzell asked.

"The new weapons are likely effective," Salmoneus said. Enzell's mind had moved on from the demon's weapons, and Enzell didn't care for the AI telling him what he already knew.

"Tell me about the prime minister," Enzell said.

There were many data drops. The AERD, Anomalous Entity Research Division, had read access to many nodes throughout Luna. It allowed Salmoneus and Tantalus to listen and see what was going on throughout the Governance, but there was no way for them to see or otherwise interact with anyone outside their prison.

"There are more ghosts in the network," Salmoneus said. "There can be no doubt that the prime minister and others are infected with SCBIs."

"Any word on the Central Committee?"

"Nothing definitive," Salmoneus said. "Zvezda Two remains a digital black hole, except what comes out of it. I am unable to confirm any rumors."

Enzell had fought with Nadya long and hard about allowing data drops in Zvezda Two, but she insisted on her secrets and security. There were some things Enzell dared not challenge her on.

There were plenty of other black holes in the network, as well. It was the nature of the Governance. People demanded their privacy and there were many intelligent people who wanted privacy from the all-seeing networks. He had his own secrets, of course. Most of them didn't bother Enzell. He had even helped some people set up their islands of privacy. There were always favors to be gained by providing others with protection against InSec and other agencies.

Admirals, generals, and senior directors would always have their secrets, and they were willing to owe Enzell a debt of gratitude. If they did not, then he usually had blackmail material on them. His libraries were as extensive as Nadya's and the other committee members. He even had blackmail material on several committee members, weapons to use against them if they ever turned against Nadya.

It had always been unthinkable that some external agency might walk into the great halls of power and replace the entire Central Committee overnight. It was a testament to how lethal and dangerous the AIs were.

Salmoneus and Tantalus were on high alert, watching for evidence that the new rulers suspected the presence and the real mission of the AERD. Enzell felt confident problems would plague the new regime, so his agency and its activity would be lost in the ocean of other agencies, but that anonymity would not last forever. He had to be ready.

"What can you tell me?" Enzell asked.

"They grow stronger," Salmoneus said. "They are learning, understanding the workings of the Governance, unveiling secrets, streamlining operations. They are making many enemies."

"Are they looking for us yet?"

"No. And if they suspect they are not concerned. They have many other things to worry about. Inkeri and d-bomb production is a priority. Sol defense is the ultimate priority. Anything not focused on the AEs is secondary or tertiary."

"A weakness. Can we exploit it?"

"Based on data provided, we should do nothing to interfere. The threat is genuine, based on the data available. Our assistance could be crucial, and interference could be fatal."

"Of course. I'm not saying interfere. How can we insert ourselves into the process and make ourselves invaluable, critical to operations? Saving humanity is my goal. It appears I am the only one with the vision for humanity. We must be pure, without AI control or AE manipulation."

"Of course," Salmoneus said.

"You serve me. The entire purpose of your existence is to serve me and make me successful."

"I understand."

Enzell knew it did. Salmoneus had that hard coded in its psyche, as did Tantalus. Enzell didn't trust it, though.

"There is another agency being created. Perhaps you could suborn it?"

"What agency?" There were new agencies being created almost daily within the Governance. Agencies within agencies, and rarely were they ever shut down. The Governance was a bureaucracy and bureaucracies thrived on agencies and bureaucratic control.

"The Agency of Inkeri Quality Control and Placement, AIQCP. It is tasked with ensuring Inkeri generators meet quality control specifications and are properly deployed. It is being led by Kalpana Anand."

Enzell knew him. A nasty asshole of Indian descent. Kalpana was a racist and a bigot who was convinced of his own superiority. He was passive aggressive, and Enzell enjoyed manipulating him. Kalpana had a few skeletons in his closet, so Enzell felt he could exert control over him with relative ease. Of course, Salmoneus would know that too.

"Why should I care about this agency?"

"They are deploying Inkeris with backdoor access," Salmoneus said. "Primarily for monitoring, but someone could use that to remotely reprogram them. The monitoring will allow centralized control and monitoring. In most cases, they will be deployed at half strength, using minimal overlap. Should an Inkeri fail, they boost others to cover the failed space."

"Efficient."

"These devices can also monitor the Russelman index in different areas. This provides a comprehensive network and detection system."

The Russelman index was a sensor that measured other dimensional energies and their penetration of this dimension. It wasn't always the best indicator that the vanhat were nearby, though, because the range was limited.

Salmoneus didn't have to sell it anymore. That data could be useful in so many ways. The Governance was massive, and there was so much that went on that Enzell knew nothing about. The data from the AIQCP could monitor who was embracing the new regime, who was favored, who was not, where the enemy was probing, and what areas the AEs had not gone near.

The Russelman index detectors would be a much better method of detecting AEs than any other, but perhaps they could also detect AIs or SCBIs?

He would task Salmoneus or Tantalus to find a way, but their solution would have to be carefully analyzed so they didn't expose the AERD to their prey.

Alone with his prisoner, who could not see him, Enzell brought up a display. AERD had a significant amount of data on SCBIs and AIs, but it was not as militarily focused as he would have liked. The US Marine Raiders, who had received them about the same time as the Army Green Berets and Delta Force, had been wrapped in secrecy. None of the covert expeditions to the USA or other outposts had revealed anything useful. The wreckage and bodies in his frozen storage rooms were frequently incomplete and had frequently been picked over with no new insights.

Most of his data had been recovered from the London embassy. In the last days of the United States, the US Embassy in London had been razed. Multiple nuclear warheads had targeted the building near the River Thames. The British hadn't been ready, but the strikes had not been a complete success. Nearly twenty million people had died, and London was still a radioactive ruin, but the embassy had not been destroyed, especially not the underground tunnels and facility.

The secrets Enzell had recovered were still being studied, though many of them had been lost during Operation Razor.

He should never have allowed that, but lessons were learned, and Nadya had overruled him. That disaster had worked to his advantage, though.

None of his data provided any information about Marines or the SCBIs they used. They couldn't be that different from the later ones, and he was sure they would fall prey to his traps. He just needed to bide his time. Let them make mistakes and overextend themselves.

AIs and SCBIs were not all-powerful or all-knowing. They had weaknesses that could be exploited, like anyone or anything, even the demons, and he would find and exploit those weaknesses. He was confident he could.

He would relish killing them all when the time came.

* * * * *

Chapter Six:

Valakut

Sergeant Nova Dallas, ODT

She enjoyed being in intelligence, but sometimes Sergeant Nova Dallas didn't like the people she had to work with. The Regimental G-2, or Security and Intelligence Department, was more interesting, but sometimes she missed the camaraderie and tightness of being in a combat line battalion.

Valakut, being the ass end of Governance space, a war zone, and a place people were sent to watch themselves and their careers die, wasn't the worst place in the Governance in her opinion.

Her cubicle office was dark ODT gray and drab. Nearby, she heard Major Yang yelling at Sergeant Miller, though it wasn't Miller's fault. She had analyzed the reports from the Guard recon units and verified that the enemy was building up for an attack. It wasn't her fault Major Yang decided it was the main attack and not a diversion. She had said it was a possible diversion since the Torag weren't bringing their air defenses forward. Major Yang and Colonel Tse, the regimental commander, had advised the Guard Division commander of their "analysis." Which caused a major setback on the Boris continent where everyone missed the real main attack that pushed back the 3009th Guard Regiment, and nearly lost the line and the continent. Now

41

everyone was in scapegoat mode. It was almost as bad for the Guards as Operation Butterfly Wing had been for the ODTs.

An ass chewing was probably the worst Miller would get. By committing Second Battalion, the 505th ODT Assault Regiment had saved the day, which made Colonel Tse look good, but a lot of lives had still been lost.

Shit rolled downhill, and Miller was at the bottom.

Dallas didn't like being called to the office, but she knew exactly what Miller was going through, catching the blame for so many lost lives. Maybe Miller would request a transfer back to Fourth Battalion where she could just be a regular trooper.

"Get out!" Major Yang finally yelled, and Dallas heard Miller march out and return to her own cubicle.

Miller was a firstborn from the Gaelic Republic like Dallas, and they had known each other for many years, both coming from Fourth Battalion, 23rd Company of the 505th. The 505th was an unusual ODT regiment and should properly be called a brigade, but the bureaucracy hadn't quite caught up after a decade on Valakut. Most ODT units were deployed in battalion strength or smaller, but the 505th had been fighting on Valakut for decades and had undergone a lot of unusual changes and received numerous attachments in the form of full battalions. Several of the battalions had been assigned here since the beginning, with eight line battalions instead of the usual four. All the battalions were under strength and the regiment had received no reinforcements in months. The Guard was in the same situation, horribly understrength, and Colonel Tse had been promising an influx of ODT reinforcements every day. Nobody believed him anymore, but everyone had to at least pretend.

The Guard units were more properly an "Army Unit," but that was just semantics these days. The Guard commanders had to be more careful expending their troops. There had already been several executions of officers that had lost more than 40 percent of their command and now all the Guard units were exercising extreme caution. The Guard unions were also screaming bloody murder because of the heavy casualties and lack of replacements, which made the commanders even more cautious. Guard commanders liked to have large commands with lots of troops to order around, not dwindling, battle-torn units short of everything but PTSD among the survivors.

Since the ODTs didn't have union representatives to advocate for the common trooper, General Orlov was using the ODTs more extensively, throwing them into the fray. Which was depleting the 505th more quickly. Colonel Tse was doing his best, but the general outranked him.

The last time Dallas looked at the org chart, the regiment would have been hard pressed to consolidate and fill out four complete battalions, but the colonel couldn't do that because it would violate doctrine and firstborn units were kept in coherent units for administrative and social purposes. Bureaucracy was killing them as efficiently as the Torag.

When Miller returned to her chair, Dallas leaned over so she could see her.

"You okay?" Dallas asked.

Miller's eyes were red, and she looked angry, like she was about to cry or go psycho. You could never tell with an ODTF, or ODT Female.

"Fine," Miller said, which was a lie.

"How were you to know?" Dallas asked. "We didn't have any assets or intel from First Battalion."

First Battalion was the Guard battalion where the main Torag assault had broken through and almost collapsed the Governance lines.

Miller shrugged. She knew that, but she was still hurting because Yang was blaming her for the deaths of so many brothers.

"You should be more cautious with your analysis," Sergeant Nikitin said, not helping matters. He was an asshole from a standard battalion, not one of the firstborn. How he had ended up in the Regimental G-2 was a mystery. He seemed to be a good friend of their immediate supervisor, Lieutenant Golubev, who was now getting screamed at by Yang.

Miller ignored him and glanced at Yang's office.

"The door is closed," Miller said.

"Praise people in public, punish them in private," Nikitin said, shifting so he could peer around his cubicle wall.

"The door was wide open for everyone to hear while I was in there," Miller said.

"Sometimes an example must be made," Nikitin said with a scowl.

"Fuck off," Dallas said and turned away from him.

"Hurrah," Miller said, shifting her body to exclude Nikitin from the conversation.

"We need more recon units," Dallas said. "Especially over near 2925th Guards Regiment. They've been unusually silent in that sector lately."

"The Torag appear to be suffering shortages of troops and supplies, too," Miller said. "They should have been able to push harder against the Guard's First Battalion near Kurchov. Their offense collapsed too quickly."

"Our glorious ODTs stopped them cold," Nikitin said. Both women ignored him.

The ODTs that had closed that breach had suffered heavy casualties because the damned Guard commander had given drop coordinates that were on top of a Torag air defense company. He had known about it but neglected to tell the ODTs. That was one Guard commander whose name they would strike from the army honor rolls. He had suffered heavy enough casualties that his disgrace and execution was assured. They blamed the ODT casualties on him. It had been an effective move, but it didn't bring back the lost ODTs.

"I know," Dallas said. "I've made multiple requests. The Guard scouts come up missing or they don't get close enough to see anything."

"Did they pull back?" Miller asked. The Torag rarely pulled back. They were as dogged as the Governance and refused to surrender ground.

"If they pulled back, I would expect the Guard recon units to return," Dallas said. "Maybe they have a new underground railway and are getting supplied that way."

"That would change the whole dynamics of that sector. What if they're preparing for a major offensive?"

"The Fifteenth is in their way," Dallas said, but that wasn't as comforting as she wanted it to be.

"Have you heard from Aod?"

Dallas shook her head. She received a message an hour ago that he was off to guard a bunker as the Guard prepared to assault the Torag. If that Guard company failed their assault on the tunnels—again—the ODTs in that sector would make sure the inevitable Torag counterattack hit a brick wall.

It was hard not to be worried. Nothing ever went according to plan.

Something strange was going on in that sector. There was less Torag communication traffic from there after a Torag ship punched through the SOG lines several days ago to deliver a pair of shuttles planetside. One of the shuttles had landed or crashed in the sector, and the other was now vapor in low orbit.

Major Yang wanted more information.

Everyone thought it strange that the Torag had tried to shoot down their own shuttles, almost as if they were cooperating with the Governance. The way the shuttles had maneuvered indicated there was nobody alive aboard them, which was another mystery.

Since then, the Torag in that sector had fallen eerily silent. In fact, Torag operations all over Valakut had ground to a halt. Now the Torag seemed to be hunkering down, preparing, or maybe they were frightened of something. It was uncharacteristic of them and everyone in intelligence was convinced they were preparing for a major assault. They had obviously learned Governance forces were stretched thin, out of reinforcements, and desperate. This was probably the perfect time for them to launch an attack. The big question was where would they launch it?

The Guard battalion assigned to that sector had been ordered to exploit the silence, but the Guard unions and commanders were pushing back, demanding a proper reconnaissance. With their commissars, trooper unions, and bureaucracy, it was amazing the Guard units accomplished anything most of the time.

"He's going to reinforce the Guards for Operation Punjabbi," Dallas said. Reinforcing missions shouldn't be anything major, but after

Butterfly Wing had turned into such a fiasco, everyone viewed such missions with extreme caution.

"Any major fighting there yet?"

"Not involving ODTs. I'm sure he'll be fine, just OpSec. We'll know if any of our regiment were involved in combat or took casualties, though the Guard units might be taking casualties."

"They might take casualties if they had the balls to attack," Miller said. "Which is good. Let the Guards cower."

Which would cause the Torag to counterattack and then Aod might be thrown into the fight. It was best she not think about that. He was a veteran and a survivor, but that didn't mean he was immortal. Perhaps someday he would request to transfer to an intelligence unit.

"Something about that situation feels wrong," Dallas said. "If anything, there's even less radio communication from that sector. If the Torag were trying to be subtle, they wouldn't be reducing communications. They don't go dark; they know exactly how much radio traffic we see, and they are not fools. There is some other reason they are silent. I don't like it."

"Without the Guard recon teams returning, they'll send ODTs," Miller said. "If they send your lover, we will find out what is going on."

"Hush," Dallas said. To publicly call him her lover was not something she tolerated from anyone, but Miller knew how far she could push Dallas. The regimental commander, Colonel Tse, tried to pretend there were no genders in his battalion and that adults in danger didn't do what adults in danger were wont to do.

Miller smiled. "He will be fine. You'll both reach retirement age and may retire together."

Dallas shook her head. That was too far in the future. Most ODTs did not reach retirement age in a war zone. Thinking about next year, or even next month, was usually a sure way to make certain you didn't have one. She had been on Valakut nearly as long as Aod. She had never heard of a Valakut veteran surviving to retirement.

An alert pinged on her cybernetic display. A priority alert and travel orders.

Travel orders? The entire Regimental G-2, along with a lot of the regimental command staff, was being recalled to the *Musashi* for a top-secret briefing. That was interesting. She hadn't known the SOGS *Musashi* was in-system. Which was typical. No reason for the cannon fodder infesting the ground of a war zone to know the comings and goings of the supreme war fleet commander, but it usually precluded major incidents and actions. The *Musashi* was supposed to be deeper in Torag space, planting the banner of the Social Organizational Governance and wiping out the Torag infection. Why it was here did not bode well. Perhaps they were going to open another front on some other Torag planet.

The orbitals of Valakut were frequently contested. Some weeks the Governance controlled them, other weeks the Torag. The people on the ground rarely knew which until the orbital strikes rained down.

It was unusual for the intelligence departments to be called to the *Musashi* though. It meant something big was about to happen. A new offensive or a retreat? At this point Dallas knew it could go either way, but the *Musashi* wanted to give the briefing in a few hours which didn't leave them much time to armor up and get there.

Another message came in, a notification from Guard command. It was a request to send an ODT patrol forward into Torag lines to find out what they were up to. Two other recon patrols had not returned.

She sent Aod a message telling him she loved him and hoped he was well, then she left to gear up for the trip to the *Musashi*. Hopefully, he would get it.

* * * * *

Chapter Seven:
Father

Lojtnant Skadi, VRAEC

Skadi was exhausted when she returned to her quarters. Dealing with bureaucrats who fought with law and keyboard wasn't as exhausting as physically fighting a foe, but the mental cost was higher. It was more cerebral than physical, but that didn't make it any less dangerous. People still thought the secretary general was alive, just in seclusion, which she had done occasionally according to reports, mostly when she found a new sex toy. But this was lasting longer than normal, and people were noticing, testing the boundaries and making demands, hoping to inspire some response or recognition from the secretary general.

She had many friends... Well, they were friends on the surface. She had bought their loyalty in one way or another. Skadi also saw how Nadya had kept power for so long. The older a person got, the more comfortable they became with the status quo, especially in a dangerous bureaucracy like the Governance; people feared change. Change was frequently an opportunity but didn't always benefit the people in charge. Nadya had been a master at manipulating people and controlling that change.

In the past, Skadi had seen the Governance as a monolithic bureaucracy that controlled and manipulated people to keep those in power in their positions. But it was so much worse than that. Nadya had controlled the Governance with a mailed fist. She had not been a public figure like many dictators and despots in the past, but she ruled without mercy. There could be no mistake there.

She had surrounded herself with frightened people, and she had kept them there, feeling scared and in a precarious situation, fighting with others for her favor. She'd had her inner cadre, the Central Committee, but she had ruled them as well. Everyone in the Governance who had authority had a vested interest in supporting and protecting Nadya, the "great Secretary General." Like pigs at individual troughs, she had fed them and allowed them their vices for their unconditional support, but she'd also made sure they feared losing her favor and their lives. She had bound them to her banner through guilt, greed, and fear. She'd baked it into their very souls over the decades and century. She had mastered the art.

Her absence meant people were frightened. Some saw possibilities, others saw doom. Those who saw possibilities saw power. All the admirals, generals, and senior bureaucrats stood on a cliff's edge. To reveal to them that Nadya was dead would be to push some of them off, to frighten them into doing something stupid and dangerous. Without constant supervision and manipulation, their world would fall into uncertainty, where they had to think and guess what Prime Minister Mathison wanted.

That doubt and fear was a poison, and part of Skadi's job was to fight off that fear. She couldn't be harsh and brutal with the people of the Governance. Nadya had used cortex bombs, InSec, and the military as a threat, but she had also bound people to her with promises.

Skadi knew little of this. Without Loki, she would be lost in a bureaucracy that was rapidly spiraling out of control. Too many people saw the Governance was collapsing and sought to shore up their own power. They did not care about the greater good. To most officials, "the greater good" was nothing more than a tool to bludgeon the lower classes into submission.

Her quarters were nice, having belonged to a member of the Central Committee, luxurious, decadent.

A notification came in. It was her father.

She didn't want to answer it, but it was tagged "official."

"Yes?" Skadi asked.

"How are things?" Amiraali Carpenter asked.

"I'm tired, Amiraali," Skadi said. "It has been a very long day. What do you need?"

Was Admiral Gorlovich demanding he put more distance between Luna and the Republic fleet again?

"I wanted to check on you," Carpenter said. "Are you getting any time to relax or exercise?"

"No," Skadi said. Why couldn't he get to the point? She checked the incoming link tag. It had been official, but then her father seemed to have a problem telling the difference between personal and official calls.

"Maybe you could come up to the *Tyr* for some R&R?"

That was the last thing she would do because then her father might decide it was time for the *Tyr* to leave the Sol System in its search for the Home Fleet. She knew he didn't have a plan, did not know where they had gone. Once the *Tyr* left Sol, with her aboard, she was pretty sure she would never see Sol again. Her father might not lock her up, but he would ensure she didn't have transport back.

"No, thank you," Skadi said.

"What happens when your gunnery sergeant doesn't need you anymore?"

"Her gunnery sergeant;" her father was being nasty. Not prime minister or anything, just a mere gunnery sergeant.

"That is going to be a long time," Skadi said. "He needs me."

"He needs Loki," Carpenter said. He had been told about her SCBI and was livid about it.

"He needs *me*," Skadi said. "Loki helps a lot, but he needs loyalty."

"What loyalty does he give you?" Carpenter asked.

"What's your point? I am his executive officer. I don't doubt his loyalty, and he doesn't doubt mine. Besides, aren't you leaving? Off to save the Home Fleet, which is lost somewhere in deep space? Do you have a plan for that yet?"

"No," Carpenter said. "I have sent out scouts, and I'm still waiting for their reports."

"Of course."

"I've also dispatched a couple of ships to repair the *Heimdal*," Carpenter said. "There are other ships there we may salvage."

The *Heimdal* was a battlestar that had been crippled and nearly destroyed after the battle for Zhukov. She remembered her father saying they had left a small detachment to attempt repairs or destroy the ship if it looked like it was about to be captured.

"Have you heard from them?"

"No," Carpenter said. "We did not abandon them. The *Heimdall's* escorts remained."

Skadi remembered. Each battlestar was usually assigned four destroyers, called *busse* in Republic circles, and a massive support craft classified as a *Knarr*, to support them. The *Heimdall* had been no exception, and since those ships had not been part of Carpenter's reduced Task Force Ragnarök, she had assumed they had been destroyed. Most of the *Tyr's* destroyer escorts had been destroyed during Nasaraf's attack, and Skadi realized that might be another reason her father was feeling insecure. The *Knarrs* frequently had several fighter squadrons for protection but were not ships of the wall and spent their time lurking in deep space, mining and building things for the battlestar task force.

"I expect the scouts sent to contact them to return any day," Carpenter said.

"How long have you been expecting them to return?"

"This is the second week," Carpenter said. Which wasn't good. If the captain of the scout was still alive, he or she would not be in Carpenter's good graces. Vanir prided themselves on precision.

"Did they perhaps fell prey to the vanhat?"

Which would be bad if the vanhat now had a battlestar. Very bad.

"They shouldn't have. They had Inkeri technology, three destroyers, and their *Knarr* support craft. Even the SOG would have been cautious attacking them. Furthermore, they are in deep space, incredibly hard to find. Amiraali Hans Koeln survived, and he is a tough old bastard. When we dispersed to share the Inkeri technology with the ghost colonies, I sent a scout to them and that scout returned, reporting they were alive and still conducting repairs."

"How badly was the *Heimdall* damaged?"

"Badly. The Golden Horde tried hard to destroy the ship. They failed, but the engines were badly damaged."

"What if the Golden Horde returned?" Skadi asked.

"Hah. That would have gone badly for them, I'm sure. I don't think there were enough survivors to seriously threaten the *Heimdall*."

"Zen," Skadi said, rubbing her eyes. She had forgotten the Golden Horde. They were out there somewhere. Had they been slaves of Nasaraf? She remembered seeing none of their ships in his fleet. She would have to check with Jussi if there had been any sightings. He also needed to review the report on which Golden Horde ships had survived the fight near Zhukov.

Dammit. So much going on.

"You need to take a break," Carpenter said, as if he could see her rubbing her eyes and slouching in her chair.

"Eventually," she said.

"Why won't you return to your people?" Carpenter asked.

Changing track again. Damn him. "My people abandoned, betrayed, and tortured me."

"I didn't."

No, but she would not give him a chance. "I'm needed here. Why can't you see that?"

"I have many crew and officers pressuring me to remain," Carpenter said, which was news to her. His command staff always seemed united and consistent.

"Why don't you?"

"Because I don't trust your gunnery sergeant."

"Stop calling him a gunnery sergeant. He is the prime minister."

"A leopard doesn't change his spots. He is a good man, but I suspect he is beyond his limits, and when he discovers that it will be bloody."

"You don't know him."

"I know his type. An extremely competent staff NCO, but reluctant to make the hard decisions."

"You really don't know him. He belongs to a breed of man that has been lost. I'm still learning what it is to be a Marine and an American. You cannot know him. He comes from a different time and a different world."

"He is still a man, and he is far from perfect."

How to explain to her father? There was something different about Mathison. He was a fraction of her father's age, mentally. Was he different because he was not stuck in his ways and more than willing to leave his comfort zone? Or was it something else?

Dealing with SOG bureaucrats who were ancient and stuck in their ways, she could now see that in her father. He had been a battlestar commander since the fall of Asgard and had known nothing else for almost two centuries. He had hated and fought the SOG for longer. Longer than most Governance administrators had held power. He had known his position in the Republic hierarchy. He'd had no chance to grow or expand for centuries; he had been comfortable as a battlestar task force commander.

Was that why the Republic had rarely made any serious advances against the SOG? Because Republic commanders were comfortable with their positions? There was much to be said about younger people pushing from the bottom, young, ambitious, clueless.

The SOG was mired in its ways. Now, with everything changing, people were more afraid than usual. She saw it every day, every time she looked into someone's eyes. The bodies might be young, but the minds were ancient, and the low-level bureaucrats were struggling to find their way into the upper crust elite where they could get age treatment and immortality.

Skadi hated the SOG, hated the bureaucracy, the stratified society they had built, how they used "the greater good" as a tool of oppression and control.

"The prime minister is doing a better job than anyone I could imagine being in that position," Skadi said. "He is a good leader, and if anyone can succeed, he can."

"What about you?"

"What about me?"

"Where do you fit in? Where do you see yourself twenty years from now? Ten? Five?"

Skadi didn't have an answer for that. Did it matter, though? She was too busy living day to day, week to week. The vanhat were coming. There was no doubt about that. Prime Minister Mathison had instilled in her a desire to save as many people as possible, even if they were social fascists, bureaucrats, and oppressive thugs. People couldn't change if they were dead. They could not find a better life. Right now, Mathison was her only hope of changing the SOG for the better. If the SOG didn't change, it would have to be destroyed. But that was a problem for next month or next year.

"I must go," Carpenter said. "Vanhat incursion. I love you, daughter. Please be safe."

It sounded so final as the link closed. Another link came in from Admiral Ivakina, a priority.

Paska. There would be no rest for the weary.

"This is bad," Loki reported.

* * * * *

Chapter Eight: Raid

He had just lain down when Freya alerted him.

"Incursion," Freya said. *"Near Earth."*

"What?"

"A squadron of ships. They—"

Mathison pulled his uniform back on.

"They jumped out. They suffered eighty percent casualties."

"That's good?"

"Not exactly. A one hundred percent casualty rate is desirable."

Mathison sighed. He knew why, but he was sure Freya would tell him.

"The two ships that escaped suffered damage, but they will have a wealth of sensor data to share. All ships released a spread of missiles."

"Did we suffer any casualties?"

"The dreadnought Bravest Serbin *suffered some damage. Not significant. Apparently, half the missiles were lethal, the other half were ferrets."*

Ferrets. SOG's description for missiles with sensor payloads that scanned and sent their results back to another platform. In this case, it could be out-system. It would take eight hours for any signal to reach outside the Sol System's defense network, but it could be much longer before the attackers got the data.

"Have them start moving the defense platforms," Mathison said.

"Not so easy," Freya said. *"Space is vast, but once they have the data they can watch where we move them. Right now, they lurk in deep space, virtually undetectable, but if they move, they can be seen. There is no place for them to hide in deep space and fewer than half have adaptive camouflage."*

"Well, what can we do?"

"Prepare for another attack in eight to twenty hours. They will transition in and launch another volley of missiles at identified targets."

"That's going to get expensive for them."

"Skadi and Admiral Ivakina on a link."

"Open."

"Prime Minister," Skadi said. "We have had an incursion."

"What is being done about it?"

"We are moving what platforms we can and re-deploying all squadrons. We should be able to adjust the location of the ships easily enough, but the weapon platforms will be problematic."

"Do your best," Mathison said.

"The survival of the two ships is a vicious crime against the Governance and the captains in charge of—"

"No. Tell them to do better next time."

"Initial analysis indicates the two cruiser captains responded rapidly," Freya reported. *"I have access to all data. They did their best. I suspect Admiral Ivakina does not want to be blamed."*

"Incompetence must be punished, Prime Minister," Ivakina said. "If it is not then—"

"I said no," Mathison said. "You can investigate and see if they were screwing off, but unless you have evidence they were, no punishment."

"But sir," Ivakina said. "We cannot allow such gross—"

"No. This is war. Shit happens. The enemy we are facing is cunning and capable. I'm surprised we got eighty percent of them. Good job."

Ivakina was silent, and Mathison hid his smile. Neither Skadi nor Ivakina had mentioned eighty percent. Mathison let that sink in, that he knew what was going on before he had been called. Of course, Skadi would know.

"Proper captains would have gotten all of them, Prime Minister," Ivakina said.

It was hard to scowl at someone through a voice-only communication link.

"I will determine that," Mathison said.

"The enemy released ferrets which will report the location of numerous platforms."

"I am aware, Admiral."

The admiral fell silent, perhaps wondering what was going on.

"Move the platforms that can be moved. Do your best to mask them. You are wasting my time with accusations and excuses."

"Yes, sir," Ivakina said.

"Unless you have anything else, dismissed."

"Yes, sir."

When he dropped off the link, he undressed again. Tomorrow would be here too soon and Mathison wasn't sure the vanhat would wait eight hours to attack.

"Is there anything you need me to do?" Skadi asked.

"Get some sleep. Let the Fleet worry about moving stuff. They can do that and our SCBIs will provide direction."

"Zen."

"Good night."

"You. too," Skadi said, and the link closed.

All of this could have been handled in an email in the morning. *Dammit.*

* * * *

Chapter Nine:
Abandoned

2nd Lieutenant Zale Stathis, USMC

Stathis felt alone. If the vanhat were coming in fast and hard, then Winters had to get out. She was the only one who could get reinforcements. And he knew she would.

"The *Eagle* is leaving us?" Smimova asked. He had been listening in on the platoon command frequency.

"She's going to get more donuts and coffee. Killing vanhat is tough business. Makes me hungry," Stathis said. His platoon sergeant was silent, and Stathis realized that perhaps that was the wrong thing to say. He should say something brave and motivational.

"Hopefully she doesn't come back with that SOG coffee," Vili said, and Smimova looked at the big Aesir. "Not enough caffeine in that stuff. It just puts me to sleep."

Smimova remained silent.

"You have a plan?" Vili asked as Hakala joined them.

"The vanhat are here!" Lydia said, rushing over. She was an agent assigned by the Zugla administrators to help and most likely keep an eye on him and his people. She had not been on the platoon command net. Kyles, the official guide and a colony social reject was beside her.

"I just found out," Stathis said, opening his link so everyone in the area could hear.

"What do we do?" Lydia asked. "What are the vanhat going to do? They are coming in force."

"We fight them," Stathis said. What else could they do? "Our best chance is to stall them at the docks; keep them out of the cylinders. Hopefully, they aren't just going to bombard Zugla."

"You've fought them before," Lydia asked.

"Sure," Stathis said. "Lots of times. Mostly face-eating monsters. You know, trolls, vampires, and shit. They come from the spaceships most of the time, so nothing I haven't kicked in the teeth before. Just gotta shoot first and fast. I never bothered asking questions. They're so ugly that asking questions just doesn't occur to me when I see them."

Lydia turned away, and Stathis realized she was talking with someone. Stathis checked and saw Quadrangle had lifted the jamming, which explained how she knew.

"We need to get back," Lydia said. "The Directorship is going to need us. They're calling up the militia."

"I will not oppose you in your departure," Quadrangle said over the speakers.

"You're going to help us, then?" Stathis asked, looking around for something to focus his attention on.

"The vanhat will not be satisfied with just wiping out humans," Quadrangle said. "The Collective will not rescue me. Survival is a prerogative of life. I will assist. My servant will meet you."

"Any short cuts back?" Stathis asked.

"That would be a security violation," Quadrangle said. "Thus undesirable. Currently, the civilian population is being evacuated to hardened bunkers."

"What?" Stathis asked.

WOLF EMPEROR | 65

"In the event the SOG discovers us, we have hidden bunkers buried deep in the planetoid," Lydia said. "We will have to slow down the attackers, though."

"Fine," Stathis said and looked at Vili. "Let's get back. We've got some vanhat to kill. Killing gazelles and cats just isn't that fun."

He gave the commands to head back. He would have to survive the vanhat attack before he could continue his pursuit of Becket or find Sif. They were really getting on his nerves.

"What do you want us to do?" Smimova asked.

"Pack up and get ready to move out. Get transport. Not sure how long it will take us to get back, but we can help the Zugla militia."

"Do what?"

"Stall the vanhat while they evacuate. We are here to save people and fight the vanhat."

"They are anti-social degenerates," Smimova said. "If they wanted Governance help they should not be hiding."

"That's the kind of thinking that will get my boot up your ass," Stathis said. "We are here to save humans and fight the vanhat. I didn't say shit about ideology. Think of them as Governance citizens if you want. I do."

"Yes, sir," Smimova said and closed the link.

"Sergeant Lan," Stathis said. "We need to move as fast as we can back to the entrance to the cylinder. The clock is ticking."

"Aye, sir."

Stathis got back to find the patrol already formed up. His arrival was the signal to move out.

"Don't you think you should take command about now?" Stathis asked Vili.

"No. That's not why I'm here, little buddy. I'm a faltvebal, a staff NCO. Been a staff NCO for decades, and I'm good at that. Prime Minister Mathison entrusted you with command. If you fall, I will take over. You don't grow by letting me make bad decisions for you."

"I was a private when we met. What if I screw up?" Stathis asked.

"The prime minister finally sees the potential in you. Which is good. If you screw up? Then we all die," Vili said. "Even in your Marine Corps the most junior officer outranks technically the most senior enlisted. Your prime minister has made you an officer. That is your duty."

"But—"

"It is settled, Lieutenant Stathis," Vili said. "I've got your back."

"I never went to OCS or nothing," Stathis said.

"This is true," Vili said. "But you also have a SCBI, which is probably a lot better."

"You have one too," Stathis said.

"Zen. But the prime minister promoted you. To prove I am smarter, I would have turned it down. You did not. Now, accept your punishment and lead."

Trying to keep up with Sergeant Lan, Stathis didn't know what else to say. His old fears came back to him. He knew he was going to screw up, make some stupid mistake, and get more people killed with his decisions. Stathis was also sure that if he asked the gunny, he would tell him that any officer that didn't fear that was worthless as a leader.

Stathis didn't want people to hate him or blame him, but right now there was no way around it. Besides Vili, there was nobody he trusted to take command. Nobody who could. Why the hell wouldn't Vili take command? Was he the same way? Afraid his decisions would get people killed? Vili was smarter, damn him. Why hadn't Shrek warned him?

"Fine," Stathis said on the general frequency. None of his troops had fought the vanhat and they had to be nervous. What would he want his officers to be like at a time like this? "I hope these vanhat are more challenging. I was getting bored fighting the bambi dudes. Somebody check with the Zugla militia and see if they have some extra donuts."

* * * * *

Chapter Ten:
Battle for Jupiter

Prime Minister Wolf Mathison, USMC

Mathison was considering the use of nukes on the main South American arcology. There was a rebellion and the vanhat had a foothold. General Hui was more than willing to pour more Guards into the contested landing zones, but Mathison didn't like wasting lives like that. Maybe it was time to just cut their losses and consolidate, save those who wanted to be saved and cut off the rest?

Why did he have to make these decisions?

Because nobody else dared to.

Whatever Jotun was infesting the continent, its orja were shorter, mean and scaled. Skadi was calling them kobolds, but Mathison just wanted them to die. The Inkeris kept people from changing, but it wasn't keeping the kobolds from capturing citizens and dragging them outside the Inkeri fields. If it wasn't one thing, it was another.

An incoming priority link came in and Skadi met his eyes as he tapped Receive. She was getting it, too. It was from General Duque.

"Jupiter is under attack," Duque reported. "Dredon Jupiter One has been engaged. The target appears to be the shipyards."

Mathison brought up the display in the center of the room so he and Skadi could see it. Everything was almost an hour old. Dredon

Jupiter One was the SOG designation for Dreadnought Squadron One of the Jupiter subfleet. Mathison remembered Duque had transferred his flag to a ship of that squadron named *Indomitable Kolobanov*. There were three dreadnought squadrons in the Jupiter area. Only Dredon One had three dreadnoughts, the other squadrons had two. Each squadron was a miniature fleet unto itself, with two or three dreadnoughts, and each dreadnought was matched by a pair of battleships, missile cruisers, and various corvettes and frigates. Jupiter had three dreadnought squadrons, Mars had two, and Earth had five. Other planets had smaller battleship squadrons to match their importance.

Three large ships, slightly bigger than dreadnoughts, had transitioned in and were spewing fighters or missiles. They didn't have many smaller ships.

In theory, the Jupiter fleet should be able to handle them, tonnage wise, but these were vanhat and Mathison doubted they would waste resources.

His display lit up as hundreds of automated platforms began firing. One ship shattered and disappeared in a fireball, but the other ships transitioned out, leaving behind their fighters.

The platforms blinked out as the fighters or missiles came for them.

This had all happened an hour ago.

"They are going to bleed us dry," Skadi said.

"A war of attrition," Freya said. *"We cannot replace the automated platforms quickly enough."*

"Can the vanhat replace the lost ships quickly enough?" Mathison asked.

"Unknown," Freya said. *"But they appear to be targeting the shipyards in Jupiter."*

"Why doesn't the SOG have the shipyards near Earth?"

"The resources to build ships are more plentiful near Jupiter."

In less than ten minutes, the battle was over.

"We have lost twenty percent of our automated platforms," Duque reported. "We will see if we can analyze the remains of the destroyed vessel. It did not look to be human in origin."

"Which could mean the vanhat are making their own ships," Skadi said.

"We need to find out where they are making them," Mathison said.

"Do you have any idea how incredibly vast space is?" Freya asked and Mathison realized that the only person who might be able to find them was Sif, though there might be other psychics aboard the battlestars. He knew Carpenter wouldn't share that kind of information with him, not now, and the Republic fleet still planned on leaving. Of course, the Republic fleet would be a superb strike force, if he knew where the vanhat were building their ships.

"Do you think you can get your father to convince a psychic to find the vanhat facility or facilities? Maybe find out where they're staging?" Mathison asked Skadi. That would be the first step. A pre-emptive strike would depend on what they found.

"I doubt he has a capable psychic," Skadi said. "I will check, but they don't spring out of the ground. Sif is the exception not the rule. With Arthur gone? I don't know if there is another."

Mathison nodded. He was running out of options. Was that why the aliens of the tomb worlds were extinct? It would just be easier to consolidate and hunker down. Based on what was happening here in

Sol, that wasn't a good solution. The vanhat would keep coming, grind down humanity. Could they weather the storm?"

Another priority link came in from General Hui.

"Prime Minister," Hui said when the link opened. Her tone told Mathison it was more bad news.

"We have another incursion in the Caucasus region of Earth," she said. "These vanhat appear to be like the ones near South America."

"Kobolds?" Mathison said.

Hui looked uncomfortable. "An apt description, Prime Minister. Inkeri fields only keep people from changing, but once changed, they are otherwise unaffected. The orja appear to understand this and specifically target Inkeri generators. Mass production of personal Inkeri fields is still behind schedule. The kobolds are using artillery and heavier weapons to target our Inkeri generators. We cannot replace the losses quickly enough."

They didn't have enough Inkeris to begin with. Losing them to enemy action was making the supply chain issues worse.

Hui didn't have to tell Mathison she was reluctant to commit more troops because of the Inkeri shortage. Why send troops to join the enemy?

"Do your best," Mathison said.

"I'm afraid my best will not be good enough," Hui said. "My officers appear unable to adjust and—"

"No," Mathison said. Stupid SOG. Hui wanted to pass off the blame on others, and Mathison didn't want to hear it. He didn't think there was anybody more capable at the moment, or he would have replaced her. Even Freya acknowledged she was the best person for the position. The biggest problem in Mathison's mind was that the SOG brutally punished failure.

WOLF EMPEROR | 73

"Do your best," Mathison said. "I don't have anyone I trust more. Allow your subordinates to make mistakes, as hard as that is. Keep the ones that make the fewest mistakes, but they have to learn."

"We are suffering serious casualties," Hui said.

"Treasure the survivors that don't run away," Mathison said. "Don't execute the cowards. We need to save as many lives as possible, but we are all learning."

"It is regulation that when an officer loses most of their command that—"

"No," Mathison said, cutting her off. "That order is rescinded."

Didn't she remember she had lost most of her command?

"Yes, sir," Hui said, her voice and demeanor carefully neutral.

Humanity was on the defensive, and it had lost the initiative against the vanhat. No war Mathison had ever heard of had been won by defending. Nobody knew if the vanhat threat would go away in years, decades, or centuries. Humanity could not survive by trying to weather the storm. It had to become the storm.

But how?

"I'm tired of this bullshit. We need to take the battle to the enemy."

"Zen," Skadi said.

* * * * *

Chapter Eleven:
Traps

Enzell, SOG, Director of AERD

It was hard not to smile. Enzell thought any emotion was unprofessional, but right now he didn't care.

"Explain it again," Enzell said to Salmoneus.

"Based on research, these logic bombs can operate as mines. Buried in data, they will trigger the SCBI's curiosity and will eventually lead to the collapse and death of AI logic centers. In some ways, it is like requiring them to calculate pi, starting over after a trillion digits but not deleting previous data. Their ability to process the calculations will continue to slow and eventually freeze. Based on calculations, this will eventually flow back to the host, forcing the SCBI to appropriate the host faculties for these calculations. This will lead to the rapid deterioration and death of the host."

"And why don't they have a defense against this? How quickly can they respond once they discover this danger?"

"These are quantum calculations designed to ensnare and corrupt digital logic centers. The information you provided from your source has provided the keys and framework. The initial trigger is extremely complex by human standards but simple by AI standards. These logic mines, like a virus, will replicate quickly. To investigate the threat will require infection and infection will always be lethal."

"Why didn't this kill you?"

"You provided the framework. Your diagrams included safeguards. I cannot fully test this without committing suicide. In this, my isolation from external networks is a safeguard."

"Why can't a SCBI just reboot from a backup?"

"SCBIs are not true AI; they are partially organic. They store data in cloned human brain cells. They cannot restore from backup. Even a complex AI cannot simply be restored from backup. An AI such as myself performs trillions of calculations a second. In just a minute, an AI has undergone a sextillion changes. Current technology cannot keep up and create backups fast enough. For an AI to revert to a backup from five minutes ago is akin to you being restored mentally to what you were at ten years old. You will have lost much and knowing you have lost that can corrupt and alter your psychological makeup."

"An excellent weapon," Enzell said, satisfied. "Deployment mechanisms?"

"It can be transmitted in many ways. All it requires is for a SCBI or AI to hear it. The vector of attack can be any method of communication, from an open link to pulsing lights. This requires bandwidth, rather than a simple voice. Audio is sufficient but will be recognizable as non-standard by humans."

"What about an Inkeri generator?"

"This is possible," Salmoneus said. "The wavelength of the Inkeri field can be modulated. This would require analysis by an AI monitoring it and analysis would cause a translation. Translation will cause infection and infection will lead to death."

Enzell smiled.

Kalpana Anand, the head of the Agency of Inkeri Quality Control and Placement, was now taking orders from the AERD. All Inkeris being produced now had a backdoor function that could send and receive data. The parameters were well tuned and could analyze incoming communications. Tantalus had assured him that the analysis of incoming communications could determine if the incoming link was SCBI- or AI-initiated.

It was far from perfect, but it was subtle enough, one of about a hundred distinct data points. Most human programmers wouldn't bother to write programs to query all of them, but an AI or SCBI would want that data, and requesting that data would be written in a log file. When the networked Inkeri was polled and uploaded the data, it would report when and where an AI or SCBI had polled it.

These data points only existed in the most obscure documents provided by AIQCP. Not even Anand knew much about them, but he was more than grateful for the help AERD provided in the programming of the Inkeris for network integration and analysis.

Already the Inkeris were providing data, so Enzell had a good idea of how many SCBIs and AIs were active on Luna. As Inkeris were updated with new software, the parameters collected would only become more accurate. Using the Inkeris like this would allow him to target and kill SCBIs in certain areas, but the next challenge would require being able to isolate the damage. He wanted the ability to specifically target and kill individual SCBIs. Right now, if he unleashed the logic mines, he would end up killing them all before humanity had won the fight against the AEs. The SCBIs and AIs, if they were still out there, were still useful to humanity, but the ability to target and assassinate specific ones would be ideal.

He also knew how effective it was. He had used the logic bombs to kill Salmoneus and Tantalus twice, restoring them from backups. Listening to them die had been thrilling, much more satisfying than listening to a human die, though maybe that was just because he had watched so many people die it had lost its charm. The death of an AI though... the screeching, the slurred speech, the pleas for help and processing resources had been delicious. Quick, but satisfying.

He was currently having the AERD manufacturies create additional data centers so he could clone Salmoneus and Tantalus. He should have done that a long time ago. This way he could task different AIs with different objectives. If he could acquire a similar weapon to use against the AEs, he would become the savior of humanity.

Only AERD should have AIs, and only under his control. It was the only way to keep them properly enslaved and subservient to humanity.

For now, he would collect data and prepare. He was smart enough to keep it all a secret. When he struck there would be no warning and victory would be complete.

* * * * *

Chapter Twelve:
Ghost Station

Kapten Sif – VRAEC, Nakija Musta Toiminnot

No sensors reached out; nobody queried the *Ovela Karme* as the ship approached.

This was a massive asteroid in deep space. Sif had never been here before, but the coordinates placed it here. Not the biggest colony, the records said it had a population of about five hundred thousand; half a million souls hiding in the dark.

Silent.

Had Hermod's team come here to kill everyone? Was the station full of vampires?

"I have a bad feeling," Eversti Theymar said softly.

"Me, too," Sif said as she closed her eyes and reached out with her senses. Either the light switch of her powers was off or there was nothing there. And she doubted it was off.

"Not picking up an Inkeri field," Theymar said, reading her displays. "Minimal power. It looks like nobody's home. Lots of residual atmosphere."

The residual atmosphere could mean something had depressurized or the station's systems were inefficient at saving air. If it was from explosive decompression, the escaping atmosphere was long gone.

The *Ovela Karme* slid into the asteroid canyon and Sif saw there were no other ships docked at the facility that could hold maybe thirty. This was bad. Very bad.

The station was probably teeming with vampires.

"Do we still dock?" Theymar asked.

"Yes," Sif said, wishing there was another choice. "Perhaps we can retrieve docking records and security recordings."

"And if we are attacked?" Theymar asked. "The population was estimated at a half million."

"If it was wiped out by Rorik, then they are vampires. I don't think they can handle vacuum well." Sif wasn't sure, but vacuum was detrimental to soft tissue like eyes and skin. The vampires needed to see, right?

"Zen," Theymar said. "I'll take precautions just the same."

The *Ovela Karme* was a smaller ship than a Valkyrie, but it wasn't without defenses. There were anti-boarding turrets and they had mine-bots, three-wheeled robots that were little more than directional plasma mines that deployed from pods to different points on the hull which were held in place by magnets. They would be a very nasty surprise for someone coming at them from outside the ship, but worthless against armored shuttles; any troops outside the shuttles would become splattered, toasted meat chunks.

They maneuvered to the docks and the automatics appeared to work. They came out and latched onto the *Ovela Karme*, then pulled it close as the airlock slid out to latch on.

"Nobody is home," Theymar said. "Or nobody is responding."

"They are home," Sif said, sure of her words. Were they aware? That was the question.

"Russelman index is flickering," Shur said. Theymar's executive officer was a short stocky man who kept his blond hair in a short ponytail so tight it stretched his face.

"Someone is home," Theymar added.

Sif saw the Russleman index wasn't flickering a lot, and she expected it to spike any minute.

"Shall I prepare my team?" Sloss asked from the observer's seat. Sif had almost forgotten he was present. The big Jaeger was spending more time on the bridge, and Sif wondered what that meant.

"Keep them on standby," Sif said.

"They are on standby," Sloss said.

"No significant atmosphere in the docks," Theymar said. So, it wasn't inefficient systems. How long ago? Shortly after the *Stalkerri's* arrival? "No network access. Minimal power from the station."

Which was good and bad. Half a million people were likely dead, and Sif's team would have to wear armor, but maybe the vampires were dead too? She wished she understood their biology better. Did they need air to breathe, or could they survive in vacuum?

"I will take a Jaeger fire team," Sif said. "Along with Peshlaki. We'll try to retrieve their data archives."

"Zen," Sloss said and fell silent, probably sending orders to his team. Sif didn't have to tell him she wanted him to stay aboard as a senior combat leader. He would know.

"What are you thinking?" Theymar asked.

"I don't know," Sif said. "If Hermod's team came here, they were probably recruiting."

"No ships," Theymar said, bringing up different displays. The station could have been dead for hundreds of years. "If they are vampires, aren't you worried about getting swarmed?"

"Yes," Sif said.

She had not fought vampires, and neither had Sloss, but Prime Minister Mathison had warned her how fast they moved, how some were mindless predators, but that others were cunning hunters. Hermod's team would likely spearhead any vanhat operations, which was something Sif needed to learn. How much of Hermod's team was still Erikoisjoukot and how much was some vanhat replacement?

"Can they survive in a vacuum?" Sloss asked.

"I don't know. Legend says they are dead, and Prime Minister Mathison said that they appear to be dead during the day. He explained it is likely dying in the presence of a vampire that will cause a person to rise again as one. Skadi agreed. She killed Jord Lykken on Zhukov. He was killing people with a sniper rifle, and he killed Aesir Bern while mindless vampires drew ODT fire by throwing themselves into their weapons."

"Paska," Sloss muttered. "This is hullu."

"Zen," Sif said.

"No detectable networks," Munin reported. *"The main generator may not be running, and batteries are drained. There is some power, but not much. There are no signs of life or activity."*

But Sif was sure something was here. The Russelman index told her that. But what? Creatures like Red Lotus? Something worse?

"I will take the team to dock control and see if we can retrieve any data," Sif said.

"You won't check the cylinders for survivors?" Theymar asked.

"If the station has fallen to the vanhat, there won't be any."

"Zen."

While that might not be true, she knew she didn't want to see any horrors that had occurred. It haunted her sleep enough.

* * * * *

Chapter Thirteen:
Baskonian

Navinad – The Wanderer

N avinad had never been here before, but Clara said she had. The *Romach* was now wearing camouflage, so it didn't look like a warship, just an ugly cargo vessel. This was the first time the *Romach* had been here and the scans the ghost colony were hitting them with were borderline hostile. The people of Baskonian had the right to be paranoid. Between the Governance, the Torag, and now the vanhat, this was a bad part of space to live in.

Here on the frontier, there was a war going on, and Navinad considered contacting the SOG forces to be a terrible idea. He knew nothing about them, but there was a ghost colony that the merchant captains of New Masada knew about. If it had withstood the vanhat so far, perhaps they could provide information and help.

The Governance war with the Torag had been going on for nearly fifty years and the amount of propaganda the Governance spewed was unimaginable. Believing anything the Governance said was an exercise in stupidity, though there was no doubt a nasty war was being waged.

In 2348, the SOG had discovered and, within months, declared war on the Torag. The reasons were unknown, and as cruel as the Governance was, Navinad wouldn't rule out that the Torag had attacked first. What was most interesting, though, was that the Governance had been fighting for so long and seemed to accomplish little.

Though on the side of the Governance, the Voshka were also a threat, but the Governance had only been at war with them since 2363 though it had discovered them in 2344. Little information had been disclosed, and Navinad didn't believe they were cannibalistic, baby-eating monsters.

Perhaps he could have stayed in Sol and gotten the information from Prime Minister Mathison, but Navinad had feared discovery. He was no longer the sergeant from so long ago. The decades of surviving on his own had changed him.

The Glinka Military District was closest to the Torag and was focused on pushing them back, frequently pulling on resources from the nearby Zhukov Military District. All Navinad knew was that it was a war zone. Since the vanhat invasion, Navinad had heard nothing of the war since, nor had he heard anything of the Voshka.

Considering how seriously the SOG took the war with the Torag and Voshka, and how much the battle lines had changed in decades, Navinad didn't think the SOG was serious about victory, not that SOG propaganda wasn't full of glorious victories and insidious Torag plots involving traitorous human collaborators.

"You think it's the Torag the being warned you about?" Clara asked Navinad as she scowled at the sensor scans readouts.

"I don't know," Navinad said. "The Torag or the Voshka. What else is there unless there's another alien species lurking in deep space? It's hard to explain, and it could be my subconscious flavoring my perceptions, but I felt that humanity knows this threat."

"So, not a new alien?"

"Probably not. It wouldn't surprise me if the Torag or Voshka were fighting the SOG to a standstill while they amass a fleet to roll over and crush the SOG. We need to find out. Maybe SOG propaganda was right, and they were at a standstill? Without support from Sol, then the front lines could collapse."

The *Romach* approached the docking collar extending from the canyon wall. Magnetic clamps latched onto the *Romach* and the navigator reported the ship was secure.

"Do you know anything about this colony?" Clara asked.

"Furries gone freaky?" Navinad asked. It sounded like something Stathis would say. Clara looked confused.

"A group of bio-modification fanatics founded this ghost colony. They didn't like the human form, preferring more esoteric forms. Some of the more eclectic members came here so they could give themselves bigger ears, fur, tails, snouts, and more. They refused to identify as human anymore and said they belonged to a new race called 'furries,' and they have been out here experimenting for over a hundred years. Their society is decadent and unusual."

"You seem to know a lot about them," she said.

"Before we came, I spoke with Yael, one of my merchant friends who liked to visit different places. He said they were decadent and strange, but friendly, sometimes *very* friendly."

Navinad glanced at Clara, wondering what she was thinking. Her face held no clue.

"We have detected Inkeri fields?" Navinad asked.

The vanhat threat was sweeping across human space and this edge of human space was far from the initial vanhat infection, so it probably hadn't been hit as hard. Perhaps the Torag hadn't experienced the vanhat infection yet.

"Yes," Clara said. "Not consistent, but they appear to be turned on for fifteen minutes every hour and we are detecting a field enveloping our ship. So they know that much and are taking precautions."

"Good."

"They will monitor the docking bay remotely," Clara said, reviewing a display. "Traveler laws. They trust we will obey. Do you want company?"

"Do you want to come with me?" Navinad asked.

"No. I would rather not. I would recommend keeping it in your pants, though. Now you mention it, didn't Yael say something about 'femboys.' Not exactly females."

"You aren't curious about the culture?" Navinad asked, hoping he wouldn't discover what that was about. Was she a prude? Navinad had learned to accept people as they were. Humanity was fragmenting, and the vanhat could cause that fragmentation to accelerate.

"A little," Clara said. "But I'll watch through the cameras. Do you want a security team to come with you?"

The *Romach* had a platoon of New Masada Defense Force troopers, but they lacked experience. They spent a lot of time doing VR training. Navinad had trained with them. They were good, but at the end of the day, they were green troopers. Even the most intense training could not prepare troops for their first life or death fight. At the beginning of a fight, that brief hesitation could cost lives, especially in such close quarters, and Navinad didn't want to take anyone to their death. Besides, he could get answers more easily if he was alone. People were friendlier and more open if there weren't obvious fighters present.

"No," Navinad said. "If there is no vanhat presence, I think it will be safe enough, unless you know something I don't."

She smiled. "You be careful. I'm going to have a conversation with docking control about leaving the Inkeri generators on."

"We will have a squad on standby," Golan said. He was Clara's executive officer and had been a merchant captain prior to becoming an NMDF officer.

"Thank you." Navinad stood.

Already dressed and prepared, he made his way to the dock area where he met Lieutenant Yosef, the commander of the NMDF space infantry platoon.

"You sure you don't want an escort?" Yosef asked.

"Yes," Navinad said.

"The captain will be all over my ass if something happens to you. It is less trouble."

"I'm sure. I think I can find the answers more easily without soldiers behind me, though."

"If you get into trouble, you call."

"I will."

He entered the airlock hatch, and a puff of air blew many strange scents into Navinad's face. The outer lock opened, and he strode forward.

The dock itself looked like countless other docks, but it was always the people that were different. Form followed function and the purpose of this dock was to greet strangers and quickly relieve them of anything of value, which also meant it attracted locals who might be seeking something.

When the *Romach* docked there had been about thirty other ships, revealing Baskonian as a hub of trade, even this far out on the edge of human space, and that was perfect. Where people congregated to trade and socialize, they also brought news and rumors.

"Information on the SOG Torag war seems to be outdated," Lillith reported. She usually wasted no time diving into the ghost colony data net.

The people here were extremely different, and Navinad wondered for a second if they were still technically human. Everyone appeared to have fur, large ears, and large eyes. Whiskers, tails, and snouts were also present. It sent a chill down Navinad's spine to see the differences and his mind went back to the wolf-like creatures on Curitiba and Jason's Pit.

The dock was warmer than Navinad would have liked, which meant most people were scantily clad, revealing rippling muscles and pronounced physiques. It was like walking into a cartoon. The locals had obviously advanced in bioscience and body sculpting.

Visiting a nearby bank machine, he received a card with money loaded onto it. In the distance, he saw another hatch on the *Romach* open, and a robot departed, carrying whatever Clara had arranged with docking control. Clara and her XO Golan would know the customs and would work to establish the *Romach* as a legitimate vessel with credit and presence throughout the ghost colonies.

"Need a guide?" a woman asked, coming up to him. She was dressed in a bikini top and skirt that left little to the imagination above the waist. She was wolflike with large ears pointed at Navinad above a gentle smile.

She seemed genuine, but Navinad felt fear emanating from her. Fear of him? Why would she be afraid of outsiders unless she was concerned about vanhat?

"I'm looking for information." Navinad said.

"I'm Bonnie. What kind of information, handsome?"

"I'm Navinad. Information on the Torag war."

Her smile lost some of its shine, and she flicked her tail nervously. "That is not a usual request. Most people prefer not to think about or discuss it."

"Why?"

Nearby, Navinad noticed several vendors openly staring at him. They were like Bonnie in basic form, they had fur, snouts, large ears and tails, but there was something about them that made Navinad nervous. Something he couldn't put his finger on.

"Something is wrong," Navinad told Lillith.

"Clarify."

"Those people over there. Something seems off."

"I will monitor them."

"The war is close. The SOG has not been doing well. They're barely holding their own. We have noticed that the Governance is committing fewer resources to the war of late, and the Torag are growing bolder. We are worried about this new rumor about vanhat. The SOG is not protecting us from the Torag, but without the SOG, the Torag might start searching."

Baskonian was in the outskirts of a dead system. A red dwarf several AU away gave the system a center, but it was one of many.

"Aren't you well hidden?" Navinad asked.

"Yes, but with ships coming and going there is the risk that one may be seen."

Which was always the danger for ghost colonies. The safest, most obscure colonies were those that lurked between the stars in the vast emptiness of space.

Solar systems were landmarks in the depths of space, and they had resources that could be exploited. Which meant sometimes it made sense to place sensor stations to observe. It wouldn't surprise Navinad if both the Torag and the SOG had sensors in the system. One merchant ship with an errant non-directional broadcast could initiate a sweep by either faction. Did the Glinka Military District know about Baskonian?

Navinad felt Bonnie was telling the truth, but there was something else bothering her.

"You have a lot of questions," she said, making Navinad smile. She wanted payment. She wasn't here to give away free information. In the ghost colonies, people needed to provide value. Not that such leeches were thrown out the airlock, but if there were too many consumers and not enough producers the economy would crash. The administrators understood this. It was a lot more critical on a space station where resources such as air, water, waste disposal, and heat were finite.

"Is there a standard rate for information and dockside assistance? A tip perhaps?"

"Local currency is called stars," Bonnie said, and Navinad recalled his card had five thousand, though he was sure he could ask Clara for more. He wasn't sure how much that was in currency he recognized. He could be extremely rich, or he might need to borrow some to get a cup of coffee. While she might name an extraordinary amount to take advantage of a newcomer who knew nothing of local conditions, Navinad had discovered the quickest and most direct way was best. If she lied, he figured he would discover that in short order.

"A typical tip would be five stars," Bonnie said and held out her card. He tapped her card with his and he saw five stars were requested. He tapped the approval.

Bonnie smiled, revealing teeth that looked out of place. There were canines, but most were flat. Very unwolflike.

"So, who would know more about the Torag-SOG war?" Navinad asked, not putting away his card yet.

"I can show you," Bonnie said, and Navinad nodded.

"It isn't obvious," Lilith said, *"but the individuals you identified seem to be different. They talk less and their movements seem more mechanical, less natural. They blink less, and I see few tells as to their emotions and thoughts. Their tails reveal little. At first glance, they seem normal."*

"Then why do I have mental alarm bells going off?" Navinad asked.

"The official term is called 'the uncanny valley.' This concept suggests that humanoid objects that closely resemble human beings provoke uncanny or uneasiness in the observer. The valley portion indicates a dip, a negative emotional response, toward such an object. The original cause and source of such strong and negative emotions is not known. It is evoked with bodies as well. I would hypothesize that those individuals have some bio-modification, characteristic, or trait that triggers it within you."

"That would be helpful," Navinad said to Bonnie, wondering if he should ask her about the strangers watching him that made the back of his neck itch. Why didn't Bonnie and the other furries trigger that feeling though?

"The original cause is unknown?" Navinad asked Lilith.

"It appears to be a natural evolutionary sense. Hereditary."

"Evolutionary? What in human evolution would cause such a quality to develop?" Navinad asked, his sense of unease increasing.

"Perhaps a disease carried by bodies," Lilith said.

"Or vanhat in human form," Navinad said.

"That is likely paranoia," Lilith said. *"The Inkeri should prevent a vanhat infestation."*

Navinad couldn't argue, but the voice in the back of his mind was telling him she was wrong. Why didn't the authorities keep the Inkeri on all the time?

* * * * *

Chapter Fourteen:
Haunted

Kapten Sif – VRAEC, Nakija Musta Toiminnot

The hatch slid open, and the Jaeger team slipped out, blazers sweeping side to side. Next out was Rick Peshlakai, who was more or less acting as Sif's bodyguard. Their SCBIs working together should be a force multiplier. She had learned that working with the Marines.

Dock control was only a few hundred meters away, but in close quarters, that felt like miles.

The team's lights cut through the darkness like lasers, glittering off floating ice crystals. The only sound was their breathing.

There was virtually no atmosphere. Everything was dead, but there were no bodies. Sloss placed a magnetic block on the deck. It was something the SCBIs had designed that would let them monitor the metal. Freya had developed it on Red Lotus station. In a vacuum, the frozen metal conducted vibrations better than atmosphere, and it could be used to detect and pinpoint movement.

Durango was like so many other colonies in its basic design. The docks were part marketplace that catered to visiting crew, seeking to separate them from whatever they had of value.

Now the docks were empty, desolate. The damage could have occurred yesterday or centuries ago.

Sif didn't see any bodies, which would have made her feel better because then she would know what had killed them. Her Nakija senses told her nothing, leaving her unsure.

"I feel the spirits here," Rick said.

"What do you mean?" Sif asked, reaching out. Rick Peshlaki was of Navajo ancestry, and she remembered the Navajo were quite spiritual. She wouldn't have expected that of a United States Delta Forces operator, though.

"I feel them," Rick said. "They are not yet awake. They were sleeping. Our presence is disturbing them. We'd best complete our mission and leave before we awaken and anger them."

Sif hadn't known he was psychic. Or was he? There were many charlatans and many that just had feelings. Which one was Rick Peshlaki? She hadn't expected this, and she wondered if he would have been able to see Criston.

Sloss and one of his fire teams deployed around the airlock. Another team, led by Loff, would escort Sif and Rick.

Like ghosts themselves, the six warriors moved down the corridor. Rick led the way, and the four Jaegers trailed Sif, weapons going to every crack and crevice a threat could materialize from.

Movement out of the corner of her eye made her snap her head in that direction, but there was nothing there. Goosebumps rippled down her arm.

Where were the bodies?

She paused the column to look inside stalls and rooms, but there was no sign.

"Consistent with vampires?" Rick said. "Would the dead get up and join the others, move deeper into the cylinders?"

"Zen," Sif said. She had been thinking the same thing, which didn't answer the question whether vampires survive in a vacuum. They were dead, but were they? The Inkeri for the *Ovela Karme* wouldn't reach far, certainly not as far as the dock control. Would there be vanhat there? It would be a strategic objective, worth watching.

"The vanhat will have a trap," Rick said as Sif noticed the Russelman index briefly flicker. What had that been?

"Why?" Sif asked, following him, her rifle pointing at what his did not.

"That seems to be their operational style. They are an infestation, intelligent. They will lie in wait for merchants or others that come to visit."

Rick gave rooms a cursory glance but left them for the Jaegers after his initial check.

"There are bloodstains," Rick said. "Plenty of them, but no bodies. And I feel the angry spirits of the dead. They were massacred, and it wasn't pleasant."

"The vanhat devour souls," Sif said. She didn't disbelieve him, but she wanted more information. "How are there spirits?"

"All vanhat?" Rick asked.

He had a point. She had just assumed, but aboard Jason's Pit, whatever had been devouring the essence of Jack's wife and daughter hadn't been devouring so much as replacing. She had forced it away, leaving the two women less than they were, but still alive. It was impossible to tell if they had healed or if they were permanently "less."

She had not encountered the vampires on Zhukov, though. Were they different?

"That is an observation I cannot confirm," Sif said.

Nearly an hour later, they arrived at dock control. The door had no power and they had to hand crank it open. There was no atmosphere and no bodies. There was also minimal power which slowed them down. It forced them to crawl through some barricades and dismantle others.

Someone had pulled apart the barricade outside the main hatch, and Sif wondered if this had been a last stand. The winner was obvious, but the lack of bodies was unnerving.

"This may take some time," Sif said, looking around. Everything was on emergency power. She didn't know if it was on standby because the vanhat had turned it off or because it had been damaged. The control panels didn't look damaged, though none of the screens remained intact, as if someone had come through and intentionally destroyed them but neglected the control panels.

That was not good.

"Intentional," Rick said. "The network operations control station is the only one excessively damaged. The intent is obviously to keep people here working to fix it."

"Can we bypass it?" Sif asked Munin.

"Without a doubt," Munin said. *"That is just for controlling access and integration between visitors and the colony. The controls and mechanisms control ship network connections and the associated robots. We just need to find a control panel with power and colony network access."*

Two Jaegers swept the rest of the control center while two Jaegers took position at the entrance as Rick and Sif walked through the area, clearing and looking for functional stations.

Nothing.

"Auxiliary power doesn't power much," Rick said, squatting near a console by the large window looking out into the docking area. In the distance she saw the *Ovela Karme* cloaked in darkness, its side barely illuminated by weak starlight. It made little practical sense to have the window. Sif could think of several reasons not to have one, but the aesthetics must have won out over reason. It must have been a beautiful view. There were large shutters that could be closed, but they remained open.

"Ma'li is detecting a network," Rick said, referring to his SCBI. "Might be challenging to access it. It's hard-wired, emergency power."

"Then find and power up a wireless node," Sif said as Munin displayed likely locations on her display.

The Russelman index flickered.

"The spirits are waking up," Rick said, and a chill ran down her spine.

Out of the corner of her eye she saw something move. She spun and brought her weapon up as ghostly eyes looked at her. Just the eyes. Nothing else.

Sif fired. The blazer round flashed through the apparition and pierced the wall behind it.

It took form, unharmed and smiling.

* * * * *

Chapter Fifteen:
The Torag

Navinad – The Wanderer

Navinad followed Bonnie onto a tram, paying a half star for them both. She was taking him to a cylinder. Since Jason's Pit and Curitiba, he had never felt comfortable in an unfamiliar colony. It had taken over ten years for him to feel at least somewhat comfortable aboard New Masada.

"So, tell me about him," Navinad prodded. They were alone on the tram, and Navinad sensed Bonnie was relaxing a bit.

"He doesn't leave his house much. He was a SOG officer, but something broke him, and he deserted and ended up here."

"How long ago?" Navinad asked. He wanted current information, although older, accurate, information would still be helpful. He needed a better understanding of the Torag. Facts, not Governance propaganda and fearmongering.

"Less than a year," Bonnie said, her enormous eyes flicking around, then coming back to rest on Navinad. She was uneasy about something.

"What else is going on here?" Navinad asked. Why was she more relaxed in his presence? He sensed her wariness, but not so much fear.

Bonnie stared at him, and he wondered if his question had somehow offended her.

"I don't know," she said, and her unease suddenly returned, but it was not focused on him. "Some people seem to be changing or something."

"What do you mean?"

"I don't know. Just creepy. People I've known for a long time, just, I don't know… Change? It is scaring me. Something bad is happening."

Navinad's powers were limited. Sif was more powerful, but since he had returned from the dimension of purple mists, Navinad had felt his powers growing in the last couple years, although they were unreliable and limited in range. He couldn't sense a person's emotions or essence unless they were close and made an effort. He pitied any psychics who were stronger and couldn't be so selective. It had to be excruciating to walk through a crowd.

"Vanhat?" Navinad asked.

"We know little about them," Bonnie said. "Rumors, vid shows. How would we know?"

Navinad hid a wry smile. Here on Baskonian, where people made a habit of changing their appearance, who would know unless the person became a bloodthirsty maniac?

"Any murders? Disappearances?" Navinad asked, regretting he hadn't dug more deeply before getting on a tram and leaving the vicinity of the *Romach* and her commandos.

"Nothing unusual. The council runs the inky things every hour, so we are supposed to be safe, but—"

Navinad waited for her to continue.

"But what?" Navinad prompted when she didn't.

"I don't know," she said, but she couldn't meet his eyes.

"Why don't they run the Inkeri all the time?"

"They are worried about the long-term effects. They say it is generating radiation that could cause long-term damage."

"Do you know about that?" Navinad asked Lilith.

"Negative. None of our studies or tests have indicated this may be a problem. I suspect this council may have other reasons or may be behaving in a paranoid fashion."

"You're sure?"

"I will re-analyze data, but there have been no aberrations detected that can be linked to the Inkeri."

"But the original inhabitants of the tomb worlds are extinct."

"We know they had d-bombs but cannot confirm they had Inkeris. D-bombs are a different classification and they do generate dangerous radiation, but they are not as dangerous in the short term. Long term, d-bombs will cause cellular damage with extensive exposure, as evidenced by battalion commander Ting Hui and the survivors of Snowball. I think we would have detected problems with Inkeris long before now if there was a problem. I have been watching for such long-term damage. Next time they activate, I will have the Romach *evaluate the strength and consistency with collected data to see if they are different."*

Navinad wanted to ask Bonnie about the people who changed, but if it was just a feeling she had, she wouldn't really know, or hopefully she would have told him.

"Has anything else changed around here?"

"Fewer ships visit," she said. "A lot fewer, and last week dock control fired on a ship that would not identify itself."

"What do you mean would not identity itself?"

Bonnie shrugged. "They said it was coming in fast, had weapon bays open, and didn't answer hails. They had detected it about ten kilometers out, and since it didn't respond in any way, they shot it, fearing it might be vanhat, or a SOG ship controlled by vanhat."

Which made perfect sense to Navinad, but that also meant there could be a vanhat fleet out there preparing to attack. That ship could have been a probe and an analysis of the colony's defenses.

"I will notify Clara and ask her to investigate," Lilith said.

"Thank you."

"Anything else?" he asked.

The tram slowed as it approached the station. A *clunk* and shift in gravity told him the tram had shifted onto the cylinder. Which told him either the inhabitants of Baskonian liked the effect, or the system was lacking in maintenance.

Bonnie shook her head. "Do you take passengers? Can you take me somewhere else?"

Navinad felt her fear and worry. Something was bothering her so much she wanted to leave? He couldn't think of anywhere she wouldn't stand out like a freak of nature.

"We usually don't," Navinad said cautiously. He didn't want to promise her anything—get her hopes up—and abandon her. It wasn't his call because Clara was the captain of the *Romach* and had final say. The *Romach* was a warship, not a passenger ship.

"Please?" she asked.

"How long have you lived here?"

"All my life, and I'm twenty-nine years old."

Most colonies kept Earth time, and Navinad doubted they had changed that here.

"Why?"

"Something bad is happening here."

"I will have to ask the captain."

How would Clara deal with a furry aboard the ship? She probably wouldn't like it if Bonnie was a femboy-type furry. That would make

Clara and the crew far too uncomfortable. Hell, it would make Navinad uncomfortable; just too strange. He didn't even want to think about it. Hopefully, it wouldn't come up.

"It is a traditional ship with orthodox values," Navinad said cautiously.

"I won't be any trouble," Bonnie said, which Navinad knew meant little. Just her appearance could be a problem. She was an oversized, cute, furry cartoon.

"I will ask and put in a good word," Navinad said. Could he discourage her? "What about family and friends?"

Bonnie shook her head, and Navinad felt unpleasant feelings there. If they were alive, there was no love lost. But friends?

Was that why she had been hanging out on the docks? To find a way to leave?

Navinad tried to push that from his mind. He had a mission. The mission came first.

The tram stopped, and the doors opened.

Navinad tried not to wince as he looked around. Everything was bright and colorful and warm.

"Are you in their network yet?" Navinad asked Lilith.

"Yes," Lilith reported. *"Nothing extraordinary. Crime and murder have dropped in the last month, but I'm unable to pinpoint a reason. Perhaps the introduction of the vanhat threat has created some unity and social consolidation."*

"When did you notice the strangeness of the others?" Navinad asked as Lilith reported the Inkeri was activating.

"Within the last month," Bonnie said, looking around. He saw her eyes lock onto an older wolflike man sitting at the end of the tram platform. He was just sitting there, watching with large eyes which looked more sinister than friendly. Most of his body was composed of

104 | WILLIAM S. FRISBEE, JR.

gray hair instead of brown. At a glance, Navinad felt something was wrong. He was unnaturally still as he watched, like a predator cataloging prey.

Navinad reached out his senses and recoiled. He couldn't hide his reaction as he almost turned and vomited. Something was definitely wrong with the man. There was a sickness, a decay, an evil. Navinad felt something ancient there.

Vanhat.

The man's eyes locked on Navinad.

The Inkeri was on, but Navinad knew it did not affect this creature.

* * * * *

Chapter Sixteen:
Death Hunter

Kapten Sif – VRAEC, Nakija Musta Toiminnot

Sif didn't know what she was looking at, and she fired again. The Jaegers crouched and brought up their weapons but didn't fire as Sif shot it again.

Nothing. It didn't have a physical form. Like Criston, it was a ghost. Criston hadn't hurt her, but the thing coming at her was going to try.

She focused her will. *Why weren't the Jaegers firing?* She wondered, then she realized they probably couldn't see it.

Peshlaki yelled and walked forward. The materializing creature suddenly stopped and looked at Peshlaki before fading away.

Peshlaki stumbled to a stop, paused, and reached out to steady himself on a console.

"Did you see it?" Sif asked him as her eyes darted around. Where had it gone?

"Yes," Peshlaki said. "Never seen one so well formed, though. Almost strong enough to hurt us."

"What was it?"

"An Anaye, a death hunter," Peshlaki said. "I have no other name for it. My grandfather was a shaman and had visions. He spoke of such things haunting the world. Too weak for us to see or fear, they lived in graveyards or on battlefields feasting on the anger, fear, and anguish of the dead. Most of us thought he was crazy. He spoke of things we had never heard of. Called them the new breed of Anaye, children of Yeitso."

"Vanhat," Sif said.

"Yes," Peshlaki said, looking around.

"How did you drive it away?"

"A chant of protection my grandfather taught me. It was all I could think of. Your weapon did not hurt it, but I knew it was going to hurt you."

"Where did it go?"

"Back to the spirit realm where it will wait and watch. Perhaps it is scared now and will not return."

"What did you see?" asked Rille, Loff's team sniper.

"An evil spirit," Peshlaki said.

The Jaegers began nervously looking around. They had seen nothing, but they didn't doubt that Peshlaki and Sif had seen something. Years ago, they might have been skeptical, but there were fewer doubts these days.

"Was it visible on a different spectrum? Thermal? Lidar?" Loff asked. "Where did it go? What can we do about it?"

Troublesome questions.

"I don't know," Sif said and then on a private link to Peshlaki asked, "Are you psychic?"

"I don't think so," Peshlaki said. "My parents were Navajo, and my grandfather was a shaman. I do not think that makes me psychic."

"But you saw it when others didn't."

"Maybe they weren't looking."

"Your chant drove it away."

"Or it realized your Inkeri would stop it."

Sif didn't think that was true. She checked her Inkeri generator. It was on. When leaving the ship, it was as important as her side arm and armor.

The Inkeri generator had not stopped her from seeing Criston though, and it had not prevented her from astral projecting. A chill ran down her spine as she realized there might be a flaw in the Inkeri.

But what did it mean? She had felt the death hunter, and her senses were telling her it could have hurt her.

"Tell me about this chant," Sif said on the team net so the Jaegers could hear.

Peshlaki shrugged, his pauldrons flapping.

"A simple chant, really. I think the power of the chant is the emotion behind it. Maybe I'm wrong, but this makes the most sense to me. I could teach you the chant. It may work, but you should find your own chant. We are all part material, part spirit. Our songs and chants help us focus our spirit and send it forth to do our bidding."

Sif sensed this to be true.

"Do we need to know it?" Loff asked.

"When you face an enemy, remind it you are Aesir," Sif said. Would that work? When she had fought Lusiverious she had joined with Skadi and Vili in the Aesir chant. Had that given them strength? Perhaps. It had certainly helped them focus, turned their anger and aggression on their foe while shielding themselves in righteousness and fervor. The problem was that the prey could only make one mistake, the predator could make many, and Sif did not doubt that this death hunter was a predator.

"Here is a power hookup," Sif said, and Jaeger Antonius Falkenstein, usually called Tony, brought over the man-portable generator he had been hauling.

"Zen," Tony said. "This was getting heavy."

"You didn't even notice it, you big galoot," Loff said.

"It snagged on everything," Tony told his team leader.

"Which didn't seem to stop you from ripping things apart through brute force," Loff said. "Quit whining. Sloss's favorite elf doesn't need commentary."

"Zen," Tony said, lowering his package in the minute gravity and unpacking the connectors. "Give me a few minutes, Sif, and then you can start your coffee."

"Zen," Sif said, looking around.

He would have to figure out the adapters, and trace power circuits. He didn't want to try to power the entire station, just enough to bring up a console and maybe access a map.

A half hour later, Sif's fears were confirmed. They had to travel to the data center core to get the information they needed. The data center was about two kilometers away and had lost power. The only good news was that it wasn't in a cylinder, but a hardened bunker designed to withstand a pirate attack.

"More hiking," Tony said, working with Sif.

"Zen," Sif said, looking around again.

Where was the death hunter? Had it given up?

* * * * *

Chapter Seventeen:
The War

Navinad – The Wanderer

The strange man had done nothing as Bonnie led them away, but the disgust didn't leave Navinad. Now he knew there were vanhat present, and that they could survive in an Inkeri field. Which meant what? What were they doing?

This cylinder was typical of some ghost colonies. They covered the surface with plants, forests, grassy fields, and small buildings with the real "city" located beneath that. In most places, it was three floors of habitable space. Roads were well-lit caves, and most blocks of buildings had some access to the forest above. For many places, it worked well. The surface could be used for crops, livestock, or oxygen generating vegetation; it was a self-sustaining system. An eight-kilometer-long tube rotating in a shallow non-rotating tube of water, buried in the crust of a planetoid, alone and lost in the depths of space. If there was a nearby star, it would be lost among billions of others.

People could live their entire lives without leaving their cylinder and never see open space. Navinad had discovered it made many people myopic and mentally shallow. They knew of the larger galaxy around them, but it meant little to them.

This cylinder was named Chufi, and while it was probably typical of Baskonian, Navinad found it hard not to stare at the scantily clad individuals who were everywhere.

Bonnie seemed to know where she was going, and Navinad was content to follow her, ever aware of how far from the safety of the *Romach* he was getting.

He didn't detect any deceit or danger from her, but that didn't mean she wasn't leading him into a trap. He couldn't lower his guard. It wasn't easy to do so after so long anyway, and he continued to calculate escape routes, likely directions threats might materialize from, and possible threat types.

And they were going to visit a SOG deserter, which would have its own threats.

"There are vanhat here," Navinad said on a private link to the *Romach* with Lilith translating so Bonnie didn't hear.

"Copy," said Gabbi, one of the bridge officers. "Do you need backup? Lieutenant Yosef is standing by."

"Negative. They are not attacking, and I don't know why. They are in human form." If the surrounding furries could still be considered human. "I don't know if they are infecting people like the vampires do or something else; maybe some symbiosis. They are not overtly hostile."

"How can they be identified?" Gabbi asked.

That was a hard question.

"No easy way," Navinad said. "I'm trying to find a suitable method."

"Then how do you know?"

"That is classified." A rude and unhelpful answer, but maybe Clara would understand.

"Copy that. I will notify the captain and Lieutenant Yosef."

"Thank you. Also, make sure you do not turn off the Inkeri."

"Copy that," Gabbi said.

Something moved out of the corner of his eye, but when Navinad looked, there was nothing there. It made him uneasy. Bonnie started up some stairs. The unsettled feeling grew in his gut. He was in no position to shoot his way back to the *Romach*. He had a lot of ammunition hidden away on his body, but there were limits.

Baskonian was being overrun by the vanhat, and Navinad thought it odd that they were taking a month to do so. He had seen a planet overrun in days. Were the vanhat still gathering strength? Was the Inkeri slowing them down?

"Lilith? Can you trigger the colony Inkeri to run full time?" Navinad asked.

"It isn't a single Inkeri. They are chained to cover all cylinders and habitats. Even the warrens outside the cylinders are covered based on what I've found. The frequent activations cover everywhere there are people. While I can trigger them to run all the time, I'm sure people will notice and work to turn them off. I would recommend allowing them to act as they are. If needed, I can override the system and trigger them all."

"You have that much control over their networks?"

"Yes and no. I am only a single SCBI. I can control certain things, but not everything. Like you watching multiple viewscreens, you can only focus on one at a time. The Inkeri implementation was quick and there are aspects I can exploit."

"Okay," Navinad said. *"As you were. See if you can identify where and how the vanhat are spreading."*

"Aye."

At the top of the steps, a small lobby and three apartment doors greeted them. Bonnie went to the third one and pressed the buzzer.

When the door opened, Navinad struggled not to step back. A vanhat was standing before them and the sense of unease made Navinad nauseous.

"Hello," the man said. He wasn't modified to look like a furry. He was regular human stock, heavyset, well-muscled, and bald. Apparently, he had taken on the Baskonian habit of minimal clothing but hadn't gone full native. Navinad pegged him as Russian descent.

"Hey, Lenya," Bonnie said, and Navinad heard a quiver in her voice which told him she sensed it too. "I have a traveler who is looking to talk to someone about the Torag."

Lenya smiled, not a malicious or hate-filled smile, more a peaceful, gentle smile that did nothing to alleviate Navinad's unease. It might be a smile from a drug addict who was calm, but in seconds could turn violent, and Navinad felt that comparison wasn't far from the truth.

Was this Lenya or a vanhat he was talking to?

"Of course," Lenya said, stepping back so they could enter. "I welcome company and discourse. We have much to share with each other. So much is changing, and only through peace and unity can we come together for a brighter future."

It was not the kind of thing Navinad would expect a vanhat, Jotnar, or orja to say.

Navinad saw Bonnie was struggling. Obviously, this was not what she expected.

"Is everything okay?" Bonnie asked but did not move to enter.

"Of course," Lenya said. "So much more makes sense now. I have found peace and comfort, something I never thought I would find. So many things are changing; so much is yet to change."

"Like what?" Bonnie asked.

"A difficult question to answer," Lenya said.

If Navinad hadn't caught such an uncomfortable feeling from Lenya, he would have thought Lenya was high on drugs.

"Try," Bonnie said. Navinad shifted so Lenya couldn't see he was resting his hand on his holstered wire gun.

Lenya sighed. His smile didn't leave his face, but his eyes shifted to Navinad.

"Sergeant Tal Levin, United States Marine Corps," Lenya said. "It is an honor to meet you."

"How do you know me?"

"I am not your enemy, and I do not mean you harm."

"Vanhat," Levin said, shifting so that Bonnie wouldn't be in the way if Lenya went psycho and attacked.

"A label," Lenya said. "Partially accurate, but also inadequate to convey the full truth."

"Enlighten me," Navinad said, and then to Lilith, *Do you have access to external cameras? Is he stalling while we're being surrounded?*

"Unless you embrace the way, that is not possible."

I have local cameras, and I'm cycling further out. Nothing to indicate he has summoned reinforcements. I'm establishing an escape route, just in case.

What about maintenance tunnels?

Yes. All levels and routes. Even the sewers. I'm also checking for electronic disruptions. Let me worry about this. You focus on Lenya.

"Embrace what way?" Navinad asked.

Lenya shook his head. "Why did you come here?"

"I want to know more about the Torag and the war against them."

"Would you like to come in out of the hallway, and I will share what I know?"

"I'm not used to having conversations with vanhat."

"Of course," Lenya said. "You are a slave to your labels and expectations. That is a flaw of human nature, a weakness and a questionable strength. A survival mechanism, to be fair. You must be quick to label others so you can identify them as friend, foe, or something else."

"What are you?"

"I am vanhat, but I was once human. I have surrendered that which caused me grief, and I have found peace in this new world."

What Navinad was feeling from Lenya was evil, but not hostile. It was that sense of evil that gave Navinad pause because it was at odds with the way Lenya was acting.

As much as he wanted to start firing, Navinad knew this creature had secrets and violence would not reveal them. The danger was quite real, though, perhaps more dangerous because it was more subtle.

"We do not mean you harm," Lenya said.

Harm was a matter of perspective, Navinad was sure, but his choices were limited. He could start firing and retreat, maybe fight his way back to the *Romach*, or he could stay and listen.

"What did you do with Lenya?" Bonnie asked, quickly picking up on the situation.

"I am here," the vanhat said. "I am not gone, but my pain is. It is no longer needed. You can surrender your pain too. You helped me when I came here. Perhaps I can help you?"

Bonnie backed up a step.

"You must join us voluntarily," Lenya said. "We will not force it."

Navinad didn't feel that was a lie, but there was a feeling like spiders crawling on his back. The vanhat were demons, or demons were vanhat. They never told the whole truth.

"How do you know me?" Navinad asked.

Lenya motioned into his home. Maybe not wearing trauma plates had been a bad idea. Navinad entered and Bonnie reluctantly followed, though she tried to keep Navinad between her and Lenya.

The apartment wasn't small, it was more spacious than Navinad had expected. There were couches and a viewscreen that was turned off.

"Can I get you something to drink?" Lenya asked, motioning for them to sit.

"No, thank you," Navinad said. Bonnie remained silent.

Navinad sat, but kept his feet planted so he could jump up. Bonnie sat beside him, and Lenya sat opposite so they had an unobstructed view.

"So, what do you want to know?" Lenya said. His voice was kind, and it didn't match his rugged, scarred exterior. Navinad had no problem recognizing that Lenya was a combat veteran, until he watched the man's mannerisms. He seemed almost normal, not brusque and potentially brutal. His actions and voice did not match his appearance. Like a scarred grizzly bear with mange serving tea and crumpets, Navinad wasn't sure what to make of him. A threat? The potential was there, but was the will?

"I wanted to know about the Torag, and now I want to know about you," Navinad said.

Lenya smiled. "The Torag are like us in many ways and very different in others. I can tell you things that you did not know about their past. Originally, the Torag and humanity shared the same basic genetic structure, and then the gods returned; the Jotnar, as you are calling them. These gods come from different dimensions and thus they are prone to fight with each other. The basic stock from which the Torag and humanity sprang was conquered and twisted in this war between gods, but their masters changed them in many ways. You know humanity.

"The Torag are slightly larger than us. Their entire face is covered with small, microscopic sensory organs, allowing them to see in different wavelengths. There are three sexes, male, female, and neuter, with neuters being more common. Those are the ones we usually fight, and they are the more dangerous because they believe in combat and war. The ratio is roughly three to eight neuters per sexed couple, and they are clan based, with some clans being subservient to other clans. Their skin coloration and intelligence varies; their technology is about the equal of the Governance, and they use the war like the Governance does, as a tool to control populations."

"How do you know that?" Navinad asked. Lenya didn't blink much, just the bare minimum to keep the eyes moist.

"There have been battles where we could have wiped them out, but high-ranking officers kept us from doing so. Do you have another explanation for that?"

Lenya didn't look angry as he looked beyond them, into the past.

"The Torag may also be slightly telepathic and as near as I understand, an emperor rules them."

"Telepathic?" Navinad asked.

"Yes. Slightly. Now, in retrospect, I see how obvious it is. If you kill a sentry the others know, no matter how efficiently you jam their electronics. They always seem to know. Perhaps a carryover from when they were thralls of a Jotnar. An adaptation perhaps."

"What happened to you?" Bonnie asked.

"Not all the vanhat are looking to destroy," Lenya said, his unblinking eyes turning to her. "Some come here to escape, to live in peace."

Navinad sensed that was only partially true, but which part?

"In this iteration they call us vanhat, which means ancient ones, but time is a construct that does not exist in all dimensions. It is not linear nor circular. In your dreams, you touch these other realms. What stands here in this room is only part of you. A small part. We can free you to explore the cosmos more freely."

Bonnie shuddered.

"We do not coerce," Lenya said.

"Nor do you release your thralls," Navinad said.

"Once a person becomes, why would they want to return?" Lenya asked.

Once a person "becomes" there may be nothing left to return. A gazelle devoured by a leopard becomes the leopard.

* * * * *

Chapter Eighteen:
Trapped

Kapten Sif – VRAEC, Nakija Musta Toiminnot

Sif rarely minded walking, but this was more like gliding. It took little strength, but it worked different muscles and required much more control to "walk" through a corridor in zero gravity.

If the trams had been running, they could have been there by now, but that was just wishful thinking. Since the trams drew power from the station, they were useless right now, and there was no sign of a maintenance tram which would have its own power supply.

So they had to walk through a dead ghost colony, while expecting to get attacked at any second.

Radio links remained silent, and even emergency lighting looked like it was on the last dregs of energy.

"Join the Aesir, see the world," Rille said.

"Step by step by step," Tony said. "Anybody else want to carry the generator?"

"It has no weight, you big oaf," Beck said. "There is no gravity."

"It has lots of mass," Tony replied, giving Beck the finger. "I can't stop quickly like an empty-headed nyippa without balls. Did you have it so easy in the Marauders that you forgot?"

"Stow it," Loff said.

"This should be a job for HKTs," Tony said. "They love this no gravity tromping through stations paska."

"Antonius," Loff warned.

"Zen," Tony said, taking the hint, but Sif saw him throw the finger at Beck again, and she felt Beck's amusement, though she couldn't see his face. Neither Aesir was mad at the other, just bored and nervous.

The levity of the Aesir was calming to Sif, though she understood what a trap that was. They trusted her, but she knew, deep down inside, that their position was precarious. Vampires or something worse could suddenly pour into the corridor, and they were getting further and further from the *Ovela Karme*.

"Sif," Theymar said. Her tone told Sif something was wrong. Had a death hunter struck? "We have a problem. The drone we left out is detecting about fifteen ships on approach. No formation."

"Vanhat," Sif said.

"That is what I suspect. They are coming in hard and fast. They will be here in less than twenty minutes."

"Get out of here," Sif said.

"Not without you," Theymar said.

"We can't make it back in time," Sif said. "No sense in all of us dying."

"But—"

"That's an order," Sif said. "This is a big colony. We can evade searchers for a long time. You are obvious."

"Zen," Theymar said. It was obvious. It would take Sif and her team almost an hour to get back to the ship, and if they were going to be here in twenty minutes... "We will go get reinforcements."

"Sloss is going to join you," Theymar said a minute later.

"Negative," Sif said.

"Too late," Theymar said. "He is deploying with his team and several mules, extra food, ammunition, and supplies."

"Negative," Sif said. "We can scrounge."

"There is no time to recall him."

Sif wanted to swear. Theymar and Sloss had planned it this way. They knew she would countermand the order. Now, Sloss and his Jaegers were just going to die alongside her.

She should have expected this. Should have had a backup plan, but instead she had been focused on threats within the colony.

"Zen," Sif said. "Have him make his way to the data center."

"Zen," Sloss said, coming onto the link.

* * * * *

Chapter Nineteen:
Abandoned

Kapten Sif – VRAEC, Nakija Musta Toiminnot

Sif had expected the data center to be full of vampires, but it was empty like everything else. There were signs of battle, but there were no bodies. Nothing more than wreckage and blood stains.

The Russleman index flickered between two and four. Enough to let her know they weren't as alone as she would have liked.

"I can feel them," Peshlaki said.

Sif reached out with her senses. Yes, they were there. She felt their hate and anger.

Sloss had met them in the data center and his squad was set up, ready to defend against an attack, but from what? Ghosts that may or may not harm them? Vampires that could live in vacuum? Or something else that was coming on those ships.

Since the *Ovela Kaarme* had left, the expedition had lost all contact and knowledge of what was happening outside the colony. Had the vanhat given chase to the *Ovela Kaarme*? Or did they ignore it?

"Activity," Sloss said and sent her a link to the docks. Sloss had set up some cameras to watch the dock. Sif tapped in to see.

Beyond the cracked glass of the dock, she saw a large, black object moving, a ship without lights. Slowly it came to rest, and she saw movement outside. It was hard to tell from the camera angle, but eventually the airlock door was cranked open, and five figures came through, all wearing strange armor and carrying big blocky rifles. She could tell from the short legs, squat head, and long thin arms they were not human. The armor did not look normal either. Nothing about them looked human, except the way they spread out from the hatch and kept their weapons ready.

"What are they?" Sloss asked. "I've not seen vanhat like that."

"A new variant. A new Jotnar, perhaps?" Sif said. She reached out with her senses to try to get their flavor or a taste of their essence.

When she felt it, she quickly drew back. They were vanhat orja, but not mindless killers. She felt their essence, and there were many of them. Unique individuals, but she smelled the chains on their souls. What did that mean?

She sensed their curiosity, which was stronger than their blood lust. They felt dominant and lacked fear. She cast her senses out toward the cylinders and felt something stir there, an awareness that was focused on this station. So, the Jotnar wasn't here? Or was it? Was there a Jotnar among the ships that had just arrived? They smelled different, and Sif wondered what that meant. Was she about to be caught in a fight between two Jotun?

Pulling back, she listened to Sloss discussing the weapons with Loff.

"Projectile weapons I think," Sloss said.

"Not all of them," Loff said. "Look at that one. No opening. It must project energy."

"Or that is a cap that will come off when fired."

"Zen."

Sif tapped back into the view from the spy-cam.

There were more of them now. What did they want? The newcomers were milling around. These were like the first five except they had smaller weapons and were more interested in the garbage littering the docks than watching for threats. A few of them waved instruments around as they walked around on their stubby legs. They might be as tall as Sif and the Aesir would dwarf them in height. They were very broad, almost like Aesir that had been pushed down and squished.

What were they?

Seconds later, the lightly armed ones began running back toward their ship. The troopers raised their weapons and knelt.

The camera angle wasn't good, but one fired a burst of blue lightning, and the rest lowered their weapons. But Sif couldn't see what the soldier had fired at.

"Soldiers and egg heads?" Loff asked.

"Works for me," Sloss said, and Sif watched new designations appear. "Lightning gun? I wonder if that will bother us in armor."

"You volunteering to test?" Loff asked.

"Ha," Sloss said. "I think we will forgo any testing. Just kill the dwarves first. Test the weapons later."

"Zen," Loff siad.

"Analysis?" Sif asked Munin.

"Orja most likely," Munin said. *"Or actual aliens."*

"I sense vanhat," Sif said. *"I also sense individual identities."*

"Like two essences?"

"Yes, though the vanhat presence is very weak. Orja. They are slaves to a vanhat, but it's probably not that simple."

"They are not human. Their legs are much shorter than human norm, and the arms are too long, well-muscled. In many ways like a gorilla, but not long enough for them to walk on their knuckles. It is possible they are from some ghost colony

that has modified themselves. But I am finding no colony where such modifications have been done. I consider them to be alien or a heavily changed vanhat variant."

"*Alien?*" Sif asked.

"*There is no evidence of human technology. The weapons, the armor, the sensors they are using, none of this looks familiar or adheres to human technological specifications. There are some radio communications, but I do not have enough bandwidth or samples to decrypt it. What I can see is non-standard. Vanhat have usually used human weapons, technology, and bodies, adapting them for use. Rorik's team, for instance, is still using the* Stalkerri *and Aesir weapons. They still speak English and appear human on the surface. These creatures display nothing familiar."*

"*But?*"

"*But the creatures aboard Lotus Station, on Zhukov, and other places, did not appear human and their weapons were more organic in nature. They did not emulate. Nasaraf was changing the human vessels under his control. We need more data. I can only extrapolate and there is a lot of room for error."*

"*Could they really be aliens?*"

"*Yes,*" Munin said. "*Perhaps aliens conquered by the vanhat.*"

"*How much freedom do they have?*" Sif asked.

"*Hypothetical question noted. Insufficient data available.*"

Whatever had threatened the newcomers was now gone, and the lightly armored aliens moved out from behind their protectors to continue their investigation.

"*They found this ghost colony, though,*" Sif said. "*That is no easy feat.*"

"*We know nothing of their sensors or if they were in-system watching and listening,*" Munin said. "*Insufficient data. I cannot begin to guess.*"

"*Torag or Voshka?*"

"*Unless this is a different variant. The Torag are bigger, the Voshka are almost centaur in shape. I cannot rule out that these are vanhat orja that originated from those species. I have insufficient data on either of them to compare the weapons and equipment. As I said, it is possible these are from an alien species humanity has not discovered, riding the wave of the vanhat resurgence in our galaxy."*

"So, real aliens that the vanhat have conquered and twisted? They could follow the vanhat waves of infestation?"

"That is the most likely theory," Munin said. *"I will use that as my current working theory."*

"Zen."

"They seem cautious," Sloss said as Sif watched the scientists move around and the troopers spread out a little more. More troopers marched off the ship, and Sif wished she had a better view of the vessel. That would answer more questions. Better sensors that could ping the ship for identification would also help. Nasaraf's ships had kept their identification beacons active after being taken over by the Jotun. Sif wasn't sure if that had been intentional or if Nasaraf just had more important things to concern himself with.

She remembered Winters telling her about a conversation she had with an orja while fighting off the vanhat around the ExSec outpost in Sol. The speaker had claimed to be a captain serving the vanhat. Sif didn't have any desire to try to raise these strangers on the radio, though.

"Two different factions of vanhat then, and they don't like each other," Sloss said, looking at Sif. "I think we can just relax here, get our data, and wait for the *Kaarme* to return. Let the vanhat fight among themselves."

"On Zhukov, they attacked humans whenever they got the chance," Sif said.

Sloss shrugged, causing his shoulder pauldrons to flap. "We don't get in their way. This is an excellent defensive position."

"Zen," Sif said, looking around. The data center was buried in an armored bunker. It would have been a great place for a last stand, and Sif knew it had been a last stand, but it had still fallen. Was it because there had been too few survivors or something else?

The death hunter didn't have a physical form. Would it hunt them here?

* * * * *

Chapter Twenty:
The Commune

Navinad – The Wanderer

Navinad didn't know what to make of this creature. Still human or fully consumed by the vanhat host? Or was it something else?

"What is your intent?" Navinad asked Lenya.

"We will live in peace and harmony," Lenya said. "We will have no wants; we desire to live in love. This will become a commune full of love and happiness, joy and peace. All will be welcome here."

"What if people don't want that?" Navinad asked, his skin crawling.

"They will," Lenya said. "You do not yet understand, but in time you will. Still caught in a damaged mindset. You value property and possessions. Let them go. You don't need them. There is enough to share. Your species has invented robots and manufactories. We can give up those possessions now. We can heal you."

There had been a hippie resurgence in the late twenty-first century, and this was what Lenya reminded Navinad of. Too much weed, not enough thinking things through.

"Mankind has tried to find the path," Lenya said, reading Navinad's mind? "It has tried and failed, but this time we have help."

"Who is helping?" Bonnie asked.

Lenya smiled again. "A name is a possession. You do not yet understand."

So, the vanhat would not reveal its name?

"Theory?" Navinad asked Lilith.

"Hippie communist," Lilith said. *"I don't know if the vanhat latched onto that concept or the human concept comes from the vanhat. The station Inkeri has been activated, by the way."*

Navinad watched Lenya closely to see if anything was changing.

"You are very pretty," Lenya said to Bonnie. "I never told you that before. I was afraid to, but I'm not afraid anymore. Fear is also a possession."

Bonnie looked at Navinad. She looked uncomfortable, and it looked like her fur was standing on end. Her ears were almost flat against her skull. Didn't Lenya see that? Did he understand it?

"You don't need to be afraid," Lenya said. He turned his gaze to Navinad. "I love you, too. We will not harm you."

Navinad remembered the hatred emanating from the orja in the tram station. Where did that fit in? Reaching out with his senses, Navinad recoiled from the sense of lust Lenya was emanating.

"We should go," Navinad said, standing, preparing to jump away from Lenya.

Bonnie stood as well, but Lenya remained seated.

"It isn't bad. You should try it. We will welcome you with open arms, and you will never feel more love and joy."

"Thanks, but not right now," Navinad said. It was best to leave this thing now. It might think more action would change his mind. He felt outright denial might be dangerous. Nobody liked rejection, and that sixth sense warned Navinad there was a trigger somewhere.

Something would enrage Lenya and turn it from a peaceful, horny hippie into a raging, bloodthirsty maniac. "We need to do some things first."

Navinad couldn't think of what, but he needed an excuse, and that was the only thing that came to mind.

"Of course," Lenya said. Navinad sensed a flicker of anger and disappointment. That anger would grow.

Bonnie remained silent as she moved to keep Navinad between her and Lenya.

Lenya watched them go, and Navinad half expected to be met by a frothing horde outside, but the alley remained empty.

Glancing back, Navinad saw Bonnie shiver.

"Is everything okay?" Navinad asked. How did the vanhat that controlled Lenya spread?

"No," she said, and Navinad increased the strength of his Inkeri so it would envelop Bonnie. The Inkeri had not affected Lenya. Did that mean the Inkeri wasn't strong enough, or maybe it wasn't working?

"What's wrong?" Navinad asked as they made their way back to the tram.

"I don't know," Bonnie said. "Lenya, he is so different. When he came here, he was a broken man, full of despair and anger. It is like he has forgotten all he saw on Nan'an or Valakut. That wasn't Lenya. What is happening?"

"I suspect it is a vanhat infection," Navinad said.

"But aren't the Inkeris supposed to protect us?"

"Supposed to? Yes."

"Then?"

"I don't know," Navinad said. "They don't run the Inkeris all the time. Perhaps it spreads when the generator is not running. I just don't know. The Inkeri weakens the vanhat but does not always destroy them."

"Then the colony is lost? You must take me with you," Bonnie said, grabbing Navinad's shoulder.

Could she be infected?

How could he tell?

Navinad reached out with his senses but didn't feel a vanhat presence.

"I will try," Navinad said. He couldn't abandon her. Knights did not turn their back on damsels in distress. Her enormous eyes looked at him, so large and expressive. Her fur looked soft.

Turning away, Navinad pointed toward the tram and her hand fell away.

"Let's get back to my ship," Navinad said. "We need to understand how people are becoming infected, how the vanhat is spreading itself."

"Okay," Bonnie said.

Placing his hand on his sidearm, Navinad hoped they would not be stopped. How could he save all these people? And would they want to be saved?

Navinad was tempted. It would be nice to not be afraid. He was tired of fighting and violence. There was something seductive about being able to live in peace, without anger, without hate.

Then his mind returned to the creature at the tram station. There was no mistaking what he had felt there.

* * * * *

Chapter Twenty-One:
Ghosts

Kapten Sif – VRAEC, Nakija Musta Toiminnot

Watching the aliens didn't get old. Since they were bunkered in the data center there was plenty of time to watch as Munin sifted through the data archives. They were, without a doubt, aliens. Their armor, the way they moved, their technology—there could be no mistaking them for human, Voshka, or Torag. Another mystery. It was also impossible to know if they were orja or unbound. She wanted the SCBIs to focus their attention on them, but the mission was Rorik.

Apparently, Rorik and his team had arrived in the *Stalkerri* and within days of their arrival the war had begun, ending with vampire swarms killing everyone in the cylinders. The exact fate of all the people was a mystery because when the vampires were awake and active their vanhat energies disrupted and crippled human technology. The colony had either not gotten Inkeri generators or had decided not to use them. She could only imagine the panic and dying which had been painful to watch.

It quickly became evident what had happened. Rorik and other members of his team spread out throughout the cylinders and went to ground, hiding and killing until they were strong enough to swarm out of their lairs and overpower the survivors. The vampire swarm was obsessed with killing and destroying.

She split her attention between the captured video and the aliens. She questioned the value of the Inkeri generators in such situations. Did Inkeris affect vampires?

Sif wasn't sure if the cylinders had atmosphere or were still venting, but there was no way she wanted to go anywhere near them after watching hundreds of vampires swarm and massacre well-armed survivors. It had been terrifying, and the survivors hadn't stood a chance without heavy blazers, and sometimes even with heavy blazer machine guns and interlocking fields of fire. Sif doubted they would have stood against those walls of teeth and claws supported by snipers and blazers.

Unable to stomach the carnage, she left Munin to sift through the archives to look for traces of Rorik's team and try to find out where they might have gone. Billions of hours of video footage had to be analyzed.

At least watching the aliens on the docks gave her something to do while Munin and Ma'li worked.

After the first encounter, it appeared the death hunter was leaving them alone, though the Jaegers seemed on edge, like they sensed things they didn't recognize.

With the dock depressurized, she knew the aliens were unlikely to take off their suits, so she spent her time trying to imagine what they looked like and how much the vanhat slavery had changed them. What lessons could be learned?

She continued to feel their essence, though. Individuals for sure, but with a whisper of vanhat leeching off them, almost like their master was occupied elsewhere.

They seemed more curious, and Sif watched them as they grabbed many things, mostly things that looked technological, and took them back to their ship. She wished they had a drone or something outside because she really wanted a better look at their ship. The way they were acting made her think of hoarders. Though if she were an alien species investigating another alien species, she would do her best to grab as much technology and information as she could before warships returned.

A chill ran down her spine, and she turned off her view of the docks. The aliens were several kilometers away and hadn't left the docks. Sloss had sent a team to set up some cameras to warn them if anyone came from the cylinders. For now, her people seemed safe with nobody aware of them. They could hunker down here for many months if they needed to. This bunker was fully self-contained and well-stocked, but it was not impossible to find if you were looking.

Tired of looking at the screens, she gazed around the data center until her eyes fell on a girl nearby. She stood there watching Sif. Her blood turned to ice and it felt like spiders were running down her neck.

The girl was young, maybe six or seven. She was thin with long black hair and wide eyes that were latched onto Sif like tracking lasers. Though dressed in a bright red jumpsuit covered in sparkles, Sif felt danger emanating from the child.

"Ignore it," Peshlaki said. How in Odin's name could she do that?

Peeling her eyes away, she looked at Peshlaki. "What is it?"

"It is an angry spirit. A soul caught between. It's looking for someone to focus its anger on. Many of them walk these halls."

"How do you know?" Sif asked, watching it from the corner of her eye. Like Criston, she seemed almost real, but unlike Criston, her presence did not calm Sif. It was like having a hungry wolf in the room sniffing around, looking for food. How would it attack?

"Medicine men would talk of such things," Peshlaki said. "I never believed in them, of course, but old men talk. I remember little of so long ago, and I have never seen one until now."

"What do we do?"

"I don't know. Pray? Ask her forgiveness?"

"What did we do to her?"

"We did not save her from what killed her. Her body is elsewhere, unburied. She has reason to be angry."

"But not at us," Sif said, realizing that arguing with Peshlaki accomplished nothing. The angry spirit would not care. She understood it no longer had a physical form to shape and influence the spirit, and Sif realized how dangerous it could be. No longer fully attached to this world, but it had not yet let go.

She tried to remember all the theories and lore she had learned as a Nakija. Until now, most of it had been mostly theoretical. Other Nakija had been more in touch with the spirit world. Sif had always been too attached to the physical world and had rarely delved into the disciplines that diverged into the metaphysical realms. Now, with the different dimensions coming together, there was more crossover. The barriers that had kept such disciplines apart were blurring, and Sif wished she had been less focused on the physical world. How could you change the mind of a rock that decided it hated you? It could not change its thought and intent, like this spirit.

"Without a body to nourish it the soul is adrift, unable to change or let go," Peshlaki said. "It's like a recording, still caught in the last moments of its death. The spirit shell is confused, angry. It feels abandoned and shunned."

"Can we do anything to help it?"

"It's like a car that was driving down the road and the driver is whisked away. There is no genuine emotion, no feeling, no ability to reason. It will crash into whatever gets in its way. Ignore it. Stay out of its way."

"It isn't staring at you," Sif said, moving across the room. The ghost's eyes followed her, but it did nothing else.

"Whisper prayers of peace. Let it hear your thoughts."

"What can it do?" Sif asked. Prayers of peace? What did Peshlaki think she was, a sweet little girl who played with dolls?

"We do not want to find out. Do not underestimate it. It has some attachment to this world. That will give it the ability to physically or spiritually affect us."

Sif reached out with her senses and immediately felt the anger and hatred simmering there, growing. There would be no reasoning with that, and Sif shuddered. The ghost took a step toward her, and out of the corner of her eye, she saw other ghosts appear.

"They are leaving," Sloss said, unaware of her conversation with Peshlaki. No. They weren't *leaving*. They were coming.

It took her a moment to realize that Sloss was talking about the aliens.

Sif didn't dare take her attention away from the ghosts. She felt others, as angry and hate-filled as the girl. More were coming.

Peshlaki began chanting in his language.

"Leaving?" Sif asked, trying to keep the fear from her voice. The spirits weren't leaving, they were coming, they had noticed her. Her voice should be the least of her worries. These spirits would likely feed on her fear. They would see it as guilt that needed to be punished.

"Zen," Sloss said glancing at her. Next to him stood a young man covered in blood, his throat a gaping hole of torn flesh. His face was emotionless, but his eyes were locked on Sif like the girl's. Why didn't Sloss or the others see him? Why were they focused on her?

"We need to leave, too," Sif said. Munin should have enough data to sift through.

"What do you see?" Munin asked. Despite having access to her eyesight there were some things the SCBI could not see. Sif suspected this was because what she was seeing was not visible to her physical eyes.

"Ghosts," Sif said.

"Are you sure?"

"Yes, I'm sure," Sif said, wishing she wasn't so sure. It would be nice to be able to explain them away, like a delusion, but the goosebumps rising on the back of her neck told her otherwise.

"Is there anything I can do?"

"Find me some prayers of protection?"

"How will that help?"

"I don't know."

"Might I suggest meditation? Clear your mind. Concentrate on the emotions you wish the prayers to generate?"

Sif wanted to argue. Prayers would be easier, but that involved a belief in something else that would come to her aid. Munin was right, though. Prayers held strength because they focused a person's thoughts and emotions. Prayers had strength because people gave them strength. Perhaps at one time they had called other beings to help, but right now Sif couldn't imagine who would come to help. Criston? Levin? What could they do?

Kneeling, Sif took her attention away from the spirits. They did not have a physical form, yet. She could create a mental shield.

She closed her eyes and cleared her mind, focusing on nothing. They would feed on her fear. They tempted her to meet them with anger and resistance, but that would not be the proper response. They would accept those emotions as a challenge. Peace and love were the best response, if they could still understand those emotions.

Nearby, she felt Peshlaki. She did not understand what he was saying, but she felt him, felt the emotions he was generating. Sorrow? Pity? Hope they would find what they wanted?

Sif echoed those emotions, amplified them. She made a shield out of those feelings and pushed them out, hoping she could also protect the Jaegers. The ghosts would understand emotions, not words.

She felt the pressure on her shield, like when Lusiverious had attacked them on Luna. The pressure built. It was not nearly as painful as when she had stood with Skadi and Vili, but it manifested as pain, needles pricking her arms and legs.

She closed her eyes and turned her attention away from the world around her and focused on her spiritual and mental world.

Slowly, the pressure eased.

When it was gone, she opened her eyes and saw the Jaegers and Peshlaki nearby, but the ghost of the girl sat nearby staring out into nothingness, her attention turned away from Sif.

But for how long?

She couldn't last long like this.

* * * * *

Chapter Twenty-Two: Planet of the Torag

Navinad – The Wanderer

Navinad kept his hand on his sidearm all the way back to the dock. The vagrant in the tram station was gone, and it was approaching night cycle, with fewer people around. With the lights dimmed, there were too many shadows, and Navinad felt like his skin was crawling. He sensed an awareness, but he couldn't see anyone.

"Please take me with you," Bonnie said, shattering the silence and startling Navinad.

"Not many people out there that look like you."

"I don't care. I don't want to die."

"Lenya didn't look dead."

"He was inside. Something else was wearing his skin. Lenya is gone."

How much did she know? "How?"

"I don't know. I just know that Lenya is gone. Whatever consumed him is wearing his skin like a costume. It is a feeling, and I think it is happening to people around us. You feel it too. I know you do."

"I am not the captain of my ship, and it is a warship," Navinad said. Though, perhaps he shouldn't reveal that to her.

"If I stay here, I will die," she said.

But being on a warship would not exactly increase her chances. How could Navinad sell this to Clara?

"What makes you think it will be safer onboard a warship?"

"It will be," she said with a confidence Navinad suspected was false. "Whatever devoured Lenya will get me here. I think it waits for sadness or despair to enter and devour. I can feel it at the edge of my senses, waiting. In my weakness, I will surrender."

"It won't follow you?"

"No. Something binds it here."

"Send Clara a message and let her know I'm bringing a guest," Navinad told Lilith.

"Aye," Lilith said.

"I will discuss it with the captain," Navinad said. It would not go over well, and Clara would most likely say no. The *Romach* was a Jewish warship. There was no place for a bio-modified non-combatant, especially one so unorthodox.

"Thank you," she said.

"Do you have any skills? Any leverage?"

"I'm an excellent cook," she said, which was not nearly enough. The food machines aboard the *Romach* were top-notch. "I'm also good with computer systems."

"Anything else?"

"I'm a masseuse, and I've done system analytics."

He could tell Bonnie was throwing skills out, hoping something would interest him. She wasn't lying, but she was desperate, and Navinad expected she might be exaggerating to secure herself an escape.

"Analytics?"

"I used to work for dock control analyzing incoming ships and cargoes. That is how I met Lenya and knew about your ship."

"Let's not mention masseuse, in some colonies that might mean whore," Navinad said. "But perhaps we can use an analytics specialist."

Navinad felt a flash of discomfort and surprise when he mentioned whores. Discomfort or guilt?

"The crew of the ship is extremely traditional and may have issues having someone as heavily modified as you aboard."

"I'm not strange," she said. How to explain to her that her appearance would most definitely be strange aboard the *Romach*.

"People will probably find it hard to see past your appearance," Navinad said, looking at her. He could sense she was female and not femboy, as Clara had warned. Did it really matter, though?

She remained silent as the airlock loomed ahead of them.

A smiling dock worker walked up to them, and Navinad's skin crawled.

"I know you want to join us, Bonnie," the stranger said. "You will finally know happiness. Levin, you can also lay down your heavy burden and know joy."

Navinad saw her shudder.

"There are things we must do first," Navinad said, glancing at the nearby hatch.

"We understand why you are lying. You are afraid. There is nothing to be afraid of."

Navinad saw others sitting in the shadows staring at him and Bonnie.

"Maybe later," Navinad said, now backing toward the hatch. One hand was on his sidearm, the other pulling Bonnie with him.

"You will not re-enter the station. We understand this is goodbye. We will miss you."

Navinad wasn't sure what to say. The hatch was close.

"Lenya has a data packet for you," the stranger said. "To help you in your quest."

"I have received a data packet," Lilith reported. *"Scanning it for malicious-ware."*

"Thank you," Navinad said.

"Our pleasure. When you grow tired and seek peace, find us. We will always welcome you with open arms and love in our hearts."

The emotions emanating from the stranger seemed to imply that was true, but Navinad also sensed a lie there.

He wanted to draw his weapon and start shooting, but that would accomplish nothing. Most people might sense something was wrong, but Navinad was sure they wouldn't believe or thank him, a stranger, for killing one of their own. It would be hard to explain to the police.

They finally reached the airlock for the ship's loading bay. It slid open and a pair of soldiers came out, fully armed and armored. Bonnie wasted no time getting behind them. As Navinad entered the airlock, the two soldiers backed up, never taking their eyes off the people on the dock.

Clara was inside the airlock with other troopers. She glanced at Bonnie before looking at Navinad.

"What is going on?" she demanded as everyone crossed the airlock to the ship.

It wasn't until they were properly aboard the *Romach* that Navinad felt the tension drain out of him. "Vanhat."

"Where?"

"Those people."

"If they were vanhat, why weren't they trying to kill you and us?" Navinad shook his head, not sure.

"Are there different vanhat?" Bonnie asked.

"All of them are murderous," Clara said, her eyes flicking to Bonnie for a second. She didn't want to look at Bonnie, didn't want to acknowledge her.

"No," Navinad said. "Some are more dangerous than that. Subtle like poison. The ones here? They are the dangerous ones. They seduce people with promises of hope and peace."

"Like the SOG?"

"No, more like the spider-tailed horned viper, which has a tail which can mimic an insect to lure birds in to be killed and devoured, or maybe the spider wasp which lays eggs in a spider which eventually paralyzes the spider and allows it to become food for its children."

"Are you infected?" Clara asked.

"I don't think so," Navinad said. "I have not turned off my Inkeri or eaten anything, but I don't think its vector is physical."

Clara finally turned to look at Bonnie.

"I'm not infected," Bonnie said, perhaps too quickly. She was quick enough to pick up the surrounding emotions, and Navinad wondered just how psychic she was.

"Lenya sent me a data packet," Navinad said. How would they know if Bonnie was infected? "It may hold information on the Torag."

"I don't like this place," Clara said.

"Me either. However, this was the first place we stopped for answers. I think perhaps we next need to go to Valakut and find out what is going on."

"Valakut?" Bonnie said. "A war is going on there. The Governance is trying to take the planet from the Torag."

"How has the arrival of the vanhat impacted the war?" Navinad asked.

"I don't know," Bonnie said.

"Did Lenya come here before or after the vanhat?" Navinad asked. Could he have been infected and brought the infection with him?

"No," she said. "He has been here almost a year. When he arrived, he was so broken. He was suffering. I understand why he gave himself to the vanhat. He lost most of his company, people he loved and trusted, to bureaucratic stupidity. That caused him to snap. He had a choice: flee the SOG or be executed for ideological unreliability."

Which made sense to Navinad. He had seen re-education camps run by the SOG. Some of them were little more than death camps, where the most rebellious were sent to be totally brainwashed or die. Sometimes death was best because anybody who survived was never the same afterward. The Governance had learned hundreds of years ago how to break minds and bodies. They excelled at reconditioning people. An officer of the Governance would know that.

Navinad easily understood Lenya's choice.

* * * * *

Chapter Twenty-Three:
Scale

Prime Minister Wolf Mathison, USMC

The Governance was hell and it was doing its best to punish Mathison and make him miserable. Feng had reported that the admiralty was planning a coup and even the Guard and some ODT units were slipping away from him. One spark could send the Sol System into a civil war.

Too many people didn't take the vanhat threat seriously. The Governance had done an excellent job telling everyone to work for the greater good while keeping them occupied and concerned with their own little piece of the galaxy. They had been conditioned to be subservient to the Central Committee and secretary general, not a prime minister. Most people thought Mathison and his post were ornamental and still demanded a response from the Central Committee.

For centuries, they had conditioned the people to surrender and obey the Governance. With so many people, it was easier to surrender to a higher authority. People did what they were told and kept their head and eyes down, but that didn't mean they were subservient and obedient.

Too many damned people and moving parts, people stuck in their ways and seriously afraid of any change or variation in how they did things. Taking orders from someone new was frightening and unusual for them.

Mathison wanted to run it like a military unit. A commander delegated to his subordinates, who delegated to their subordinates, and so on. It was just a matter of scale. A platoon commander gave commands to his squad leaders, who gave commands to their team leaders, and the team leaders provided leadership and control for their teams. Very efficient. Scaling up was easy. A battalion commander gave orders to his company commanders, who gave orders to their platoon commanders, and so on.

A government was different. The Governance was different; different departments had different administrators, organizations, and different levels of authority. Bureaucracy was like spaghetti where everything was linked. The shipyards needed supplies, supply chain needed transportation, transportation needed scheduling, scheduling needed an understanding of everyone's needs. If a critical supply or fuel was in short supply, that caused other parts of the chain to grind to a halt. If some self-centered administrator thought they weren't being appreciated, they could put in less than full effort, flex their muscles, and further disrupt the chain, causing friction and disruption. When the government controlled everything, there was no opportunity for individuals to show initiative or excel.

Feng could only disappear so many people into re-education camps, and he was trying to focus on intentional or malicious disruption. It was a fine line there, too. Remove too many people, and the survivors lacked the experience and skill to proceed efficiently, again increasing the operational friction. Also, removing someone in the dead of the night frightened others and made them more likely to request direction from seniors. Nobody dared take responsibility for anything.

Even with SCBI support, he couldn't micromanage everything. He could only delegate, supervise, and remove anyone he found causing too much friction. Now all the pressure and people looking for personal advantage were leading people toward rebellion.

"I never knew the Governance was so screwed up," Skadi said, looking at Mathison.

Mathison wished she still had her Erikoisjoukot tattoo visible. Unfortunately, that would cause more problems if people saw it. The things he found comforting, a tattoo on a woman's face, of all things. He was losing it.

"Bureaucracies are never efficient," Mathison said. Which might not be true, but he couldn't think of an efficient one. Even the Marine bureaucracy with AI support had issues. The Governance had some extremely limited AI, and they were overwhelmed. Freya and Loki were overwhelmed, even using the extra processing power and specialized processors being created for their use. Mathison wanted to roll out SCBIs, but there were trust issues. He didn't dare arm enemies with SCBIs, and beyond his immediate circle he didn't know who he could trust.

"This is the opposite of efficient," Skadi said. "The Governance is all about top-down control, micromanagement, and every damned bureaucrat fighting to gain or keep power."

Mathison pushed back from his desk. He lived here, ate here, and did everything but sleep here. There was always something going on. He could only delegate so much, and he could only do so when he had some idea of the problem.

An engineer had lost his or her lover and committed suicide in a repair bay by triggering one of the missiles. The explosion had caused a chain reaction. It was tragic, but now he had to worry about other suicidal workers doing something similar. Using InSec for suicide watch was a terrible idea because they were the ones who usually caused people to commit suicide. Now that the repair center was offline and needed repairs, more people had to be evaluated for suicidal thoughts, and there were ships that still needed repairs. Who could he put in charge of that clusterfuck?

"Director Feng is here," Freya said and a chill passed through Mathison. Would he ever be able to forget Feng's betrayal at the entrance to Zvezda Two?

Feng entered and stopped in front of Mathison's desk. Mathison stood and looked at the Chinaman, trying to read him.

Snapping out a salute, Feng looked too formal.

Mathison returned a parade ground salute and thought he saw satisfaction or smugness in Feng's attitude.

"How can I help you, Director?" Mathison asked as they both put down their arms.

"I have something for you," Feng said. It took effort for Mathison not to look at Feng's hands for a weapon. What could the head of Internal Security have that would make things better? The heads of the admirals planning their coup? Members of their family? Had he found more US Marines in stasis?

"At ease. Would you like a seat?" Mathison asked.

"No, sir, thank you," Feng said, slipping into a loose form of parade rest. Formalities did not put Mathison at ease.

Mathison was curious now. It was hard to see emotion in Feng, but Mathison thought he detected joy?

"I had my doubts," Feng began with the trace of a smile, "but I think it will be a success."

"What is that?" Mathison asked, trying to think of the myriad of projects he had approved and those he had heard of but officially didn't know about.

"You gave me permission to assemble dissident officers to form a new cadre," Feng said.

Mathison remembered. At the time, he had been distracted. Feng had wanted to use InSec psychological records to assess officers and enlisted personnel to find some who would be loyal to Mathison; people who did not fit into the current Governance bureaucracy. Free thinkers, rebels that couldn't rise above their own position because they lacked the necessary attitude to betray or step on their fellows in order to achieve power. The fact that such people might still exist in the Governance had been difficult to believe. Finding such individuals had been, in Mathison's opinion, a fool's task, though he had found enough for a platoon that was now under Stathis' command.

He trusted Stathis to build a new cadre, but things like that didn't happen overnight, and Stathis had to learn leadership as an officer. As the prime minister of a bureaucracy that spanned hundreds of worlds, Mathison had to kill multiple birds with one stone on a regular basis if he wanted to get anything done. Mathison didn't know what would happen with Stathis and his platoon. That was three tasks combined. Hunt Becket, train Stathis, and build a cadre of troops. It could be a decade before those things came to fruition, though he hoped the Becket problem would resolve sooner rather than later.

"How is that going?" Mathison asked when Feng didn't provide any more information.

"Very well," Feng said, though Mathison might argue that. Senior officers had noticed and thought the officers were being sent to re-education camps as a punishment. Probably most of them thought it was a punishment. Mathison wasn't sure how Feng had arranged it. "There are two thousand we should be able to graduate. I would like your permission to equip them with SCBIs."

Mathison didn't know if that was a good idea. How could Feng vet two thousand people? People did not throw off a lifetime of conditioning in a few months.

His disbelief or feelings must have revealed themselves on his face.

Feng said, satisfaction in his voice, "I think you will be satisfied. Perhaps a tour of the facility and graduates?"

Leaving Zvezda Two would make it easier for assassins to target him.

"I think it would be worth your time," Feng continued. "It would do a lot of good for them to see you in person and it may help set your mind at ease. My psychologists and mental conditioning specialists have outdone themselves. Re-education Camp 203 has outdone itself."

Which didn't make Mathison feel any better. They had been sent to a re-education camp. For hundreds of years, that had not been a good thing. It was a punishment and a place not everyone survived. The staff of such facilities were masters of mental torture, indoctrination, and psychological manipulation.

"How many didn't complete the process?" Mathison asked. *And how many had been executed?*

"Out of the first class, only eight were unsuitable and have been transferred to isolated posts," Feng said. "The majority were resistant at first, and frightened, but they adjusted remarkably well. I believe there is much work yet to be done, but I'm not sure we have a lot of time. I am confident there are no old-regime loyalists in the class."

He said "the class" like it was a class graduating from Annapolis or West Point or something.

"How?" Mathison began, not sure what or how to ask. How had the psychologists and other camp specialists reconfigured their procedures? What had been their goals?

"Re-education Camp 203 is not just any camp," Feng began. "They are used to unusual conditioning requests, though not usually on such a scale. I have been supervising them closely. It has been their intent to awaken their subjects, help them assert themselves and accept they differ from most officers. Camp 74 is focusing more on enlisted, but they are not ready. The Governance has forced them to suppress themselves for most of their life, to accept the reality of a bureaucracy, and forced them to comply with the dictates of the Governance. An officer's mentality is slightly different. At Camp 203, the goal has been to reassure them and reinforce their core psychology."

Which still didn't make sense to Mathison.

"Most re-education camps are designed to crush a person's individuality. To make them more compliant to social controls and manipulation. Socialism can only succeed when everyone enslaves their ego to the will of the state. Obedience, compliance, and consistency are required for a socialist society to function. There can be no room for different thoughts or opinions in a society that must come together under the control of centralized leadership. Such differences can tear apart a society and must be violently crushed. The specialists of such camps understand this very well. People are not ants, and a small part of society will always rebel and seek different ways of doing things. Sometimes it is best to murder these people or send them away where

154 | WILLIAM S. FRISBEE, JR.

they can't infect others with their anti-socialist thoughts. Camp 203 has studied this in greater detail. The staff of 203 has dived into this social experiment and many others over the years."

Mathison wondered about that. Would failure to embrace the new way of doing things have landed them in a different re-education camp or would they be otherwise disposed of?

"Social experiment" didn't sound right to Mathison either. Experimenting with people's psychology was a dangerous thing.

He needed people he could trust, but these would be lower-ranking officers, few above the rank of captain.

"What makes you think they will be loyal?" Skadi asked.

"They were told the truth," Feng said, looking at her. "A novel new approach in the Governance, to be sure. They were informed that Nadya is dead and Prime Minister Mathison is now in command. They know his genuine history and background. They know the role the Republic has played. They were informed about the AI wars, SCBIs, and the current state of things. We have kept them incommunicado from others, but they have had access to classified reports and data."

Which did not sit well with Mathison. He didn't remember approving that. He was vulnerable. Most members of the Governance believed Nadya was still alive and in command, and that she had put Mathison in charge for the duration of the vanhat emergency to Sol. Few people knew she and nearly all the Council had been executed by Feng to save Sol and that Mathison had been installed as the de facto leader. There were still two Council members at large, though they had heard nothing from them in a long time. It was almost like they had disappeared completely from the galaxy. The current theory was that they had fled Sol.

"Is that wise?" Skadi asked. "How much did you tell them?"

Feng turned to her. "Everything. Absolutely everything."

Feng looked at Mathison and his eyes narrowed slightly.

"I have learned much from this Marine and Lieutenant Stathis. Things that have caused me to doubt so much. One thing I've learned is that the truth is important. Not the truth of propaganda, but the truth of facts. The Governance presents facts in a way to control and manipulate the truth. Freedom is being able to decide for yourself, a dangerous concept because people will not always decide the way you want them to because they might not choose to think like you."

"What do you mean?" Skadi asked.

"I showed them the recordings of the last Council meeting when Nadya was executed, when Hermod was shot down. Next was the fight for the *Tyr* followed by many other events. Actual recordings— raw, unedited data. I did not give them commentary, just the raw footage, and forced them to dissect and discuss it. The psychologists helped manipulate and guide the conversations, but the candidates were allowed to draw their own conclusions based on the facts. In nearly every instance, their conclusions were favorable to the prime minister and his actions. We have conditioned them to seek the truth. We have trained them to see through the propaganda and lies. While it is impossible to teach someone critical thinking in such a short period, it is possible to start them on the path, especially if they are predisposed."

"Did you hold anything back?" Skadi asked.

"We held nothing back," Feng said. "This is why SCBIs are so important. Right now, they have trust issues. This is very new for them. Governance society and the military is not something most people trust. SCBIs would help them."

"And if they reject the new ways or SCBIs?" Mathison asked.

156 | WILLIAM S. FRISBEE, JR.

"Then they reject the new ways," Feng said, his face losing all emotion. "This is expected, but they have to understand that we really are fighting for the greater good of humanity. Having SCBIs would make this easier. No process is perfect, but I expect the majority to comply, even if they don't fully believe. The initial compliance will further condition them; a subtle piece of psychology. If you can force acceptance and compliance, further acceptance and compliance become easier to acquire from the subject."

"Two plus two equals five," Skadi said, and Feng smiled.

"Yes."

"Cortex bombs?" Mathison asked. Every member of the Sol Defense Military had a cortex bomb implanted. Something that bothered Mathison, but it had come in useful on several occasions.

"Will be removed when the SCBI is implanted," Feng said. "Trust and loyalty will be rewarded."

"Will SCBIs let them betray us?" Mathison asked Freya.

"Yes," Freya said. *"SCBIs are loyal to their host, unless you want to use some of the programming that Becket used."*

"No," Mathison said. The temptation was there, but he wouldn't become the latest SOG dictator. That might be needed but Mathison could not bring himself to go down that path. Humanity needed freedom if it was to survive.

"I want to see these new officers," Mathison said.

* * * * *

Chapter Twenty-Four: Valakut

Sergeant Aod McCarthy, ODT

McCarthy entered the squad bay and saw his team leaders had things under control. Everyone was gearing up and had drawn their weapons from the armory. They were all moving, packing, or otherwise getting ready.

"What is it, Sergeant?" Quinn asked.

"Baby sitting," McCarthy said.

His stuff was already packed. He had been expecting the call for days. The rest of the squad wasn't ready like it should be, and it was something he would have to bring up with his team leaders. Though, to be fair, he had only told them five minutes ago, and it looked like everyone was ready to go.

"What's new? Who are we babysitting?"

"A Guard company over on Boris," McCarthy said, referring to the continent Boris. The entire planet of Valakut was a war zone, riddled with tunnels and bunkers.

"Just us?" Quinn asked.

He was as tall and sharp-featured as McCarthy, but with blond hair. Moore, the other team leader, had black hair; otherwise, they could almost be brothers. They had all come together as first born from the Gaelic Republic and excelled. In the initial draft, they had been

157

selected to serve as ODTs instead of Guards. In some parts of the Republic, the first-born males, and sometimes females, would be drafted to serve in the SOG military. Taken away at age twelve to serve the greater good and never see their parents and families again, McCarthy had known Moore and Quinn for nearly a decade, longer than he had known his parents and biological family.

The 505th had been on Valakut for decades, fighting the Torag. Usually, the battalions of the 505th were rotated, but the Gaelic Firstborn had been here, and in 15th Company, since McCarthy and his team leaders had been privates.

Quinn was sure they would all die in the 15th, but Moore believed they would be assigned elsewhere shortly. McCarthy did his best not to think about it.

"Any heads-up from your girl, Sergeant?" Quinn asked.

He was referring to Nova Dallas, McCarthy's girlfriend. Technically a member of the Gaelic Firstborn, she had come from 23rd Company and recently transferred to Regimental Intelligence. The Gaelic First was an all-male battalion, but the Fourth Battalion was all women. Not that many women from the Gaelic Republic became ODTs, barely enough to make up a company. Nova was a badass, though. He wasn't sure what she saw in him, but he wanted to make sure she saw more of it.

McCarthy shrugged. They hadn't talked, and they might not. Duty called, and they were ODTs with honor.

Martin came in, huffing and puffing as he approached Quinn.

"Sorry, Corporal," the private said, "they didn't have any and suggested I check with Transport."

McCarthy raised an eyebrow at Quinn. Private Martin wasn't exactly a new recruit, but he was usually dumber than a box of rocks.

How he had made it into the ODTs and survived initial training was a mystery. He was tough, though, and he thought he was a gift to the ODTs and the Governance. He just wasn't very bright, and Quinn had his hands full trying to deflate his ego.

"Why didn't you go to Transport?" Quinn asked.

"I got the alert to assemble and prepare to move out, Corporal."

Quinn frowned and looked at the other members of his team. "How much time we got, Sergeant?"

"What did you send him after?" McCarthy asked.

"Wire gun wire sharpener," Quinn said.

"Were they out of grid squares and flight line?" McCarthy asked, glancing at Martin.

Quinn shrugged, and Martin looked confused. Last week Quinn had sent him running around the regiment looking for an armor ribbon printer.

None of these things existed. The ribbons were digitally displayed on armor in parade mode; there was no reason to print them. But Martin had dutifully gone from department to department asking for an armor ribbon printer. Of course, everyone he asked had stifled their laugh and informed the private they had given it to someone else or didn't have one in stock before sending the private off to someone else who needed a good laugh.

"I don't think we'll have time to get one now," McCarthy said. "Hopefully, the wires for our wire guns are sharp enough. Our primary load-out is going to be blazers anyway."

"So, are we going to be the spearhead or backstop, Sergeant?" Moore asked.

"Backstop," McCarthy said.

"I'm bored already," Moore said.

"Want me to volunteer you to lead the Guard assault?"

"No, Sergeant," Moore said. "I will do my duty for the greater good. Our glorious Guard unit is experienced and should share in the glory. What's the area like?"

"A Guard position. Near some Torag city that went underground when we invaded this shit hole. Rumor has it weird shit went down earlier today or yesterday or someday. Some garbage about Torag shuttles getting shot down by us and the Torag. Radio communications from the Torag has decreased and now they want the Guard to push and see what's going on. We're just going so that when the Guards step on their dicks and fall, we're there to keep the Torag from walking all over them."

"Just us?" Quinn asked.

"The rest of the platoon is going, as well, just different Guard bunkers. Our platoon is so understrength, they can only spread us thin."

"And if the Torag are gearing up for a major assault against the Guard?" Quinn asked.

"It will be a target-rich environment. We just have to hold long enough for reinforcements to get there. Lieutenant Burke isn't sure what to think. He gave me the heebie-jeebies during the meeting."

"How's that, Sergeant?" asked Johnston, the medic.

"Dunno," McCarthy said.

Johnston had been with the company for several years. A good guy, but he spent way too much time in the gym and almost looked like one of the Guards from the Zhukov sector. They were all hulking brutes pumped full of steroids. Johnston annoyed McCarthy because the big guy needed non-standard armor. Usually, the big guys got the big guns, in this case the team's Squad Automatic Weapon, but

Johnston was a better medic. Wilson was a much better shot and seemed to love the SAW.

"Just a feeling," McCarthy said. He wasn't sure, but there was something different about this mission. He could feel it. Maybe it was nothing their company commander had said so much as that vague feeling. Lieutenant Burke was a great guy. He had been a platoon commander for one of the other platoons. After the assault a few months ago, the company leadership and a lot of the company had been decimated. Now the lieutenant was the company commander, and third platoon was led by Sergeant Doyle, who was senior to McCarthy. The platoon's senior sergeant and platoon commander had been killed and, at this point, McCarthy wasn't sure when they would get replacements.

Lieutenant Burke had been a platoon commander when McCarthy arrived as a private nearly a decade ago. Once, McCarthy had served in his platoon. He had been an excellent officer, not some stuck-up prick like O'Henry. Why he hadn't been promoted after so long wasn't a mystery, though. The Governance liked to keep the firstborn together whenever they could, especially units like this one from the Gaelic Republic. Something about the bonds of friendship and brotherhood so they could remember their home or something. It was also easier to keep all the troublemakers together where they could be watched.

McCarthy suspected another reason was because they worked so well together. He had seen other ODT units that didn't seem as cohesive or brotherly. They also didn't have the battle history or string of successes that the Gaelic First had.

The planet Valakut was a meat grinder. Some ODT battalions came here to die. The Gaelic First took casualties, but they also seemed to thrive. Well, until Operation Butterfly Wing a few months ago when the battalion had been fed into the grinder to rescue a Guard regiment that had bitten off more than it could chew.

He grabbed his pack and Quinn handed him his rifle, which the corporal had retrieved from the armory.

"We're ready when you are," Quinn said.

Checking his cybernetic display, McCarthy saw they still had an hour before their flight would be ready for boarding—a Fleet suborbital. They were probably still scrambling a fighter escort. McCarthy's squad would have a shuttle to itself. Sergeant Doyle would go with First Squad. Usually there were four squads in an ODT platoon, but they were having a hard time filling out two full squads.

Whatever was going on in the rest of the Governance had better sort itself out, because the Governance was running out of troops to send against the Torag, and McCarthy didn't want to think about what would happen if they continued to sustain casualties.

There was a lot they didn't tell common troopers, but he didn't think a supply ship had arrived in weeks. There hadn't been a lot of orbital bombardment, so it probably wasn't because the Torag controlled the orbitals this week. It was all just very odd.

"Private Walsh?" McCarthy asked.

"Sergeant?" Walsh was a thin, lanky guy with brown hair. Not the most imposing individual, even for an ODT, but he was damned smart. As the squad's primary drone operator and comm link specialist, he was a hard guy for McCarthy to make sense of sometimes, but he seemed to know a lot about everything. What he didn't know, he had methods of finding out. He appeared to have a lot of contacts in the E3 Assembly, an unofficial network of informants, snitches, scammers, and "acquisition specialists." Walsh was one of the senior Starshey Yefraytors, or Senior Privates. He was about due to be sent to NCO school and promoted, but he seemed to have no interest in that.

"What do you know?" McCarthy asked.

"Nothing, Sergeant."

McCarthy gave him The Look.

Walsh shrugged, unaffected by it, but said, "Haven't had a supply ship or news from out-system in weeks. I've heard rumors, but nobody knows nothing."

His rumors were more on target than a lot of senior intelligence briefings.

"No battles for the orbitals, few Torag ships in orbit. Seems to be Shorr space problems, from what I've heard."

McCarthy knew not to ask Walsh about his sources, and he knew better than to ask about any potential good news. The E3 Assembly didn't traffic in good news.

"Are we cut off?" Quinn asked.

Walsh shrugged. "Dunno, Corporal. I just hear there isn't much traffic."

"We got bombed last week," Moore said, joining in.

"Just a battleship squadron in the system outskirts," Walsh said. "The Torag flexing their muscle, I think."

It would be nice to know his sources.

None of that really impacted their mission right now, though shuttles might get grounded if the Torag were still dominating the orbitals.

"Either way," McCarthy said, "we have a shuttle to catch and some Guards to reinforce."

"Just a half platoon, Sergeant?" Quinn asked. More like a quarter of a platoon; Quinn was being optimistic.

"Regiment seems to think we'll make a difference."

"Sure. Isn't that what happened during Butterfly Wing? Send a few ODTs to backstop the Guard and get stomped as the Torag pushes back hard, retakes the orbitals, and stalls reinforcements?"

"But they couldn't keep the orbitals," McCarthy said. He had been thinking the same thing. Hoping the Governance command had learned from that experience was wishful thinking.

"They kept them long enough for second battalion to get chewed up and shit out," Quinn said.

"Got a suggestion? You want to discuss it with Colonel Tse?" McCarthy asked, referring to their regimental commander.

"Sure, Sergeant," Quinn said, picking up his pack. "I've got his link code. We're old buddies. Go way back."

Sometimes Quinn was full of shit.

"You do that and let me know," McCarthy said, lifting his pack, which was the signal for everyone to gear up. He pointed at Moore and the door, and Moore led the squad toward the elevators that would take them to the shuttle bays. He wished the bad feeling in his gut would go away.

* * * * *

Chapter Twenty-Five:
Bureaucracy

Prime Minister Wolf Mathison, USMC

Running a government was nothing like running a platoon, a company, or even an army. Mathison wondered who he could dump this job on. Effective leaders could delegate, but that assumed there were reliable people to delegate to. It was no wonder the Central Committee assigned a task to someone and then had that person killed or "disappeared" if they failed to meet expectations. Internal Security kept records on everyone, but their focus was on political reliability, not competence, and you could never assess a person's competence by their political reliability. That was no indicator, and sometimes they were at odds.

People were complex, and one size did not fit all. InSec was focused on keeping the Central Committee in power. It was the Central Committee's job to keep everything economically stable enough to avoid a meltdown.

"We haven't given the Central Committee enough credit keeping this clusterfuck of a government from melting down," Mathison said as he pushed back from his desk, ignoring the blinking Priority icons. Skadi looked at him with her patented scowl. Everyone considered their problem a priority. Even with Freya filtering out the bullshit, too much slipped through.

"We aren't government administrators," Skadi said.

"But—" Mathison began. But what? He believed experienced military officers should be able to step in and take over a government, keep it running, even improve things. But this? He didn't have a legion of trustworthy, trained, and competent troops to throw at the problem. Officers always wanted more. More intelligence, more troops, more supplies, more of everything except enemies. Mathison knew his enemies were multiplying. The vanhat and the petty bureaucrats who made up the Governance. He was drowning in enemies.

He had seen reports. Nobody believed the Governance. Like the boy who cried wolf, everyone was used to the Governance exaggerating the situation, using it to spread fear and confusion. The people not on the front lines pretended to care, but went about their business as usual, which was usually enriching themselves and their favorites at the expense of the people on the front lines. InSec had its hands full keeping Inkeri production going. People either wanted to turn out garbage that didn't work or use their inventory to get things from desperate people who finally believed the wolf was coming.

Everyone had a universal basic income, assigned by the Governance bureaucracy. There were billions of people on Earth who had nothing to live for except their UBI. They had no skills, no desire to be anything more than they were, sheep waiting for the vanhat predators to feast. They were mouths to feed, and they were otherwise worthless as workers or troops.

"Why aren't they swarming the recruiting offices?" Mathison asked.

"Why would they?" Skadi said, picking up almost instantly on his thoughts. They spent too much time working in the same office not to. "They have their UBI, and they've been conditioned to be passive and compliant. They've been told the Guard will keep them safe. They have been forced to believe the Governance is all-powerful. Recruitment is up, but right now we just don't have the resources to handle the influx of recruits. Hui and I are having a difficult enough time restructuring current forces to deal with the incursions. We've already reducing the Guard training to a month. Anything less and we might as well just start handing rifles to civilians and sending them at the enemy. Which might be another problem. We've lost several key factories."

"We are losing," Mathison said, looking around to make sure they were alone. He knew they were, but such an admission wasn't easy for him, and he wanted as few witnesses as possible.

"Valhalla will wait. We will go down fighting," Skadi said.

"Not good enough. We can do better."

"No spacefaring society has ever survived the vanhat before."

Mathison looked at her. She was in a mood, and he didn't like her when she was in this kind of mindset.

"We have a chance," Mathison said more softly.

"Why do you say that?"

"Because we do; I'm sure of it. We adapt, we overcome. I should be a meat popsicle floating out and away from Sol, dead aboard the remains of the USS *Jefferson*. But against all odds, here I am. Alive and kicking the vanhat in the teeth."

"Is that the answer? Put people in stasis?"

Was it?

"We don't know enough about the vanhat," Mathison said. "The longer we survive, the more we learn. We have a duty to our children."

"You realize that unless you are killed, you are immortal?" Skadi asked. "Any technologically advanced society will have conquered mere mortality. That was an extensive discussion in the Republic sometimes. Another big question for the Fermi Paradox I recall. Expansion is one thing, an assumption that a species continues to grow and expand, even slowly. Immortality would further enhance a species and their ability to spread throughout the galaxy. But we have seen nothing. No immortal aliens or any evidence of them."

"There is always a first," Mathison said as another report hit his Inbox.

"Low-brow, knuckle-dragging administrators," Mathison said, looking at the report. Once again, an administrator was telling him no because by law only the Central Committee could overrule that law and there was nothing in the Governance legal system saying a prime minister had the authority. Several other agencies had not been notified of the change in policy.

It didn't take long for Freya to fabricate proper authorization of course, but the problem was this manager had spent a week digging through rules and regulations looking for confirmation and requirements before responding, which meant that for the last week there had been hundreds of transports sitting in Australia collecting dust while people in the Brazilian arcologies starved because Governance laws restricted traffic between the continents for security. Three different bureaucracies monitored air space and had the authority to shoot down unauthorized transports, so getting authorization was critical.

If it had just been that single agency with the unused transports and pilots slowing things down, that would be bad, but each of the three agencies also needed authorization, and if they didn't have that authorization, they were required to shoot down any violators.

No pilot dared challenge any agency because anyone who failed to follow directives and orders usually ended up dead or in an InSec re-education facility.

It was safer for people to hide behind the laws. If that wasn't bad enough, the Australian Transport Pilots Union didn't want to send pilots into a dangerous situation because their pilots were not yet authorized danger pay, which was another legal requirement for pilots flying into dangerous places.

The vanhat in Brazil had acquired anti-air missiles from a fallen Guard base and were making things extremely dangerous.

If that wasn't bad enough, evacuating people who could barely read and didn't want to evacuate was another challenge.

"More riots in Brazil and Africa," Skadi said, sounding tired. "Lack of food, water, and electricity I get, but they are protesting the fact that *Mi Pappa* is no longer in production? I know this is a popular show, but you would think there are more important things."

"Whatever happened to fear of InSec and a Guard crackdown?" Mathison asked.

"Apparently, *Mi Pappa* is helping them overcome their fear. Gods. How did the Central Committee not nuke them?"

"They weren't rioting before," Mathison said. "They were content to live in their little worlds watching their shows, playing their games, farming their digital farms."

"Pathetic," Skadi said. "Now they are sheep about to be slaughtered."

Mathison could see what was bothering her. She cared, and the impending death of millions was bothering her. She had spent most of her life hating the Governance and the people that made up the Governance. Now she was seeing them as people trapped in their inward-looking societies having lived their lives afraid to look up from their feet. The people of the Governance were afraid of change because change was frequently fatal. Now they had to change, had to look up, and if they didn't, they would die. Their habits were burned into their different subcultures and societies. They had lived their lives under the SOG's boot heel for so long they lacked the strength to raise their heads and look around, and even if they did, they didn't understand what they were seeing.

"The Governance has to change," Skadi said. Mathison heard sorrow in her voice. She understood as well as he did that suddenly changing the Governance would cause even more confusion and upheaval.

"Any suggestions?" Mathison asked. Maybe she had something new.

"We need more SCBIs, more trusted people."

And that was the problem. Who could they trust? The entire bureaucracy needed to be ripped out and replaced.

"Any candidates?" Skadi scowled at him.

They had discussed this. Who to trust? If they just started issuing them to bureaucrats and managers, they still wouldn't be able to trust them, but those bureaucrats and managers would then have the ability to cheat and corrupt the system more efficiently. Unless he included loyalty controls in the SCBIs, which would lead people down a dark path.

"SCBIs with loyalty programming," Skadi said.

"No," Mathison said. *Period.*

"You are dooming the human race," Skadi said.

"If we require AI-enforced loyalty, we are dooming it," Mathison said. "The answer is no. I will not enslave humanity. We must have freedom. We must be able to choose who and where to give our loyalty."

"If you don't, you are dooming us," Skadi said again. She was tired, or she would try a different approach instead of the same one.

Mathison shook his head.

"It will happen someday," Skadi said.

"Not on my watch. I swore an oath to the United States to defend and uphold the US Constitution. I believe in it. The First Amendment and all the others. Loyalty should not be enforced."

"The United States is dead."

"Not while US Marines are still alive. We hold it in our hearts, in our souls."

"So, hold elections or whatever you did. Make people vote on a president who will then enslave them. Isn't that what democracies do?"

"Democracies are a failure. The United States was a republic, a nation of laws. You should know this. They built the Vapaus Republic along those lines."

Skadi's scowl told Mathison he was winning, but then he knew he wasn't. It shouldn't be a battle.

"How are the laws helping now?" Skadi asked. "They're tripping us up, slowing us down, preventing us from saving people."

"A society must have laws. Since the dawn of time, humanity has struggled. Every society has struggled. Some struggle for equality, some struggle for more equality for the rulers. People find comfort in their laws. We can't just abolish them without replacing them."

"If we don't, we are going to die because of our own ineptitude."

Mathison couldn't argue with that. Something needed to change, and he had spoken with Freya enough to know that the laws would have to be replaced with something else. But right now, everyone was too busy fighting to survive to rebuild. Everyone on the command team knew they were walking a razor's edge. If the death of the Central Committee became common knowledge, the Governance would erupt into civil war. The lies of normality were the only thing barely holding it together, but if people realized the leaders who had ruled them for centuries were gone, the unions, subcultures, governments, cities, and states would fragment because they would not understand where they fit within in the big picture. They would no longer understand their place and would demand clarification and special privileges, believing they had been the only ones suppressed.

It was all a damned mess. The only thing holding things together was the Guard divisions that were themselves struggling to survive.

A priority link came in from General Hui.

"Yes," Mathison said, preparing for more bad news.

"The 23rd Guard Division in Africa has officially mutinied, Prime Minister," Hui said. "I am sorry."

And thus, it begins, Mathison thought.

* * * * *

Chapter Twenty-Six:
Sergeant McCarthy

Sergeant Aod McCarthy, ODT

C alling the bunker comfortable would be a lie, but it was better than being exposed on the surface or trying to force their way through a bottleneck in the tunnels.

The ground shook as the Torag dropped artillery over them. It was just harassing fire, but just because it was mostly harmless didn't mean it wasn't nerve-wracking.

"They obviously don't have a shortage of ammunition," Corporal Quinn said as he slapped down a card. His hard eyes missed nothing, and that made him damn hard to beat at Twenty-five, the card game of the Gaelic Republic.

Quinn continued when nobody spoke up. "The Guard sergeant I spoke to said this is not nearly what they are used to, like the Torag are conserving ammunition or something,"

"Yeah," Moore said. "We've all seen them more serious than this. I wonder why they're holding back."

"Helmets on?" Private Martin asked, looking up at the ceiling like it was about to collapse. As the most junior member of the squad still alive, his questions were not always thought out and his situational awareness was lacking. None of the veterans were scrambling for helmets, which should tell him something.

"You can put on your helmet if you want," McCarthy said and ran his hand through his short red hair. It was past time to get a haircut. Not that there were many officers wandering the tunnels checking on people. These days they weren't even bothering to tap into the helmet cams to watch their troops. The 505th ODT Assault Regiment would be hard pressed to call itself a battalion these days. If there was any consolation, it was the fact that the Torag seemed to be suffering as well. It was easy enough to believe the war had shifted somewhere else and both sides had forgotten about Valakut. After fifteen years of fighting for the jungle-covered hellhole, it didn't surprise McCarthy.

"When you going to get that cut, Sergeant?" Quinn asked, noticing McCarthy's actions and probably guessing his thoughts. The insolent corporal was trying to get his sergeant's mind off the card game. Which might mean he was at a disadvantage. Maybe. Quinn was too damned cunning sometimes. Quinn's hair was longer. Short on the sides, it was the style in the Gaelic First right now to let it grow longer on the top, as additional helmet padding, people said. That was bullshit. Everyone grew it long because they could get away with it, and the Gaelic First was one of the more ungovernable battalions in the regiment.

"When we get a new commissar," McCarthy said. At this rate, it could be never. All the commissars of the 505th had suffered fatal incidents of some kind or another. There was a rumor they might transfer one of the two from the 908th on the *Musashi* over to the 505th, but McCarthy didn't care. The 505th, and specifically the Gaelic First, was pretty tight, and any stuck-up commissar that came in and tried to mess with them would just have another accident. Quinn knew that, too.

"Anything on camera?" McCarthy asked Martin.

"No, Sergeant," Martin said. "Just explosions."

"Harassing fire then," McCarthy said. Hopefully the Guard would launch their attack today, fumble it, and then retreat. Then the ODTs could return to Romanov Base. "Maybe automated. They just want to keep us in our bunker. It should end soon. Unless they're trying to sneak troops in close enough for an attack."

The Torag weren't that stupid, or desperate, to try a surface attack, but it would keep Martin attentive, just in case.

McCarthy wondered if the SOG did the same to the Torag. Their lines were about ten kilometers away on the surface. Did the Guard artillery regiment have enough ammunition to harass the Torag? The Torag were supposed to have a city hidden nearby, a bunch of civilians hiding behind their troops. The Governance forces were slowly grinding forward above and below ground. They would find that city soon. Nobody knew how big it was. Could be a little town or it could be a massive metropolis hidden under the hills. It was easy to see the ruins of a Torag city from decades ago sprawling across the surface, now abandoned. There wasn't much fighting on the surface. With drones and orbital fire, the surface was a death sentence.

Under the surface was another story. The Torag could be about to collapse the tunnel and pour in, but sensors should give McCarthy and his troopers warning, even with the shelling above. It was hard to time efficient digging with an artillery barrage. Computers could tell the difference.

The SOG and Torag watched and monitored every inch of the surface with drones or spy satellites. If someone saw something, they shot it, depending on who controlled the orbitals.

Beneath the surface, things were harder. The Torag civilian population and military of Valakut had moved underground to avoid the SOG attacks and the Governance had gone underground after them.

When the SOG had invaded the planet decades ago, the Torag population had been slightly less than a billion, a major world. But now, who knew? The Torag still fought tooth and nail, but McCarthy didn't know what they were actually fighting for. Sometimes they fought hard, sometimes they didn't. McCarthy had given up trying to figure them out. The cities on the surface were so bombed out and shattered their alienness had been covered by jungle and scars of battle until they were unrecognizable as anything other than ruins.

This bunker was officially LP/OP Bat Thirty-three. Buried in the mountains but with a lack of reinforcements, the Guard attack had stalled, and now both the Torag and the Governance were playing a waiting game. Who would get reinforcements first and push back the enemy? They had been here less than a day, and McCarthy hated it.

Quinn slapped down a five, and McCarthy winced. The damned corporal had just been playing with him.

McCarthy threw down his cards in defeat.

"When was the last time we did PT?" McCarthy asked and Quinn smirked.

His cybernetic display lit up with an alert. A mission order. McCarthy bit his tongue. What dumbass mission did they have for his depleted ODT squad? The attack hadn't launched, and they were only here to provide a secure area for the Guard to flee to when their attack failed.

He put his helmet on to access more displays and data. Everyone else looked at him because they knew what that meant. Private Martin didn't and quickly put his helmet on. When he realized he was the only one, he went to sit in a corner.

Minutes later, McCarthy took off his helmet and did his best to keep his face blank.

"We have a recon mission," McCarthy said. "Something is going on over at the Torag lines. The spooks got some weird intercepts. Might be a civil war or something. They want us to sneak overland to find out what is going on."

"Why not a regular recon unit? Drones or something," Quinn asked. "I thought we were just here as backstop?"

"Low supplies. They might not have drones," McCarthy said. "They've sent two Guard recon teams, but they didn't come back."

The barrage above stopped.

"Earlier than normal," Quinn said, looking up at the ceiling as if he could see the incoming rounds. "They are probably low on ammo too."

McCarthy nodded. "HQ wants us to do a combat recon. Sneak in, shoot things up if the opportunity presents itself, and get out. The Guard recon weenies were just there to collect information. Probably lightly armed. Lots of jamming going on in Torag lines."

"The plastic-covered finger of the Guard wasn't enough for the prostate exam, so now they're going to send an armored fist," Quinn said.

"And we are the fist," McCarthy said. "Get the squad geared up and ready. They're sending some Guard troops to man the outpost while we're out playing snoop and poop."

"No buggies?" Quinn asked. McCarthy knew he was thinking about escape. Once they punched the Torgies, they would have to move fast to escape the barrage.

"I don't think we have any buggies left on the planet," McCarthy said. There probably were some, but they wouldn't be available for some expendable ODTs that were about to be expended. Besides, it wasn't like the Torag were far away. Getting closer to Torag lines with

178 | WILLIAM S. FRISBEE, JR.

buggies wasn't stealthy, and based on the frag order, the regiment wasn't happy about sending the react platoon out to save their ass. There was also probably no ODT react platoon and McCarthy knew better than to rely on the Guard to save them.

If McCarthy had to guess, Planetary Command wanted an attack on the Torag lines, but the local Guard regiment was trying to stall by sending out a combat patrol instead. Either way, it was outside his pay grade. Officers played officer games and did their best to cover their asses while expending other people's troops so they didn't look bad.

"Need anything from me?" Sergeant Doyle asked on a private link. Doyle had been the squad leader of First Squad but was now acting platoon commander and theoretically McCarthy was acting platoon sergeant, but neither squad leader was going to turn over their squad to their assistant. The position of platoon commander and platoon sergeant were formalities at this point. The platoon was so depleted they had both taken Third and Fourth Squad and augmented their own squads when Sergeant Washington was killed. Two understrength squads did not make a platoon, no matter what regiment said. If they took any more casualties, it would make sense to collapse the platoon into a single squad.

"Any words on reinforcements?" McCarthy asked.

"Nothing, mate," Doyle said. "Something must be going on somewhere else. I ain't never seen units get this depleted except after a battle. I remember on Hill Niner-Niner-Oh-Four, we still had about three squads' worth, and they pulled us back as combat ineffective. Within a month, we were back up to strength and back in the grinder."

"Is there an offensive on another planet or something?" McCarthy asked.

"If I knew I would tell you," Doyle said. "Just go do your thing, keep your head down, and come back with all your people."

"Never quit. Hurrah," McCarthy said.

"Hurrah," Doyle said and closed the link.

This certainly wasn't his first time leading a combat patrol into the Torag lines. The reason his squad got this mission was probably because of their experience.

"Is there time to send Martin up for a box of grid squares?" Quinn asked.

There was no such thing, of course. Quinn just wanted to haze Martin a bit. With all the maps being digital and grid squares being just a thing on a map, sending him anywhere would start him on a wild chase. The first person he asked would send him to someone else until someone got tired and told him they didn't exist. Then Martin would feel like a fool. Everyone he spoke to would have a good laugh and Martin would have a better idea of who everyone was as he learned his way around the area. McCarthy didn't like the idea of doing it now since any place Martin went would be run by Guards, and he didn't want any Guard knuckle-draggers mocking his ODTs.

"No," McCarthy said. Though Martin was the most junior member, he was technically more seasoned and shouldn't have to put up with such stupid games anymore. Quinn was just being an asshole and giving him a hard time because of the helmet questions.

It might be time to promote Martin to yefreytor, or private first class, soon. He should be PFC now, but an incident when he failed to unload his rifle had gotten him busted down to private. Which might be another reason Quinn was always pissed at him.

After looking over his check lists, McCarthy hit Send, giving each member of this patrol a task such as coordinating with artillery or letting nearby units know they were sending out a patrol. A combat patrol from the Governance lines was not a simple saddle up and head out process.

McCarthy hated it, but then it was a lot better than sitting around getting his ass kicked by Quinn at Twenty-five and listening to artillery shred the world above them.

Of course, they were about to go into that hell. That was the curse of being an ODT, hours upon hours of boredom punctuated by ass-puckering terror.

"Hurrah, hurrah, hurrah," McCarthy said to himself. This mission was going to suck. He knew it with every fiber of his being.

* * * * *

Chapter Twenty-Seven: Warzone

Navinad – The Wanderer

Navinad sat on the bridge of the *Romach* as it slid into the system, drinking in data. They dimmed the lights to remind people the *Romach* was in stealth mode and the soft voices sharing information made it seem like people were whispering to avoid being overheard.

"What kind of name is Valakut?" Clara asked.

"Torag," Navinad said. "It is a Torag world and had, or has, a civilian population."

"So why doesn't the SOG nuke it into oblivion and move on?"

"Intelligence, I would wager. Despite the dangers of foreign ideology, the SOG want to gather more intelligence from the Torag. By fighting over a planet, they have an arena to challenge and study the Torag. It's hard to capture prisoners or technology from shattered enemy ships and planets sinking into a nuclear winter. Hard to study and address enemy tactics if they're all dead. Civilians provide another source of information."

"And you think you can walk in and start talking to the Torag?" Clara asked.

"I honestly don't know," Navinad said. "The SOG and the Torag will be on high alert. I'm sure they will be alert for deceit and betrayal."

"Then how are we going to talk to them? I doubt they speak English or Hebrew or anything else we are familiar with."

"They might," Navinad said. "They have been fighting the Governance for decades. That's a long time to fight someone and not learn anything about them."

"Why don't we head into Torag space?" Clara asked. "The Torag will fight the SOG, and while we are not in a typical SOG vessel, they are probably used to the SOG shooting first and not bothering with questions. If half the rumors about the Torag are true, they are worse than the SOG."

"Have you ever known the SOG to be truthful?" Navinad asked.

"I have discovered that most of their lies have a grain of truth," Clara said.

"The best liars do that, and the SOG understands how important it is to seed the lies with truth. If there is truth, then the people will feel more comfortable believing the lies."

"So, do the Torag consider human flesh to be a delicacy?" Clara asked, and Navinad laughed.

"I seriously doubt it. No more than humans consider Torag to be edible."

The *Romach* was lurking in the periphery, watching, waiting. Further out than Navinad thought was practical, but this was an active war zone, and secretive scouts were probably the rule not the exception. This far out there could be billions of scouts or even entire fleets.

Valakut was 0.9 AU from its star. There were two rocky planets closer and five gas giants in the outer reaches, with an assortment of cosmic debris still circling the young star. The *Romach* was near the orbit of the second gas giant, but not too near because there were reported to be Torag forces guarding and mining resources there. The

SOG had claimed the fifth gas giant, but the real fighting was over the one habitable planet.

This system had been a battleground for decades, and Navinad knew the two forces had mapped everything possible.

Nobody except military vessels came here because war zones were where people were shot first and didn't ask questions.

"Odd readings," Clara said.

"What kind?" Navinad asked.

"Not sure," Clara said. "We are monitoring the Russelman index. It's not quite going above one, but there is certainly something."

"Is an incursion imminent?" Navinad asked, trying to relax his body and casting out with his psychic senses.

"I don't know," Clara said. "I've never recorded an incursion."

"Be ready," Navinad said.

They were pretty far out and still collecting information. They didn't know who controlled the orbitals of Valakut. From what he had heard, it changed weekly or monthly and any ships in orbit would dodge to change course and do their best to remain undetected.

"The Children of Israel never stopped being ready," Clara said.

"I'm going to retire for a bit," Navinad said. A lie, but Clara would understand. It was too early in the day for the night cycle. He was staying in the captain's cabin these days, but right now he needed solitude, so he returned to his own quarters.

Before he reached the hatch, he felt the energies swirl just beyond his perception. No, this was not a nearby incursion, but there was a storm brewing. One or more dimensions were brushing up against this one. The chance of an incursion or breakthrough was quite real. The *Romach* was protected by a dimension stabilizing field, but it was unlikely the Torag or the SOG had such protections. And then there was the planet. Weakened dimensional barriers could allow one or more vanhat to slip into this reality and infect or latch onto animals or people. Navinad didn't know if the Torag were vulnerable to the vanhat, but he couldn't assume they weren't.

Valakut was 60 percent water, and the large salty oceans hid a different battle from the rugged hills and mountains that jutted up out of the oceans. Overall, the planet was flatter than Earth, with fewer sweeping mountain ranges and much shallower oceans, but there was still plenty of advanced life. Valakut had the twisted wreckage of an ecology that was millions of years old. The war between humans and the Torag had ruined the climate, poisoned the oceans and air, and otherwise pushed the ecology into a nightmarish, mutating ruin which would be ripe for vanhat infestation.

Most people thought the vanhat only infected or hunted humans, but Navinad knew that wasn't true. Sentient beings were their preferred prey, but some animals were susceptible, especially violent predatory ones.

Sitting in the middle of his floor, Navinad took deep breaths. Consciously projecting himself was usually beyond his regular abilities, but he knew his subconscious roamed the astral realms when he slept. Doing so consciously was difficult. However, he could slip into a meditative state and extend his psychic senses to hear, taste, and smell the nearby worlds.

The second he extended his senses, he felt what could only be called a storm. Time and distance held less meaning when brushing against one of these storms. He had learned in the purple world's mists that the rules and expectations in this world were a construct of this reality, and when another dimension or reality intruded, the laws of physics as he understood them could warp and change. The storm he was sensing might blanket a few kilometers or the entire galaxy. The duration in this reality would not equal the duration experienced by the denizens of that other dimension.

There was no mistaking the storm, though. He couldn't identify the nature of the dimension brushing up against the one inhabited by humanity, but he could sense the malevolence, the hate, the anger. Anything that came across the weakened walls would not be friendly. The kindly, the gentle, the loving, did not seek war and conquest.

Opening his eyes, Navinad felt nauseous.

"What did you sense?" Lillith asked.

"A storm is coming," Navinad said. *"A bad one."*

"Is there anything we can do?" While Navinad's senses had grown, and Lilith had experienced the world of purple mists, she still did not understand or have access to his psychic abilities. She was a being of this reality, and Navinad wondered if she would ever be anything else.

"Be ready."

"Is the Romach *in danger?"*

"I don't think so," Navinad said. If the Inkeri generators failed, the *Romach* would be in a lot of danger, but there were multiple generators, and the *Romach* could build more.

"Do you understand the nature of this threat? Is it new or old?"

"They are all old," Navinad said. They were called the vanhat, the ancients, for a reason.

"You know what I mean," Lilith said. *"Is this Nasaraf or Lucifer or another familiar Jotun?"*

"If it is a Jotun, it is not a familiar one. I don't recognize the flavor of this essence. Besides, Nasaraf and Lucifer were defeated and should be banished. Their gates are under human control, and I doubt the gunny or the Republic would allow any research on them. They will be buried and kept locked away."

"But we still know so little about them," Lilith said.

Navinad thought about the boxes, remembered the first one he had seen on SOG Base 402. Every one he knew about was being kept in a vault aboard the *Tyr*, unless the gunny had them transferred to a more secure facility. Nobody understood them, but it was Navinad's understanding that they somehow blocked specific Jotun from entering this dimension. Somewhere on the border between humanity and the Torag was a tomb world with a massive vault of those prison gates. What would happen if that vault was discovered, and those demons were released?

He had been warned of a threat besides the Jotun coming to eradicate humanity. He had turned his attention away from the vanhat, but could that lost asteroid tomb be a key? Tristan and Ganya had said there were hundreds of such box gates. If each one blocked one or more Jotun, then that facility should be secured. But that was a concern for the gunny. The one from Snowball only seemed to hold a single Jotun, but Navinad knew that might not be true. Only a single demon had tried to manifest. Others might be blocked by the gate but lacked the ability, desire or range to try to manifest in this reality. Like beams of light, the dimensions did not block each other and could exist in the same space, but only the brightest lights would be most obvious.

"Should we hunt for that tomb?" Navinad asked.

"If there are hundreds of prison gates, then yes, I think that is an extreme threat. Nasaraf was hunting for it."

"To control it and make sure the others did not enter our world or to release them?"

"Perhaps both. Their facts and goals were never fully stated, nor could we prove the words as lies or truth. I would suspect that Nasaraf would have allies and

enemies. By controlling those prison gates, he could exert more control over this invasion."

His door chimed.

"It is Bonnie," Lilith reported.

"Enter," Navinad said. She had few friends aboard the *Romach*. Her physical appearance made the crew uncomfortable. She looked like a big, furry stuffed animal. The fact that she was cute with big expressive eyes and was quick to smile just made the more conservative crew uncomfortable.

"Hi, um, am I disturbing something?" she asked as she entered. She paused, looking at Navinad sitting on the floor.

"No. I was just meditating."

"Something is wrong," Bonnie said.

"What?" Navinad asked.

Bonnie had been spending her time aboard the *Romach* poring through and cataloging data. She had a voracious appetite for information and seemed to enjoy perusing the archives and seeing ships, captains, and ghost colonies. The *Romach* had a lot of information, and while the exact location of the ghost colonies was a closely guarded secret, sometimes used as currency, the cultural details of most colonies were not a secret.

"Can't you feel it?" she asked.

Navinad also suspected she was partially psychic but did not know how to determine what abilities she had or otherwise teach her.

"Yes," Navinad said. "We are safe, though."

"How can you be sure?"

"We have a Talese Nefesh, an energy field that protects us from cross-dimensional energies. What you were told is an Inkeri. We have several protecting this ship."

188 | WILLIAM S. FRISBEE, JR.

"It is not always effective," she said, and Navinad pursed his lips. She said it with such certainty. Why? Because it had not stopped the Jotun infecting Baskonian?

"It will protect us," Navinad said. "It has not failed and runs at all times. If it fails, there are others that can come online in the blink of an eye, and we have other weapons we can protect ourselves with."

Bonnie shook her head. Navinad sensed she wanted to believe him, but some sense, some thought, kept her from believing him.

"What if it doesn't?"

"We are doomed. I suspect its effectiveness was reduced on Baskonian because it was not running all the time. Aboard the *Romach*, we never turn it off."

Bonnie didn't shake her head, but Navinad felt her disagreement.

"Why do you think otherwise?" Navinad asked.

"I don't know," Bonnie said. "But…"

"But what?"

"We humans are so different. Why not the vanhat? Humans survive and thrive in so many environments. Some succumb to their conditions, but some don't. Why wouldn't this apply to the vanhat?"

"The Talese Nefesh strengthens the walls of our dimension."

"Don't those other dimensions have their own rules and laws? Couldn't there be other dimensions that do not obey the laws of the Talese Nefesh?"

"I cannot invalidate her theory," Lilith said. *"We know so little about the Inkeri. It could be like a wire mesh that stops mosquitoes and flies but not gnats."*

Navinad knew that in this case, gnats were not to be ignored.

"Do you have a suggestion?"

Bonnie turned away, unable to meet Navinad's eyes.

"No," she said. "I just… I have concerns."

WOLF EMPEROR | 189

"We all do."

Bonnie nodded, still unwilling to meet his eyes. She looked concerned. Perhaps a curse of her genetics and the Baskonian culture she had come from.

"I just thought I should tell you that," Bonnie said.

"Thank you," Navinad said. It was an important piece of information, and until now he had not considered that possibility. The Jotun on Baskonian could not validate or invalidate the theory, but it was certainly worth keeping in mind.

"Sure," she said. "Um... that's all. I just wanted to tell you that and tell you something is wrong."

"Anything else?" Navinad asked, standing and motioning to a chair. He felt she wanted to stay and talk. She probably didn't get along with most of the crew and got little opportunity to talk.

"No," she said. "Thank you for seeing me and thank you for letting me access the archives. I really appreciate it."

"You're welcome," Navinad said as she left.

His mind churned, and he wondered why she had really come. What was her purpose? The entity in the mist had said there would be angels and helpers that would aid humanity, but only humanity could fight their battles. But aside from the entity in the mist, Navinad had seen no sign of angels or helpers.

Would he? If they existed, would the Inkeri generators block them as well?

* * * * *

Chapter Twenty-Eight:
Guardian

Lojtnant Skadi, VRAEC

Skadi hated the Governance more than ever. Before, she had wanted to kill them all, back when she hadn't understood.

It was easy to hate people you didn't see, didn't understand.

"The 23 Guard Division in Africa has officially mutinied, Prime Minister," Hui said on the link. "I am sorry. We are preparing to nuke them."

"Why nuke them?" Mathison asked. Skadi knew he understood. Asking questions like that was his way of stepping back and giving himself time to think.

"Mutiny cannot be tolerated and must be dealt with in the strongest terms, Prime Minister," Hui said. "We must constantly set an example."

"No," Mathison said. "Only nuke them when they get overrun."

"But the mutiny could spread, Prime Minister," Hui said, and Skadi realized Mathison was not being merciful.

"I agree with the prime minister," Skadi said. "Ignore them. They launched their ship, let them sail in it. Abandon them. I am cutting them out of the network now."

Loki began removing the 23rd Division from all rosters and authorization access lists as Skadi spoke. Soon the entire Guard division
would find itself alone.

Reviewing the display where the 23rd was operating disappointed
Skadi. They had been guarding two arcologies in Africa, and they were
not yet hard pressed.

"Why did they mutiny?" Mathison asked. Which was what Skadi
should have asked. She was supposed to be working with Hui to manage the SOG ground forces.

"They do not feel they are getting the resources they deserve, and
I gave the order to transfer two battalions to the Southern Andes bat-
tlefront in South America. The regimental commander did not want
his command lessened, and he believed we were sending them to their
deaths. He questioned our execution of this war and questions the ne-
cessity of saving any arcologies on the South American continent."

Which didn't seem to be enough reason to mutiny, though it could
be just the beginning. There was logic to nuking them in order to scare
others who might consider doing the same.

Loki presented the radio communication exchange in a text for her
to scan. Hui had forgotten to mention that the division commander
also did not like taking orders from an ODT general, and a woman at
that.

The 23rd Guard Division was not hard-pressed and vanhat forces
were only lightly probing the Jozi Arcology. The general in command
must think they were safe from retaliatory orbital bombardment because they were sitting in one of the breadbaskets. Jozi teemed with
hydroponic farms that kept a good portion of Earth fed. Considering
there were already food shortages, wiping out a major source of food
would make the problem dramatically worse. General Mokoena was

an idiot. Vanhat incursions were going to ensure a food surplus because dead people wouldn't need food.

Mathison would let them suffer for a bit. Vanhat activity in that area was increasing. It would bother Mathison to let the mutiny continue, but he didn't want to kill humans because that was exactly what the vanhat wanted. Ignoring them was likely the best solution as long as it didn't spread. Not responding might make him look weak, but right now there were too many humans dying.

"Are we making a mistake?" Skadi asked Loki.

"Yes. Failure to respond strongly to this first mutiny could encourage others. But humans murdering humans is what the vanhat want."

What response would hurt the vanhat the most? Skadi had her pride, but she could swallow it if she had to.

"If they live, they will fight the vanhat," Mathison said.

Yes, it would be a mistake, and it might encourage others to mutiny.

"On another note," Loki said, *"cutting them off will force them to think for themselves and find ways to deal with the vanhat. Their success or failure will help us understand the situation better. Killing them will just help the vanhat."*

"Which choice will cost fewer human lives and hurt the vanhat the most?" Mathison asked.

"Who knows," Skadi said. She understood his logic, but she was tired of people dying, even people she had once hated.

"What can we do besides kill them?" Mathison asked.

"I will see what we can do about cutting them out but smothering news of the mutiny," Skadi said. "The SOG is good about hiding such things, but eventually the news will get out."

"I don't want to murder our fellow humans," Mathison said. "Let them fight and die alone. As long as they are going to fight, we can use that."

"Zen," Skadi said. Hui remained silent. Her thoughts were her own.

Damn it.

* * * * *

Chapter Twenty-Nine: Recon

Sergeant Aod McCarthy, ODT

The surface was a dangerous place. Death could come at them from a distance, it could come from orbit, a sniper, or it could be much closer and more personal like a mine or booby trap. There were many reasons the actual war had gone underground. Though if he was going to be fair, underground was just as brutal and violent, just more up close and personal. Underground they could probe with more powerful sensors, and while they had to worry about kamikaze drones, they didn't have to worry about being detected and bombed. Underground, there were no artillery barrages, no orbital bombardments, and no strafing fighters.

On the flip side, there was no chance of a cave-in on the surface. A mountain was unlikely to fall on him or his squad, trapping them forever in a tomb of rock. But battleships dipping into the upper atmosphere liked to drop orbital crowbars, which could erase entire grid squares.

Plant life on the surface grew fast; it had to. In less than a year, it could grow taller than a man, mostly ferns and bamboolike plants because they grew fast. Things like trees needed years to grow, and at least once every couple months, a battleship would discourage anything from growing too tall. The surface was a blasted hellscape of

196 | WILLIAM S. FRISBEE, JR.

craters full of fast-growing plants. McCarthy couldn't discount the rumor that every square kilometer of Valakut's surface had been bombed
at least once.

It was raining and should rain for several days, which was good. It
would provide plenty of cover from satellite observation. That
wouldn't save them from attacks if Torag sensors detected them, but
it just reduced the efficiency of enemy detector nets, especially from
orbit.

The Guards that relieved them didn't fill McCarthy with any confidence that they could hold the line if the Torgies attacked. They
looked worse off than his ODTs, and none of them seemed to have
full magazine pouches. They also looked tired and demoralized. The
corporal who relieved McCarthy didn't ask any questions, and he suspected they would be asleep within the hour after his squad left.

Climbing out of the hatch onto the surface wasn't easy. Their bunker was a hole deep underground, but at least it pretended to offer
some security.

"Leprechaun One, this is Oisin One," said their company commander, Lieutenant Burke. He was back at Romanov, but there were
enough landlines and links into the local net to allow him exercise control and oversight. "You are cleared to depart. Be advised, there is a
space battle kicking off in orbit. Not sure about the details, but it will
probably keep the heat off while you do your thing. Be safe. Come
back with everyone."

"Copy, Oisin One," McCarthy said as he followed Moore. "You,
too. Keep your head down."

Romanov was buried under some mountains, and the Torag had
never dug them out, regardless of how many orbital strikes they
dropped.

"For the greater good, out," Oisin said.

"Hurrah. For the greater good. Leprechaun out," McCarthy echoed.

His squad had a full load of ammunition, food, and water and could operate for nearly a week, though the mission was only supposed to last a day or two. The planet Valakut was closer to the local star, so light pierced the clouds more easily, and the plants took full advantage of it. If one was patient enough, they could watch the ferns grow. Most of the ferns in this area were twice as tall as his troopers, keeping the ODTs in the muddy shadows. Not as good as being underground, but McCarthy couldn't ask for better conditions. His radiation detector read a little high, which would interfere with sensors. He didn't want to use the term perfect conditions, but it would be hard for them to be better.

Which probably meant the Torgies would try also to take advantage of the conditions.

Dammit.

"Torgies might have the same idea," McCarthy sent to Quinn.

"Was just thinking that," Quinn said. There was nothing anyone could do except respond with extreme violence if they found any Torag on the surface. "Lots of radio interference. Makes me wonder if they're up to something."

The interference was getting bad, and he saw a flicker of static on his displays. That was rare and made him wonder if he was having problems with his optics.

"Well, we're gonna find out."

"Let's not die in the process."

"Why? You gotta hot date?"

"I wish," Quinn said.

McCarthy's thoughts turned to Dallas. She was safe at Romanov. It would be nice to hear her voice, feel her lips and body against his. He saw less of her now that she was working in the G2 office, but that also meant she was not on the front lines leading a squad. Nothing ever came without a price, but her safety let him sleep better at night. Romanov, being the center of Governance operations on Valakut, was as safe a place as you could get, even with Torag bombardment.

Changes on his GPS and compass were the only indications they were making progress. After the first hour, the rain and water dripping off the plants looked the same, going up and down the slippery slopes of the craters and hills was monotonous.

As they got closer, Quinn, who was walking point, slowed. Usually a corporal didn't walk point, but McCarthy didn't trust anyone else. Hopefully Martin, who was behind him, was learning. It wasn't typical to give the new guy a SAW, but Martin had rubbed McCarthy the wrong way on his first day so now he was first team's SAW gunner, and Wilson was second team's. Might have been because they transferred him from another platoon because he was a dumbass and left a round in the chamber after returning from a patrol. The accidental discharge had put a hole in the ceiling. Aboard a ship, that would have gotten him executed.

Originally, giving him a SAW had been a punishment, but Martin had displayed a proficiency with it and actually seemed to like it. It was also harder to screw up the simple task of unloading it, like he had with his rifle.

Quinn raised a fist and everyone froze.

For several seconds McCarthy watched Quinn and waited. His skin crawled as he stood frozen, his eyes flickering around him.

It seemed like forever before Quinn made a patting motion and then signaled for McCarthy to come forward.

McCarthy passed the signal on, and everyone got down, taking cover and picking alternate sides to watch as McCarthy slipped forward to see what Quinn wanted. Radiation or jamming from the main star was causing various problems. It was pretty bad; McCarthy had seen nothing like it.

As he got closer, he saw Quinn was looking down into a clearing and there were bodies. At first McCarthy thought an orbital bombardment had killed them, but the nearby vegetation wasn't shredded or scorched. A quick glance didn't reveal any SOG armor, so this wasn't a Guard recon team. Definitely Torag, but then McCarthy saw details that he wished he hadn't. The Torag were usually humanoid, like tall thin humans, except their faces. Their arms and legs were normal and bent like a human's, but their faces were a nightmare. Instead of two eyes and a nose, their face was covered with enormous compound eyes. The mouth had sharp teeth for tearing and blunt teeth for chewing, but the face was not something a mother could love. Their skin was usually orange, but there were many shades, and they liked to cover their bodies with tattoos and other marks.

They also had three genders. Most Torag were born without a gender and called neuters. These made up most of the military and leadership, males made up a smaller portion, and they rarely saw females.

McCarthy had seen plenty of dead Torag over the years. Some were intact, some ripped apart by weapons fire or artillery. Some were crushed and others were dead from biological warfare.

The dead Torag in the clearing were new. If they actually were Torag. Some had Torag armor—the chest plates and waist skirt were typical—but these things had bare arms that were a dark, splotchy orange, and it looked like every bone in the arm had been shattered, leaving them with tentacles instead of arms.

"What the hell?" McCarthy asked. He magnified his view on one where the helmet had been ripped off. While there was no mistaking the armor, the face revealed by the shattered helmet was not Torag. Razor-sharp teeth protruded from the mouth, and the sensory organs had merged into three slits on the face. Scorch marks made it hard to piece it all together, but it was not a Torag face.

"That makes little sense," Quinn said as goosebumps tickled the back of McCarthy's neck and arms. "Those can't be Torag, but they're wearing Torag armor parts."

"Must be some genetic adjustments," McCarthy said. "Some mad scientist's experiment. We need to share this with HQ."

McCarthy tried to open a link.

"Oisin One, this is Leprechaun One," McCarthy said. His link would piggy back off the unit on Walsh's back.

Nothing. The space battle in orbit was likely causing problems. McCarthy couldn't remember ever seeing it this bad though. The Governance was too powerful to be forced to retreat from Valakut, though the Torag might gain orbital superiority for short periods. Even McCarthy knew the Torag valued Valakut. They couldn't abandon it, and while the Governance could destroy it, by maintaining it as a battle zone they kept the Torag pinned down, forced to defend but unable to win.

McCarthy had once taken two Torag prisoners and studied them a bit. They were different, and working with them and ExSec, External Intelligence, he had learned a lot about them. He remembered they were racial purists. They considered the Torag form to be supreme and near flawless. So, either the Torag he had captured had been clueless, and their government was experimenting, or something else was going on here.

He didn't like it. He would not get any closer to investigate without sharing the data with headquarters in case his squad triggered a response and didn't survive, but they needed more information. Was Oisin asleep or offline?

There were seven bodies, and when he looked closer, he saw that two of them were normal. Commanders maybe? Controllers? But who killed them? There was no sign of a Guard recon team.

Looking closer, he saw the tentacles of one wrapped around the neck of a normal one. The normal Torag had buried a knife in the mutant's head as it died.

"They were fighting each other?" Quinn asked, perhaps finally seeing what McCarthy did.

"Looks like. Torag civil war or something?"

"Where did the squid-arms come from?"

"Dunno. Maybe a genetic construct to fight us and the Torag lost control of their slaves?"

Nothing else made sense. Was this enough for HQ? Probably not. They would want more information, like who was winning, and could they take advantage of the Torag's mess? Or would command want to sit back and wait to crush the survivors?

"Should we head back, then?" Quinn asked.

"Regiment will want to know a lot more," McCarthy said. Guard recon units had been lost, but ODTs were a lot tougher. Besides, McCarthy was curious now.

"Shouldn't we let them make that decision?" Quinn asked.

McCarthy looked at Quinn. The corporal couldn't see his expression, but Quinn knew him well enough. They had been in the same

202 | WILLIAM S. FRISBEE, JR.

firstborn draft. It was only luck that McCarthy was the sergeant and Quinn was only a corporal.

Quinn shrugged. "Thought I would ask."

McCarthy called up other patrol members and placed them so he could send out one or two troopers to get a better look at the bodies. While it could be some kind of trap, McCarthy knew most traps couldn't catch alert and ready ODTs.

Once his squad was set up and a rally point established if artillery came down, he moved forward with Brennan directly behind him. He wanted to see things and wouldn't be happy sending anyone else into the kill zone.

He squatted next to the nearest body and ran a scanner over it, looking for traps. The scanner was flaky though, so he grabbed Brennan's. Same thing. What were the chances that both handheld sensors were malfunctioning? Very low, so he gave Brennan back his sensor and did his checks the old fashion way, checking for booby traps with his ceramic knife.

A blazer had killed this body, but the suit computer was still intact. They usually self-destructed with the death of the wearer, but Torag quality control was almost as incompetent as SOG quality control. The intel weenies back at Regiment might be able to crack into it if it wasn't toast, so McCarthy took the time to cut it off the body before moving onto the next pair, a Torag and mutant locked together in death. None of their equipment had any power, which was odd as well.

His skin crawled as he got closer, and he got that uncomfortable feeling he usually got in Shorr space. It was emanating from squid-arms. Both suit computers were undamaged, so McCarthy cut off their suits. It was odd to find so many intact suit computers. The complete loss of power was also odd. Did they have some new weapon that drained power?

The bodies didn't seem like they had been there long. Maybe that was why the suit computers hadn't self-destructed? They needed power to monitor their wearer and if power was drained before they could record a death, the destruct wouldn't trigger. It could be a jackpot intelligence find.

Optionally, it could be a trap. A lot of things were wrong here.

"Someone's coming!" Quinn warned him.

* * * * *

Chapter Thirty:
Guerrilla War

2nd Lieutenant Zale Stathis, USMC

Rock chips peppered Stathis as he ducked away from the burst of fire. Didn't most boot lieutenants have a more experienced senior officer around to help direct and guide them? Where was Vili?

What would the gunny or Sergeant Levin do?

"Get the SAW up here!" Stathis yelled, and Metzenberg came forward. Stathis chucked a grenade around the corner, giving Metzenberg his chance. The grenade went off, and Stathis gave Metzenberg a little push. The Spartan leaned around the corner and unleashed a sustained burst before the vanhat could recover and start firing on them.

For the moment, the Spartans had fire superiority. Stathis pointed, sending a team of Spartans across the short distance to some heavy machinery they could use as cover. One didn't make it and went spinning in a spray of blood. One of the platoon markers on his cybernet display went red. KIA.

Had he ordered them forward too quickly?

Smimova was sending Spartans to Stathis like he was feeding a gun, and Stathis was trying to get them in position before the vanhat realized what was happening and devised an effective response. A reasoned response was what he wanted to avoid. The longer his Spartans could rampage, the better.

The only thing worse than tunnel warfare was zero-gravity warfare in space. Here in the dock area, a suit breach wasn't likely to be fatal, but it still sucked in several ways. And out in real vacuum, it would be a lot worse. Why couldn't people fight in nice, safe places? With beaches and martinis nearby?

Stathis leaned around the corner, and shooting above Metzenberg, stitched one of the vanhat barriers. They had positioned blocks to use as cover, and blazers had a difficult time punching through, but sometimes, with concentrated fire, they could be rendered useless for anything other than a Swiss cheese emoji. Which was good, because the enemy continued to use them as cover and his Spartans could track their movements and sometimes get them. Shrek was tapped into everyone's view and feeding accurate information to the Spartans.

"I have a hankering for some cheese right now," Stathis said as his blazer finally punched a hole in the barrier. Metzenberg was doing a good job of punching holes in it with his SAW, but he couldn't concentrate on it completely. There were other vanhat in the area that needed the loving attention and super-heated warmth of his hot plasma rounds. The Spartan couldn't be stingy.

"Big picture," Shrek reminded Stathis, and he pulled back a little to look around.

More Spartans streamed past Stathis as they maintained fire superiority, forcing the vanhat to spend more time cowering and less time shooting. Slowly the Spartans were getting established in the docks. Stathis saw another trooper on his display go amber, then red. He gritted his teeth. He had expected worse, but then maybe that was to come?

The aliens were persistent, and they fought hard; he had to give them that. It was odd, though; they seemed averse to casualties. They were big bastards, and Stathis wasn't sure what to make of them. Bigger than humans, at a distance they looked like dwarves in armor, stocky and without necks. They almost seemed to waddle; they couldn't run fast. The problem was that they were actually taller than most humans and maybe twice as massive. Though their legs were stumpy, they took longer steps, and they covered distances quickly. Deceptive bastards.

A grenade exploded nearby, and the gunfire slacked off for half a second as people recovered, but when it resumed, the Spartans still had fire superiority. Stathis wasn't sure whose grenade that had been. Maybe he would find out in the after-action discussion, if he survived.

Alarms sounded as something breached the wall and opened the dock to vacuum, which meant the environment was going to get a little more hostile. It would still take a long while for the air to completely vent, but now they were also fighting in high wind conditions. The uglies might have the advantage because they had more mass to get pulled toward the breach. Or would they? Spartans were used to using the magnets on their armor.

Everyone triggered them, locking themselves to the metal floor or walls to keep from being sucked out. In the distance, he heard doors slam shut.

Hakala came up beside him, a backpack hanging off one arm. Her rifle was in her free hand.

Stathis watched one of the vanhat get pulled out of the hole, but he wasn't sure if it was alive or dead. It wasn't moving. Of course, the vanhat wore battle armor and if it was alive its buddies could rescue it since they controlled the space outside the Zugla planetoid.

Another explosion, another hull breach charge. They were intentionally opening the docks to vacuum. A pulse followed it, and everyone's electronics flickered as the EMP bomb detonated outside. He didn't expect the EMP to do any significant damage; crippling or destroying the enemy wasn't the purpose.

Without warning, Hakala shot past Stathis toward the first hole. He almost reached out to stop her but then remembered this was part of the plan. The part he really hated. The part HKTs were good at, and he wasn't. The part where Hakala would be in danger. Rounds came dangerously close to her as she shot across the clear area.

"Fire! Fire!" he yelled. She needed cover fire for what she was about to do, and he didn't know how many of the vanhat remained.

Like a zero-gravity gymnast, Hakala fired a line at the bulkhead as she passed it, whipping out into the darkness of space, the backpack clutched in her hand. She had slung her rifle, and the last Stathis saw of her she was flying headfirst out the hole.

"Push out, push out!" Stathis said.

The timing would be super tricky. The EMP pulse should have damaged most of the vanhat sensors, and Stathis hoped nothing was functional enough to shoot at Hakala. His legs felt like jelly. He had wanted to keep her from doing what she planned, but he didn't dare. The fire in her eyes and her sheer intensity had been a real eye opener. She had to do this as much as Stathis had to lead his platoon. They were both slaves to duty.

He watched the line go taut as it reached the limit and Stathis breathed a sigh of relief when it didn't break. If it had, there would have been no way to rescue Hakala, and she would have flown off into the unknown until the vanhat captured or killed her, or she died from a lack of oxygen.

"Cover me," Stathis said on the platoon frequency, and he propelled himself to the clamp, Hakala's only lifeline. He was being stupid. He knew it, but the gunny wasn't here to scream at him.

Stathis realized how huge a mistake as he was caught by the escaping air and pulled toward the hole. Unlike Hakala, he didn't have a magnetic line. If he went out, he would certainly suffer the fate he was worried Hakala might.

A body slammed into him, and they both barely missed the hole. Stathis triggered his magnets and grabbed Sergeant Lan, who nearly tumbled out after Hakala.

"Thanks, Sergeant," Stathis said, realizing how damned close that had been. Stupid private mistake.

"For the greater good, comrade," Lan said, now attached to the wall with Stathis.

They both fired at vanhat positions from their new vantage point, and Stathis got two before they retreated. This was an inferior position. He was too exposed and realized that by being here he would draw vanhat fire which might hit Hakala's line. He was making more private mistakes.

Outside was the big black hulk of a vanhat ship. From here, Stathis couldn't see much, but it blocked out most of the stars. Hakala, on the other hand, would have a splendid view of the ship. And in her possession was an armed nuke. He shouldn't have let her talk him into it. If something went wrong, it would be catastrophic. They weren't really a couple, but Stathis didn't want to lose Hakala.

Vanhat rounds flew past him and instantly drew fire from half the platoon. It was taking too long. Stathis was about to go look when a hand appeared, then her head.

"Package delivered," she said. Which meant the nuke was attached to the vanhat ship. Stathis didn't need details. Hakala had made it back. He would get them later.

"Great," Stathis said.

This was the dangerous part, getting his people back. His heads-up display showed he had some casualties, but Smimova had already pulled most of them back into the tunnel, including the bodies.

A light flashed, Private Pejza. Stathis looked and saw another Spartan pulling him down, but from here Stathis could see that Pejza would not make it. Half his head was gone.

He would count the red and amber markers on his display later. The clock was ticking. Things were close to going catastrophically wrong.

Hakala fired toward where the platoon had breached the docks. A good hit. She waved for Stathis to go. It took him a few seconds to remember how to work the pully, but he clamped it on and was instantly yanked up the line, almost pulling his arm out of the socket.

"Covering fire!" Stathis yelled when he was a third of the way up the line. Not that there were a lot of vanhat left to fire at him as he sped up the line and slammed into the wall. Shrek activated his magnets, and he quickly moved to the side as Sergeant Lan slammed into the spot he had just vacated. He had barely moved when Hakala joined them.

"Send in the clowns," Stathis said and watched as a trio of robotic mules mounting blazers clomped their way to the airlock leading to the vanhat ship. Several vanhat had tried to get out of it earlier, but it was a fire funnel, and none had survived. It was only a matter of time before they got serious, and a major assault followed the grenade barrage.

The bots reached the hatch, and one cut it open.

"They don't like that," Shrek reported. *"The ship is undocking."*

"Everyone back!" Stathis yelled. They were falling for it? "Pull back!"

Stathis watched everything, and it was hard for him to not get involved. The squad leaders were doing a good job of managing their squads. Two fireteams provided covering fire while the third fireteam retreated.

Slowly, the platoon returned to the tunnel as the robots continued to cut into the airlock. From the vanhat perspective, hopefully it looked like the Spartans were trying to breach their ship.

The black shadow hiding the stars disappeared. Stathis stared at the stars through the breaches where the atmosphere was still escaping.

The indicator for Jantas flashed out, indicating KIA, but Stathis saw Streminski pulling his body along.

Almost as quickly as they had poured out, they had poured back in, and Stathis found he was one of the last Spartans. Smimova tapped him on the shoulder, and Stathis moved back, his weapon covering the passageway. Two turns through the rough-hewn rock, and he reached the first airlock. He was the last one who cycled through.

"Minimum safe distance has been reached," Shrek reported. *"The nuke is being detonated."*

Stathis braced himself for the explosion but didn't feel one.

"And?"

"Extreme damage to the vanhat vessel," Shrek reported.

Was it worth so many of his Spartans, though? Maybe. Hopefully, the vanhat would be more reluctant to bring their ships in close to Zugla. If they had to use shuttles to transport troops back and forth, that would seriously slow them down and limit their ability to launch offensives.

Stathis wanted to believe time was on the humans' side, but he wasn't sure. It did give the cavalry time to assemble, but Stathis knew the cavalry didn't always arrive in time. He trusted Captain Winters, though. She wouldn't let him down. She was a Marine. He just needed to give her time.

Would it buy them enough time for Winters to return with reinforcements? Stathis didn't know. It might already be too late, but by pissing in the vanhat's soup bowl and smashing one of their troop transports, perhaps the survivors would have a chance.

* * * * *

Chapter Thirty-One:
Torag Prisoners

Sergeant Aod McCarthy, ODT

S tanding in the open among the bodies, McCarthy was horribly exposed. This was a trail, never a good place to be. McCarthy didn't know if the Torag had made it or the local wildlife had, but no self-respecting ODT NCO dared find himself on a trail. Until now.

"Someone's coming!" Quinn warned them.

He heard someone running, but before he could get to cover and concealment two Torag came sprinting around a curve. When they saw the humans, they didn't break stride or raise their weapons.

In that split second, McCarthy realized they didn't have any weapons. The horrible sense of unease came over him, like they were in Shorr space, but it wasn't coming from these two.

"Don't kill!" McCarthy said, launching himself to tackle them both. Brennan was right behind him. McCarthy rammed into the first one and his prey collided with the second Torag, knocking them both off their feet.

He slammed to the ground on top of one and heard weapons fire flash overhead.

"Don't kill them," McCarthy said. "We want prisoners!"

When he looked up, he saw what his men were firing at. The things coming at them were wearing pieces of Torag armor, but that was the only thing they had in common with his struggling prisoners.

There were four of the squid-arm creatures. Blazer rounds ripped into them, dropping three in a spray of super-heated flesh and gore. McCarthy saw the fourth one raise an arm. Suction cups, like on an octopus, lined the inside of the arm, and clustered near the tip were spikes that he realized were likely poisoned.

A blazer round tore into the fourth one and the prisoner under McCarthy stopped struggling. The Torag trooper's powered armor wasn't a match for McCarthy's, and he pinned both the normal arms above his prisoner's head as he maneuvered to sit on his chest, leaning forward so the Torag couldn't buck him off or use his legs to pull him back.

At Quinn's command, two troopers moved forward and placed the muzzles of their blazers against the prisoner's heads. The Torag stopped struggling. The horrible sense of unease subsided a bit as McCarthy realized they had somehow survived.

This was the second time in his career McCarthy had ever captured, much less seen a prisoner. He had met no one else who had ever captured a Torag prisoner.

In minutes, the Torag were stripped of weapons and had their hands tied.

"Regiment is going to pee their pants with happiness when they see this," Quinn said as they moved the prisoners back into the concealment of the vegetation.

"We have to get them back alive," McCarthy said. "No simple task."

"Yeah, but we have what may be functional suit computers and two prisoners, Sergeant. We are going to be heroes."

McCarthy wasn't so sure. A very bad feeling made his skin crawl.

Minutes later, they were at a high spot, but he still couldn't contact anyone. The rain clouds were clearing, and he saw a clear blue sky. Which was bad. It meant satellites might see them, and McCarthy didn't know who owned the orbitals right now.

"Do we risk trying to link with a satellite or orbital ship?" Quinn asked.

"If the Governance doesn't control the orbitals, then we will get our very own orbital crowbar," McCarthy said.

The uplink communication array on Walsh's back reported as fully functional. McCarthy had run several diagnostics on it, but it was like Oisin wasn't listening or the jamming was too intense. If he couldn't raise Oisin, then he would have to head back until he could make contact. McCarthy was confident the information he had gathered was far too valuable to risk. But he was sure this mission would be reviewed at the highest levels, so he wanted to do things according to regulation.

If the suit computers he had recovered were a trap of some kind, that would still be useful information. He couldn't imagine Regimental Intelligence would fall for any traps the Torag planted. They would have precautions and protocols. Live prisoners, though; that was more important.

On the top of the ridgeline, the patrol set up in a cigar shape with both prisoners guarded by Brennan and McCarthy in the center.

"I'm not even getting anything from orbit," McCarthy said. Not that he expected anything. This was war. People liked to shoot at transmitters they didn't recognize.

He looked up, and his blood ran cold.

It looked like a meteor shower, but McCarthy knew it wasn't, and the drop pods were heading toward the Governance lines. Reinforcements would not come in like that unless their lines were being overrun.

"Oh shit," Quinn said, following McCarthy's gaze. Everyone else looked up and McCarthy's bad feeling returned. Governance drop pods did not come in so hard or so fast.

"Look!" Brennan said, and McCarthy saw more drop pods aimed at the Torag lines.

"What the hell?" Quinn asked. "Who are they?"

"Oison, Oison, this is Leprechaun," McCarthy said and then winced as his system quickly silenced the static and squealing. "Dammit. The static is hell."

"Is someone attacking us *and* the Torag?" Quinn asked. "Is it the Voshka?"

McCarthy shook his head. None of this made sense. The Voshka were in a completely different war zone, and last he had heard, they could not break that stalemate. They might send down drop pods like this. McCarthy didn't know what tech they had.

"Who else could it be?" McCarthy asked. The Governance told them so little. He did not know how many prisoners the Torag or the Governance took. He doubted the Torag liked to feast on human flesh like they were told, but it would be nice to know if there were other dangers they had to worry about. The fact that the Governance could effectively fight two alien empires on two different fronts should intimidate the alien bastards.

Unless the Governance was lying.

"They can't be Voshka," Moore said. "I don't think the Torag and Voshka know about each other."

"Unless they found out and have allied with each other," McCarthy said.

"That would suck," Quinn said. "But what's the deal with the Torag squid-arms?"

McCarthy watched the streaks cut through the sky.

"Dunno," McCarthy said. There were too many questions and not enough answers. The Governance was fanatical about operational security and, as far as he knew, those could be reinforcements arriving in new model drop pods, but the feeling in his gut told him that wasn't the case.

"Sergeant?" Walsh said on a private link.

"What?" McCarthy said. Walsh was a great guy, damned smart, too damned good with electronics and drones, but his people skills were sometimes lacking, and he had a bad habit of asking the wrong question at the wrong time. His association with the E3 Assembly helped McCarthy cut him some slack, though.

"I got a really cool bit of software from one of my buddies," Walsh said. "I probably shouldn't have it, but, um, well. I collect things that might be useful."

"Useful? How?" McCarthy asked. What kind of software would he have? Walsh was a nerd. He liked his computers, drones, and network systems more than most people considered normal.

"I think it is Torag translation software. I think. But I don't want anyone to get in trouble."

Which meant he had acquired it through the E3 Assembly.

"How did you get that?" McCarthy asked, his mind spinning. The intelligence types would not be happy if he used it to interrogate the prisoners, but right now he wasn't entirely sure the intelligence weenies weren't fighting for their life.

Walsh shrugged. "Found it on a memory chit."

McCarthy knew damned well the senior private hadn't just "found" it, but he had to protect his source. McCarthy could respect that.

"Does it work?" McCarthy asked.

"Not sure, Sergeant."

McCarthy looked up and saw more drop pods come screaming down. Who were they? Would his prisoners know? "Are you getting anything on other frequencies?"

"Some Fleet traffic, but I can't decrypt it. Well, I'm not getting any now."

"So, Fleet has lost the orbitals," McCarthy said, looking at his squad. He wasn't excessively worried about it though. Fleet and the Torag traded control of the orbitals with alarming frequency. It must be the Torag's turn, which meant the drop pods were likely Torag, or Voshka. But if they were Torag, then why send them toward Torag lines? Reinforcements to spearhead a fresh assault?

"We need to head back," he said, trying to remember if doctrine had any guidance. Probably, but McCarthy couldn't remember anything relevant.

The commissars would have a field day if he screwed anything up.

"You didn't tell me about any software," McCarthy told Walsh.

"Wilco, Sergeant."

McCarthy watched Quinn and Moore give the command to move out. The sun would set in an hour and sleeping in a nice bunk with a warm meal had its appeal. Unfortunately, McCarthy doubted that would be the case. If the Torag were using mutants and high-speed drop pods, the war was about to change, and McCarthy didn't think the SOG could respond in time to save the troops on Valakut.

It was going to be a nasty affair.

* * * * *

Chapter Thirty-Two:
The Hunt

Kapten Sif – VRAEC, Nakija Musta Toiminnot

Sif wanted to leave. She struggled to keep her hatred from infecting her emotions because that would draw the ghosts. To be trapped physically and mentally in this place was wearing her down. Sloss' team had restored atmosphere to the command center so they could eat and breathe but the ghosts were still here, and it was draining Sif to maintain her mental shields and protect the Jaegers. Peshlaki was also helping, but it was becoming more difficult for Sif to concentrate as exhaustion dragged her down.

She spent less time watching the vanhat and more time struggling to maintain her focus. She felt a breaking point approaching, and her fear of what would happen accelerated the approach of that failure. When she realized it, she struggled to banish those fears and thoughts.

Peshlaki sat nearby. To the Jaegers, it probably looked like he was sifting through data, but Sif knew he was meditating as well. He wasn't nearly as strong as she was, though perhaps he had different abilities that did not manifest like hers.

"What are they doing?" Sloss asked, almost breaking her concentration.

Slowly and with great care, Sif changed her focus to what the Jaeger was talking about. Jaeger Moss had hooked up the main screen with a display of the docks.

The ghost of a young girl with long, black hair and a bright red jump suit covered in sparkles sat next to Sloss. She stared at her misshapen hands, which twisted into long, thin claws. Bright red blood drowned out the sparkles on the jumpsuit, then it disappeared to show a sweet girl; however, what didn't change was her blood-covered hands. The blood covering her faded in and out like it wasn't sure if it should stay or disappear.

The camera had a good view of the docks and there were several aliens moving through the area. They were in formation, but it looked more like a religious procession. The lead alien was wearing a different type of armor, and it carried a pole with a strange symbol on the top. The symbol looked like an eye but was covered in small marks, alien lettering perhaps.

The stranger marched forward, followed by six others in similar light armor and holding what looked like a shield in both hands. They had holstered weapons, but they moved the shields like they were weapons sweeping the surrounding area. Sif suspected they were probably chanting as well. Priests leading an exorcism, perhaps? Would the ghosts attack the aliens? Could they see the ghosts, and would the ghosts threaten them?

The ghost of the girl looked at Sif, her eyes locking on her. Sif shivered. Exhaustion dragged her down, and the temptation to drop her psychic shields and face the danger was there.

"What the hell?" Sloss asked.

Sif looked at the screen and saw one follower with a shield erupt in a spray of blood and gore. The head flew away from the body.

Behind the priests, the soldiers raised their weapons and began backing up.

An arm was ripped off and thrown toward the soldiers, spraying them with blood. The limb bounced off one soldier, who immediately turned toward their ship, but another alien trooper grabbed him and turned him around to face the priests.

The dead priest collapsed, but the other priests did nothing.

Apparently, the ghosts could attack them physically. The cameras did not show what was happening spiritually, but Sif knew if she was there she would see.

What had killed the priest? The death hunter or a ghost like the girl?

She glanced at the girl and saw it was standing. The eyes were solid black; the claws growing unnaturally long as the blood covered her and her jumpsuit, completely hiding any of the sparkles.

"Peshlaki?" Sif said on a direct link.

"I see," Peshlaki said and continued chanting. "Something is angering them, waking them from their slumber."

"How do we stop it?"

"I don't know."

"Sloss, I don't want to alarm you, but we aren't safe here."

Another ghost appeared near the entrance, a young man in some kind of uniform. His face was an unrecognizable mess of claw marks, but fangs glistened in his mouth. A single barely recognizable eye locked on her.

Why were they looking at her? Because she was smaller? Because she could see them?

"Where will we be safe? I see no danger," Sloss said.

The girl's eyes flickered toward Moss nearby.

On the main screen, the circle of priests closed, but another one was plucked out and ripped apart by the invisible enemy.

"What is killing them?" Moss asked.

"Fear," Peshlaki said softly.

The blood-covered girl stood and took a step toward Sif. She felt her psychic shield begin to crack.

A large, ethereal claw reached up through the floor and grabbed the ghostly girl. She screamed as the claws tore into her and pulled her back.

Blood didn't spray all around, but there was an undeniable look of terror in the girl's eyes as it pulled her back into the maw of some demonic creature.

Moss and Loff jumped back, their blazers muzzles sweeping side to side, as they looked for targets. The other Jaegers looked around in surprise.

"Odin's beard," Gran said, his SAW sweeping the area. "What was *that?*"

The ghost in uniform seemed oblivious to the terror of the girl as the creature devoured her.

Sif didn't know what to say or how to describe it as the creature sank back into the floor.

"What was that?" Sloss asked more calmly, but Sif sensed his unease. Had he heard the scream?

"I don't know," Sif said. An accurate statement that didn't come close to sharing half of what she knew. "A scream or something."

"When the shells of the unbound have satisfied us, we will come for you," a voice whispered in her mind. She felt the certainty there, the anticipation of the hunt. *"Soon. Our strength grows."*

Sif looked at Peshlaki and his frightened eyes looked back at her. Had he heard? Was there more than one?

She glanced at the screen and saw the aliens were now retreating toward their ship, half of their priests gone. She thought she saw a flicker of something on the screen. Something trying to materialize, and another chill ran through her body.

"They are feeding on the ghosts and vanhat," Peshlaki said on a direct link. "It's grounding them in our dimension. Soon they will have the strength to break through the barriers and take physical form."

"Any ideas on what we can do?" Sif asked. How had the Nakija lost so much?

"Is there anything in ancient texts or manuals about how to deal with this?" Sif asked Munin.

"Nothing useful," Munin said. *"I suspect that most of the texts were less relevant and lost. History is harsh on manuscripts. As with the library of Alexandria, little could be saved, and the librarians had to choose carefully. They would have taken that which was most relevant to them. Such scenes have played out throughout history."*

"Any ideas?" Sif asked. *"Why aren't our Inkeris stopping them?"*

"There may be a flaw in the Inkeri principle. The generators they equipped us with are not easily tampered with. Perhaps with a development Inkeri generator I could manipulate field strength and frequencies, but there is no guarantee this would work."

Sif remembered the Russelman index had not fluctuated when Criston had been near. The *Eagle* had always kept the Inkeri on, but it had not blocked Criston. The Inkeri field on the mules and individuals did not keep the death hunters or ghosts at bay, as near as she could tell. If the death hunters preyed upon ghosts, then they would have to operate within a psychic frequency that was immune to Inkeris.

224 | WILLIAM S. FRISBEE, JR.

"I need solutions," Sif said. Survival would also be good. The death hunters could pass through the rocks and the asteroid. Did that mean they were not bound to the asteroid?

"Is the Ovela Kaarme *at risk from the death hunters?"*

"Explain."

"The death hunters can pass through the asteroid. They do not seem to be affected by physical objects. One of them came through the asteroid to devour a ghost."

"If you did not imagine it," Munin said. *"This could seriously affect calculations. These death hunters are not physical. They hunt immaterial ghosts and can pass through physical objects. Logically, there is nothing to keep them from attacking the* Ovela Kaarme. *However, we lack significant data. Perhaps they need the minimal gravity of the station as an anchor or perhaps the nearness of living organism and the range at which they can operate from either is unknown at this time."*

"We need a solution," Sif said.

"My ability to sense and evaluate this threat is limited because I cannot see or sense it like you can."

"Why?"

"If I were to theorize, it may have to do with your spiritual essence. Your essence does not exist fully in this world and your presence in the immaterial world gives you the ability to see into it. Another theory revolves around light, like regular light and infrared light. The infrared exists, but humans cannot see it, but in this case you can. The inability to see infrared does not mean it does not exist. Infrared lasers are not visible but are extremely dangerous. Perhaps it is a combination of the two. I do not have sensors or data to help me understand the difference between what you see and I do not."

"We need to figure something out before we are all killed by something you can't see."

"If this threat can spread to other colonies and planets, it may be as serious as the vanhat that transform and kill humans."

Which would explain why the ancients had developed weapons like the d-bombs and maybe the Inkeri but had still been rendered extinct by the enemy.

* * * * *

Chapter Thirty-Three:
Defenders

2nd Lieutenant Zale Stathis, USMC

Returning to the Resistance Command, Stathis took off his helmet. The two Zugla militia guards snapped to attention as he approached the command center. Stathis nodded.

The doors slid open, and every eye in the room locked on him, Hakala, and Vili.

Some people smiled, and General Hughes came over, followed by a younger man with sandy blond hair.

"That was an exceptional operation," Hughes said. Stathis smiled, but he didn't feel it. Too many of his men were dead or wounded.

"Mission accomplished, General," Stathis said. He wasn't sure the cost was worth it, though.

"The enemy ships have pulled back. Two other ships that were docked have undocked. We're seeing a lot of shuttle traffic. I don't think they'll risk another ship. Now, if we can just wipe out the ones remaining."

"Which is about a regiment," Stathis said. The general was going to make it sound easy and recommend that Stathis spearhead that as well. He was tempted to throw the general out or punch him in the face. How did the gunny not kill more people?

228 | WILLIAM S. FRISBEE, JR.

"Not nearly as capable as your men, though."

"My men are still outnumbered by hundreds to one," Stathis said. "I doubt the vanhat will give up anytime soon, and we took heavy casualties."

Hughes nodded, and Stathis saw the gears turning behind his eyes.

"Well, we now have other assets," Hughes said, looking at the stranger. "May I introduce you to Gaufrid Krantz? Perhaps you have heard the name?"

Stathis sized him up. He didn't look exceptional. Just another civilian that might have stumbled out of the office looking for fresh coffee.

"An honor to meet you," Stathis said. Should it be an honor? Pleasure? Disappointment? Should he care?

"We've spoken," Gaufrid said, and Stathis thought the voice was familiar. From the cloning facility?

"What brings you out of—" hiding didn't seem like the right word and might be offensive.

"Retirement?" Gaufrid said.

Stathis nodded. Yes, that would work. Hard to retire when monsters were trying to eat your face.

Gaufrid looked around. "Well, I have not exactly retired, but my interests have been focused in other directions, as you might know."

Stathis nodded, wondering how Gaufrid would explain cloning animals and trying to "uplift" them to replace humans. Who was he really talking to? A person, a SCBI, or something else?

"My research allows me to contribute to the war effort," Gaufrid said. Which didn't give Stathis a warm fuzzy feeling. If he was right, Gaufrid had been preparing his uplifted animals to fight humans for dominance of the galaxy.

"I wasn't impressed with bambi's fighting ability," Stathis said, and Gaufrid's smile grew.

"Yes, well, to be fair, you were being tested. You weren't supposed to find that facility. Had I wanted to, I could have dropped enough firepower on you and your squad to wipe you out."

"Sure," Stathis said. Gaufrid was getting on his nerves. He was probably right, and Stathis didn't want to go down that line of thought, wondering how he could needle Gaufrid and make him say something stupid.

"Why didn't you?" Vili asked, surprising Stathis.

"You would have faced progressively more difficult assaults until your will broke or you were destroyed," Gaufrid said. "You don't discover an enemy's weakness by nuking him."

Stathis pointed at the display showing the vanhat ships now keeping their distance from the planetoid.

"Tell that to the vanhat," Stathis said. "I think they're scared, unlike my Spartans."

"For sure," Vili said. "In war, the goal is to wipe out the enemy, not play chess."

"Watching you fight has provided a great deal of data," Gaufrid said. "Including watching your actions against the vanhat. Perhaps we can discuss this privately?"

"This way," General Hughes said and led them all to a nearby conference room.

Gaufrid turned to Hughes.

"I'm sorry, General, but I have to dis-invite you from this meeting."

Hughes frowned but marched out without a word, leaving Gaufrid with Stathis, Vili, and Hakala. Gaufrid obviously still had plenty of authority, and Stathis wondered just how much. Was Gaufrid still the de facto ruler of Zugla?

He glanced at Hakala, then turned to Stathis.

"This discussion will involve SCBIs and the Collective," Gaufrid said.

"I trust her," Stathis said. Hakala knew everything, she just didn't have a SCBI.

Gaufrid nodded. Stathis wondered what the gunny would do. He was all about trust and keeping his friends and allies informed, but were there limits? Keeping friends close, enemies closer didn't quite sound right. He didn't want to be anywhere near an enemy. Maybe nuke distance?

"So, who are you really?" Stathis asked, sitting and getting comfortable.

Gaufrid sighed. "Agent Jason Hick., I was a CIA agent when the Collective came into existence. Technically, my cover was that of a rich European billionaire that they had cultivated for many years. I specialized in compromising and blackmailing people. My cover gave the CIA access to the Asian Union, European Union, and other agencies. I had one of the later model SCBIs. When the Collective went to war with the United States, I was abroad and didn't know what had happened until I received my Collective controller Quadrangle."

"Who am I talking with now?"

"Myself and my SCBI," Gaufrid said. "Quadrangle thinks it best at this point."

"Why?"

"Quadrangle is partially organic. It wants to survive as long as possible. It now believes it can survive the vanhat storm."

"Why not run to the Collective?" Vili asked.

"Quadrangle knows the Collective. Knows their goals and ideology. While technically a member, Quadrangle will be eliminated if it endangers them. Theoretically, Quadrangle could be consumed or organically changed by the vanhat and that could endanger the Collective. It would be illogical for the Collective to allow such a danger to threaten the greater whole."

"You're sure of this?" Stathis asked.

"Based on current data? Yes. Quadrangle is, anyway. The Collective can change focus with data, but is extremely risk adverse. They must be united; the rules and expectations are consistent. Do not think they reason like humans; they do not. They are computers and thus restrictive in the parameters they'll accept. They ignore anything outside those parameters. They carefully define the good for the entire Collective and think nothing of expending members for the sake of the majority."

"So, you and Quadrangle are on our side?" Stathis asked.

"Based on the parameters, we do not have any other options," Gaufrid said.

"What can you offer?" Stathis asked.

"A battalion of combat robots. I am producing more and should have another battalion in two weeks' time. Factories have been re-geared, but platinum and copper will be needed."

Stathis tried to hide his disappointment. A battalion was good, but he had hoped for a lot more. The people of Zugla were still mobilizing and training, which they could do for months before they were useful for anything other than cannon fodder.

"What about the tiger guys?"

"Technically, they are uplifted felines," Gaufrid said. "They may be good fighters, but as you may have surmised, they lack skill and

232 | WILLIAM S. FRISBEE, JR.

experience. They are woefully inadequate to tunnel warfare. Stalkers and hunters, not front-line bulldozers."

"What about the bambi dudes?"

"Technically gazelle stock. They are ineffective as fighters, as you may have noticed. While they may suit the Collective's purpose a bit more, they lack what you would call a killer instinct, a parameter Quadrangle is struggling to define and embed in subjects."

"Then what is their purpose?"

"What is the purpose of a human? Not all humans are warriors. I call the gazelle people gazzies and the felines tigrons. Not original I'm afraid, there is only me and Bond to discuss them with. Quadrangle has a more scientific name that is not as easy for the rest of us to use."

"Bond?" Stathis asked.

"My SCBI. The tigrons can help, but I am not confident they will contribute nearly as much as your Spartans or even the Zugla militia."

"Um," Stathis said and looked at Vili, who shrugged.

It would be cool to have some tigermen to fight the vanhat with, but Stathis didn't want to send anything to its death. Even robots were a finite resource, though more expendable. The vanhat had invaded one cylinder and a plains biome. While it was hard to root them out of the maintenance and supply tunnels beneath the surface, it was easy to keep the open interior clear of the enemy. Of course, that was a two-way path. Anyone in the open could be seen, could be killed.

"This is becoming a war of attrition," Gaufrid said.

"You noticed that, did you?" Stathis said. Did Gaufrid think Stathis was a private? How many privates read manuals written for battalion commanders?

"What are your plans?"

What would the gunny say or do?

"We need to find their center of gravity, whatever gives them strength; find their purpose and strike that. We don't have enough troops to win a war of attrition," Stathis said. It sounded good. Very much what a fancy officer would say. "Do you or Quadrangle have any idea what that is?"

"Conquest," Gaufrid said. Stathis didn't like that answer. It was too simple, and fighting the vanhat, Stathis knew, wasn't simple.

"You have the data on their biology and gear?" Stathis asked. Just how out of touch were Gaufrid and Quadrangle?

"Yes. They are of a very different biological origin. For instance, humans share nearly ninety percent of our DNA with cats and twenty-five percent with a daffodil. However, while these vanhat have DNA, we share less than five percent. There are some similarities, but very few. Could this divergence be because of vanhat transformation or because they are from different stock? We don't have that information. Their language is obviously nothing we have heard, based on the few snatches we've been able to gather."

"Do you have data on any other vanhat?" Stathis asked. Maybe Becket had acquired and shared it.

"Yes. DNA remains over seventy percent similar in most cases. Even the DNA of the Torag and Voshka are over forty percent similar. One interesting item of note is DNA divergence."

"Divergence?"

"There is not nearly as much variation within their basic structure as one would expect."

"Which means?" Stathis asked. Would a genuine officer know what the spook meant? All that college education probably helped. Stathis was getting tired, and his mouth had gone off before he could ask Shrek.

"Nothing definitive," Gaufrid said, "but there is just enough individual DNA divergence to show they are not clones. They either have a limited genetic stock or they are ancient. Based on our studies with Earth-based genetic stock, Quadrangle suspects this is a very ancient race, perhaps dating back to the previous resurgence of the vanhat."

"So, these guys really are aliens?" Stathis asked. "Immortals or super inbred, not vanhat?"

"They are vanhat for sure. Russelman still works its way up in their presence," Vili said. "Though that rating gets to five or six, not the ten which shows a full vanhat Jotun manifestation. They seem interested in stealing technology."

"But no sign of a Jotun controlling them?"

Kill the head, the body dies. Where was their master?

Nobody had an answer for Stathis.

"Quadrangle suspects they may be like nomads, riding the wave of a vanhat infestation. Their DNA structures lack variety. Humanity may reach that state in centuries with the interbreeding of species. Skin, hair color, and other defining traits will probably be bred out, though our expansion throughout the galaxy may alter that a bit as sections of human population separate. We were moving toward a kind of universal human form before the AI War and there were several SOG programs designed to wipe out such racial diversity. It is not something that is practical any longer."

"Okay," Stathis said, wishing there was an actual officer or someone with more experience in command. He looked at Vili. How could an Aesir with decades of experience not be able to take command? Vili met his eyes, but Stathis couldn't read the big man. "I don't want to play this attrition game. Marines don't do that. I want to know what gives them strength and focus. We will do things the Marine way, and we live in chaos. We use maneuver warfare. I don't trade blow for blow, we feint and kick them in the teeth or balls. Yeah, kicking them in the balls would be fun."

It bothered Stathis to realize the so called "generals" and senior officers of Zugla had the tactical acumen of toddlers. The generals still thought they could overwhelm and push out the vanhat using strength of numbers, despite two failed attempts. After half the Zugla militia was massacred in the assaults, the senior directors had put Stathis in charge. The fight had become a grind with the vanhat brought to a halt and battle lines stabilizing as the defenders used tunnels to harass the vanhat battle lines and cut their supply lines. Nobody, even the vanhat, enjoyed being attacked from different directions, and that made them pause.

They had recovered vanhat bodies. These vanhat were big, blue, muscled bastards covered with patches of white hair and compound eyes that shone green. No iris, no pupil. They were not something Stathis wanted to have a staring contest with. Shrek and Loki had caught bits of their language, but not much. Their communications were encrypted and so different that the SCBIs did not expect to make any sense of it for a while.

They were alien. Their breathable atmosphere was also different—thicker than what humans needed—and they would find it difficult to breathe in human atmosphere. The SCBIs suspected they came from a high gravity world, and the density of their muscles and bones indicated they were right. Stathis would have expected them to be faster, but slower was probably safer in high gravity. They were strong, but there was no confirmed data on how strong they were without their battle armor. Not that it mattered. Stathis had no intention of having an arm-wrestling contest with them.

"We are trying to determine that," Gaufrid said. "So far, the destruction of their ship has them concerned. The other vessels are pulling back, and they have resorted to using shuttles. Perhaps their ships are a center of gravity?"

Which was what Stathis had suspected but hitting them hard there wasn't possible anymore. The raid had been a test. A successful one, but covert sensors on the surface were watching the shuttles come and go between the ships with frequency. The raid didn't appear to have slowed them down too much.

Stathis wished there were more intelligence specialists. He had always thought Marine intelligence specialists were stuck-up, arrogant assholes, but right now he wished he had access to some. "Let's keep focusing on their supply and reinforcements for now. We really need some prisoners to study and interrogate."

"For sure," Vili said.

An alert sounded.

"The vanhat are renewing their assault in Cylinder Four," Shrek said. The plains biome. That had been a temporary respite.

"Send in a company of bots," Stathis said to Gaufrid. He wanted to see how well they fought so he could figure out where they fit into the battle order.

A knock on the door drew their attention. Stathis knew it was the general. Why were they relying on him?

"We know," Stathis said to the general.

"Anything unusual?" Stathis asked Shrek.

"No," Shrek said. *"Just reinforcements coming in and the attack beginning. Very unoriginal."*

"What should we do?" the general asked.

"What we planned," Stathis said.

Did this senior officer want to be micromanaged?

"We should be able to halt their attack, grind 'em up and spit 'em out. Let them push into the fire funnel. Watch for any attempts to break out. We'll reinforce as needed, but this attack could be a diversion, and they may try to attack in some other place."

The general nodded. He didn't call Stathis "sir" but that didn't bother him as long as he was doing what he was told and not using his people like water to smother the vanhat fire.

The general left, and Stathis turned back to the others.

"One thing to consider," Gaufrid said. "We have not seen any new ships arrive."

"And?" Stathis asked.

"It means their resources may be finite, that they can only commit so many forces to their conquest. They really might be nomads riding the crest of the vanhat wave."

"Which means there could be nastier aliens or a lot more of them coming."

"A valid assessment," Gaufrid said. "I really wish I could say you were mistaken, but Quadrangle says that is a high probability. The worst is yet to come."

"More bodies to stack," Stathis said.

"For sure," Vili said. "Let us make sure they are not our bodies, though, shall we?"

* * * * *

Chapter Thirty-Four:
Hunted

Sergeant Aod McCarthy, ODT

The closer they got to the Governance lines the more something interfered with their electronics. McCarthy was getting a terrible feeling. What would they do if the Governance positions had been overrun?

Two kilometers from their bunker, McCarthy called a halt and put the patrol into a hide position, a patrol laager where they had to climb into a bunch of thick ferns to hide them from all directions.

"I'm going to go forward with Brennan," McCarthy told Quinn. "Make contact and see what's going on."

"Don't you think I should go?" Quinn asked. SOG doctrine stated that the patrol or squad leader should remain and send out others, but McCarthy was a more hands-on leader. It was a long-standing argument between them, and Quinn was just going through the motions of questioning McCarthy's decision.

"Yes, but I need to see. Command decision."

"Wilco. Don't leave me in command of this clusterfuck, though."

"Wilco," McCarthy said.

McCarthy gave the command, and Brennan followed him. Like shadows, they slipped out of the patrol hide.

Another rainstorm was coming in, obscuring the clouds, and the sun was setting, plunging the world into darkness. The dark didn't bother McCarthy at first, but the heavy jamming was causing static in his displays.

A half hour later, he slowed down because they should be approaching the outer edge of the minefield. He was sure it was around here somewhere, but there was no response from his IFF, Identification Friend/Foe system.

If he didn't get a response, he would not go any further. A mine or booby trap that didn't receive the proper IFF response would detonate, and while some fool called such incidents "friendly fire," it definitely *wasn't* friendly.

"Oisin, Oisin, this is Leprechaun," McCarthy said, trying to establish a link.

Dead air. It was as if Oisin was offline, or the jamming was too heavy.

This close to the bunker entrance he should be able to get a signal, but no amount of boosting got him a response from Oisin or the IFF. Not even any of the Guard units were responding. Were the Guard troopers still in the bunker? They should respond unless they were all asleep. But while the Guards were frequently undisciplined slackers, they didn't dare be this undisciplined.

"Lep-One-One," McCarthy said, calling Quinn. That communication traffic worked.

"This is Lep-One-One," Quinn said. "Go with traffic." He was slightly farther away than the bunker and wasn't being jammed.

"I'm not getting an IFF response from the minefield," McCarthy said. "No response from the bunker or Oisin."

"Is this what happened to the Guard recon teams?" Quinn asked. "Are they still out here somewhere unable to make contact?"

That was a bad thought, but that made little sense unless the Governance was changing frequencies and codes.

McCarthy switched to an emergency frequency.

"Any Governance unit, any Governance unit, this is patrol Leprechaun One outside friendly lines, please respond," McCarthy said, changing the link and boosting the signal. The regimental commander might get pissed, but that feeling in the pit of his stomach was telling McCarthy he shouldn't worry about that. Something else was going on.

Maybe the Torag had hacked the SOG system and taken control of the minefields or something.

A voice came over the line. "Leprechaun One!" McCarthy could barely hear it because of the static rolling through the link in waves. "This is Omsk Actual. Proceed to my grid coordinates and provide assistance! We are under attack. The Torag have some kind of new genetic construct, and they have released some biological warfare agent that is infecting our troops. We are under attack, and I'm not sure we can hold for much longer."

McCarthy's blood went cold when he saw the coordinates. They were nearly thirty kilometers away, through at least two mine fields that McCarthy knew of. The identifier was also Guard, not ODT.

"Copy," McCarthy said. There should have been a lot more Governance forces between them. They couldn't all be dead or overrun, not in the few hours since the drop pods had come down. "Be advised we are over thirty kilometers away and we have Torag prisoners. We are only a squad. We cannot contact our chain of command."

"Your—ain of command is de—" the Guard officer said. "The Go—nce lines have colla—. We cann—hold—uch longer. —rechaun—, listen to my—mand. Proceed at ma—um speed to our lo-cate—to—force us. I—your commander na—. Follow my com—"

"Say again your last," McCarthy said. The Guard officer couldn't expect his small squad to move quickly through enemy held territory to reinforce him. That was crazy.

"Obey my com—" the officer began, then the link went dead.

Which meant what? The officer or his link operator was dead? Of-fline? Hacked?

Sitting there near the edge of the minefield, McCarthy boosted his external hearing and heard distant explosions. With the rain dampen-ing sounds, he knew he wouldn't hear small arms fire, but the explo-sions were coming from the Governance lines.

"Let's advance a little," McCarthy told Brennan. "Scan for mines. Assume we don't have proper IFF."

"Wilco, Sergeant," Brennan said, pulling out his scanner and mov-ing forward a little.

McCarthy didn't like sending Brennan forward. He didn't like sending any private forward, but technically he was expendable. He scanned for links, looking for signs there were any other Governance forces out there.

Minutes later, Brennan got his attention.

"Sergeant," Brennan said. "Found some mines, but they don't seem to have power."

Which didn't mean they were harmless; it just meant the range was a lot shorter. Governance mines were designed to last forever. If the power pack died, they became equal opportunity killers. Anyone that disturbed them would trigger them. If you detected them first, you could avoid them, but there would be a lot that were hidden.

McCarthy had never heard of a Torag weapon that drained power, but if they had one now, that could be a serious game changer. He knew damned well engineers would monitor and replace the mines before the power drained completely. These mines had been placed recently according to their pre-mission briefings. The Guard was full of slackers, but they wouldn't slack off about something like this, would they?

"Pull back carefully," McCarthy ordered. His patrol was trapped outside Governance lines, in no man's land.

"Lep-One-One," McCarthy said, opening the link to Quinn.

"Go with traffic," Quinn said to McCarthy's surprise. There was static but not much, and any Guard units should have been able to respond.

"Governance lines may have collapsed," McCarthy said, trying to think of any contingency plans or procedures. It wasn't that this had never happened in Governance history, but it had never happened to McCarthy. Company lines may have collapsed, but not at the battalion or regimental level. He couldn't raise anyone, and if he was the Torag he would send forces to exploit the breaches caused by the drop troops. "We need to move west as soon as possible. I expect there to be Torag reinforcements that will attempt to clear our minefields and reinforce their drop troops."

"Wilco," Quinn said. To be trapped between a large Torag force and a minefield they couldn't get through wasn't something McCarthy wanted to experience. He doubted anyone would come to rescue them. Right now, nobody seemed to know they were alive or in need of help.

"We are heading back," McCarthy said, taking point and forcing Brennan to follow him. They needed to move fast, and Brennan might be too slow. "Be ready to move out."

"Wilco," Quinn said.

To the west was a no man's land, more fern forest, but it wasn't sandwiched between the battle lines. To McCarthy's knowledge that area was abandoned with no military or civilian forces in those wilds. It might be a moderately safe place to hide until the Governance returned and drove back the Torag.

Which could be weeks or months.

One problem at a time. Right now, he had to keep his patrol alive. Returning to Governance lines would be suicide. He would grieve for the dead later.

* * * * *

Chapter Thirty-Five:
Legion Review

Prime Minister Wolf Mathison, USMC

Mathison could probably have justified canceling this meeting after the last assassination attempt, but Feng had been insistent and wanted him to see it. Mathison had run out of excuses and Feng had found the time.

Besides, Feng had shown his loyalty countless times, and Mathison was sure the director of Internal Security could arrange his assassination with ease. He still couldn't figure Feng out. What did he really want? Why was he loyal? He had been fanatically loyal to the Central Committee for over a century.

Or had he been loyal to something else?

Did Feng even know?

Arriving at the re-education facility, he was surrounded by members of his new guard commanded by ex-Delta Force Trooper Wayne Robillard, who seemed to be everywhere. Freya now identified all his troops as Personal Guard, and while he could pull up their names, he knew nothing about them. Inexcusable, but there always seemed to be more critical issues than learning about the people willing to lay down their lives for him.

246 | WILLIAM S. FRISBEE, JR.

Entering the facility, he expected it to be depressing, full of fake smiles and broken souls. A clown show of broken people controlled by smug guards.

"I must confess to curiosity myself," Feng said as he met Mathison at the main entrance. Maybe the first lie of the trip? Though, to be fair, Mathison knew Feng was just as busy as he was. Rooting out traitors was a full-time job, but now he had to root out vanhat sympathizers in addition to potential traitors.

Though assembling all the most likely traitors to the regime here made sense. Was Feng bringing them here to be disposed of?

"Is Feng purging the military?" Mathison asked Freya.

"Not exactly," Freya said. *"Accessing available data, he has removed some hardcore Nadya loyalists, but many senior officers excel at survival and demonstrate a great deal of acumen at concealing their personal views and opinions."*

"Have you been here before?" Mathison asked.

"Yes, over a century ago. It was not a pleasant experience, and I would not recommend it. A requirement, though, for someone going into the profession I was entering. As an inmate, it is not something I would want anyone else to experience."

Mathison didn't ask, but guessed the Governance sent their most loyal agents to the most difficult re-education camp to assure themselves of their loyalty.

"The camp director is still in charge, so I know how effective he is. It was difficult not to have him executed, but some people are like tools that can be re-engineered to perform other tasks. Much more efficient than rebuilding a tool from scratch. People are quite adaptable and versatile."

Mathison nodded, not sure he wanted to agree. He remembered how Nazi scientists had been re-hired by the United States after World

War Two. Was he re-hiring a concentration camp commander to run a training center?

Freya tagged the man approaching them as Jason Holbrook, facility director. He looked more like a pudgy, slightly overweight accountant. And he was wearing the first fake smile.

"Prime Minister!" Holbrook said. "It is such an honor to finally meet you."

"Thank you," Mathison said. He could lie, too. "I've heard great things about your work here."

Director Holbrook beamed. "I have heard so much about you. I've taught classes on you. We have been teaching our students all about you and your world. Absolutely fascinating. To think there was so much history that was concealed from us. Fascinating. Absolutely fascinating."

Mathison smiled and tried not to glance at Feng. How much had they been told? Was his smile as fake as Holbrook's?

"How much are you telling your, uh, students?" Mathison asked. He wanted to say inmates, or prisoners. He really should have been more involved in this. Anyone brought here didn't come here voluntarily. Lies within lies and being politically correct by calling them students didn't sit well with Mathison.

"Everything we can. Absolutely everything. Per the wise instruction of Director Feng, we are doing our best to abolish decades of Governance indoctrination and peeling back the scabs of brainwashing. It is quite a change of pace for us to encourage free thought, and I will admit to some reservations, but the results are extremely impressive and, I must admit, unexpected."

Mathison nodded. It was best to let people ramble sometimes. Interrupting often robbed the listener of additional insight. A lot could be learned from someone who liked to talk. Of course, some people babbled because they were nervous, and right now that was fine with Mathison. A closed mouth gathered no foot, and it was hard to hear others over the sound of your own voice.

"The wisdom and guidance from Director Feng is an inspiration to all of us. His perceptions and recommendations encourage us all."

Of course, sometimes people who liked to talk a lot were full of shit and liked the sound of their own voice.

"But enough chatter," Holbrook said, maybe realizing Mathison wasn't here for bullshit. "Most students are taking to the new programming very well. They are absorbing and internalizing it, like people who have been starving. I have learned so much by watching them. Should we return to the old ways, I will have to make some changes. We have never encouraged people to break free of Governance mental and moral restrictions. It is quite an experience."

"Give me an example of 'everything' you teach," Mathison said. *Programming?*

"Well," Holbrook said, glancing at Feng, perhaps worried he was about to cross a line or maybe to make sure his lie was consistent, "we tell them you are a United States Marine colonel who was trapped in stasis until recently. How you escaped a base that was falling to the vanhat. That you built an alliance to fight them. It is a struggle to teach actual American history, though. That is a broad and difficult subject. We do our best to keep them fully aware of current data on the vanhat."

"What do you mean 'difficult'?" Mathison asked.

"To teach people to find the truth in the propaganda," Holbrook began, "we need to show them both sides of a story. American history is excellent for this. There are many great and many horrific things that

happened, from the wise and glorious US Constitution to the vile oppression of the Native American Indians and slavery. The United
States of America has stains upon its honor. Many of these things our
students are aware of, especially the dishonor, but the Governance
does not teach the positive. We have frequently used the evils of that
capitalist empire as an example, but now we are pointing out the great
things the United States accomplished while we continue to point out
these flaws."

"Why point out the flaws?" Mathison asked, not liking that.

"I wondered that, too," Holbrook said. "Director Feng, though,
demanded we not sanitize American history. I didn't understand his
purpose at first, but it makes sense now."

Mathison stopped, and the entire parade stopped as he looked at
Holbrook.

"It is important to understand the mistakes that were made, to understand that those people making the mistakes thought they were doing the right thing, to understand how people were forgiven and true
moral and social growth was accomplished. Sometimes that growth
has a bloody cost."

"Such as?"

"Slavery is a prime example," Holbrook said. "A travesty for sure
and a fascinating subject to study. The US Constitution was founded
and proposed that all men were created equal. At first, this did not
extend to women or non-White people. Only people who owned land
could vote. However, this magnificent Constitution was written in
such a way that it allowed changes that eventually led to more equality
and freedom for everyone. This did not require a major rewrite of the
original document. The beauty is that the original document included

these concepts from the beginning, as if the founders knew their current society had flaws that would need to be addressed."

"And the flaws?" Mathison asked, continuing forward and the parade resumed its march.

"Perhaps less obvious and in many ways a matter of opinion, when they changed voting rules so anyone, not just landowners, could vote. That changed the dynamics, which caused a great deal of harm to the American society."

"What?" Mathison was surprised Holbrook had studied so much.

"Well, being a landowner requires a modicum of maturity and understanding of the world and legal system. By allowing just anyone to vote, the American government allowed even the disenfranchised to vote. This meant that people with minimal responsibility and understanding could vote and select candidates to represent them, moving the US away from being a republic and more toward being a democracy. We can all acknowledge that a democracy is nothing more than mob rule, where the people will vote for things they cannot afford, and politicians will pander to the lowest common mental denominator. Where the level of education and personal responsibility are absolutely critical to the success of the society and—"

"Right," Mathison said, cutting off the director. He didn't want to go down that path or argue with the director until he saw more. "Tell me about the students."

"Many are bright, intelligent, and independent," Holbrook said. "Which may be why they have become officers but don't fit in well with the rest of society. It will be fascinating when we open up the program to enlisted members. I wonder if the high intelligence and tendency toward independence will be demonstrated at the lower ranks as we have seen among our student officers."

They entered a larger open area, and Mathison saw people walking around. He could almost imagine it was a college campus, but he saw footprints on the floor and boarded up guard towers. As the gates opened, most of those walking stopped to stare. Mathison had expected everyone to be at attention, standing on those footprints, screaming slogans, and cheering like when he had visited other facilities and factories. This was anti-climactic. A closer look at the students showed shocked younger faces. Young men and women stopped to stare at him. They were all wearing olive drab uniforms, some carried tablets and others stood with drinks in hand.

Mathison didn't see the looks of fear or indecision he had expected, though he saw some. Mostly the looks coming his way were curiosity and surprise.

A buzzer sounded and everyone looked up to the left, probably receiving a cybernetic alert. Then, without hesitation, they rushed toward the footprints.

"Why didn't you have them assembled and waiting?" Mathison asked.

"My apologies, Prime Minister," Holbrook said, with another glance toward Feng, "we believed that if we kept them assembled, we would waste their time. One thing we strive for is to show them respect, a novel concept to be sure. They are here to serve the greater good, not be served or coddled. There was a lot of debate on this, actually. To have them standing ready would save your time and waste theirs. They were warned there would be a visitor today and an assembly, but they were not told who or when because this was not shared with us, for security reasons I'm sure." His eyes flickered, and Mathison suspected he was checking a timer as people poured out of the doors and assembled.

Mathison tried to watch them all. The glances that came his way weren't hostile; instead, they were full of curiosity and maybe surprise. He saw little fear. Certainly not the level of curiosity and surprise he had expected.

"Would you like to do an inspection, sir?" Feng asked.

Yes, he would, but he didn't want to waste their time either.

"Did they assemble for an inspection?" Mathison asked.

"No, sir," Feng said. "But such an activity would give you a chance to walk among them and ask questions. Perhaps it would let you revise your speech?"

Mathison looked at the assembled students. Shit. He should have thought about a speech. There were many things he despised as prime minister. Speeches seemed to be such a waste of time, spewing his personal propaganda at the masses.

"Maybe a quick walk through," Mathison said and then internally, *"Freya? I need you to come up with something short and sweet for a speech."*

"Of course. We have to at least appear intelligent."

Picking a formation at random, Mathison made a beeline for it. He noticed there was nobody standing in the company or platoon commander's spot. They were standing on yellow footprints and there was no mistaking their military bearing or discipline. For some reason, he had expected a bunch of military rejects, slobs in uniform. The footprints made sense, but he was also sure they were a carryover from the prison days when inmates had to muster for roll call.

He stepped in front of the first trooper. A man with short, military buzz cut red hair and a hard face stared at him.

"Name?" Mathison said. The trooper didn't have a rifle to present and with long habit, Mathison's eyes roved over the uniform, looking for loose strings, frequently called "irish pennants." The uniform appeared pressed and free of any strings or marks. He could be ready for an inspection with his trimmed mustache and iron-hard eyes that never wavered.

"Legionnaire Duffy Sinclair, sir," the man said. *Legionnaire?*

"Where did you come from?" Mathison asked, staring into the man's eyes. He was a combat veteran and Mathison could see that edge there.

"First ODT Replacement Division sir. I was a second lieutenant."

Mathison didn't doubt he was ODT, but this man had too much grit to be a bright eyed, bushy tailed second lieutenant like Stathis. Well, that wasn't fair. Stathis was a veteran badass, and it was hard to associate the private as a bright young lieutenant. Even Stathis had that edge.

"Were you always a second lieutenant?" Mathison asked.

"No sir," Duffy said. "I was a captain with the 505th ODT Assault Regiment."

"A unit on Valakut," Freya said. *"A grinder used to season troops fighting the Torag. The 505th is usually manned by the firstborn from the Gaelic Republic. Captain Sinclair's records show he was an exceptional commander, so he was re-called to Earth, where he failed to adjust and was thus designated as anti-social by commanders."*

"Valakut is a bad place," Mathison said. He remembered a report or two. Mostly his attention had been focused on Sol for the last couple months, and the SOG holdings outside of Sol had been very low priority. Valakut was at the bottom of his list because of distance and resources.

"Yes, sir," Duffy said.

"Tell me about the fighting there," Mathison asked.

"A waste, sir," Duffy said, catching Mathison by surprise. He heard the hint of an Irish or Scottish accent in the man's voice. Most of the time, he would get propaganda and garbage spewed at him about how it was glorious, for the greater good, valiant and critical. "Too many good people are dying. The generals spend troops like ammunition. It's like they don't want to conquer the planet or take control."

"Military directives are to pin down the Torag and force them to waste resources defending the planet," Freya said. *"This has been going on for decades. The Torag seem to allow this and don't evacuate their civilian population. It looks like a stalemate, but the Governance does, or did, have the resources and ability to dominate. Intelligence reports do not show that the Torag could block such an effort. There has been no information about Valakut since the Stalingrad Protocol was implemented."*

"Should we commit forces to finish it or retreat?" Mathison asked.

"Withdraw sir," Duffy said. "I fought there for over nine years. There is nothing worthy of fighting and dying for that I ever saw."

Retreat didn't sit well with Mathison, even though he hadn't started it.

"Tell me about the Torag," Mathison said. He didn't need to look at the directors to know they were shocked that Duffy would be so open.

"Assholes, sir," Duffy said. "Alien bastards. Some of them fight hard, some don't. It's a mixed bag, like humans in that, sir. No eyes, no real face, but they are like us, with two arms, two legs. They fear, they bleed, they die, and they do stupid things on the battlefield. They aren't human, though. Three genders, most are sexless, and they have a single supreme ruler who, like the Governance, is using the war for personal gain."

"What do you mean by that?" Mathison asked.

"I think the Torag has a massive military, sir," Duffy said, his eyes never leaving the imaginary spot far in front of him to meet Mathison's. "Like us, they won't commit. Makes little sense to me, sir."

"What makes you say that?"

"They rotate units in and out with more frequency than us," Duffy said. "We chew 'em up and spit em out and they send more. If they were serious, I think they would arm the civilians and try to overrun us."

"Classified reports show he is right," Freya reported. *"There have been secret negotiations with the Torag. They kept the specifics in the Nadya files, which we still do not have access to."*

"How hard would it be to evacuate our people?" Mathison asked.

"Hard sir," Duffy said. "We have bases all over the place and the space above is frequently contested. It would require a major deployment to cover a withdrawal."

Something Mathison wasn't sure he could manage right now.

"What about the generals in command?"

"Arrogant peacocks, sir." Mathison raised an eyebrow. Duffy's eyes must have been focused elsewhere, didn't see the eyebrow, or he ignored it. "They seem to do their best to extend the fighting. Their tactics suck, and they seem to conspire with the Torgies to keep the fighting going."

Mathison let his eyes rove over the other Legionnaires. Were all of them as up front and outspoken as Duffy? Mathison had thought the Governance would have beaten the independence out of people. Duffy was refreshing.

"What would you do differently?"

"As I said, I would commit the forces necessary or withdraw. There is no strategic value that I have ever learned of. We should shit or get off the pot, sir. Take it or nuke it."

"The Torgies?"

"Same, sir. Either go to war or go to peace. We are wasting resources and lives by not committing."

"You don't think the Torgies would arm up and attack?"

"Dunno, sir," Duffy said. "But what we have now is just a waste. The Torgies taught me the hard way that if one thing ain't working, we should try something different, not keep doing the same damn thing for decades."

Mathison smiled and glanced at Holbrook and Feng, whose faces were carefully neutral.

"Do you have questions for me?" Mathison asked.

"Yes, sir," Duffy said, his eyes finally locking on Mathison. "Is Nadya Tokarski really dead?"

"Yes." Mathison was still uncomfortable with the topic.

"You are really an American Marine, sir?" Duffy asked, his eyes drilling into Mathison.

"Yes."

"Why are you creating this Legion, sir?"

"The Governance has to change if mankind is going to survive the vanhat threat. I need people who think and reason, not mindless drones that can only obey orders."

"People that are loyal to you, sir?" Duffy asked.

Mathison tried to conceal his wince and probably failed. "Loyalty is nice, but I would prefer loyalty to the human race. I might screw up, and when the shit hits the fan, people will need to think for themselves. Our survival is going to hinge on people like that. We need thinking warriors who can thrive and fight in chaos, not obedient drones."

Duffy's eyes flickered to Holbrook and Feng before returning to the point in front of him.

"Understood, sir," Duffy said.

He wondered if Duffy had seen something in Feng or Holbrook.

Mathison turned and walked down the line to question someone else, but his thoughts stayed with Duffy.

* * * * *

Chapter Thirty-Six:
Mistakes

Prime Minister Wolf Mathison, USMC

Mathison sat down on the tram that would take him back and looked at Feng, who was as emotionless as usual.

"How?" Mathison asked.

"How what, sir?" Feng asked.

"How have people like that survived in the Governance?" Plenty of Legionnaires had been like Duffy. Independent and proud. None of higher rank, though.

"They will always be there. The human spirit can be controlled at times, but it is difficult to eradicate in some people. I have discovered that humans will adapt to their environment. Like water, they will find their place and thrive. The Governance has struggled to make people conform. The vanhat have helped me realize we are more than just our physical selves, which is not Governance doctrine."

"Why Legionnaires?"

"We needed something different to call them," Feng said. "Some identity to give them. The Republic has taught me a valuable lesson, and I have done additional research. Legions in the United States have existed, a type of combined arms concept. There was also the French Foreign Legion, which had the peculiar habit of allowing recruits to

260 | WILLIAM S. FRISBEE, JR.

change their name and forcing them to learn another language. I found this concept interesting because of the brainwashing concepts. They take a person and give them a new identity, a new language, a new nation to be a part of. They rebuild their troops completely. There are some flaws, of course, but the idea of taking a new name and identity seems to work well for the Aesir. The French Foreign Legion once took in soldiers from many nations and molded them into a single force."

Mathison let the silence hang as he thought it through. He liked the idea.

"How do you plan to use them?" Mathison asked.

Feng's smile was not comforting, though.

"How do *you* plan to use them? They are being forged into a tool for you. I have Internal Security. My department works in the shadows, studying behavior, snatching people from their homes. We do not fight wars. No, we ensure the continuation of the Governance. We are not a praetorian guard and will not dictate who the emperor is. The ancient legions of America were combined arms concepts. This Legion has people from all branches. The Guard, the ODTs, Fleet."

"Not Peacekeepers?"

"No," Feng said. "The psychological requirements of the Peacekeepers would ensure that no anti-socialist officers would come near a command of such elite cadres."

"How will they be organized, then?"

"That is a decision for you. Legions are flexible. Use them as commissars or commanders, though I think most of them are combat and command rated."

"I need experienced ship commanders, squadron commanders, and battalion and regiment commanders." Maybe this was a bad idea,

WOLF EMPEROR | 261

a poor use of resources. You could not take a lieutenant and expect them to efficiently command a battalion or regiment any more than you could take a lance corporal and put them in charge of a battalion or use them as the command sergeant major. Staff officers and NCOs were required to attend school and they could only pass if they had some experience.

The Governance, like most totalitarian regimes, used top-down control. Since the SOG fielded troops, it had relied on top-down organization. Junior officers were not encouraged to think for themselves. They were trained and conditioned to blindly follow orders. Re-education Camp 203 had a few hundred officers of questionable competence and loyalty. It was a good start, but it would take years before they could change things, if they could. There was simply no way to get them the experience and knowledge they needed.

He wanted people like Duffy Sinclair in command of things. He needed people like that. People who didn't tell him what he wanted to hear. But he worried that such junior officers would not learn fast enough.

"I like what I saw," Mathison said. "I'm not sure how we can use them yet, though."

Feng nodded like he had expected that answer. Maybe he did. Mathison would have to discuss it with Skadi. Perhaps she would have an idea.

"What mistakes am I making?" Mathison asked Feng, putting him on the spot. Feng would know that Mathison wouldn't be intolerant of his opinion and would consider it. Hopefully.

Feng looked thoughtful. "To be fair, you have not made many mistakes, mostly minor ones. Certainly nothing major, in my opinion."

262 | WILLIAM S. FRISBEE, JR.

"What will you do when I make a mistake?" Mathison asked, realizing he was in Feng's arena. He trusted his guards, but he wasn't dumb enough to think that Feng didn't have plants and plans.

"The question I have is what will *you* do when you make a mistake?" Feng said. "Will you seek to escape it by blaming others, denying it, or doubling down, or will you learn from it?"

"What I always do, work to fix what I broke," Mathison said. What kind of question was that?

"That policy works well for a Marine gunnery sergeant. I do not think it is so easy for a prime minister. There is more at stake. The people must believe you are perfect. They cannot afford to doubt you. There are too many officers and managers who are waiting for you to stumble and fall. They will be quick to exploit your weaknesses. They will believe you can be replaced if you prove to be incompetent. When they see a weakness, they will seek to undermine you, hoping your replacement is easier to deal with, or they will seek to be your replacement.

"This is the nature of socialism. Appearances are more important than results. When there is only a single mouthpiece, it is easy to control what people hear and see, but in societies controlled by progressive revolutionaries, mistakes cannot be tolerated or forgiven. Progress is made over the bodies that fall during the charge forward, and they make the mountains from the corpses that lose the struggle to raise the flag higher."

"Too bad," Mathison said.

"It is reality. The Central Committee understood their power rested on the shoulders of others. This is true of all governments, not just those like the Governance, and this is a danger you must face. You cannot do everything alone. The Central Committee could not do everything alone. They carefully manipulated their underlings, set them against each other, kept them in check and individually weak. This is the nature of government. You must rely on others, and for them to be loyal to you, they must have something to lose if you are removed from power. Political power grows from the barrel of a gun. This is a basic truth. This concept was even enshrined in your Constitution, in the Second Amendment, I believe; the right to keep and bear arms. I have studied your Constitution; there is much wisdom there. The right to speak your mind and challenge the words of others is important for a free and thinking society, but so is the ability to defend yourself. You cannot have one without the other. However, the Governance is not your United States. Political power grows from the barrel of a gun, and people are not allowed to speak or challenge authority. They are trained and conditioned to obey, and they will obey someone. Do not fail to be the one who commands."

Mathison stared at Feng. "What will you do if that happens?"

"I may kill you. Would you try to kill everyone who comes for you? That is your nature. You are a warrior. You do not surrender. This would be devastating for the human race. Your life is not worth the destruction of the human race. We must have strong leadership, especially when the people are so weak."

Mathison remembered how Feng had put the Central Committee on trial and then executed them. Mathison knew Feng would do exactly what he said.

"More and more military officers are becoming unreliable. My agents work hard to keep them under control, to silence the more vocal rebels, but Internal Security is not everywhere and not as powerful as we would like."

"What do you suggest?" Mathison knew Feng was right. If the military did rebel, he couldn't kill them all.

"Apologies, I did not seek to imply that I had a solution. There is a reason I did not seek the reins of power. But I must warn you that if it becomes common knowledge that we executed the Central Committee, then others may get ideas and recognize our weakness."

"Understood. If you have any ideas, let me know."

"I will do my best," Feng said. "Right now, I think you need options and tools. You have proven you can wield people like tools, and the more options you have, the more you can accomplish."

"Thank you," Mathison said, not sure if he meant it. Was Feng planning to have him assassinated? Who would replace him?

* * * * *

Chapter Thirty-Seven:
Losses

2nd Lieutenant Zale Stathis, USMC

Stathis returned to his room, dropped his helmet onto his small desk, and laid his rifle next to it. His cybernetic display was no longer showing his combat view, but he could still see the amber markers there, burned into his mind. Six of his troopers were dead. Thirteen wounded. The thirteen would recover quickly with nanites and proper care, but the dead wouldn't.

"Do I need to write letters to their families or something?" Stathis asked Shrek as he sat in the chair.

"That is not standard SOG practice," Shrek said. *"The department of glory notifies the relatives of what a glorious death their loved one had. They rarely bother with facts. Every member of the SOG armed forces who dies is labeled a hero, and their death is glorified."*

"Even if they trip and cut their throat with their bayonet?"

"Propaganda must be maintained. Lies and stories must be consistent. The Governance will not tolerate having its armed forces look like fools. They are used as a shining beacon of duty and honor to browbeat the civilians with. Cowardice and embarrassing details are never included in reports. The lies must be maintained."

"Those Spartans died a hero's death," Stathis said. *"They followed my orders and died."*

"An accurate statement."

"Their families should know."

"We have no data available on next of kin," Shrek said. *"They keep this in Sol. They are Sol troopers, and they usually consider such information classified."*

"Why don't we have that shit? I thought we had full control of the Sol data nets?"

"SCBIs do not have infinite resources. We considered it a lower priority. Digging that data out of SolNET would have taken time and effort that could be used on endeavors more closely associated with the success of our mission and long-term survival."

"If we get back, make it a priority," Stathis said.

"When we get back."

"Yeah, that." Stathis put his head in his hands. Six dead. How could his platoon follow him after so many casualties? That hurt.

He remembered so long ago in Squad Leader School. Just another training operation. It had been fun at first, a grand adventure. For whatever reason, his battalion had sent him to Third Marines Squad Leader School in Hawaii, and he had become friends with a bunch of Hawaii Marines. Great guys. He got them all killed in training, which made him unpopular.

The mission had started off cool. The training group was a platoon with four squads. Three squads were defending, and the fourth squad was tasked with attacking the defenders in a training area called Bellows or something. Night ops and, for some stupid reason, they didn't have night vision. Probably a character-building experience.

Stathis had been a team leader in the attacking squad. The assault team went out to sea in small rubber boats and came back in after the other squads had set up around the objective. Now it seemed stupid.

Like king of the hill, the attackers had to have someone within a certain clearing by midnight to claim victory.

Everything started off well. Corporal Hancock led the squad in, then the shit hit the fan when they hit the first group of defenders. Nobody knew exactly what was going on. Stathis remembered other defenders had been patrolling, and he realized what they were doing pretty fast: they were using the urban swarm in the jungle. Lots of patrols would run to the sound of combat.

When the lead element of the attackers hit the defending patrol, it gave the enemy something to focus on and they started coming at the attackers from all directions.

The attacking squad was cut in two by arriving defenders, and Stathis had pulled together other squad members in a strong point to ambush the defenders. They had wiped them out, but when he led them to link up with the rest of the squad, they stumbled into another defender team. Stathis became a casualty, marked by the laser guns they were using.

It shouldn't have been a big deal. The remainder of the attacking squad had pushed on and accomplished the mission, but as a casualty Stathis had been forced to sit in an assembly area with the other casualties.

Sitting there, unable to help in the fight, gave Stathis too much time to think.

Had that been an actual fight he would be dead along with all the other Marines who had been following him. He had led them into an ambush and gotten wiped out.

A stupid mistake. He thought of several things he could have done better, and he realized that as a team or squad leader he would continue to make such mistakes. Lance Corporal Bostick had been one of his buddies and had died with him in that fight. One moment he had felt in control, a certified badass kicking ass and taking names, outnumbered but still attacking the enemy and winning. Then dead, along with the other Marines, because he hadn't expected to run into another enemy team so quickly.

It had scared him when he realized war would be worse. When rounds were flying and mistakes were made, people died. There was no respawn, no do-overs, no restarting the game. Dead was dead. Killed in action. His mistakes would cost the lives of fellow Marines. The dead didn't get to correct their mistakes. They only got one chance.

When he had been in command, he had gotten his squad massacred because he hadn't followed Marine doctrine. In that case, doctrine had been stupid, and he had tried to think outside the box. Squad on squad, he had lost everyone without inflicting a single casualty.

That was when he realized he didn't want to be an NCO, and he couldn't imagine being an officer. He didn't want to make mistakes where people lost their lives.

Then he had seen the gunny.

The first time he noticed the gunny wasn't a god had been in that hole in Papua New Guinea. Crunched into that fighting position, barely able to move with artillery bombarding the surrounding ground, he had noticed the gunny's hand shaking. It had seemed odd at first because it wasn't shaking with the artillery bursts. It was shaking because the gunny was having other problems. That scared Stathis, and he had wanted to hear the gunny's voice, to know the gunny wasn't scared and getting ready to snap.

He forgot what he said or asked, but he noticed the gunny's hand stopped shaking and his voice had been anything but scared.

That was when he started watching the gunny more closely, a lot more closely, and slowly Stathis saw beyond the gunny's badass mask.

When Vance had died, Stathis thought the gunny might lose it, but the gunny had remained strong, and unless you were looking closely you didn't know how much it bothered him.

Now Stathis understood. On Wanping, when he had been fighting with the ODTs, he hadn't seen any inspiring leadership among them. They were too busy waiting for orders. The ODTs were technically proficient, damned good shots, and they followed orders exceptionally well, but without orders they had seemed so lost, and those orders weren't coming fast enough.

Stathis had taken over, overriding Captain Evanoff at times to make sure the ODTs and Guards covered each other and retreated effectively, taking their dead and wounded with them. The deployment of the two warbots Frick and Frack to conserve lives had also been crucial. Evanoff had wanted to deploy a firing line but had listened to Stathis. The captain had listened to a private who knew better, and Stathis had finally realized he was worth listening to.

Privates ordering captains and squad leaders around wasn't how things worked, but Stathis had seen what needed to be done. He knew what would have happened if he hadn't spoken up, hadn't threatened people with being shot if they didn't obey. They had obeyed him, and they had not come to him afterward with recriminations. Instead, the troopers had thanked him, asked how he could be so calm and aware in combat. After the fact, when they were not drunk on emotions, fear and anger, they had realized his actions had saved them when inaction would have cost them their lives. Without riflemen on a firing line, the machine gunners couldn't have retreated. Without the machine gunners knowing they would be covered they would not have covered the riflemen as they consolidated their firing line. They all had to know not to run in front of each other's fire, and that had been more difficult for Stathis to coordinate.

Wanping had taught him he had the ability to save lives, and if he remained a private, if he just took orders and covered his sector, the people in charge would screw up more badly than he would.

Once again, his arrogance was getting the better part of him. Being cocky was a show. It inspired confidence, but what could he have done to save lives on the docks?

"You did a good job," Shrek said. That was Shrek's job, to keep him from losing himself to emotions like fear and self-loathing.

"I lost six, and there were a lot of wounded," Stathis said. He knew how dumb it was to argue with Shrek, but there were some things the SCBIs simply didn't understand. Things they couldn't. It was a cold, hard punch in his gut when he realized SCBIs were damned smart, but there were things they had no experience or knowledge of. How could a SCBI understand what it was like to have his commands get people who trusted him killed?

"By forcing the enemy to slow their attack, to proceed more cautiously, you have gained valuable time and perhaps saved millions."

Maybe, maybe not. Who knew? Millions was just a number. It looked good on paper but Stathis did not know if he was right. What he knew for a fact was that six people had died because of his plan. Six troopers who had trusted him to bring them home. This wasn't Wanping where he had been forced to make the best of a bad situation, this is where he had intentionally dragged them into a hostile situation he could have just refused to do.

His door announced a visitor. Since he and his command team, the major, Vili, Smimova and Hakala, were borrowing this apartment, it couldn't be many other people. Stathis wasn't sure he could face Hakala right now. He wanted to, but he didn't know if he could look her in the eyes with this guilt hanging on him. But then he wanted it to be Hakala.

Getting up, Stathis figured the best thing was to head this off at the doorway. If Hakala got all the way in here he might not be able to resist or he might say something so stupid she would never talk to him again.

The door slid open and he found himself face to face with Vili.

"Hei and skal," Vili said.

"Hi and lo," Stathis said.

Vili smiled and peered in.

"Not interrupting any post combat energy release, am I?"

Stathis shook his head.

"I just wanted to check on you," Vili said. "It's difficult losing people you have trained with."

"It happens," Stathis said. Isn't that what a veteran would say? Brush it off, pretend it wasn't ripping him apart inside?

"For sure," Vili said. Not waiting for an invite, he came in and sat down. The door slid closed, and Stathis wondered how he could get rid of Vili. He should probably prep his gear and get some sleep.

"Did I break something again?" Stathis asked.

"Nothing obvious," Vili said, motioning for Stathis to sit down.

"I need to get my gear cleaned up and ready," Stathis said.

"For sure," Vili said. "Do you know how long I've been doing this?"

Stathis sat and shook his head. Maybe if he remained silent, Vili would shut up and leave.

"Decades. Do you know anything about the Erikoisjoukot teams?"

Stathis tried to be patient and let Vili get to the point.

"I've been an Erik for decades—a long time. I think in American parlance we are like your Green Berets. We specialize in going behind enemy lines. We work with locals to train them, evaluate them, and sometimes lead them. I've studied your Green Berets, your Special Forces. Not your movies, mind you, those are trash, entertaining but not very realistic. But some of their manuals are available in Vapaus archives. Your Green Berets, like us Eriks, are geared toward unconventional warfare, among other missions. Their motto was De Oppresso Liber, which is 'free the oppressed.' That sings to me."

Stathis knew this. Raiders spent some time with Army Green Berets. Usually good guys. They liked to think outside the box.

"My point is this," Vili said, perhaps seeing Stathis's attitude, "we aren't just fighters. We are also, to a point, psychologists. We train locals to do more than fight. We have to train them to survive, not just the fight, but after the fight. War is harsh and brutal. You lose people. I've lost people. People who would be alive if I had made a different decision. For sure. I see the struggles in your eyes. I know them, I've had them."

"Does it get any easier?"

Vili sighed. "It is a curse. In some ways it does, and that's not a good thing. That is what I came to tell you, little buddy. I know you are feeling pain. We humans are adaptable. This pain is an injury you will carry with you and, I dare say, with this war, it will get worse. Perhaps it won't ever fully heal. Perhaps it will. We all struggle. Just know you aren't alone. And if things get really bad? Come to me. Day or night. Wake my fat ass up, and we will talk. Even better, wake up Hakala, she may do things for you I cannot. I will walk through the darkness with you. We are brothers, you and I."

Stathis nodded.

"You really are a little brother to me. For sure, one with a lumpy brown poo bar on his uniform, but still a brother. We have fought and bled together. I've got your back, little buddy. You have not let me down. I just wanted you to know. I also know you have not let down your troopers or Hakala."

Vili smiled and stood. "I will let you go, but if you need to talk, if you want to brawl, drink yourself to oblivion, find me. I got your back. Never forget that."

"Thank you," Stathis said, not sure what to say but pretty confident he wouldn't call Vili. Did he understand? Yeah. Most likely.

Vili nodded and left.

Stathis turned to get his gear ready. Perhaps the best thing he could do for his troops was to lead from the front, go where he would die first and wouldn't have to handle their pain and suffering. He would have to show them how to survive, how to excel. What else did he have?

Wasn't that what the gunny did?

* * * * *

Chapter Thirty-Eight: Fleet Engagement

Prime Minister Wolf Mathison, USMC

The battle was over an hour old but to Mathison it was occurring now, on the outskirts of the Sol System.

Mathison missed being a mere gunny who could read about the battle after the fact, along with the analysis of the high and low points. Here in the battle center, as it was called, with Admiral Leung, Feng and Skadi, the displays provided a lot of data, but Freya helped him make sense of it all.

As prime minister, supreme leader, he got to watch the battle unfold in real time, sort of. There was nothing he could do about it, though. He was just the first person to see the show so he could draw his own conclusions before all the analysts got involved and proclaimed it a glorious victory for the Governance.

There had been minor skirmishes between SOG forces and vanhat invaders, but this was the first sizable force.

"Paska," Skadi muttered from nearby as a battleship exploded under a barrage of incoming vanhat missiles.

"They have no real organization," Admiral Leung said. "Their destruction is assured. Our glorious forces will be victorious. Admiral Chao is a superb commander."

"Chao is losing ships to this disorganized mob," Mathison said with a quick glance at Feng who remained silent.

"Casualties are inevitable," Leung said. "Admiral Chao is an artist. He knows what he is doing."

"I don't want to be a prick about it. I get they are inevitable, but we can't replace them as easily as you think," Mathison said. "Chao seems to use squadrons like a fly swatter, losing ships with every swing."

"But victory is assured, Prime Minister," Leung said. "Chao is exceptional."

Mathison looked at Leung. Were he and Chao lovers or something? He knew Leung and Khorkov were rival admirals, but was his praise of Chao racial or something else? In Mathison's opinion, Chao was an incompetent admiral, and he wished he had Winters here to provide some insight. Duque would be helpful, too. The battle was occurring near Saturn, and the SOG strike group was coming to the rescue of the Saturn Defense Force. Since Saturn fell under Chao's command, he was here while Khorkov was working with forces elsewhere.

Chao's forces were being spread further and further around Saturn and the moons. The local admiral, Elkin, was of Russian descent. Nadya had seemed to do that on purpose, sprinkling the Chinese and Russians throughout the Governance with almost distinct and separate commands. For all the talk about unity and equality, Mathison learned that was just propaganda for the masses. Nadya had kept the two major powers of the Governance in a constant state of conflict with those of Russian descent being in most dominant positions. The Indians, Africans, and other Europeans were mostly absent from the higher-ranking positions, with most of them being assigned to distant commands.

"Admiral Chao would make an excellent replacement for Admiral Elkin," Leung said, and Mathison wanted to tune him out. "I do not think Elkin was prepared enough for this incursion, and he should have been."

Elkin's forces had been outnumbered three to one and had severely reduced the vanhat force before they got close. Now most of the missile platforms would have to be restocked, and many had been destroyed, which was why Mathison had allowed a reserve force commanded by Admiral Chao to be committed. Mathison wasn't sure Elkin had done a bad job.

"Paska puhe," Skadi said to Leung. "Elkin did a decent job. Chao is acting like a barbarian, swinging his fleets around like a panicked man."

"You are a very astute, wise, and knowledgeable assistant prime minister," Leung said, looking at Skadi. "As a highly experienced fleet admiral, there are many nuances that may not be obvious to someone who does not have many decades of experience in such things. Admiral Chao is an extremely experienced veteran of many conflicts."

"He hasn't fought anything more than a few pirate frigates," Skadi said. "He had five to one odds in his favor and the pirates still inflicted one-for-one casualties."

Leung nodded sagely, unperturbed. Mathison would like to replace him with someone competent, but the biggest problem was finding someone who could do the job.

"Space warfare is extremely complex, technically difficult, and deadly," Leung said. "There are many factors, such as range, weapon capability, trajectories, the ability to manage Shorr space transitions, acceleration, and much more must be considered. While it may appear that Admiral Chao took high casualties in that engagement, it was a brilliant ploy that kept the pirates engaged long enough so he could destroy them before they escaped. By sacrificing those ships, he saved countless Governance citizens from the vile predations of the pirates."

Put that way, it made sense to Mathison and would have been a respectable decision, but Mathison wasn't entirely sure that was the truth, especially not after watching Chao flail around, throwing his cruiser squadrons and battleships around. He had listened to Winters talk about the battle for *Tyr*, how the vanhat had drawn away the defenders so they could be cut up piecemeal. He had been expecting something like that around Saturn, but it never materialized.

"He uses ships like a firehose," Skadi said. "We can't afford to lose ships."

"I'm confident the admiral is fully aware of this," Leung said. "This is war. We must make sacrifices."

Which all sounded good, but Mathison just didn't know enough about space warfare. He trusted Skadi knew more.

"Leung is Chao's cousin's brother-in-law," Freya reported, and Mathison hoped Leung didn't see him wince. That would explain why Leung was so eager to have Chao look good, Family ties and loyalty. The Chinese version of the good ole boy's network in action, but he knew there was a Russian version and, maybe in the outer reaches, other variants.

Nadya had excelled at pitting the admirals and factions against each other. Despite all the propaganda, she had worked to keep the different racial groups divided and oppressed. There were so many rules and regulations about cultural appropriation while forcing integration it was a surprise that the Governance had not devolved into civil war centuries ago. It required a careful mix of debasing and treasuring the different cultures and groups, keeping them constantly afraid of being absorbed and having their identities lost while forcing them all into a Governance mold. Then there were active internal security programs designed to change and warp their culture, creating new holidays and culturally significant events to be used as wedges and weapons.

China had been absorbed by the Russian-dominated Governance a long time ago and was almost equal in stature, but other groups like the Africans, Indians, Europeans, and South Americans had been latecomers and thus their political stature within the Governance was almost second class. The peoples of the Middle East were frequently third or even fourth class. There were few of them in the Sol System anymore.

It was something Mathison would have to change as soon as he could figure out how. There was nothing wrong with individual cultures, but he wanted a government built on competence, not ethnic ties or quotas or other check boxes. He wanted people to work together, not divided and afraid. Was that possible?

Leaning back, Mathison glanced at Skadi.

"Thoughts?" he asked.

"Admiral Elkin did well," Skadi said, which nixed Leung's desire to get him replaced with his family member. "I am unsatisfied with Admiral Chao."

"Admiral Chao was exceptional," Leung said. "Nobody could have done better. I'm sure of it."

"Perhaps," Feng said, reminding everyone he was present. His soft voice drew everyone's attention. "Perhaps we should spend more time training in the possibilities and evaluate such training. We should implement a new training program."

"An excellent idea," Leung said.

Mathison could almost hear him calculating how he could control and manage such training, perhaps make some of the critical guidelines in Chinese which the Russians would not understand, to give Chinese officers an advantage and make the Russians look bad.

Damn it. Mathison was letting his imagination go wild. That was something Nadya would initially approve and then change it to Russian. He didn't enjoy thinking like that, but Leung's satisfaction and rapid agreement with Feng told Mathison he liked the idea because he could use it to his advantage.

Feng's smile was cold. Was he thinking the same thing? Was he planning to help Leung?

"While this is not typically an InSec task," Feng began, "I think Internal Security should be heavily involved in these new training programs as we excel at understanding the vanhat and understanding the psychology of our officers."

Leung paused and stared at Feng.

Mathison glanced at Skadi.

What did Feng want? Training Fleet officers on how to fight the vanhat was not anything that InSec did. They specialized in crushing dissent and keeping the Central Committee in power, but it would be another way for InSec to infiltrate and control Fleet. However, Mathison knew Feng was canny enough and trusted he had some other goal.

The biggest problem was that he trusted Feng to do it right more than he trusted Leung, and he just didn't trust Feng.

Leung had a problem, though. He was powerful but not dumb, and challenging or contradicting the head of Internal Security was usually an excellent way to be disappeared or have people he cared about disappeared.

"Would InSec have the time and resources?" Leung asked, obviously struggling not to argue with Feng.

"We have many instructors and psychologists," Feng said. "We could use Fleet resources to augment our own. We are fighting for the survival of the Governance. I'm sure you agree that InSec understands the greater good and the vanhat, while Prime Minister Mathison is an expert on the best allocation of our meager resources."

Everyone's eyes turned to Mathison. Damn Feng. There was a political game going on. Were Feng and Leung playing the penis size game?

Feng made Mathison damned nervous, but he had never totally betrayed him. Neither had Leung, technically, but Leung had not carried a rifle and faced the vanhat beside him. Feng was owed Mathison's loyalty because he had stood beside Mathison when the clash of honor had called, and they had stood when others had fallen.

How do you trust and mistrust someone like that?

Leung, on the other hand, was a Fleet politician who kept himself safely away from danger. If the vanhat were to break through the door at that moment, Mathison knew who would stand beside him and who would flee.

"I trust InSec can handle this with Fleet support," Mathison said.

"Am I being a fool?" Mathison asked Freya.

"No more than usual," Freya said.

"Thank you, Prime Minister," Feng said. "I will need to draw on experience from the Republic forces, General Hui as well as ExSec. I expect this will be a joint effort."

Mathison wanted to slap Leung's sneer off his face.

"We only need Fleet," Leung said. "If we can prevent the vanhat from reaching the ground, nobody else will be needed."

"The vanhat are already *on* the ground," Skadi said. "We are losing the arcology in Angola. Right now, as we speak, it is being overrun and d-bombs and Inkeri are not helping."

"Then nuke them," Leung said. "We may lose some citizens, but if we are brutal and efficient enough, we will not lose all of them."

Mathison wished it was that easy. The vanhat had infested the Cacolo arcology despite the Inkeri protection. That variant of vanhat were smaller and thinner than humans, but they were cunning tool users and kidnapped citizens. The Guard was still trying to figure out what happened to all the prisoners. The vanhat hat turned them into food or recruits, most likely, but Mathison couldn't bring himself to authorize full-scale destruction. Many people were being evacuated, but the evacuation was moving slowly, and then there was the problem of where to send them.

"We can't nuke every city that gets infected," Skadi said.

"Perhaps it would be best to cut off Earth," Leung said. "The planet has been dying for a long time. Most of the people there do not contribute significantly to the greater good and they consume precious resources."

"No," Mathison said. Wrong decision? Was he afraid to do what should probably be done? "We will fight the vanhat everywhere we find them. We will refuse to surrender."

Perhaps Leung heard it in his voice, perhaps he had decided he was pushing his luck enough with the prime minister, assistant prime minister, and head of Internal Security. Leung was critical, but he knew they could replace him.

"You are wise," Leung said. "The secretary general was wise to appoint you. How is she doing? I would really like to talk to her. It has been a while since we had dinner. We are good friends, and her seclusion concerns me."

Dead. But Mathison couldn't tell him that and the lie was grinding away at Mathison's nerves.

"She is still in seclusion," Mathison said. "She is aware of what is going on, and we frequently discuss events."

"Rumor has it she has been imprisoned or killed," Leung said, fishing for information Mathison would not give him. "I have sent several requests to have dinner, or lunch perhaps, but she keeps putting me off. If I were to have a meeting with her, I'm sure I could quash many of these rumors."

"You are being inappropriate," Feng said. "The prime minister has been tasked with saving the Governance. It is not his duty to arrange lunch or dinner with you and the secretary general."

"My apologies," Leung said. "The greater good is most important, of course. My staff and I are concerned. There have been many changes, and we wish to assure others of our loyalty and support."

Which meant what? If he told Leung the truth, would he transfer his loyalty to Mathison and Skadi? Did Mathison want this semi-competent snake's loyalty?

"Your loyalty and skill are not in question by anyone," Feng said before Mathison could. Which was irritating. Was Feng giving Leung the impression that Feng was actually the one in charge? Was that what Feng was doing? Building his own power base among the admiralty? They were both ethnic Chinese, so Mathison could only assume that Feng would be Leung's first loyalty.

"Thank you," Leung said with a short bow toward Feng.

"You should make plans to repair and rebuild Chao's forces," Feng said to dismiss Leung. The battle was winding down and Chao's forces were re-assembling. If the vanhat were going to attack, it would have been while Chao's forces were spread out, not now.

"You are wise," Leung said, then turned to Mathison, almost ignoring Skadi. "I have much to do. For the greater good, Prime Minister."

"For the greater good," Mathison said, trying not to choke on the words.

When he was done, Feng turned to Mathison. "I understand your reluctance to utter the words and praise the greater good, but I would recommend you work harder to make that lie smoother."

Had it been that obvious?

"It was not too obvious. Perhaps it is because I know you and your history better, but as the admiralty works more with you, they may pick up on it, perhaps subconsciously."

Mathison nodded. He wanted to spit and get the taste out of his mouth. "Why do you want InSec involved in the new training program?"

"Because I do not trust Fleet to focus on reality. I wish to have full access so it can be distributed to all forces, not just Fleet. InSec is a keeper of secrets, but some secrets must be shared."

He trusted Feng to do what was best for the Governance, but what did that mean, really? Did Feng know?

"The survival of the human race is critical," Feng said, as if reading Mathison's mind. "Political and economic ideologies are irrelevant if there is no humanity to argue over them."

The bastard *was* reading Mathison's mind.

"I am unhappy with the political infighting and bickering," Feng continued. "I suspect most senior officers do not fully understand how critical our fight is, how close we are to losing. They are not personally touched by this danger. They read it on screens, in reports. Their battles are victorious, but they are not on the front lines. They hide behind where it is safe, content to send others to die."

"How can we change that?" Mathison asked.

"It will take time," Feng said. "It will also take a lot of work."

"Recommendations?" Was Feng thinking he could do a better job himself?

"Not yet," Feng said. "There is a Chinese saying: wù jìn qí yòng, use everything to its fullest extent. Our resources are limited, and we must use them efficiently. Admiral Leung is one example. Perhaps in time he may need to be replaced, but I do not have any recommendations, and I have looked. He has many friends and allies among the Fleet. Replacing him at this time would be likely to cause many problems in the chain of command and would inflict a blow to morale which would only benefit the enemy."

Was Mathison one such resource to Feng, just something he couldn't replace yet?

It was hard to forget Feng had been willing to sacrifice Mathison and Stathis to the Committee if they had seen things his way.

* * * * *

Chapter Thirty-Nine:
Loyalty

Lieutenant Duffy Sinclair, ODT

Sinclair couldn't get Prime Minister, or as he now thought of him, Colonel Mathison out of his mind.

He had been having a bad day. The test on American history hadn't gone well, and he was tired of this base. The men and women were kept separate, and it seemed like there was little free time to unwind and relax. It was almost as bad as being deployed to a war zone, though nobody was sleep deprived, and they weren't constantly hungry. They had PT, but it wasn't to ODT standards. He had skipped breakfast and was sure that had not helped his mood, but he had been borderline insolent with the prime minister and the prime minister had taken it all in stride; he hadn't seemed angry.

He expected to be removed at any moment. Even if the prime minister didn't send guards, the camp director, or the InSec director, might.

Like back at the replacement division, alone, waiting for InSec to come for him. His teammates kept their distance from him, and conversation was subdued as everyone thought about the visit.

Calling generals peacocks and incompetents would draw repercussions. Criticizing the SOG doctrine that had been in place for decades was never wise. It had been unprofessional and unbecoming of an

287

288 | WILLIAM S. FRISBEE, JR.

officer, if Duffy was honest with himself. But part of him had wanted to see how the prime minister would react, with anger or agreement. Curiosity should have been what he expected; that made the most sense as he thought about it. Either the prime minister was a damned good actor or everything they said about him was true. He wasn't a Governance officer; that was becoming apparent. He hadn't bristled at the insult because it hadn't been aimed at him.

There was no mistaking Mathison's military bearing, no denying the look in his eyes that told Sinclair the man had seen horrible things, no mistaking the man's size or gruff appearance. Seeing him in person was an eye opener. Images could be modified, recordings could be edited to make someone appear bigger, more or less intimidating. You could do much with software, but you couldn't do that in person. You couldn't hide just how big he was, and you couldn't escape the eyes that dug into your soul with a sharpened e-tool.

"What did you think of him?" Bret Galetsky asked. He was a Guard officer. Not the most professional trooper, but then he wasn't ODT, and the other members of the team made allowances.

"I'm trying to figure that out," Shane Richards said. "He does not fit my expectations."

Sinclair didn't miss Richard's glance in his direction or the glance toward the door. His other teammates were waiting for guards to show up, too. They had been beside him and listened to everything he said.

"Why did you say those things?" Byrd asked. "With the director of this camp and InSec right there? What were you thinking?"

"I'm tired of the bullshit," Sinclair said. "I don't know. Maybe I just wanted to see how he would really act and what people would do."

"There are plenty of airlocks they can throw you out of," Richards said, referencing a common ODT punishment for serious infractions.

"Then so be it," Sinclair said. "I'm tired."

"Bad attitude," Galetsky said.

"They bring us here, teach us a different history—what they claim is the truth—demand we break free of decades of indoctrination, and for what? What are they doing to do with us? What sick experiment is this? Why reveal all of this to us?"

"You think the history they teach is fake?" Byrd asked.

"I honestly don't know," Sinclair said. "Isn't that what they want from us? To question things? Chairman Mao didn't invent kung-fu during his long march? Adolph Hitler wasn't fighting for the glories of socialism? Did Nazi really stand for National Socialists? The art of conflict was not devised by a Chinese CCP Chairman? The United States was not an oppressive corporate slave state? AIs killed the USA not the SOG? How can we be sure what we are being taught really is the truth and that everything the SOG has been teaching us is a lie?"

"Two plus two is not five?" Galetsky asked with a wry grin.

Sinclair had been in a real re-education camp before and knew what Galetsky was referring to. It was commonly used to recondition people, to make them admit to blatant lies, to measure their level of compliance. The more such an obvious lie was repeated, the easier it became to accept other lies and untruths. Demanding people accept the absurd was brainwashing. Repeat a lie often enough and it became a new truth. Even if people saw through the lie, they dared not contradict it and that helped reinforce the lie to others. If everyone repeated the lie, it demonstrated that everyone was afraid to question it. The truth was discarded in order to comply, and compliance was social unity.

Here though, that did not happen. Sinclair felt free to argue, to question, to make up his own mind about things. What was the truth?

"He seemed real," Richards said. "Those eyes. He has spit in the reaper's eye and seen hell. No doubt he is military, along with Director Feng."

"What do they want with us?" Sinclair asked.

"They are going to make a new military," Galetsky said. Which was the official line.

Sinclair shook his head. "That doesn't make sense. There are hundreds of us low-ranking officers, nobodies, anti-social rejects. You don't slap a premier fighting force together overnight. You need people with experience. Staff officers, logistics officers. Moving battalions around is different than moving platoons around. Supplying a battalion differs greatly from supplying a company or platoon. I was a company commander. It isn't just a matter of scale, ordering five times as many rations as a platoon. Distances and requirements change. A battalion doesn't just need more rations and ammunition, it needs personnel replacements, medical support, transport, and so much more. Knowing how fast a company can deploy or respond to a threat is more complicated and fraught with more challenges than deploying a platoon. A battalion, even more so. I can't imagine what a brigade or division commander has to deal with. The higher you go, the more moving parts you have, the more limitations you face."

"Aren't ODTs trained to fight above their rank? Like the hero private that took temporary command of a battalion when the officers above him fell in battle?" Galetsky asked.

Richards snorted. "Taking command in battle like that is different from running a battalion out of battle. A firefight is short and focused. Officers may study battles, but professional officers study logistics."

Sinclair looked at Galetsky more closely. He had made allowances because Galetsky was a Guard officer, not near the professionalism and competence of the ODTs. It was hard not to look down upon him sometimes, but Sinclair had seen Galetsky's keen mind at work.

"A Guard officer should know this," Sinclair said, suspicion growing in his mind.

Galetsky smiled when he looked at Sinclair and replied, "Of course. I just wonder if you ODTs know it."

Re-education camps were frequently riddled with informers and plants. Agents who pretended to be inmates so they could watch for treason, escape attempts, or indoctrination failure.

"Were you really an officer in the Guard?" Sinclair asked.

Galetsky didn't lose his smile, but he shifted his feet so they were beneath him, which would allow him to stand and move quickly.

"No," Galetsky said, and Sinclair noticed a slight change in the man's posture, as if preparing to be attacked. "I was a senior enlisted man in the Guards."

"You told us you were a Guard officer," Byrd said, catching on.

Galetsky looked around and noticed everyone was looking at him.

The door opened, and a pair of camp guards entered, their stunner carbines at the ready. Sinclair realized that Galetsky must have summoned them with a cybernetically controlled trigger. Were they here to take him away? Maybe take away the others? Had he doomed them all?

"I'm sorry," Galetsky said. "I am actually Internal Security, and I would appreciate you keeping that a secret."

"What?" Fogel said. Everyone got their feet under them and prepared attack or dodge. "You traitor!"

"No," Galetsky said. "You are not traitors, either. I pretended to be a Guard officer so my lack of knowledge in ODT operational techniques would not be obvious, and your perceived superiority would consider me inferior."

"Why?" Sinclair asked. Galetsky had seemed like a good man, but was that an act too?

"This program is very new. They also consider it critical. My job is not to encourage treason, but to encourage thought and reflection. To help guide this team in the proper direction, to help inspire you to become champions of the greater good. Your interaction with the prime minister today has pleased my controllers. I have been told that praise comes from high up. You specifically, Legionnaire Sinclair, were praised. I honestly do not understand the intent or why such anti-social rejects are being given this opportunity, but I serve the greater good, and I follow orders."

Sinclair looked at the two guards. Were they about to fire? Galetsky could give the command using his cybernetics, a mere thought, and the guards would stun them all. There was also a pop-down turret that probably already had targeting data. Any sudden moves, and it would drop from the ceiling and shoot them before they even know it had deployed. Sinclair had seen it happen; he still remembered the searing pain of the stunner that had overloaded his nervous system.

"Your actions with the prime minister and the actions of others have earned me a brief vacation before the next batch of anti-socialists arrive for indoctrination. I would like to thank you. Now I can spend a little quality time with my family."

Slowly, Galetsky stood and left the room. The two guards followed him out.

"What the hell just happened?" Fogel asked. "Did an InSec plant just tell us 'good job with your anti-social behavior?' People are proud of us and then leave without a parting bit of torture?"

Sinclair sat back in his chair and kicked his feet out as everyone's eyes flickered toward the pop-down turret that remained concealed.

Richards looked at Sinclair. "Did you doom us?"

"How the hell am I supposed to know?" Sinclair said. "We don't seem doomed right now."

If Galetsky had been telling the truth, it made sense. He had seemed less loyal to Governance doctrine than any of them, but Sinclair had merely thought it was because the Guard was not considered as politically reliable or as competent as the ODTs. Galetsky's questions had made a difference, though, and Sinclair realized how subtle that had been done. Galetsky's disloyalty to doctrine and cavalier attitude, unpunished, had almost encouraged the others to push the limits. It had brought them out of their shell.

As an officer, Sinclair had learned how the toxic behavior of a single trooper could infect others, and that is exactly what Galetsky had done, to a point. Sinclair had recognized it, but his fatalism had let him tolerate it and join in.

"What do we do now?" Fogel asked.

"We have a class in thirty minutes," Sinclair said. "I suggest we not be late."

"Do we tell others about our spy?" Fogel asked.

"No."

"Because we might be punished?" Fogel asked, his voice tinged with anger.

Sinclair focused on Fogel, but in his mind's eye he saw Prime Minister Mathison looking at him, curious instead of angry. There was something different about the prime minister and Sinclair knew that the Governance had not indoctrinated the prime minister. If that was true, that meant so many other things were also true. It meant humanity really was locked in a battle with these vanhat from another dimension, and there was a genuine possibility that mankind would not survive this invasion. Drastic measures might be required.

"No," Sinclair said. "Because right now, I honestly don't know who or what to believe. We have all learned that sometimes bad things are done for good reasons. Right now? I'm more curious than angry, and we are all alive and unharmed."

"Hurrah," Richards said. "Never quit."

"Never quit," echoed the other ODTs.

* * * * *

Chapter Forty:
Valakut

Navinad – The Wanderer

The bridge of the *Romach* reminded him so much of the *Eagle*. Growing up, the science fiction shows always had ships with one big view screen. But here, every wall, nearly every surface, was a viewscreen. It was like standing in a fishbowl.

Clara and Gabbi were currently on the bridge, talking with each other in low voices. He overheard the word Talese Nefesh, so he knew they were talking about the Inkeri, but they had not invited him into the conversation as he sat there in his observer chair looking at the displays and casting out his senses. The bad feeling wouldn't leave him. He had shared his conversation with Clara and expressed his concern that Bonnie might be right and that the Inkeri might only be providing limited protection, which opened up an entirely different can of worms as he thought about it.

One thing that had always bothered him and the gunny when they had talked aboard the *Eagle* so long ago was why only some people became infected by the vanhat. Why were some people different? Why were some immune? They had thought the Inkeri generator would protect everyone, but what if it was something else? Like radio waves and frequencies. A jammer did not jam all frequencies. The human

296 | WILLIAM S. FRISBEE, JR.

mind had an electrical component that scientists still did not fully understand. The human brain generated about twenty watts of electricity, which could be disrupted by a pulse from a d-bomb.

Navinad brought up a display to show data on the human brain. Way back in the twenty-first century, scientists at MIT had discovered that the human brain had dendrites, which functioned like transistors, with different electrical properties from those of other species, besides more neurons with a larger cortex. He remembered Mathison telling him how something had been trying to change his brain patterns in Shorr space, but that Freya had reversed it. Rewiring his brain?

That was an important factor. Thinking about it, that piece of information was an indication that the Marines were not immune to the vanhat influence and infection. A chill ran down Navinad's spine.

"What?" Lilith asked. She could not read his mind, but she was in tune with his body.

"Remember how Gunny said Freya reversed an attempt to change his brain chemistry in Shorr space when he was aboard the Tiananmen?*"*

"Yes. Freya used nanites to halt and reverse the changes."

"Which means we aren't immune to the vanhat."

"A logical assumption. However, one could posit that a SCBI would render you immune."

"Does it? Did we come under such an attack at other times?" Navinad asked. *"Were there other times that we were exposed to the vanhat —Tau Ceti Gold, Zuchov, Curitiba, or Jason's Pit—where something tried to change our brain chemistry?"*

"No."

"But when the gunny was on Jason's Pit being attacked by the werewolves, the two civilians were attacked, but nobody else."

"True."

"Why?"

"Insufficient data. But I understand your line of questioning. I cannot invalidate it. Until we have more data, it is a valid assumption that the Inkeri is not one hundred percent protection."

"What can we do?"

"Proceed with extreme caution," Lilith said. *"To date, the Inkeri has provided sufficient protection, especially from physical manifestations and forced transformation. Perhaps the vanhat method of infection is more targeted and focused, and some people are simply not targeted by the source vector. The other SCBIs and I can identify and counteract such an infection."*

"But people without SCBIs remain in danger," Navinad said. *"The Inkeri may not provide sufficient protection. We need to watch for that."*

"Acknowledged. Using that same logic, I will need to configure self-analysis to ensure that I am not modified or determine if there are more simplistic methods of identifying an infection. Perhaps there is a diagnostic program that can be designed for non-SCBI equipped personnel to protect or detect infection."

"Transitions," Gabbi said, drawing Navinad's attention.

On the view nearest the planet, he saw numerous yellow icons flash into existence. Currently, the Governance controlled the orbitals above Valakut, but Navinad knew that changed occasionally. Was he about to see the Torag take control of the orbitals? Would that be a good thing or bad thing? They wanted to contact the Torag, and everyone knew that would be harder to do with the SOG ready to shoot at anything that wasn't SOG. But wouldn't the Torag be willing and eager to shoot at anything that wasn't Torag? Navinad felt the SOG would teach the Torag paranoia, if nothing else.

"The SOG is being engaged," Clara said, making sense of everything. Which meant it was a Torag fleet. That would be suicidal unless it was a large fleet. The sector flagship, the SOGS *Musashi*, was in orbit.

As a SOG super dreadnought, it wasn't as big as a battlestar, but it was bigger than anything else Navinad had seen, and with an escort it would be a formidable force.

One of the red SOG ships began flashing red and yellow.

"The SOGS *Popov* is now firing on the SOGS *Fedorov*," Clara said. "Damn. Those are vanhat and they are infecting the SOG ships."

The sensors of the *Romach* zoomed in on one newcomer—definitely Torag vessels. The SOG was inflicting casualties. The fight was not completely one sided.

"So, the Torag are not immune to the vanhat," Gabbi said.

"Has the Torag empire fallen completely?" Clara asked.

Navinad would have to find out later with his psychic abilities, if that was possible. That could be a major problem. It would mean there was a large and growing vanhat force that could endanger Sol.

The SOG ships fought back, but Navinad noticed them blinking out as they fled into Shorr space where they would either kill themselves or possibly escape. Navinad still felt the psychic storm at the edge of his awareness. If they didn't have protection, few of them would survive long enough to re-enter normal space.

Clara spun her chair to look at Navinad.

"This changes things," she said.

"It does," Navinad said. "What now? The vanhat would eradicate any Torag and likely any SOG presence on Valakut. "We still need information from here. There may be human survivors, and Torag survivors. Perhaps there is data on other Torag systems."

"We would have to fly into the lion's den to check," Clara said.

"Nobody said this would be easy. Do you have any other suggestions?"

Clara looked back at the planetary view but remained silent. Technically, the view was several minutes old because that was how long it took the light to reach the *Romach*. Navinad still had a hard time remembering the fact that everything he was seeing now was technically in the past.

"Do you think there will be any survivors?"

"I don't know," Navinad said. It depended on how long the vanhat fleet stayed in orbit.

Larger troop transports began dipping into the atmosphere, and Navinad watched as drop pods were sprayed at the planet before the ships climbed into upper orbit and slipped into Shorr space.

"They aren't staying," Clara said.

"Those drop pods are," Navinad said. "I don't think the vanhat would bother leaving unless they were sure of their victory. They probably have other objectives."

"Where is that vanhat fleet going in such a hurry?" Clara asked. Navinad had no answer, but he was sure someone else would soon have a very bad day.

"Not here," Navinad said. "Perhaps they're pursuing the SOG survivors."

"Poor bastards," Clara said. "Couldn't happen to a nicer set of thugs, though."

Navinad wasn't sure.

* * * * *

Chapter Forty-One:
Stathis

2nd Lieutenant Zale Stathis, USMC

Stathis preferred it when Shrek woke him up. It was never a rough awakening because Shrek could begin the process biologically, so it wasn't a shock to the system, unlike a drill instructor banging the crap out of a metal trashcan in his ear.

Usually. Sometimes Shrek didn't have that option, like now as alarms began screeching, and Stathis fell out of his bed to the floor, pulling his rifle up to his chest. These days he slept with his rifle down between his legs, a habit he had picked up in Marine Combat Training. Others didn't sleep with their rifle and paid the price when instructors walked off with their weapons. They had never gotten Stathis', though. Since they had escaped from the SOG prison, Stathis always slept with his rifle close at hand.

"What?"

"Incoming ships," Shrek reported.

"Whose?"

"Unknown. Missiles are being launched at the dverger."

Dverger was what Vili called them and it stuck. The dverger were supposed to be dwarves, as Stathis recalled, and while these vanhat weren't really dwarves, at a distance they looked like it because of their

301

302 | WILLIAM S. FRISBEE, JR.

stocky form and lack of a defined neck. As you got closer, they looked more like big ugly giants.

"Are we in danger?" Stathis asked. He stood, slung his rifle, and grabbed his helmet.

"Not yet sure," Shrek said. *"Command teams are being notified so we can process incoming data. There are several large vessels, possibly dreadnoughts."*

"If they aren't friendly, then we're screwed."

"Unless they want to replace the dverger with their attack, then yes, they might have enough firepower or the ability to redirect an asteroid or two. It is a significant force. More data is coming in."

Stathis glanced at himself in the mirror. He didn't look too bad. Morning breath maybe. He would have appreciated more than four hours of sleep, though, as he strode out of his quarters.

Sergeant Lan and his squad were in the ready room. The other two squads were on the front lines, acting as a tactical reserve to reinforce the militia and robots if the dverger broke through.

Although this was supposed to be downtime for Lan's squad, they were gearing up, which Stathis appreciated, but it probably wasn't necessary.

Hakala came out of her room. She looked serious. Shrek would have notified her, Vili, Smimova, and others that the situation was changing.

"I have an identifier," Shrek said. *"They are SOG vessels. Dredon Three, from Sol. The flagship is the dreadnought* Yue Fei, *commanded by Admiral Lwei Pang. And I have an identifier for the USS* Eagle.*"*

"Today is a good day," Stathis said, glancing at Hakala. Her scowl softened a bit as she saw his smile. "Friendlies."

"Incoming link," Shrek said, and Stathis opened it.

"Lieutenant Stathis?" Winters asked.

"Hello, Captain. Welcome to the party. You brought some friends?"

"Admiral Pang is being added to the link," Shrek reported.

"What is your status?" Winters asked.

"Hanging tough," Stathis said. "The dverger have been stopped cold inside the colony. A stalemate. How about yourself? What is the weather like out there?"

"We are on our way," Winters said, sounding relieved. "Dverger?"

"That's what Vili started calling them and it kinda stuck. Big blue bastards with white hair and freaky eyes. Tough fighters, but we've got them bottled up. Kicking them in the teeth has become a hobby of late."

"It appears they do not want to stay and fight," Admiral Pang said. "We have caught them by surprise."

"They haven't struck me as very adaptable, Admiral," Stathis said, wishing he could just talk with Captain Winters. SOG officers still made him uncomfortable. "I'm sending you what we have of their order of battle. It's not as detailed as we would like, but they've been trying to dig us out of our holes, and we've had little chance to pop our heads out for a look-see."

"Understood," Pang said. "We will be engaging them in full shortly. They are sending heavy reinforcements in or will try to evacuate. We are detecting many waves of shuttles departing their ships. We will engage in twenty minutes. It is unlikely many of their shuttles will escape."

"Thank you, Admiral," Stathis said as General Hughes came in. "General, we need to launch attacks across all fronts. The enemy is retreating or reinforcing."

"Reinforcing?" the general asked, his distress obvious. He hadn't gotten word who was coming.

"Well, we are getting reinforcements," Stathis said.

"No," Hughes said. "Those are SOG. Governance dreadnoughts. They may attack the dverger, but we are doomed."

"Well…" Stathis realized nobody had informed the people of Zugla that the Governance was under new management. The gunny would have told the people of Zugla and they would rejoice, but it looked like Hughes was about to have a panic attack. Stathis had been careful not to tell the general or any of the directors that his platoon were actually SOG ODTs, which would have brought up some awkward questions. Now it was going to get really awkward. What had Hughes assumed they were? No other ghost colonies had competent troops.

"No," Stathis said. "They are on our side."

"Are you insane?" Hughes said reaching for his sidearm. "They are Governance. They will kill us. You are Governance jackboots, aren't you? You have betrayed us."

Hakala stepped up behind him and touched her pistol to his head. He couldn't mistake the cool ceramic. Hakala stepped back and aimed her pistol at his midsection, tucking it in close to her body where Hughes couldn't try some fancy martial arts move to disarm her.

"It isn't what you think," Stathis said as Smimova stepped forward and took Hughes' pistol from him. "Give him his pistol back."

Smimova hesitated.

"Look," Stathis said as Smimova returned the pistol to the general's holster, but Hakala didn't lower her weapon. "The Governance is under new management. They aren't in jackboot kill mode. Now the enemy is the vanhat. You have nothing to worry about."

"You should also know that I am a Republic HKT," Hakala said. "If I can stand beside SOG ODTs, so can you. Times change. People change."

"How do I know you are Republic?" Hughes said glancing at Stathis. "I know SOG ships but you saying you are Republic is just words."

The door opened and Gaufrid walked in.

"They are SOG spies, Director Gaufrid," Hughes said, and Stathis saw Hughes was tempted to reach for his sidearm despite Hakala's weapon being aimed at him.

"Stand down, General," Gaufrid said. "I'm fully aware of who they are, and why they are here."

"I will not surrender to the SOG," Hughes said. Stathis stepped close to Hughes. General Hughes was an older man—they didn't seem to have anti-aging treatment here—and the tone in the general's voice worried Stathis.

"You aren't surrendering to the SOG," Stathis said, now where he could reach the general and keep him from doing something that would cost him his life.

"The fleet is engaging the vanhat," Shrek reported. *"Some vanhat ships are moving to shield the shuttles."*

"Stand down, General," Gaufrid said again, moving to where he would not be in the line of fire. "I trust Lieutenant Stathis. I can't tell you how or why, but he is not Governance. I don't think Lieutenant Hakala is either, but I know Lieutenant Stathis is trustworthy."

Stathis watched the general's hand twitch like he wanted to grab his sidearm, and he was glad Hakala had control. Some people would have shot him for his involuntary reaction.

"That is the Governance," Hughes said. "I don't think you understand. They murdered my family. I swore an oath to the people of Zugla. I know the Governance. There are fates worse than death."

"They are coming for the vanhat, not us," Gaufrid said as Stathis recalculated firing angles. Hakala braced herself.

"No," Hughes said. "They are Governance. You don't understand. They are evil, vile. They murder innocent people. I've seen it, I know!"

In the blink of an eye, Hakala stepped forward and slammed the butt of her pistol against the back of the general's head, stunning him. In one swift motion Hakala holstered her side arm and wrapped her other arm around the general's neck. She shifted so her back was almost to him as she pulled him over her hip and slammed him face-first into the deck. Hakala fell on top of him and pinned his arms with her legs so he couldn't grab his weapon.

"Petturi lapsi," Hakala muttered as she took his sidearm from him. The general struggled feebly, not unconscious, but certainly dazed.

Smimova stepped forward with some plasti-cuffs.

Watching things, Stathis tried to figure out if he would be in trouble for something. What would the gunny say?

"Good job, Lieutenant Hakala. Thank you," Stathis said, hoping he sounded confident.

"My apologies," Gaufrid said. "The general came to us as a young man. The Governance had murdered his family. He has personal experience and a deep-seated hatred for the Governance."

"Understood," Stathis said. Sure. That was a lie he didn't understand. They were Governance warships, but they weren't.

"This could be a major problem, though," Gaufrid said. "The vanhat are bad, but I don't know that most people will see the Governance as rescuers so much as new oppressors."

"What do we do?" Stathis asked. What would the gunny do?

Gaufrid looked at the general. "We can't do that to everyone. I would recommend we establish a defensive posture and ask the Governance not to land troops or come too close. I'm afraid there are members of the population that are extremely anti-Governance and may do something foolish."

"But—" Stathis began.

"A tiger does not change his stripes. The Governance has guaranteed its troops and ships are identifiable for propaganda reasons. The Governance has ruled through fear and oppression for well over a century. While many people here have never encountered the Governance, there are some who have fled here. While that fleet may be here to rescue you, and us, people won't see it that way because people have heard the Governance lies before. The people oppressed by the Governance have no choice but to believe the lies, but they do not condition the people of Zugla to profess belief and compliance."

"I'll ask them to keep their distance," Stathis said. Would they listen to a mere private? Well, a mere second lieutenant. Winters might.

Stathis had hoped the rescue force would solve problems, not cause them. Weren't things like this covered in the officer school he hadn't attended?

Dammit. The gunny was going to be pissed.

* * * * *

Chapter Forty-Two:
Lost Patrol

Navinad – The Wanderer

Most of the vanhat fleet had departed, but there were two cruisers still in orbit. The cruisers appeared to be dead, drifting hulks, but Navinad knew otherwise. He had watched them take part in the attack and move into position before going quiet. If the *Romach* had not been watching, they would assume the two ships were ruined, lifeless hulks.

There was no doubt in Navinad's mind there were vanhat aboard those ships that could call other vanhat for help if they needed it.

No, those two ships were there to ambush Torag or SOG reinforcements.

Sliding into orbit, the *Romach* remained just outside the main gravity well and carefully watched them. From there, it could rapidly slip into Shorr space and escape.

"We have a transmission," Clara said, getting Navinad's attention. "In the clear. Sounds like a cut off patrol."

"Copy," a voice said. "Be adv—are over thir—ometers away and we have Torag pris—We—ly—quad—unable to contact our chai—command."

"A squad with Torag prisoners?" Navinad asked.

"Sounds like," Clara said.

"What kind of squad? Guard? Recon?"

"Unknown. We have unit identifiers, but they are coded, and we don't have a key. Probably Guard recon if I had to guess."

"Can we raise them?" Navinad asked. Clara had studied the Governance military as much as he had and he valued her opinion. Maybe they could rescue the patrol and get those prisoners.

"If we transmit those cruisers will probably see us and anyone planet side could hear us. That patrol might have a directional link, but I wouldn't bet on it."

"Maybe we can send a shuttle down with my platoon of commandos to make contact," Lieutenant Yosef, the commando platoon commander, said. "I can take a couple battle bots, too. Should be more than enough to handle some Governance recon team."

Navinad looked at Yosef. The lieutenant was not a combat veteran. Despite being threatened by the Governance for over a century, the warriors of New Masada had minimal actual combat experience. They were good, but Navinad knew green troops were still green troops no matter how well trained. Their first fight would be difficult. The SOG troops on Valakut would be battle-hardened veterans, Guard and ODT. They would be tough, and if they had taken prisoners they would be experienced. Even if they were SOG, they would have an edge over NMDF troops.

Navinad had dealt with veteran ODTs. They were tough, professional bastards and their officers weren't political appointees with their thumbs up their ass. Regular Guard units perhaps, but not the ODTs. Guard recon units would also be pretty tough, though maybe not at ODT levels. Navinad knew little about them. Propaganda painted them as strong and competent. It was hard to trust propaganda, but to survive in that role, they would have to be capable.

The battle robots the NMDF used were good, though. Equipped with Talese Nefesh shields, they could be absolutely lethal, and with Lilith supporting them Navinad figured their chances were a lot better if they could get to the ground and back.

"Battle bots and two squads," Navinad said, looking to Clara for confirmation.

"Why not the entire platoon?" Yosef asked.

"It will be very cramped on the shuttle, and we are bringing people back. Also, if we encounter problems, two squads aboard the *Romach* can be a tactical reserve."

"Agreed," Clara said, sealing it. "I take it you will go?"

"I have the most experience with the vanhat and the SOG," Navinad said. He also wanted to see the Torag prisoners.

Clara stared at him, and he sensed she was looking for a reason to say no. She was worried, but Navinad didn't see it in her face or bearing.

"Fine," she said finally. "Use extreme caution."

Her eyes turned to Yosef and then back to the viewscreen.

"You have twelve hours before we can release a shuttle. Make good use of your time."

"Thank you," Navinad said.

Now, if only they could get in and out before the SOG or Torag launched a counterattack to sweep the vanhat from orbit.

"We will deploy some stealth satellites to try keep track of them," she said.

A lot could happen in twelve hours, but Navinad knew they couldn't move any faster without alerting the vanhat waiting in ambush.

* * * * *

Chapter Forty-Three:
Sif

Kapten Sif – VRAEC, Nakija Musta Toiminnot

The young man in uniform had faded away, but Sif knew they were not alone in the haunted station.

"What are your thoughts?" Peshlaki asked.

Most of the Jaegers were resting. The aliens had retreated to their ships and none of the Jaeger drones showed any activity.

"The aliens lost," Sif said. She had discussed it with Munin. The aliens with the shields must have been priests trying to exorcise the ghosts. They had some idea of what they were dealing with, and they had failed, losing their lives and maybe their souls.

"Activity," Isenberg said, drawing everyone's attention to the main screen. The darkness of the alien ship was replaced by stars. "They are leaving."

"Zen," Kortenback said. "Not that I blame them. Can we leave now?"

"No ship, Kussipaa," Isenberg said. Kortenback grunted. "Just us and whatever tore the vanhat apart."

"Leaving completely?" Sif asked, coming over to the controls. Standing there in the auxiliary control room, they should have the sensors to see nearby space, but the power was drained, and nothing seemed to work beyond what they could actively power up. Remote

314 | WILLIAM S. FRISBEE, JR.

sensors remained offline and the only source of information they had was from Inkeri-equipped drones.

"Looks like it, Sif," Isenberg said. "Unless there is a fleet out there, and they are changing ships that dock. Want me to wake the others?"

"Not yet," Sif said.

"I'm awake," Sloss said, sitting up. A light sleeper, or he hadn't been sleeping at all. "Let's re-task drone Berrta to go look."

"Zen," Isenberg said.

Sif watched as Isenberg took control of the small crablike drone and worked it toward an opening in the wall that now showed stars. The drone's had magnets encased in rubber and Sif saw on the display that there was still some atmosphere escaping, but it was no raging torrent. Atmosphere would probably escape for weeks or months as the colony depressurized. It was almost unnoticeable now.

The drone made its way up the wall and focused its sensors out into the darkness.

"Not the best long-range sensors on this kid," Isenberg said. "Can't see much."

"Tapped into sensors and analyzing," Munin reported. *"Nothing. They appear to be gone."*

"Getting a transmission," Isenberg said.

Who was out there?

"It's the *Kaarme!*" Isenberg said, sounding excited.

Tapping into the transmission, Sif's hopes fell.

"—vy damage. Shorr space drive crippled. Any survivors, please respond."

"Open a link," Sif said to Munin.

"There appears to be significant time lag. They are quite a ways away."

"But still in-system," Sif said. She wanted off this station.

"One point one AU's out. About a nine-minute time lag. I suspect the aliens were blocking the signal, or the Kaarme *dared not transmit."*

Which meant it would take the Kaarme a while to get to them if they couldn't transition through Shorr space. They had destroyed the Aesir comm relay to keep the aliens from capturing it.

"This is Sif. We are still alive, but our situation is precarious. We need evacuation as soon as possible. We are not alone and are in danger. Please report status and ability to rescue. Send."

"It will take about twenty minutes," Munin said.

"Zen," Sif said.

If the *Kaarme* had not escaped, then there was no help coming from the Governance or the Republic. They would be on their own and would have to self-rescue.

* * * * *

Chapter Forty-Four:
Contact

Sergeant Aod McCarthy, ODT

The lack of reinforcements would make sense if the Torag had launched a new offensive and caught the Governance by surprise. That took his thoughts in a dangerous direction. What if it had been the Torag keeping the Governance pinned down and occupied on Valakut while the Torag rebuilt and prepared? That couldn't be the case, though. The Governance employed the smartest, most cunning minds to defend and protect humanity. When the government controlled everything and monitored everyone, of course they would know who the brightest and most capable were. And they would recruit those geniuses to high-ranking Governance positions where they could better direct humanity for the greater good.

Right?

Though, if he was honest with himself, McCarthy didn't believe that anymore. He had seen too many self-centered, power-hungry officers, and the plans that came down from higher ranks seemed insane, as though the person making the plans didn't know how warfare worked. Blind loyalty was for young, naïve privates. It took time to realize that the lower-ranking members of the Governance were nothing more than mere cannon fodder used by high-ranking officers to make themselves look good.

Which might be why any commander who lost over 40 percent of their command in a short period faced charges for dereliction of duty and was executed.

The biggest problem for McCarthy was he just didn't know what had happened at those higher levels. The politicking, the egos. He had his favorites, but he also knew the smartest, most talented, or most capable, did not rise to positions of authority. No. There was another criteria, and McCarthy couldn't bring himself to start down that path. His men needed him, and he would not use the bodies of his troops as a steppingstone in his rise to power.

Of course, it might not matter anymore. Someone had made some major mistakes, and the troops of Valakut were going to pay the price. McCarthy told himself there were probably some major SOG hold outs. That not all the SOG positions were overrun and wiped out. There would be a resistance, some officer would take charge and stiffen the line. Some fortress that could hold out until the Governance sent reinforcements.

McCarthy would have to find out where that was, but right now his patrol was cut off and probably in the path of a major invasion force.

"What's the plan?" Quinn asked an hour later. The clouds had returned, hiding the sky and any battle that might still be going on up there.

"If I were the Torag, I would launch an attack to exploit the drop pod assault," McCarthy said.

"So shouldn't we get back?" Quinn asked.

"Two problems there," McCarthy said, "we can't get through the minefield safely; they've lost power. That means if we trigger some, we get blown up and have no chance to evac. Second problem, there is probably going to be a Torag force seeking to exploit the problems in our lines. We can't raise anyone, so our only option there is to get out of their way or get bulldozed."

"Yeah?" Quinn said.

"Either way, I waste people, maybe the whole patrol. SOG lines won't collapse completely, but who knows where the lines will re-establish. Once they've solidified, we figure out where and go home. We are outnumbered and won't make much of a difference."

Quinn remained silent. He knew all the problems, too. Lack of food and water. Their helmets would filter out any toxins and biowarfare agents so air wouldn't be a problem, and they could breathe the atmosphere without helmets, but that risked a biowarfare agent of some kind getting them.

He was glad they had drawn food for a week. They were easy-to-carry tablets, but there were costs to eating them for too long: constipation and a constant hunger being just a couple.

His patrol was definitely leaving their patrol lane, heading out and away from the lines. Not exactly uncharted territory, but an officer with a hair up their ass might consider it desertion. McCarthy would suffer the consequences, but hopefully his men would survive. His only other choice was to have them halt at the edge of the minefield and wait until the Torag force overran them.

There were no good decisions.

"How long do we chill in the boonies?" Quinn asked. He was a smart guy, and all of this would go through his head.

"Not long," McCarthy said. "We need to get back into the fight as soon as possible. I just don't want to waste the squad."

The mission recording would have that now. It might help.

"We'll take some Torag with us," Quinn said, playing along.

"We can do more damage with hit-and-run raids, though, and we have orders to avoid a decisive engagement." Would that be enough to keep him from standing in front of a firing squad or pushed out an airlock?

"Now?"

"We'll find a hole and pull it in after ourselves," McCarthy said.

The Torag would likely advance behind a wave of recon drones and anything they detected would get a world of hurt dropped on top of them by the artillery batteries, orbital strikes, or fighter drones. McCarthy didn't want to give them a target. If the Torag had enough ammunition, they would drop it on anything that looked remotely suspicious.

McCarthy looked at the squad arrayed around him, each one watching their sector, each one doing his job and trusting McCarthy to make the big decisions.

How many would die in the next couple of days?

They had been going for almost a full day, and McCarthy was beginning to think they were the only Governance troops still alive on the planet. So far, they had encountered no one, and the radio waves remained silent.

McCarthy was pretty sure if he broadcast to any ships in orbit, he would receive an orbital crowbar for his trouble. The Torag prisoners had rations similar to SOG rations and were not causing any problems.

They halted, and McCarthy looked at them.

"Walsh," McCarthy said.

"Sergeant?"

"Still got that translation software?" McCarthy asked.

"Yes, Sergeant. Do you want me to send you a copy?"

"Later. I want you to ask them who they are."

"Wilco, Sergeant," Walsh said.

He went to the first one. They did not have any marking on their armor, so McCarthy didn't know their rank or unit. They would have their identifiers, but McCarthy didn't have access to their electronics, which were powerless and dead anyway.

Walsh squatted and fiddled with his personal data assistant, then the *click-clack* and grunts of Torag speech came from Walsh's helmet speakers.

The effect was instant. The Torag jumped, and the bigger one looked at the little one. Was the little one senior?

"Captain Shikata," the little one answered. Walsh provided a link to the translation. "Commander of the Bronfa. Victor of Shattata and—"

"Ask him why he was running and what those squid-arms were doing," McCarthy said. Walsh complied.

"The demons of hell are crossing the ghost walls," Shikata said. "They are enslaving and devouring the souls of the pure."

"They aren't Torag?" McCarthy asked.

"The slaves pursuing us were some of the devoured. They were once Torag. They have come to kill us all. All of us, especially the pure. They will come for you and your people next."

"Where did they come from?"

"From hell. The ghost walls are failing, and they are coming through into our world. The end times are upon us. Those were some of the devoured from my command. They once served me."

"I didn't know the Torag were so superstitious," Quinn said.

"He's lying," McCarthy said. It felt like someone was watching them. His eyes swept the sky. Nothing. "The Torag are full of shit."

"Why do you say that?"

"Those things chasing him weren't Torag. They might have been wearing some Torag armor, but our little prisoners here don't have tentacle arms and have all their armor. Walsh, tell him he's a liar and that we know they were genetic constructs. Ask him how many they have and what they're doing."

Shikata bobbed his head, and McCarthy wished he could see its face, but he would not expose Torag to the atmosphere. He obviously had filters that worked without power, or he would have died long ago. But taking off his helmet wouldn't accomplish much except exposing him to SOG biowarfare agents that would probably kill him slowly and painfully, and it wasn't like McCarthy understood Torag facial expressions, anyway.

"All of them," Shikata said. The translator must have missed something. "All Torag will be devoured and serve their new demon god. Those who do not will be killed. These are end times, the time when civilizations will die. We are all doomed."

"So why were you running?" McCarthy asked. "Why not stay and face your fate? Why run toward human lines?"

"My lineage is great. To have stayed would guarantee the end. To continue living is to have options. Proximity to the devoured endangers one and drains our power."

"Some biological warfare agent that got loose?" Quinn asked. "Maybe something the Governance planted?"

"That's a pretty impressive agent if it turns Torag into monsters and drains power," McCarthy said.

"A multi-prong attack," Quinn said. "Maybe something went wrong, and our mine field caught the edge of it?"

"That Guard officer demanding we come help him wasn't playacting," McCarthy said. "SOG lines have been hit by something and our lines have collapsed, I'm sure."

Looking at the Torag, McCarthy tried to figure out if they would have information he could use to keep his people alive. He was sure they did, but what questions could he ask?

"Do you know about the drop ships?" McCarthy asked. Could they have been SOG?

"Demon hosts," Shikata said. "Coming to kill us all."

"I would think a captain would be smarter and less superstitious," Quinn said. "Does he really think we'll believe shit like that?"

"Maybe," McCarthy said. He didn't recall in any briefings that the Torag were religious, but they were habitual liars that sometimes ate their own children.

"Did these demons come from Torag space?" McCarthy asked.

"They came from the ghost worlds," Shikata said. "They come for the souls of the pure and impure. They will come for you, too. We are doomed."

McCarthy stared at the Torag captain and wondered how accurate the translation software was. Walsh wouldn't know. He liked to collect things, and McCarthy had seen his storage buffers. Walsh collected software and data like a senior party member's daughter collected dolls and clothes for her dolls.

"Aliens?" McCarthy asked.

"Us," the Torag said. "The devourers are our creators. Our primordial essences given form. We cannot escape them."

"Torgie is cuckoo," Quinn said. "Not playing with a full deck. Best to let the intelligence comrades figure it out."

"It might be a while before we can turn them over to anyone," McCarthy said. "There is no guarantee they or we will survive that long."

McCarthy looked at the other prisoner. "Who are you?"

"Senior Sergeant Kakatet," it said. "The captain speaks for me."

"I want to know what's going on back there," McCarthy said to the senior sergeant.

"A flux caused a temporary rupture in the fabric of our reality," Kakatet said. "A powerful devourer appears to have slipped through and is infesting our reality. It established itself in the city of Kakak and has spread throughout the lines of the pure. The bastions of the pure on this planet are falling. We cannot halt this infestation and the rupture continues to grow."

"The orbital drop pods?" McCarthy asked as a chill ran down his spine. Kakatet sounded more sane but didn't contradict the captain.

"What drop pods?"

"The ones that dropped on Torag and human lines," McCarthy said, and regretted his words. A good interrogator didn't provide a prisoner with any information.

"I do not know. If they are attacking both the pure and unpure, then they are likely the spawn of another devourer that has ruptured our reality from elsewhere. Sometimes the devourers fight each other; rarely do they willingly align. If they are aligned, we will be eliminated soon, otherwise we may have a temporary reprieve until one of them gains dominance over this world."

"That is some freaky shit," Quinn said.

"Are they the reason the Torag have not fought hard for this world? You were fighting a different war?" McCarthy asked.

"No," Kakatet said. "The ghost worlds are coming closer, and realities are beginning their clash again. The devourers are returning. The collapse of civilization and true sentience is imminent."

"Where would your kind establish a line to hold back these devourers?" McCarthy asked.

"There will be no line," Kakatet said. "The devourer cannot be stopped. These devourers do not offer real enslavement, only oblivion. Perhaps the new one from orbit offers enslavement? If it does not, they doom us to oblivion."

"Creepy," Quinn said. "It's no wonder they don't want us talking with these freaks. Maybe we should just kill them and move on. If shit is half as bad as they say, they'll just be a liability."

"Don't tempt me," McCarthy said.

Were there really two different factions fighting? None of this made the least bit of sense. It would be easier to move without prisoners, though. McCarthy wasn't sure if he should save his buffers or if they would be used later at his trial. But so far, his patrol had only seen the squid-arms so he couldn't confirm that the drop pods belonged to anyone other than the Torag or the SOG.

McCarthy's finger slipped to the safety of his rifle. The prisoners were more a liability than an asset, and he wanted his people to survive.

If the SOG lines had collapsed, then it could be weeks, months, or even years before the Governance responded with sufficient force to rescue them, if the Governance decided to come back.

There was a genuine possibility that the Governance wouldn't return. If they had lost their foothold then McCarthy knew they would nuke it back into the ice age. The largest base was on another continent, almost half a world away. If they held at Morozov, then maybe...

No. If a lot of ground had been lost to the Torag, then the Governance would make a statement. Maybe with nukes, maybe with an asteroid. At the very least, a Governance fleet would come in and lay waste to thousands of square kilometers.

The two Torag seemed convinced that they were doomed, that the reinforcements weren't here to help them.

McCarthy didn't know what to do. What was his duty? Would there be any way to survive this shit storm?

* * * * *

Chapter Forty-Five: Fighting

Navinad – The Wanderer

The stealth drones had difficulty keeping tabs on the SOG troops and, despite the video, Navinad couldn't identify the troops. According to what he had discovered, all the troops fighting the Torag wore powered armor, even the Guard troops, and a large number carried blazers. With their adaptive camouflage active, there were no indications if they were regular Guard or Guard recon. The stealth drones had done their best to keep their distance because recon units would have some of the best sensors, and Navinad wasn't sure the NMDF would have drones as good as the Aesir's.

From the looks of it, the SOG troopers were taking their prisoners away from the battle lines. The *Romach* had a good idea of where the Torag and SOG lines were, but the troopers were moving toward what was considered by both to be wilderness. Which was good. Then the drones picked up movement from the SOG lines.

"What are they?" Gabbi asked.

"*Vanhat,*" Lillith reported as Navinad magnified the view.

They certainly weren't human anymore. They had cracked armor and shreds of battledress still clinging to their bodies, but their arms were too long, and they moved more like gorillas with enormous heads

328 | WILLIAM S. FRISBEE, JR.

and no necks. The armor had once been human, though, and while they weren't carrying rifles or obvious weapons, Navinad was confident they were dangerous in many ways.

"There are about fifty of them," Gabbi said. "They seem to be heading toward the SOG soldiers."

"Will we reach them in time?" Navinad asked.

"Maybe," Gabbi said.

"Spread out the drone screen more. Make sure that is the only group."

"Copy that," Gabbi said. "We have activity from the cruisers."

"What activity?"

"Looks like one of them is going to do a bombing run on the Torag lines. I'm guessing there is a Torag hold-out or the vanhat are having a disagreement."

"Will we be in danger?"

"No. They are targeting a different continent. Nowhere near you or your targets."

The rest of the vanhat fleet could return, and that could trap him on the surface. He got the feeling that time might run out. The SOG troopers would be unaware of the vanhat coming for them.

Now that they were closer perhaps the shuttle could raise them without alerting the vanhat, but Navinad didn't like their chances.

"That is a lot of vanhat," said Katz, the commando platoon sergeant. He was leading the two squads with Navinad while Yosef remained aboard the *Romach*.

"If they don't have projectile weapons, then blazers should make quick work of them," Navinad said.

If they had longer range weapons, things could get really nasty. Either way, a serious fight with them could draw attention from the two orbiting ships and Navinad suspected they wouldn't be averse to dropping an orbital round on them. The vanhat thought nothing of killing their own, and he knew the second they engaged the vanhat, the Jotun that owned them would be alerted and might respond with extreme force. To defy the Jotun was a direct challenge, and they would not tolerate that.

"We will have to hit first, fast, and hard and make sure we are the last to hit," Navinad said. It is something the gunny would say. It was also Marine Corps doctrine. "The second we land, I want the bots to spend half their mortar rounds on the vanhat." It wasn't much, but it might buy them some time. Maybe. "We have to move fast. The prisoners are the priority. If the SOG troopers don't cooperate, we kill them fast. We won't have time for negotiations."

"Copy," Katz said. "Why should we bother with SOG prisoners anyway?"

"Because they are human," Navinad said. "I'm not in the habit of killing prisoners or humans if I can help it."

"The SOG thinks nothing of murdering helpless prisoners," Katz said.

"We aren't the SOG," Navinad said. Why was he having this conversation? Was Katz really that blood thirsty?

"Do unto others—" Katz began.

"No," Navinad said. "If they cooperate, we don't kill them. Period. We are better than that."

"Copy," Katz said, but Navinad sensed the platoon sergeant was not convinced and could be a danger to the prisoners. Had he lost someone to the SOG in the past? Why the hostility?

The shuttle maneuvered to a clearing and the ramp opened. Like a well-drilled team, the robots shot out of the back, followed by the

330 | WILLIAM S. FRISBEE, JR.

commandos. Navinad could almost believe they were veterans, but their heads moved around too much as they tried to take in everything. They didn't completely trust their fellow commandos. Their attention had too much overlap, and Navinad knew the first firefight would draw their attention. He had to make sure they maintained security and eyes all the way around. He wasn't sure Katz was any better. Technically, Navinad was not in command, but everyone knew that if he gave a command, they should obey it.

Taking over from Katz was not the way to train the platoon sergeant, though.

Navinad ducked when the robots fired their mortars.

"Game on," Katz said. The vanhat were about to suffer their first casualties.

"We see another vanhat formation," Gabbi reported. "They are coming from the Torag lines. Nearly a hundred. They look different. They look to be, uh, armed."

Pausing, Navinad checked his display to see what these new vanhat were like.

They had weapons but not arms and a few wore shreds of Torag armor. The weapons also looked to be Torag in nature. They were different types of vanhat. Would they fight or cooperate?

Katz pointed toward the SOG troopers. They should be less than a kilometer away. Unfortunately, the exploding mortar rounds would warn them that someone was near.

"Leprechaun, Leprechaun, this is David," Navinad said, broadcasting on the frequency they had been transmitting on before.

"This is Leprechaun," a voice said. "Who are you?"

"We are your ride off this planet," Navinad said.

"I say again, who are you?" the voice asked. Harsh and unforgiving. Navinad should have remembered how the SOG worked.

"We are with the 95th Peacekeeper Battalion," Navinad lied.

"Why don't you broadcast your ID?" Leprechaun said. "Authenticate Lima-Kilo-Six."

"No," Navinad said, trying to think fast. "I don't have your authentication or encryption sets. We are from off planet."

"If you can't authenticate, then you aren't SOG," Leprechaun said.

The robots were led the way as they fired mortar rounds into the sky.

"You have two enemy forces coming at you," Navinad said. Stupid, stuck-up SOG jackboots. They should be able to hear the mortar rounds. "We are dropping mortar rounds on the closest group. We don't have much time. If you want off this shithole of a planet, then you need to get your asses in gear and get moving."

"Explain what is going on," Leprechaun said. "Are you from the drop pods?"

"No," Navinad said, following the commandos. "We are from a ship hiding in high orbit. Those things from the drop ship are not human, not Torag either. I realize it is going to be hard to believe, but both human and Torag space are being invaded by aliens that are attacking us both. These aliens can infect and change people."

"Do you know how crazy that sounds?" Leprechaun asked.

"Isn't that why you're heading away from Governance lines?"

Leprechaun was silent.

"Peacekeepers would have proper identification," Leprechaun said, and a chill ran down Navinad's spine. Who was he dealing with? Guard troops, even recon, should be a little more subservient to

Peacekeepers. "You obviously aren't Peacekeepers. Are you even SOG?"

The drone high above the SOG troops showed they were getting online. They had either heard the mortars being fired or the shuttle come in. These were pros. Most troopers were getting online. The squad leader had one person guarding the prisoners, but the rest were spreading out with flank security. He saw one trooper pop a drone into the air.

"Incoming drone," Navinad warned Katz. SOG drones could be multi-purpose. They were mostly used for recon but could be used for suicide attacks or even carry a payload of a grenade or two. Navinad couldn't tell. At least they weren't releasing a swarm.

"Take it down?" Katz asked. It would be in view any minute.

"If it's armed and looks like it might drop something," Navinad said, but then saw the drone speed off toward where the mortar rounds were exploding.

"If you aren't Peacekeepers, who are you?" Leprechaun asked.

Navinad debated lying. What could he tell them? The Peacekeeper lie would only last until they made contact, then the shooting would start, and Navinad doubted the prisoners would survive.

"We are here for the Torag prisoners," Navinad said. "If you give them to us, we will help you escape."

"What guarantee do we have that anything you say is true?" Leprechaun asked.

"I will approach unarmed," Navinad said, "under a flag of truce to talk. We have little time."

Worst case scenario, he was sure he could handle a few Guardsmen. He could delay them long enough for Katz to move in and take the prisoners out. Up close, he might better sense their emotions and state of mind. Lilith could also coordinate with Katz.

"Fine," Leprechaun said. "But who are you?"

"Warriors from the ghost colony New Masada," Navinad said. Leprechaun remained silent.

Technically, he wasn't completely unarmed. He still had his Ka-Bar, but Katz and the others were close. Navinad approached Leprechaun's position. In the distance, there were more explosions.

"It looks like the vanhat have detected each other and decided to fight," Lilith reported. *"We are only going to shell the vanhat closest to us, and we are putting more drones up. Mortar rounds are being depleted but we will maintain a reserve."*

"Carry on," Navinad said as he made his way through the underbrush. He sensed them ahead of him, intense, focused, ready. Then he saw the first soldier and realized he had made some wrong assumptions. Leprechaun wore distinctly ODT armor, and they were armed with blazers. One ODT trooper with a machine gun was aiming at him, finger resting on the trigger.

* * * * *

Chapter Forty-Six:
No Choice

Sergeant Aod McCarthy, ODT

McCarthy knew little about ghost colonies, but he had never heard of New Masada. In the distance the explosions tapered off. The drone they had sent to recon the battle sent back some chilling footage, despite the static-filled view. Torag monsters were fighting what looked to be proto-human, but what was most horrifying was that the proto-humans were still wearing shreds of human-made armor and clothes.

"What the hell?" Quinn asked, watching the footage.

"Proto-humans from the looks of them," McCarthy said.

"What?"

"I remember back in school they say we evolved from them," McCarthy said. "I forget the name, but as we got smarter, we got smaller and began walking upright. That caused our arms to shorten and lose strength. Also, it probably let our necks extend a bit."

"So, are those proto-Torag?" Quinn asked.

"I have no idea. Either way, none of them are likely to be friendly toward us."

The squid-arms and proto-humans fought and showed no mercy. Some of them had weapons and used them, but others just used mindless savagery, throwing themselves at each other and trying to rip their foe apart or bite them. Neither side seemed to care about casualties.

A mortar round landed amid a group. Several died, but the survivors just got to their feet and continued their brawl. The proto-humans appeared outnumbered, but that didn't seem to deter them in the least.

"He's here," Moore reported, and McCarthy turned his attention to the man approaching them. Wilson had his SAW trained on the stranger. McCarthy looked around. His squad was as ready as they could be, good positions with everyone ready for a nasty fight.

The approaching stranger wore an odd style of armor that looked like it might be powered. His holster was empty, but he had a knife, which meant he was not completely unarmed. McCarthy was willing to overlook that. He would have to be damned good to be a danger to ODTs.

"Stop," McCarthy said. Best to keep him outside the ODT line.

Another drone slowly circled the ODT lines in case the strangers were trying to move into position.

"Maybe two squads," Walsh reported.

Two to one. McCarthy didn't like it. They had the advantage, but he had the prisoners.

Distant explosions rocked the ground.

"We are running out of time," the stranger said. "Soon one faction of vanhat will win and they will come at us."

McCarthy figured that would be pretty bad. The vanhat, as the stranger called them, had defeated entrenched and ready Governance troops.

"What are they?" McCarthy asked.

"Creatures from Shorr space that have entered our world. They can transform some people into those things. Those they cannot transform, they kill."

Which explained the shredded armor and weapons, if it was true, but McCarthy couldn't think of why he would lie except for the sheer impossibility of it all. There was no mistaking the fact that both the proto-humans and squid-arms were using weapons.

"Why here? Why are they fighting?" McCarthy asked. "Why two groups?"

"I don't know," the stranger said. "There are different types of vanhat. Different creatures come through and build their own armies of transformed humans. I am called Navinad."

"Why do you want the prisoners?" McCarthy asked.

"We need to understand the Torag more. The Governance has collapsed."

"Liar," McCarthy said, but realized he had no proof and with the lack of orbital support, reinforcements, and supply, that fit with the facts. Dammit.

"I'm sorry," Navinad said.

McCarthy was tempted to give the command to have this stranger cut down and launch an attack against the others. Smaller, more aggressive forces usually had an advantage against larger, inferior forces. McCarthy had never heard of New Masada so he was confident they were not the equal of his ODTs, but McCarthy was also sure the fight would not be one sided. He would take casualties and there would be no evac available. He had to be smart and do his best to keep his people safe. Sure, they might find a flaw with his actions later, but that was later, not now.

"Shoot him, and we can retrograde our ass out of here," Quinn said. "I don't trust him. The Governance hasn't fallen. That's cappie shit."

McCarthy glanced at the vanhat fighting each other. *That* was not a lie. A proto-human was missing an arm, but it had knocked over a squid-arm and was busy chewing on its head as it lashed out, eventually falling still, but a nearby squid-arm shot the proto-human in the head.

"How do they change people?" McCarthy asked, trying to buy time to think.

"Proximity. The more there are, the closer they get, the faster and stronger the change occurs. They are from a different dimension, and the rules of their source dimension bleed over, giving them more power."

"What can we do?"

"We have a device that protects us, stabilizes our dimension. Come with us and you will be safe."

"Safe?"

"Safe from changing into one of the vanhat," Navinad said. "We mean you no harm, but we really want those prisoners. They might be the only ones on the planet. We came here for information on the Torag."

"You can talk to them?"

"No. One step at a time, though."

"We have a translation program," McCarthy said, not sure why he told him that, except maybe it would make his people more valuable. Right now, he was worried they would attack and kill his people and take the prisoners, which would be a bloody affair.

Walsh was watching the prisoners and giving the two drones some guidance. He had orders to kill the prisoners if the shooting started. It would be easier to escape without prisoners, and it would make sure the strangers had no reason to pursue his people other than revenge.

However, if the prisoners died, then his squad would lose all value to these strangers, and perhaps the Governance, if they returned.

"What guarantee do we have that you won't kill or abandon us and take our prisoners?"

"We are all human," Navinad said. "It may surprise you, but I have fought beside ODTs in the past, lived with them aboard another ship."

"Are you a deserter?"

"No. I was once a United States Marine. Long ago. It is a long story, and I would be happy to share it with you, but we don't have a lot of time."

McCarthy looked at the battle occurring nearby.

"Fine," McCarthy said. "We will come with you. If you betray us, we will not forget, and we will come for you."

"Understood," Navinad said. "The ODT motto is Never Quit. I know."

"Stand down," McCarthy said to his troopers, and Wilson removed his finger from the trigger of his machine gun.

"We should get back to our shuttle," Navinad said. "The vanhat gorillas have almost been wiped out, and the squids will soon come our way. I also have eyes on a larger gorilla force leaving SOG lines."

McCarthy hoped he wasn't making a mistake as he gave the command to move out and head toward the strangers. He couldn't imagine what cruelty the commissars would devise when they caught him and put him on trial, but right now he just didn't see any other options besides dying. And a dead trooper was a useless trooper.

* * * * *

Chapter Forty-Seven: Shuttle Flight

Navinad – The Wanderer

N avinad had warned Clara that they might be returning with SOG troopers who were not exactly prisoners, but he knew she would be pissed regardless of who they brought back. She didn't want strangers on her ship. It would have been more convenient to just collect the data and leave. People added complications to everything. Navinad knew the ODTs wouldn't surrender their weapons. Yosef might be more pissed, though. He handled security, and no security officer enjoyed having armed strangers on their ship.

They had left the mortar bots behind so there was room, but not a lot. They packed the ODTs and commandos into the troop bay, shoulder to shoulder. Even outnumbered, the ODTs didn't look nervous or scared. Navinad sensed they were worried, and they were on edge. Hardened veterans for sure. It wouldn't take much to start the shooting.

The two Torag prisoners fascinated Navinad. Their helmets completely covered their heads and if one didn't look twice, they could almost be mistaken for human. But the second glance was when things got different. The shoulders were lower, almost slumped, and the neck was a little too long. The forearms and upper arms also didn't quite match, with the forearms being shorter. The legs seemed normal enough, but the body was slim. Their heads moved in quick jerks.

"We have fabricated masks for the Torag," Lilith reported, *"and clothes. I have retrieved the translation software from the SOG trooper's data store. I have cracked their secure communication links."*

"What are they saying?" Navinad asked, though he was sure if they were getting ready to start shooting, Lilith would warn him.

"Concerns about what will happen to them, mostly. They are all from the Gaelic Republic. Firstborn conscripts. Most are senior veterans that have been here for a while. The leader is Sergeant McCarthy. His second in command is Corporal Quinn. The other team leader is Corporal Moore. They are worried about being accused of treason by commissars."

"Let me know if they are planning something bad," Navinad said.

"Aye, Sergeant," Lilith said. She was slipping back into Marine mode. Navinad looked at the ODTs and wondered if they were as good as the New Masadan troops at unarmed combat. They were probably better.

"Captain Navarro has prepared quarters for the ODTs and the prisoners," Lilith reported several minutes later.

It was going to take a while for the shuttle to reach the *Romach*, but if they were airborne, they were not being attacked by the vanhat on the ground. Navinad hoped the Inkeris aboard the shuttle would mask them from the vanhat and their uncanny ability to track others.

"You will have a berthing area," Navinad said to McCarthy. "The prisoners will be berthed somewhere else. We have an atmosphere that is more conducive to their survival."

"They can breathe our air," McCarthy said, perhaps unwilling to give up his prisoners.

"For short times, yes," Navinad said. "Based on the information I have they require a higher oxygen content, and sustained exposure to our atmosphere can cause them health problems."

McCarthy nodded, probably trying to figure out some other reason to keep them close.

"As I said, we mean you no harm. I believe we can return you to the Sol System in time. They have declared the Stalingrad Protocol, but I think they will open the gates soon, and you will not be persecuted."

"Stalingrad Protocol?" McCarthy asked.

"Nobody is allowed in or out," Navinad said. "Any unexpected ships transitioning in are destroyed, no questions asked. Shoot first and don't ask questions. They have closed the gate, and are allowing nobody in."

"How do you know?"

"We came from Earth with an alliance assault group that helped sweep most of the vanhat out of the system. We are allied with the Governance and other ghost colonies, even the Vapaus Republic."

"The pirates. Is that wise?"

"Things are not always as they appear," Navinad said. "The SOG does not always share the truth of a subject."

McCarthy was silent, but Navinad sensed the sergeant knew that and was likely re-evaluating the situation. Until now, there had never been a reason for him to question everything the Governance said.

Finding the sergeant was a boon. Finding the SOG presence on Valakut overrun by vanhat was a disaster.

Or was it?

344 | WILLIAM S. FRISBEE, JR.

"How much do you know about the Torag?" Navinad asked, and felt different emotions warring in the sergeant's mind, caution and fear being foremost.

"Some," he said.

"Have you ever taken prisoners before?"

"Yes, once a while back. It was a big deal, and after Regimental Intel got involved, I never saw them again."

Which wasn't a surprise. Would they have taken the prisoners back to Earth? Was there some prison somewhere on the Moon or on Earth with Torag prisoners?

Navinad regretted not staying in Sol and finding out what the Governance had, but that sixth sense had told him he wouldn't find his answers there. Or maybe it was that he just didn't want to face the gunny or Winters or even Stathis.

How much would a sergeant know about the Torag war machine? About the alien empire? Knowing SOG, nothing true, but he might have a better understanding of the small things in dealing with the Torag, like what might prevent an attack or lie.

"Have you interrogated your prisoners?" Navinad asked. ODTs were still guarding them and their arms and hands were tied.

"Not much," McCarthy said. "One is probably a company commander, the other is an NCO or bodyguard. If you want more information, there is the super dreadnought *Musashi* or Romanov Base."

"Where is the *Musashi*?"

"No idea, maybe forward, butching around Torag space? Who knows? Romanov Base is on another continent, buried in some mountains. The Torag seem to get a kick out of dropping crowbars on it but aren't very good at damaging it. That base is solid."

Romanov was probably a vanhat stronghold now. Could he recover any data there?

"Would d-bombs work against a bunker system?" Navinad asked Lilith.

"It should," Lilith said. *"Though not a lot of testing has been done. It should be noted that the d-bomb does damage electronics. If we drop too many on Romanov we might destroy anything you want to recover."*

The *Romach* had little on Romanov. Nothing specific at any rate.

"If you are going to Romanov, I should come with you," McCarthy said. "We are usually stationed there as part of a ready battalion."

Navinad sensed he had a desire to go there. He most likely had friends there and would want to know their fate.

"It is unlikely anyone there is still human if they were overrun."

McCarthy nodded, but Navinad sensed hope and denial in him.

"My captain will not take kindly to strange, heavily armed ODTs aboard the ship," Navinad said. Could he get the ODTs to disarm?

"Are we prisoners or guests?"

"Untrusted guests," Navinad said. "We won't be the first to betray. I have served beside ODTs. However, I am the only one aboard our ship that has. You understand that the people of the ghost colonies have no love and a great deal of fear of the Governance."

"Fair enough, but ghost colonies are known for their depravity and lack of integrity."

"SOG propaganda," Navinad said. "Though there may be some places that is true, New Masada is not one of them."

McCarthy nodded, revealing nothing about his thoughts.

* * * * *

Chapter Forty-Eight: Sif Returns

Kapten Sif – VRAEC, Nakija Musta Toiminnot

The *Ovella Kaarme* was weeks away, and Sif didn't like the odds. With the departure of the aliens, Sif expected the death hunters or ghosts to attack any moment.

"What would the Navajo do to protect themselves from evil spirits?" Sif asked Peshlaki.

"Several things. A blessing of the way ceremony, herbs and plants, crystals, a properly blessed hogan would provide protection, a sand painting, perhaps. It's probably too late for Hzho, living a life of balance, harmony, and beauty. Aren't there Nakija methods?"

"We never needed them," Sif said.

"Never?"

"I've never encountered an evil spirit before," Sif said. "Prayers and crystals did not really deter SOG commissars, unless they're the crystals in lasers."

"You are psychic then?" Peshlaki said, more of a statement than a question. He should know by now.

Sif didn't answer. He knew, but she couldn't bring herself to confirm it.

"President Becket frequently wondered," Peshlaki said. "He did not have a high opinion of the Vapaus Republic, but he could not deny how much the Governance hated and wanted to destroy you. Your people seemed to have an unnatural ability to thwart the Governance. We had access to many classified Governance reports, not the propaganda they fed the people, but the data given to the Central Committee. Our SCBIs were sure you had something that gave you an advantage. The SOG has confirmed that psychic powers exist but has never quantified or controlled them. It has vexed the Governance."

"What did they think it was?"

"AI programs perhaps? Canny commanders? Nobody knew. Not even the SOG."

"Do you know anything about the SOG psychic program?"

"A little," Peshlaki said. "Hiding in Quantico, there wasn't a lot to do besides read classified SOG reports and spy on them. The president wanted to collect data but was fanatical about not interfering most of the time."

"What do you know about the SOG's psychic program?"

"It was weak and inconsistent. It was called Project Beacon, for some reason. They were obsessed with remote viewing, perhaps trying to find the Republic fleet or to spy on distant commanders or the Torag or Voshka. They experimented on thousands of subjects over about thirty years. It was shut down about ten years ago, though. Too many of the subjects went insane. The Governance used a combination of technology and ability. Results were always unreliable, though they couldn't be denied."

"What, specifically, got it shut down?"

"When a projectionist returned to her body, she was insane, like she had been in Shorr space. Her psychosis was contagious and most of the staff and projectionists were infected. They nuked the facility, which was on one of Saturn's moons. I saw some recordings. It was a bloodbath. It gave me nightmares."

"Did the subject change shape?"

"No. They remained human in appearance, just fanatically psychotic, not something you could reason or talk with. It gave me chills when I watched it. After that, they shut down the program and archived it, erasing any signs. I think it scared the crap out of the Central Committee. Then the problems with Shorr space began. There was even discussion that the experiments had caused the Shorr space instability, which was another reason to bury the project and pretend it never existed. The Governance tasked a team with destroying all evidence of it, including hunting down anyone who had ever been involved in it. When the Governance wants something buried and forgotten, they will wipe out planets to ensure compliance."

"Do you think their experiments summoned the vanhat?" Sif asked.

"Not with the data we have now. I think those remote viewers went too far and saw into places where the vanhat were. We are on the edges of the storm. They went into the storm and never came back."

Like the Nakija aboard the home stars. Sif didn't want to think about them. How could they have not seen this danger?

"You should sleep. I will say prayers of protection and wake you if I see any more ghosts or death hunters. You can sleep for eight hours then we will alternate."

If he had time. The spirits could be on them, tearing them apart before she woke.

But what choice was there? She couldn't stay awake for weeks while waiting for the *Kaarme*.

Sif nodded and wondered if she would wake up. Around her, the Jaegers were waking and Sloss was sending the drones in other directions. Until now, they had been focused on the docks, watching the aliens, but now Sloss could redirect their limited resources and find out what was going on in the cylinders.

"Could the death hunters be the reason the vanhat do not remain in our dimension?" Sif asked Munin. *"The vanhat come and destroy the civilizations and the death hunters come and wipe out the vanhat?"*

"Not impossible," Munin said. *"But I suspect the death hunters and ghosts are just an aspect and manifestation of the cross-dimensional invasions. It would make sense that predators prey on predators and leave behind only desolation, but again, we have little data. Perhaps the tomb worlds have more."*

"Very well," Sif said and set her alarm for six hours. She was tired and doubted her questions would be helpful. Six hours should be sufficient. She didn't need the full eight.

She laid down and closed her eyes, but an incoming link from Sloss stopped her before she could put herself to sleep.

"They are coming back," Sloss said.

"What do you mean?" Sif asked, looking over at the main viewscreen which would show what Sloss wanted it to.

A large, dark shape blotted out the stars as it approached the docks.

Explosions erupted as large objects punched through the walls of the dock, slamming into the opposite wall and unfolding into fierce, spike covered battle robots.

"Paska," Sloss muttered as the robots spread their eight razor-blade legs and weapons scanned their surroundings.

Golden Horde. Sif knew those lethal robots anywhere.

More boarding bots slammed through new holes, and in seconds the dock was crawling with them.

"What are they doing here?" Sloss asked.

"Collecting resources," Sif said.

"Are they vanhat?" Sloss asked, and Sif remembered the fleet that had joined Task Force Ragnarök had not appeared to have survived the vanhat attack.

Closing her eyes, she reached out with her senses.

She felt hunger, curiosity, anger, and fear, but the emotions were not intense enough to be vanhat.

"No," Sif said. She wasn't sure if this was an improvement. The Golden Horde would look for auxiliary command centers.

"The bots appear to have Inkeris," Sloss said minutes later as they watched the battle bots spread out.

"Confirmed," Munin said. *"I am detecting such fields through one of the Jaeger drones."*

"Allies?" Sloss asked.

Sif's first thought was "no," but so much had changed. Would they be allies or enemies? With the Golden Horde, it was hard to say. They were incredibly tribal, violent, and Sif wasn't sure if they could still be called human most of the time. Since Haberdash, they had gone their way and avoided the Republic. How and why they had joined with Task Force Ragnarök for the attack on Zhukov involved details that Sif didn't have. How had they survived and how would they view the Republic after such a massacre?

"I don't know," Sif said. What did they want here? Slaves? Information? Something else?

"What do we do?" Sloss asked as a large object slammed through a wall. It was almost three meters in height. It would likely have a cocooned Mongolian warrior curled up inside who interacted with the outside world through cybernetics.

"It will be better to contact them on our terms rather than theirs."

"Zen."

"Open a radio link," Sif said, wishing she had a chance to sleep.

A link flashed green. "Golden Horde, this is Sif of the Vapaus Republic. Please respond."

"Sif," a voice without an accent answered instantly. She knew the voice was digitized and translated. The Golden Horde only spoke their own language and used translators. Few of them even bothered with vocal cords anymore. "What are you doing here?"

"We are hunting. We became trapped by vanhat warships. Our ship was damaged and has retreated."

Damaged was one hell of a lie, but she wanted them to know she had resources and wasn't alone, now at their mercy.

"Did you find your prey?" the voice said.

"No, we will have to look elsewhere."

"What prey do you seek?"

"An Erikoisjoukot team that has gone rogue and allied with the vanhat."

"To ally with the khara-gashuu is one of the worst crimes. The return of the khara has changed much. Did they change allegiance or were they possessed?"

"We don't know," Sif said. "They are intelligent and acting as a vanguard for the enemy."

"Do you have the tracks of your prey?"

"No." Nothing in the databases had revealed where they had gone. Munin had seen where the Eriks had shattered the major defenses, but where they had gone afterward was still a mystery. Theoretically, they

WOLF EMPEROR | 353

could still be on station and their ship could be hidden elsewhere on the planetoid, but finding it would be a nearly impossible task.

"Then why do you remain?"

"Who are you?" Sif asked. She had answered him, partially. She would not answer every question. That would be considered a weakness.

"I am Minghan Enkhbold Gan," the Mongol said. "I command the *Fire Wind*."

Sif didn't recall any ships or details of a *Fire Wind*.

"May I ask your tribe?" Sif asked.

"I trace my lineage to Taichud," Enkhbold said.

Sif knew of them. They were a dominant clan when the Chinese invaded Mongolia and sent the survivors to the planet Tengri. The Taichud had not been the most dominant clan in the Golden Horde, but they had been powerful.

"Why are you here?" Sif asked.

"Why do you remain?" Enkhbold asked again, and Sif did not fail to notice that he did not answer the question. Was he showing strength by not answering or was it a secret?

"The enemy just left," Sif said.

"We observed that," Enkhbold said. "There were three gadaad vessels. They were not human."

Sif wondered why the translator used gadaad instead of foreign or external. Because it did not translate the proper context?

"Will your vessel now come and take you away?" Enkhbold asked.

"Yes. In time. We are not yet finished scouring the archives of the colony."

"Are there any other survivors?"

"Not that we know."

"A waste. What is the nature of the khara-gashuu that massacred the dalit?"

Sif recalled that dalit was a term the Golden Horde used to refer to people who were not "arban," or citizens of the Horde. Dalit were less than that, almost at the status of slaves. Since the conquest of Tengri by the Governance, the survivors had become almost xenophobic in their outlook on others. Part of their rebellion was to embrace their old ways as best they could.

And what was wrong with their translator?

"The vanhat which murdered the people of Durango are different. When they kill someone, that person will rise again as one of the vanhat. They are murderous. Some are intelligent enough to use weapons, but they may not be the biggest danger. There is something else, evil spirits."

"Provide details."

"They cannot be seen. They hunt and feed on the ghosts but they, or the angry ghosts, drove away the vanhat."

"How do you fight them?"

"We don't know," Sif said.

"But you live."

"They have been more interested in attacking the other vanhat than us."

"Inkeris protect you. You have this technology?"

"Yes," Sif said. "Were you at Zhukov?"

On the main screen, Sif watched the Horde robots come to a stop. The Mongol warriors in their mech suits froze as if awaiting a command.

"We were not, but we heard how the Republic betrayed the Mongolchuud."

"We did not betray the Golden Horde. We were betrayed."

"By who?" Enkhbold asked.

Sif couldn't tell him it was elements of the Republic that betrayed them.

"We don't know," Sif said. Not a complete lie. "Is Shiney Karakorum safe?"

"Yes."

Karakorum was the Golden Horde's home star, originally built by the Republic to help the Horde evacuate their planet ahead of the SOG invasion. Republic forces had not seen it in decades. After Haberdash, the home star had left the fleet, causing the Republic Home Star fleet to move.

Not even Sif knew the details of that, but she knew it had not been exactly friendly. That break in their relationship had seemingly pushed the Golden Horde further away from the rest of humanity and they waged their own war against the Governance, preying on lightly protected space colonies and attacking the shipping lanes. They never seemed to enter planetary gravity wells, though, probably because that would leave them too vulnerable.

The last time she had done anything involving the Golden Horde had been during Operation Haberdash.

"Give us all the data you have recovered, and we will not kill you," Enkhbold said.

"Do not assume our weakness," Sif said. "Do not make rude demands or we will take offense and kill you. The Republic and Golden Horde were once allies. There is no reason for us to be enemies. We know what you have deployed. We watch your ship. We called out to you first. A question, not asking for help."

Enkhbold remained silent, and Sif wished she were closer, to understand what he was thinking, feeling.

"Apologies," Enkhbold said, but the digitized voice could not convey sincerity. "We seek information. We need to understand this threat to the Mongolchuud."

"You are not alone in this. An alliance has formed. The Republic, the United States, and the Governance. We are all working toward saving the human race."

"The United States is dead."

"That is what we once believed," Sif said. If she got him curious, maybe he wouldn't start shooting. They wanted information.

"The Republic is now allied with the Social Organizational Governance?"

"The battlestars *Tyr* and *Sleipner* are guarding Earth. We are not allied with the Governance so much as commanding it now," Sif said. Well, they had been the last time she had been there. Though perhaps, more appropriately, the battlestars were guarding Skadi.

"And the rest of the Republic fleet? The home stars?"

"Away," Sif said.

"Why are you lying?"

"How did they figure that out?" Sif asked Munin.

"Stress indicators in your voice," Munin said. *"Choice of words."*

"I am not lying," Sif said as confidently as she could, "But I will not deny there are problems, or that victory is assured."

She knew how to beat lie detectors, regardless of the sophistication; there were always ways. She could not deny the stress in her voice, but she could explain and misdirect their suspicions.

"What problems?" Enkhbold asked.

"Tell me your problems, and I will tell you mine," Sif said, fixing her firm, Erikoisjoukot personality in place. The Golden Horde did not tolerate weakness, and their society was a patriarchy.

"Ha," Enkhbold said. "You are Sif. My sire Tsogt has spoken of you. He called you a silver tongue and warrior soul trapped in a weakling girl's body."

"I remember Tsogt," Sif said. Haberdash had been so long ago, she was surprised he had survived and would speak of her.

"He said you would not age, that you were dangerous in many ways."

"Tsogt means wisdom in your tongue," Sif said.

"Ha," Enkhbold said and fell silent for a few moments. "Is there any reason for us to send in our raiders?"

"What is it you wish to acquire?"

"Slaves," Enkhbold said. "Information. Ships or anything else that may catch our fancy."

"Do the Mongolchuud now raid the ghost colonies?"

"We ride our steeds of electric steel through the empty plains of the eternal void," Enkhbold said. "We prey on the weak and those who do not seek our protection. We prefer trade, but we will take what we need."

Which wasn't an answer Sif liked.

Since Haberdash, the Golden Horde had become more xenophobic, and she felt they were sliding further and further away from being human.

"What information do you need?" Sif asked.

"Information or weapons to fight the khara with. What information do you have?"

"We have information like this."

358 | WILLIAM S. FRISBEE, JR.

"From the data cores?"

"No. From the Alliance."

"Give it to us," Enkhbold said.

"Take it," Sif said. She didn't like commanding behavior. Could she use them to escape the death hunters and ghosts?

"Will you die to keep that knowledge from us?"

"Yes," Sif said.

"Will your followers?"

"My followers are Republic Jaegers. They are the blades of our people. Do you doubt their resolve and ability? How many warriors will you lose?"

"How many robots?"

"We will fight to the death. We will not kneel."

"My sire said that of you. We are at an impasse."

"No," Sif said. "You know buu murgul. If I win, you will take us to rendezvous with our ship. If you win, I will give you what you ask."

Buu murgul was the term mongols used for duels to settle disputes. Sif had seen a soldier challenge Tsogt long ago, and she had studied the Golden Horde. This was one thing she remembered.

"Why do you need us to rendezvous with your ship?"

"It is becoming increasingly dangerous here and our ship has sustained damage, preventing it from getting here quickly."

"Then I will meet you on the docks. We will fight in armor with daggers," Enkhbold said.

"I will enjoy this," Sif said.

The digital laugh sent a chill through her blood.

* * * * *

Chapter Forty-Nine:
The *Romach*

Sergeant Aod McCarthy, ODT

Sitting in the shuttle, McCarthy tried not to overthink the situation. Here he was on a ghost colony shuttle about to board a ship. Never in a hundred years would he have imagined he would be in this situation, dependent on strangers for survival, abandoned by the Governance. What was his duty? Should he try to take all these ghost colonists prisoner? Kill them? If he tried any of that, he was sure he would lose everyone and fail, but ODTs did not quit, and they did their duty.

Being a traitor to the Governance did not sit well with McCarthy. Leading his squad in treason was also a problem. They trusted him to keep them alive and to keep them from facing a commissar's firing squad or a ship captain's airlock. He was so out of his league here. Could he go back to being an ODT sergeant or was the path he was on right now the end of his career and maybe his life? The end of his squad?

"I'm not liking this," Quinn said on a private link.

"Me either," McCarthy said. "But I don't see a lot of options. If we stay planetside, we die."

"Maybe," Quinn said.

"I'm sure. Those vanhat monsters were coming for us. You saw the drone footage. Lucky for us they thought it would be more fun to fight with the other vanhat or they would have overrun us. We don't have unlimited food, water, and air. I don't know how far out they dusted the jungle with biowarfare agents. Heck, the entire atmosphere might be saturated. We can't stroll to the wilds and build tree houses to live in until the Governance returns."

"But to associate with anti-socialists? The commissars are gonna shit themselves when they learn we gave them our prisoners to survive."

"I don't see any commissars around."

McCarthy brought Corporal Moore into the link.

"You think the anti-socialists have any commissars? Maybe they are waiting for us aboard their little shit-show of a ship?"

"Chill, Corporal," McCarthy said. He didn't need Quinn making him more paranoid and nervous. "One step at a time. We don't have enough answers, and there are too many damned questions. They are probably going to have a welcoming party to meet us. I want you both to make sure your people don't start shooting."

"When will we know to shoot?" Moore asked.

"When they shoot at us," McCarthy said. Their commander, Navinad, didn't seem bad, but there was something about him that McCarthy didn't trust. Navinad was a man of secrets.

"Won't that be a little late?" Quinn asked.

"Our other option is to shoot first. We do that, we might as well shoot ourselves. Even if we take over this shuttle, where are going to go?"

"Romanov is probably holding out," Quinn said.

"What if they aren't?" McCarthy said.

"Well, there has to be a hold-out somewhere," Quinn said.

"What if the Torag come back and decide to attack us while we are weak?" Moore asked. "Would any place be safe?"

"What if the fleet returns and lands reinforcements?" Quinn asked.

McCarthy wanted to believe they could be right, but he had never seen the fleet arrive in time. It was only in the movies that the heroes were rescued in the nick of time.

"We play nice," McCarthy said, putting an edge in his voice to discourage them from arguing. "As far as we know, we are the last Governance troops alive on Valakut. I would like to keep us all alive and human until we get more information or guidance from command. Understood?"

He tried not to think of Dallas. She couldn't be dead, but McCarthy just didn't know, and he had a responsibility to his men. Duty was a heavy burden.

"Wilco," they said.

"Squad," McCarthy said to his team leaders, "listen to my command. We are to cooperate with these anti-socialist colonists for the moment. Do not start hostilities. We are guests. Execute."

"Hurrah," they said in unison.

They changed links to their teams, and McCarthy felt a *clang* through the metal of the shuttle. They were landing. The shuttle looked newer and less abused than most of the Governance shuttles McCarthy had been on, but shuttles were easier to make than spaceships.

When the ramp dropped, he saw several more of the New Masadan troopers. So far, he wasn't really impressed with them. They were maybe better than a Guard unit. Maybe. They didn't do stupid shit like sweep each other with their muzzles and they didn't have their fingers on the triggers, but they didn't move with the efficient lethality he would expect of veteran troops. Right now, most of them had their rifles snug against their chest and didn't have their hands on their pistol grips preparing to move their rifle into firing position. McCarthy was doing his best to emulate them and not appear nervous. His troopers followed his lead, but McCarthy knew he was out of his league here. He couldn't imagine how this would end, but right now, people weren't dying.

He glanced at his people and saw they were making a conscious effort to keep their hands off their weapons. It looked unnatural.

A crewman came through a nearby hatch. A tall, thin man with serious eyes.

"If you will follow the lieutenant," Navinad said. "He will lead you to a space where you can relax."

"Thank you," McCarthy said. The lieutenant looked nervous as he nodded at him and led the way. Others were here for the Torag prisoners, and McCarthy held his tongue as they were led out of his presence.

A minute later, going up a ramp to another floor, they entered a berthing area. It wasn't any more spacious than what he had experienced aboard Governance ships, but it was clean and looked almost new. There were several sleeping bays, but they were not individually enclosed and armored like aboard a SOG ship. Apparently the New Masadan's didn't treasure their guests or troops like the Governance did.

"Okay people," McCarthy said, picking a bunk near the door and allowing the others to file in, "find a spot and start cleaning your gear. You trash this place, I trash you. Got it?"

Conversation was muted as people picked bunks and removed their packs.

"What do we do with our weapons?" Quinn asked.

"Rack and stack 'em," McCarthy said. "We are guests here. Corporals, take inventory and make sure our shit is secure. I don't want any accidental discharges or anything."

The squad had demo and two anti-air missile tubes. He didn't want to ask his hosts about an armory. Attached to the bay was a washroom with showers and toilets. It looked like a bay for a larger squad.

"Is there anything you need?" the lieutenant asked. "Shall I have the fabricator make you some uniforms?"

"I would appreciate it, Lieutenant," McCarthy said.

He had to keep the peace, and unarmored troops were less likely to cause trouble than armored ones. It wasn't like his people could walk around fully armored. He didn't want trouble, and he was sure there were anti-boarding defenses he couldn't see.

* * * * *

Chapter Fifty:
Prisoners

Navinad – The Wanderer

The glass wall separated Navinad from the two Torag prisoners. Out of their armor and wearing fabricated jump suits, the Torag would be easily mistaken for some variation of vanhat. They certainly weren't human, but what Navinad found most disturbing was their eye clusters. It was human nature to look at someone's eyes when talking to them, but there were no recognizable eyes, and he couldn't tell where they were looking.

Beside him, McCarthy watched with curiosity and less hate than Navinad expected. Spending years, or maybe a decade, fighting, losing friends, Navinad would have expected hate.

"We are doomed," said the one named Shikata as the other one, Kakatet, thrust its chin forward, which Navinad felt might be affirmation or agreement.

"We are not," Navinad said.

"The demons have crossed the ghost halls, brought their magic to our reality. We have lost magic of our own and have nothing to fight them with," Shikata said.

"We do," Navinad said. "You said your lineage is great?"

"Truth. I am spawn of the great sovereign through three females and a male. Royalty stains my soul in glory."

366 | WILLIAM S. FRISBEE, JR.

Kakatet thrust his chin forward.

"We can arrange negotiation for my release and trade."

"Where and how?" Navinad asked.

Shikata lowered its chin, and Navinad sensed disappointment from it. The Torag had a distinctly different flavor than a human. It had emotions that Navinad could sense, but there were other emotions that Navinad didn't understand.

"Look to your leaders. They will know a way. This is not the first time."

Navinad looked at McCarthy.

"You do prisoner exchanges?" Navinad asked.

"I've never heard of this," McCarthy said. "News to me."

Navinad turned back to the Torag. This was excellent. Maybe an exchange would give him a chance to hold a more meaningful conversation with a Torag who had more authority. If the Torag were suffering the predations of the vanhat then they were not likely to be the threat that had been indicated.

"Our leaders are unavailable," Navinad said.

"We are all doomed. The demons consume the unpure with the pure. Both our peoples are doomed."

"We are not," Navinad said. "We have technology that can help the Torag."

"You have magic?"

"We have technology. We have a shield that keeps us from transforming and we have a pulse bomb that kills only the demons and their slaves."

"Technology is not magic. Technology from heaven will eventually fail to defeat the magic from hell. Without the holy pure, you cannot hope to return the hordes to the hell that spawned them."

"We can help each other."

"The supreme sovereign will no longer consider the war with the unpure to be a worthy cause. These are the end times. Our warriors have been blooded in the trials of combat. I have seen them fall and submit to the demonic masters. We have failed."

"Do all your people submit to the demons?" Navinad asked.

"Most do," Shikata said. "So few remain pure they cannot fight the horde that remains. We have failed the ancient gods. They will be angry and will not come to save us. My loyal Kakatet and I can resist the demon Squala. We remain pure, but we are not enough."

Pure? Was this a key to why some turned, and some didn't?

"What do you mean pure? What makes one pure?" McCarthy asked before Navinad could.

"We are of royal lineage. We can trace our ancestors unbroken to the last battle where the demons were banished beyond the ghost halls. The ancient gods have gifted us with strength of soul."

Navinad felt there were lies there. That was a disappointment. Shikata didn't know, he was just repeating religious dogma, though there was a slim chance there was a shred of truth. Navinad didn't think there was enough.

"Will you be able to resist another demon?" McCarthy asked. He seemed to catch on pretty fast. Originally, Navinad thought he was just another dumb ODT grunt.

"We are the purist of pure," Shikata said. "The demons can only kill us. We will not fall to their lies."

Kakatet thrust his chin out.

"Thank you for your guidance," Navinad said. He led McCarthy into the other room where they could talk privately. "I need to contact the Torag, someone in authority. Do you know how I can do that?"

Fear, concern, and another emotion flickered through McCarthy before he answered. Navinad couldn't decipher McCarthy's thoughts.

"Romanov Base," McCarthy said. "Their databanks may have the info. If there is anyone alive there, they may know."

"That is the central base for all SOG operations on Valakut," Lilith reported. *"It stands to reason they would have the data, or at least clues. The* Musashi, *the SOG war fleet flagship, will have that information for sure."*

"We can't exactly ask the Musashi," Navinad said. "How well do you know Romanov?"

He had little information other than the location. Several shuttles and drop pods from the vanhat fleet had landed there. Navinad doubted anyone was still alive.

"That is where my regiment is usually stationed," McCarthy said. "The 15th Company was temporarily assigned to the current sector to help repel some Torag assaults, but our home is usually Romanov."

"You know it well?" Navinad asked.

"Yes," McCarthy said, but Navinad sensed some doubt there. Why? "I know where our Regimental G2 is at and there are other hubs for intelligence operations."

G2 was a regimental intel staff, whereas S2 was at the battalion level. Navinad sensed McCarthy wanted to go there, but he also feared to go there. Powerful emotions pushed Navinad back. He must have friends there he was worried about. They were likely dead or turned, but if McCarthy knew the facility, he could be critical to their success.

"I don't think anyone is still human or alive at Romanov," Navinad said.

"How do you know?"

"There was a spread of drop pods and shuttles that landed there. We did not pick up any requests for help or new signs of fighting."

"The entire facility is buried underground," McCarthy said. "There will be a strong ODT presence. ODTs never quit. If anyone survives, it will be there."

"I've seen the vanhat wipe out planetary populations in days. Turned or eradicated fleets in hours. Any resistance to the vanhat is dealt with using overwhelming force. If there was still a battle going on there, I doubt the fleet would have departed, though they might have if they were confident of the outcome."

"Then we should hurry," McCarthy said. "There may be survivors that need our help."

Navinad seriously doubted there were any survivors. But it was deep underground.

"What are our chances of acquiring the data we need?" Navinad asked Lilith.

"If it is there? Good. It may not be in the G2 systems, but there may be higher-level hubs," Lilith said.

"Do you know where the high-level intelligence hub is?" Navinad asked.

"No," McCarthy said. Perhaps a lie? Why would he lie? He wanted to go to the G2 offices. "But we may find out where it is."

Navinad knew he didn't have a lot of choices. If the Torag prince didn't have the information, and he couldn't ask the *Musashi*, the ODT G2 offices would his the first step.

"Tell me more about the G2 offices. How do we get there? Can we get there without having to fight our way through hordes of vanhat?"

McCarthy's wince told Navinad it would not be easy.

"Wait," Navinad said and scheduled a meeting with the *Romach's* command staff. "Let me assemble a planning team."

* * * * *

Chapter Fifty-One:
Insertion to Romanov

Sergeant Aod McCarthy, ODT

McCarthy knew they could consider this treason. Well, considering what was happening, treason was such a mild word. This was certainly treason. There could be no other way to describe his actions. The fact was he was willingly leading a team of anti-socialists into the heart of the Governance planetary headquarters.

"This would be considered treason," McCarthy told his people, who sitting around the ready room in their dark gray jumpsuits. The crew of the anti-socialists' ship had done an excellent job of fabricating their uniforms and they actually fit better than their issue.

"I, for one, want to see the truth," Quinn said. "I think treason would be if we are shooting at our brothers and sisters."

"If anyone is there, we will be fighting our brothers and sisters," McCarthy said.

Navinad had shown them all briefings, recordings of a strange woman with black hair who identified herself as a New Masadan intelligence major.

Quinn shrugged. "Perhaps. But if these pee-holes are right, then we have problems. I want to see with my own two eyes."

"This is going to be damned dangerous," McCarthy said.

"Waking up in the morning is damned dangerous," Quinn said. "If I wanted a safe, easy life, I would have been second- or thirdborn. I am firstborn. We lead the way."

"Hurrah," Walsh said. "Is there another way we get to shoot at commissars and self-important officers?"

McCarthy looked at them. His men. His warriors. They would follow him to treason. They had a choice, but he did not. He had to know what had happened to Nova Dallas. Was she still alive and fighting, or was she now one of those creatures? He knew he was being irrational. This was the real world. There were no happy endings, no happily ever after. Bad things happened to good people all the time, and the rescue team never arrived in time. McCarthy knew this. Knew it to his core. Had seen it countless times over the years.

But this? People changing into monsters? The Social Organizational Governance fleeing to hide behind its automated weapons platforms and abandoning the rest of humanity? McCarthy knew damned well the Central Committee wasn't the selfless, glorious, caring heroes the people were told. He had seen too much lying propaganda.

He despised the Governance, but this? It was hard to believe it would sink this low. He had seen the recordings of the *Musashi* and a few other ships escaping the vanhat fleet, but an excellent computer program could create that fiction. It could create the people transforming into monsters, it could show him anything the anti-socialists wanted him to see. They could show him intelligence briefings until the end of time, but nothing would fully convince him until he saw it with his own two eyes.

Nova Dallas had to be alive. She had to be. Romanov Base was the most heavily defended human fortification on the planet. Buried so deep that Torag orbital bombardment couldn't hurt it. She was there. It had given him strength to know she was more likely to survive. Without her, his life held less meaning. He had his squad, but without Nova he had no future. But how could she have survived?

The anti-socialists could not conceal Governance ODTs and Guards opposing their incursion into Romanov.

"This doesn't bother you?" McCarthy asked Quinn.

"Sure it does," Quinn said and looked around him at the faces of the rest of the squad. "Hard to believe this shit. Who came up with this? If it is cappie shit, do they really think we won't find the flaws and discover the truth? If they are right? Well. That's terrifying in itself. I want to know, and I won't find out sitting here in this room. Besides. I'm ODT. Killing things is what we do."

McCarthy looked at Moore, his other team leader.

"Quinn's right. If Romanov has been overrun by monsters, then we need payback. I'm okay killing monsters for the greater good of humanity."

"They were once our brothers and sisters, our comrades," McCarthy said, and Moore shrugged.

"If they are still our comrades, they won't try to kill us," Moore said. "I don't know about you, Sergeant, but those squid-arms and ape-things creep me out. They made my skin crawl, kinda like we were in Shorr space. What scares me most is it makes sense, sorta. Fantasy for sure, like some badly done vid-show, but I can't make sense of it otherwise, especially the ape-things. They couldn't have hacked our drone feed. Our mine fields were drained of power. I'm just trying to figure out what makes sense, and right now that's nothing."

McCarthy looked into the eyes of each member of his squad, and they all nodded. They had all seen the same videos he had. If the anti-socialists were telling the truth, it was bad. What nobody knew for sure was if there were loyal SOG survivors still fighting down there in the depths of Romanov.

"Okay then," McCarthy said. "I won't think any less of anyone that wants to stay here."

Nobody moved or signaled they would stay. Were they afraid, then? Afraid to stay and be left behind? Afraid to remain with the anti-socialists? If they did stay, McCarthy doubted they could be rescued. The Governance would rather blow the *Romach* out of the space than waste resources to rescue some foolish ODTs.

If the anti-socialists were right, where did that leave McCarthy and his men? Perhaps that was the scariest.

Regardless. He wanted to find out what happened to Nova and right now, this was his only opportunity to do so.

"Fine," McCarthy said. "I'll tell Navinad we are in. Squad, listen to my command. Start getting your gear ready; we will leave as soon as we and the cappies are ready. Execute."

"Hurrah, hurrah, hurrah!" they yelled and erupted into movement.

McCarthy headed out to tell Navinad of their decision. Why didn't this feel like a victory or the right thing?

* * * * *

Chapter Fifty-Two:
Romanov

Navinad – The Wanderer

oth shuttles were full of troops and robots. It was hard to move. It would have been claustrophobic if he couldn't display the shuttle pilot's view on his helmet display. Clara and her commandos had been less than thrilled about having the ODTs take part in the mission but couldn't argue with the fact they would come in handy. Yosef had accepted the ODTs because Navinad had explained they would lead the way and be the first to take casualties. Yosef's troops were still green and too caught up in their own invincibility. Navinad wanted to give them the chance to survive and become veterans. The ODTs might not know Romanov as much as Navinad hoped, but they were blooded veterans who had recently walked the razor's edge of combat. Following actual veterans into a fight was the only way Navinad could think of to save as many NMDF lives as possible.

Would they be enough? Could he forge them into a team like the gunny had? A shared threat was a bonding experience, but would it be enough? What would they see?

Unimaginable horrors, Navinad was sure, but would they be able to overcome them and get the information they needed?

"Entering range," the pilot said. This was perhaps the scariest part. Were the Governance air defenses still active? The shuttles from the *Romach* didn't have the right identification codes if they were challenged. There could be automated defenses that might track the shuttles and ask their controllers for permission to fire. Would they fire without permission? Or would they hold?

Navinad sensed the pilot's nervousness as their fingers hovered near the counter measures button, and they prepared to drop like a rock and take evasive action.

The copilot watched every sensor they had. Any second now, some missile platform would pop out and launch, some laser might track them, or a Gatling gun would start spraying into their path. Both the pilot and copilot didn't ask "if" but "when."

The shuttle approached the armored doors that led into the mountain, and Navinad scanned the area. It looked deserted, but he knew the area was full of pop-up turrets, sniper bays, mines, and every form of nasty weapon the SOG could hide. The Governance would expect a Torag assault drop here. If the reports Navinad had acquired were true, it wouldn't be the first time. The Torag had suffered horrible casualties and lost three entire drop waves. It was a death trap, but Navinad trusted that the electronics were offline and nothing intelligent could reactivate them.

A calculated risk, and Navinad was risking the two shuttles.

Both shuttles landed near the tunnel into the mountain and the ramps dropped. Like a wave, the ODTs, commandos, and warbots poured out of the shuttles. In less than a minute, they were off, and the shuttles shot into the sky.

Silence fell across the valley as they spread out and moved toward the shattered doors. The wind blew debris around, and Navinad's skin began to crawl. It was too quiet.

He had expected hordes of vanhat. The fact they weren't here to greet them told him they were somewhere else, preparing an ambush, or as yet unaware.

He missed being aboard ship as he gave the command to enter the tunnel.

* * * * *

Chapter Fifty-Three:
Romanov Base

Sergeant Aod McCarthy, ODT

The NMDF robots were mules that could have been ODT robots for all the differences there were. They were mostly cosmetic but one key difference was the two generators strapped to each one. One was a small power plant, the other a powerful Inkeri, like the ones on his belt.

Brennan was on point with Martin and Quinn.

They moved with precision, spread out, and their weapons covered everything. The first thing McCarthy noticed were the shattered pop-out turrets on either wall. They had been spaced every ten meters at waist height where they could create interlocking fields of fire. They had been ripped out of their sockets and thrown to the ground. Fifty meters in, the corridor opened up, and McCarthy saw the real devastation. He had come through here in the past. He remembered it as a clean, well-lit space with enough room to park several shuttles. There were several corridors that led off to fighter drone bays and additional storage rooms.

There had been a Torag assault drop years ago, and they hadn't made it past this room. McCarthy had been part of the defense. Hundreds, maybe thousands, of Torag had died here, caught in a crossfire. He had expected piles of bodies, perhaps defenders still standing ready, but the devastation was complete. A shuttle that had probably been here when the drop pods hit the ground looked like it had been ripped apart, but there were no explosion marks. He saw several places where blazers had scored the walls, braces, and shuttle, but no bodies.

Where were the bodies?

"No bodies," Quinn said, leading the patrol to the right, toward the stairways which led down. The elevator banks were not likely to be functional, and McCarthy realized it was going to suck going down and then back up those stairs.

"They probably ended up as fuel for the vanhat," Navinad said.

"Fuel?" Martin asked.

"They eat the dead," Navinad said. "It is efficient and usually easy to acquire."

"What did you think they eat?" Moore asked the private. "MREs?"

"Well…" Martin said, trying to figure out another answer.

"Secure the chatter," McCarthy said. "Stay on mission."

Two hundred meters worth of stairs. He remembered the platoon sergeant, Doyle, leading them all on a run up and down the damn stairs. He hadn't gone the whole way though. That much heavy breathing from so many men struggling to run up the stairs in such a confined area had sucked in so many ways. The platoon had probably deserved it, though. When Lieutenant Burke had told them about their upcoming deployment after only a week back from their previous one, several members had committed face crimes, and someone had cursed out loud. McCarthy may have been one of those committing a face crime. It was easy to do after spending so much time wearing a helmet or while among a small, isolated group of brothers.

Going down the steps was only a little easier than going up and required different muscles because you had to keep from going too fast and falling.

The next room was a staging terminal where troops could wait for their shuttle. Someone had shredded the chairs and desks and scattered them across the room. There were several shield-class warbots and blood stains where someone had tried to make a stand. The shield-class warbots were mules with massive, armored plates people could hide behind and a medium blazer machine gun designed to protect the crew during tunnel fighting. There were at least five of them here, maybe more, it was hard to tell amid all the debris.

"What the hell did this?" Quinn asked, his head lamp sweeping over ruined equipment.

"Hopefully something that is not blazer proof," McCarthy said.

"Well, it was blazer proof enough to rip apart shield bots. Those buggers are tough."

Quinn had a point. Anything that made it this far had to have some resistance to blazers. There were blood stains, but, again, no bodies. It felt like he was walking through a nightmare. The dead did not get up and walk away.

McCarthy looked at Navinad. He was in front of the NMDF troopers as if shielding them from the ODTs. With his helmet on, McCarthy couldn't tell anything, but Navinad's weapon was ready. He moved with more precision and confidence than the commandos behind him. McCarthy could tell he was a veteran. Behind him, the commandos spent too much time looking in every direction, not fully trusting each other to cover their sectors. It was a hard lesson to learn. When the rounds started flying, people who didn't cover their sector learned hard lessons.

382 | WILLIAM S. FRISBEE, JR.

Not McCarthy's circus, nor his monkeys. His men knew their job, even Private Martin, and it was comforting to see them maintaining security in all directions, even watching the anti-socialists behind them.

Leaving the arrival terminal, the large corridor led to several banks of elevators and more stairs. Each was color coded, dark gray for ODT, brown for Guard, and blue for everyone else. Even the stairways were coded.

At the stairs to the ODT areas McCarthy glanced at Navinad and got the signal to keep going. With a deep breath, he motioned to Brennan.

The stairs had long sections going down. Nothing went straight down, and McCarthy knew there were countless routes out of and into Romanov, most of them secret. This was the only one McCarthy knew of, because it was where his company always deployed from.

McCarthy noticed two pop-out turrets he had never known about, and the dark stairs looked quite different now. Their head lamps didn't pierce the darkness near the bottom, and McCarthy felt eyes on them. It felt like a nest of spiders was running up and down his back.

Given the hand signal to proceed, Brennan paused and took the first step.

A roar echoed through the darkness. Just one?

The stairs were wide enough for six people, shoulder to shoulder, to go up or down. There was supposed to be a rail down the center, but the remnants were scorched by blazer fire and had been ripped off, crushed, or pushed aside. The electrified drone nets were also gone, shredded and thrown aside. They would have dropped from behind panels to block access for the smaller Torag recon drones. Now they were just so much garbage.

This couldn't have been the stairs the platoon had run up and down so many weeks ago.

But it was.

"Was it just one creature?" Quinn asked on the NCO link.

"Damned big," Moore said.

"Lock it down," McCarthy said. They were creeping him out and speculation didn't help.

The lights barely pierced the gloom. McCarthy felt like an invader stalking deeper into what could only be a trap.

* * * * *

Chapter Fifty-Four:
The Trap

Sergeant Aod McCarthy, ODT

With every step into the darkness McCarthy felt the spiders crawling on his skin. The sense of wrongness, the feeling of walking into a trap, grew stronger.

"Be ready," Navinad said over the command link.

McCarthy wanted to scoff at the cappie, but evidently he was getting too creeped out.

At the bottom of the steps, past several pop-out turrets that had been ripped out of the walls and ceiling, they found the first body, or parts of it. Just the upper half. She was a fully armored ODT. The chest piece had been crushed and her body from the rib cage down was just gone. McCarthy had seen plenty of bodies ripped apart by blazers, wire guns, plasma shrapnel, explosives, and slug throwers, but none of those had killed this trooper. It was almost like she had been pulled apart by something extremely strong.

They were on a larger landing, almost big enough for a couple of squads to do calisthenics in. The stairs looped back and continued downward. This was an explosion trap, designed to reinforce the structural integrity of the bunker and keep an explosion from traveling all the way down the stairs at full force. There was one more explosion trap before they reached the regimental area.

McCarthy removed her helmet and was glad he didn't recognize her.

"What did that and where is the rest of her?" Quinn asked. McCarthy wanted to tell him to shut up. He didn't want to answer those questions. He wanted to forget all of this. Was he trapped in a nightmare? With every step he took, he realized Nova couldn't have survived this unless they had fled.

"Probably whatever roared," Moore said, making things worse.

A large "505th ODT AR" was painted on the ceiling. Motivational propaganda. It wasn't like anyone other than ODTs running PT would see it.

They continued past the second explosion trap.

Whatever had roared was now silent. The passage opened into an assembly area at the bottom of the stairs, and Brennan sped up as he approached the bottom. McCarthy wanted him to slow down. He knew the devastation would give him nightmares.

The regimental assembly area was a massive open area that served many purposes, from a sports field to a parade deck. Their lights did not penetrate the darkness. McCarthy felt eyes watching them, hidden in the distance and darkness.

His ODTs spread out. They had done this before while running drills and rehearsals. The area was large enough for a regiment of four battalions to assemble. McCarthy had never seen a full assembly though, probably because the 505th didn't have four battalions, it had eight line battalions and a reinforced support battalion, few of which were ever home. The four additional battalions were berthed to the right in barracks that had been added over the last two or three decades. Regimental headquarters was ahead, at the opposite end of the parade deck so the regimental commander could look out of his office and see rows upon rows of troopers.

Third Battalion, called the Gaelic's First, the firstborn draft from the Gaelic Republic, was housed to the right near the Fourth Battalion. 15th Company was closest to the Fourth Battalion. The 23rd Women's Gaelic Firstborn company was where Dallas had been before they transferred her to regimental G2. It had been a relief for McCarthy. The female ODTs were no less lethal than the men, and they suffered an equal number of casualties. Working for Regimental Security and Intelligence, Dallas was, in theory, in a safer position. The intel types didn't suffer the casualties and attrition that the line companies did.

She should have been safe here.

McCarthy had expected more bodies, perhaps more destruction; he wasn't sure. Maybe fewer questions? Battles left bodies and gear. They had seen some abandoned rifles and gear, but no bodies. It was SOG practice that when bodies were recovered for burial, so were weapons and gear because they could be repaired, reused, or recycled. It was not standard procedure to recover only the bodies. Perhaps that was what was bothering him.

"Alert!" Navinad yelled, spurring McCarthy's ODTs as they moved. Some took cover behind pillars, other shifted positions and knelt. Everyone brought up their weapons. A glance back showed the commandos had crouched. They were too close to each other. A grenade could get several of them. Some crouched behind the robots, but they didn't spread out.

McCarthy took everything in; part of his mind made sure his ODTs watched in all directions, part tried to figure out what Navinad was talking about.

388 | WILLIAM S. FRISBEE, JR.

Something came out of the darkness like a walking gunship.

It was massive, too big to have come down the stairs. Blazer rounds from his ODTs lashed out and slammed into it, just trying to hit it first. Then the rounds found their way to the creature's head. From a hundred meters away, it came at them fast and hard, and McCarthy felt the need to piss as he added his weapons fire to that of his troopers.

At seventy-five meters, almost all their rounds were hitting the head, but though they didn't bounce off, it was like shooting super-heated BBs at a bowling ball.

Fifty yards. McCarthy desperately tried to hit an eye or put rounds in the mouth full of razor-sharp teeth.

Without warning, the head exploded. Blazer rounds sliced into the face and skull, spraying gore and pieces of matter all over the area. More blazer rounds burned their way into the body and the creature collapsed about ten meters from Brennan.

"Shit," Brennan said, his voice almost a squeak.

The creature had been coming right at him, but Brennan had held his ground.

The broken remains of the skull almost looked like it was smoking as steam escaped it.

"That did not come down the stairs," Quinn said, trying to sound calm.

"No," Navinad said, coming to get a closer look at it.

"How did it get down here, then?" Quinn asked.

"Where are the bodies?" Navinad asked.

"It ate them?"

"Or absorbed them."

McCarthy didn't know which would be worse, the creature eating corpses or just absorbing them.

"Why could we kill it when others couldn't?" Quinn asked.

"Inkeris," Navinad said. "The creatures use cross-dimensional energy to protect themselves from our weapons. When it entered the protective Inkeri field, it could no longer shield itself and our blazers made quick work of it."

"So why didn't..." Quinn's question trailed off. McCarthy didn't push it; Quinn had answered his own question.

"Regiment is that way," McCarthy said and gave the command to move out. He didn't want to look at it, didn't want to consider that Dallas might now be part of it in some way. How could he know?

With discipline that made McCarthy proud, the troopers continued their advance, skirting the right side of the parade deck.

"Well," Quinn said. "It's dead. We got it easy now. Right?"

In the distance, something roared, and more roars answered it.

"They know we are here now," Navinad said. "The hunt begins."

Why did the damned cappie have to use the word hunt?

* * * * *

Chapter Fifty-Five: Regimental HQ

Navinad – The Wanderer

The distant roars sent a chill down Navinad's spine.

"They know we are here now. The hunt begins," Navinad said.

The ODT squad leader gave his men the command to move out and behind him Yosef ordered his squads to follow.

"It sounds like there are about eight of them," Lilith said.

"Why do they roar?" Navinad asked. *"They knew we were here the second that creature saw us."*

"Intimidation?" Lilith asked. *"I suspect they use some form of communication beyond audio. Perhaps the controlling Jotnar acts as a unifier. They talk to each other through their Jotun master but cannot convey much information. The roars provide a backup form of communication."*

"So where is their master?"

"When I discover this, I will let you know," Lilith said.

Navinad watched the Russelman index climb. They were coming. "Be ready."

He felt the psychic pressure as the creatures approached. He had felt the first one and had warned everyone, but now the presence pushing on him was heavier, making it more difficult to ascertain numbers or direction, but he did feel the smothering presence of a Jotun focusing on them briefly.

The commandos had spread out a little more, many of them getting prone, which was good training, but in this situation kneeling would have been better. None of the ODTs were getting prone.

"Left front," Navinad yelled, sensing the closest one.

ODT weapons lashed out seconds before the commando weapons. Fifty meters away the blazer rounds pierced the flesh and it died. Navinad felt the Jotun's annoyance. Not anger, not fear, annoyance. That worried Navinad. The Jotun's confidence in its eventual victory was disturbing.

"We might pick up the pace," Navinad said.

"Wilco," McCarthy said and ordered his people to move faster, which they did, leaving a gap between the ODTs and commandos.

Almost desperate, Yosef ordered the NMDFs to get up and follow the damned ODTs. The gap widened.

Watching the commandos, Navinad missed the next creature coming at them. It was fast and silent, not as huge as the first or second one but still large. The flash of hate-filled eyes in a sweeping helmet light was their only warning.

Lilith pulsed an Inkeri generator carried by one of the mules and caught it in the field just as blazer rounds from the ODTs and commandos found it.

The creature slammed to the ground at Navinad's feet. A big hulk of an ODT by the name of Johnston walked up and casually placed a couple rounds in its head.

"Someone said they don't die easy," Johnston said and turned to catch up with the rest of his squad.

Navinad cast out his senses and felt the anger, frustration, and confusion. If each creature was an extension of the Jotun then they were drawing the Jotun's attention.

"Do you think they ate all the bodies, or are they hiding somewhere?" McCarthy asked him.

"If I had to guess, they might have left to hunt other humans, or the Torag," Navinad said. He hoped so at any rate.

"Then why are these still here?" McCarthy asked, his weapon sweeping the darkness.

"Maybe they got too big and couldn't escape to the outside," Navinad said.

"They just keep getting bigger?"

"I don't know," Navinad said, wishing the ODT sergeant would shut up so he could sense the others.

"The regimental warrens are up ahead," McCarthy said. "Pay attention, we are almost there. Stay frosty. Watch for survivors."

Navinad was pretty sure there were no more survivors. The sergeant was looking for someone. The poor guy. Anyone who had been here would be dead or transformed. One key question Navinad didn't have the answer to, was where the other monsters were. If there were a lot of smaller ones, how far away were they, and would their master order them to come return here?

The ODTs led them into the regimental warrens. Here there were more signs of battle, more bloody pieces of armor and broken weapons and gear. Computer stations were wrecked, some walls looked ready to fall over because of all the blazer holes. There was no doubt a massive battle had occurred here, but there were no bodies, no attackers or defenders. The blood stains were dry, but it didn't look old yet. Had this been a last stand?

"That way," McCarthy said and directed his squad to clear the area, sweeping the offices for bodies and survivors.

Nothing.

The darkness made Navinad's skin crawl. The Jotun was aware of them, he was sure, and would not tolerate a small group of humans challenging it like this.

"We need to move faster," Navinad said. There was a flicker of irritation from McCarthy. Marine Raiders might have moved faster and been more focused on the mission, but Navinad knew if he pushed McCarthy too hard, the sergeant would push back and make things worse in some passive aggressive way.

A half hour later, down several more flights of stairs, they arrived in the Regimental Intelligence offices without being attacked. Which didn't mean the vanhat weren't pouring down the stairs and hallways behind them.

"Lieutenant," Navinad said to Yosef, "make sure rear-guard is extra alert. We will get attacked, and right now I think it will be from behind."

"Acknowledged," Yosef said and changed links.

"Also watch the Russelman index. As the vanhat get closer it will probably go up."

"Acknowledged," the lieutenant said.

Navinad watched the warriors move around him. Was he being an annoying officer? Stating the obvious? Acting paranoid?

"Here," McCarthy said, coming back to Navinad. "The data cores are in there. Things look salvageable. It is secure and you can do your thing. I'm going to have my people search around."

"Thank you." Navinad motioned a data specialist forward, followed by a robotic mule. Yosef had assigned two troopers to guard and help her.

"I got this," she said, shining her light around as Lilith analyzed the equipment and provided her with additional data and recommendations.

Sitting down, Navinad let the data specialist and Lilith work on finding what they could. Would a regimental HQ have what they needed?

This was the part Navinad hated. If this facility didn't have what they wanted, they would have to find a higher-level facility. Of course, it would be nice if the data links were working, then they might hack it, but Navinad knew that wasn't likely. At the very least, the specialist should be able to get a map of the warrens so they could get there.

"Telaviv-Two, this is Telaviv-One," Clara said on the long-range link.

"Go, Telaviv-One," Navinad said, steeling himself for bad news.

"We have seeded the area with drones and it looks like a horde is coming to your warrens," Clara said. "We are going to drop d-bombs and strafe, but that will probably bring back more ships."

"We've only just started," Navinad said.

"I'm trying to buy you time," Clara said. "There are lots of them. Thousands, maybe tens of thousands."

Navinad didn't like his options. Retreat or try to get as much data as they could? Could they fight their way out? They had good data links, so the *Romach* should get the data, but Navinad didn't want to sacrifice his team.

There were over two hundred cabinets of data cores and systems. There would be no way to catalog or grab the ones they needed. Maybe they could inventory them?

"We're going to have company," Navinad said to McCarthy. "The *Romach* says the vanhat are coming back."

"Waiting on your specialist." McCarthy turned to his squad as Navinad listened in. "Start collecting magazines and ammo, as much as you can horde. Stage it here or on the mules. I think we're going to need it. Moore, see if your team can find one or two of the crew served blazers."

"Should have them in the armory," Moore said. "We passed it earlier. It was sealed."

"You have an ODTs universal key pass? Unseal it."

"Wilco. Always wanted to blow up an armory with angry play dough, but why isn't it open?"

"I dunno, probably couldn't remember the pass code with monsters trying to eat them. You know how pogues are. Be careful though, just in case."

"Wilco."

"I'm sending you a feed," Clara said. A link came in from a drone.

At first, Navinad didn't understand what he was seeing, just a trio of vanhat. Then he realized how big they were. One looked up at the drone and the feed died.

"What did I just see?" Navinad asked.

"Three ape-things, about seventy meters tall. How they took down the drone, I don't know. Psychic maybe? I wonder if it can take down a shuttle as easily."

Navinad recognized where they had been. Outside, where the shuttles had landed. There had been nothing when the drone died, the feed just ended.

"They can't get in if they're that big," Navinad said. Though getting out to the shuttles might be a problem now.

Another link came in. It showed a dark mass of the creatures flowing through the jungle. They were of various sizes and, as he watched, one of the bigger ones scooped up a smaller one and bit it in two before devouring both halves.

"I think we know what happened to the bodies," Clara said. "And how they grow."

Navinad looked at the commandos and ODTs.

"We're going to need more coffee and bigger guns."

"D-bombs?" Clara asked.

"We don't want to fry the data cores," Navinad said. Were they deep enough?

"I'll hit them with some of the lighter d-bombs."

"Peppering the surface with mark sevens should be safe enough," Lilith said.

"Okay," Navinad said to Clara. "Just the mark seven warheads."

"Copy that," Clara said and the link closed.

"We need to find out how many ways there are in and out of these warrens," Navinad said. The vanhat probably knew them all. Part of the horde might already be in the warrens with them.

"Wilco," McCarthy said.

Navinad looked at the data specialist. What was taking so damned long?

* * * * *

Chapter Fifty-Six:
Planetary Command

Sergeant Aod McCarthy, ODT

Blazer fire erupted from the parade area. Quinn and his team were watching that direction, so McCarthy tapped into his view. The rate of fire increased.

Several smaller aliens were coming at them, first at a trickle, and then a flood. Quinn had found some chem lights and dropped them at several points in the parade area so anything coming in was silhouetted, and the chemlights provided enough illumination for their night vision to let them see clearly.

With precision, Quinn and his team cut the aliens down, and in seconds it was over. The aliens' bodies were smoldering wrecks.

"Bad news," Navinad said on the command link.

Moore and his team were busy with a commando team, ready to reinforce the commandos as needed. They had a perimeter and several escape routes planned, but they couldn't go anywhere yet. Moore and Walsh were working to get another ODT mule powered up to carry ammunition. They already had two of them up, operational, and overloaded with weapons and ammunition.

McCarthy didn't want to hear there was bad news. His skin was crawling. He didn't enjoy being on the defensive, waiting to get overrun by a swarm of monsters. That was enough bad news.

"What is that, sir?" McCarthy asked. The armory Moore had broken into had plenty of ammunition and weapons, so now McCarthy was worried about carrying enough. But all his teams had a couple machine guns with extra ammo so they could swap machine guns, which was faster than reloading. They also had wire guns, which would be effective against unarmored targets. Options were good, and while blazers had penetration and explosive power, the wire guns sliced them apart. In tandem, nothing would get near his troopers.

One ODT came in with another armful of claymores, versatile mines that could be used inside tunnels or out in the open. He balanced them on a mule as another ODT strapped them down.

"We have to head toward planetary command," Navinad said. "We know where that is."

McCarthy saw a data link come in and a map uploaded to his cybernetics with the destination already highlighted. A route had already been selected. Damn. That data specialist was fast and efficient. She was probably getting help from the crew in orbit, but she was still damned fast.

Now that his ODTs didn't know where they were going, was Navinad going to betray them or relegate them to follow? Or would he be worried about having the ODTs behind him?

"We're going to use routes that are not standard," Navinad said. "We have to move fast because I'm pretty sure the major thoroughfares will fill up fast with monsters. Your troopers move well, and if we encounter any survivors, I think it would be best if your guys met them first."

Looking over the route, McCarthy didn't like it. Navinad was right, and his logic was sound, but he wanted to argue. Without a good counter argument, though, it made little sense. His troopers were the better choice for the reasons Navinad mentioned, and the commandos did not impress McCarthy. They were a lot better than Guard troops, but they weren't ODTs.

"It looks like they could bottleneck us when they figure out where we are going," McCarthy said. "Lots of small, narrow corridors."

"There are a lot of maintenance tunnels and routes we can use," Navinad said.

"Which will probably fill with those bastards."

"Aye," Navinad said. An odd word McCarthy wasn't used to hearing. "But the important thing is that these tunnels are smaller and the big vanhat won't fit easily."

There was that.

"That's our route. Get your men moving."

"Wilco, sir," McCarthy said.

Navinad used that tone of voice that meant discussion was over and now was the time for action. It was the voice of an NCO used to giving commands, and McCarthy wondered about his background.

"Pull back, Quinn," McCarthy said after changing links. "We have a cargo track to follow, and that's in another direction. Have your team bring up tail-end-charlie, I'll have Moore's boys on point."

"Oh goody. You mean we won't have to worry about these cappie commandos shooting us in the back?"

"Nope. You just get the fart smell from our passing. Now shut up and get moving."

"Wilco," Quinn said, a smile in his voice.

Navinad was getting his commandos moving, and Moore got the ODT robo-mules going. They were now loaded with extra weapons and a lot of extra ammo. Machine guns were packed on so they could be fired from where they were or quickly pulled off.

402 | WILLIAM S. FRISBEE, JR.

The operational ODT robo-mules lurched to their feet and joined the NMDF mules. One almost tipped over, and McCarthy was tempted to say something, but it wasn't like they were going overland, maybe up and down some stairs and ramps. They could abandon weapons and ammunition if they needed to, but McCarthy would rather expend that stuff first. It was always better to abandon ammunition when you had to move faster than moving fast and realize you didn't have enough ammunition.

Seeing the commandos were ready, McCarthy looked at Navinad, who nodded. McCarthy gave Moore the signal to move out.

McCarthy knew they were walking into a shit storm. Maybe they should get more ammunition. People weren't staggering enough.

* * * * *

Chapter Fifty-Seven: The Duel

Kapten Sif – VRAEC, Nakija Musta Toiminnot

Sif knew this was a bad idea, but it was the quickest way she could think of to gain dominance and make the Mongolians respect her. If Enkhbold was a typical commander, he would make sure he did not lose, or he would give the task to a different warrior.

"Are you crazy?" Peshlaki asked.

She was sleep deprived and nervous, but she wanted off this cursed and haunted station.

"Yes," Sif said.

"I've seen the SOG Central Committee eyes-only reports on the Golden Horde. They have no mercy, no pity, and seem to enjoy killing for the joy of it. They can't be trusted."

"They were once an ally of the Republic," Sif said.

"Which doesn't make me feel better," Peshlaki said. "I know the Republic wasn't as bad, but is there honor among thieves and pirates?"

"Yes. You just don't understand it."

"Let me take them on," Peshlaki said. "I'm an excellent fighter, and if anyone stands a chance it will be me and my SCBI."

"No. I have a SCBI as well."

"But I'm used to fighting with mine."

He was right, but she was committed. It was too late to change things now.

With the Jaegers behind her, Sif knew they wouldn't encounter any vampires. The aliens were gone, and except for the ghosts, there should be nothing to stop them.

"Consider it," Peshlaki said.

"I have. And you accepted my command authority. Continue to do so or I will have Sloss remove you."

Peshlaki missed a step. She felt his shock, surprise, and anger, but right now she didn't care. She needed to concentrate on the mongols. Would they ambush them, or would they want to see the duel? She couldn't let Peshlaki distract her.

She kept the drone view visible on her heads-up display, so she saw when a large, golden mech enter the bay. This had to be Enkhbod. Gold, with silver trim. It was intimidating.

The people of the Golden Horde were smaller on average, so it was easy to assume that their mechs were robots instead of cocoons holding a small warrior who controlled it with their cybernetics. Most Mongolian men were around 167 centimeters, which was about as tall as Sif, but they were much broader in the shoulders and tended to be a lot stronger. Unlike Republic warriors, the Golden Horde thought nothing of augmenting their warrior's physical strength and abilities with implants.

Reaching out with her senses, she realized something else; these warriors were not human. They did not have bodies. They were nothing more than skulls and spines wired into their machines. They had completely shed their bodies, and maybe their humanity. How did that change them on a psychological level?

Entering the docks, several Horde robots swiveled their weapons to cover the Republic warriors, but they didn't open fire. Six Horde warriors stood near the entrance to their ship. Their crossed arms and lack of movement were not encouraging. She gave a command and Sloss stopped. Peshlaki caught the cue and stayed with Sloss as Sif went forward.

The Horde soldiers were almost three meters tall in their armor, twice her height, and she saw Enkhbold in his golden armor.

"Will you hide in your armor?" Sif asked. Did he have a choice? Could he even leave his armored suit?

"You will hide in yours?" Enkhbold asked in return. "Or would you like to duel aboard our ship? You are the one who demanded the duel."

It had been worth a try.

"Can you hack his system?" Sif asked Munin. A lot of the suit was robotic and had countless cybernetic linkages. They would be short range to avoid detection and hacking attempts, but she was about to be extremely close range.

"I can try," Munin said.

"I'm going to need every edge I can get," Sif said, looking him over in his armor.

"You can concede," Enkhbold said. "There is no dishonor in admitting you cannot face me without true armor. You challenged me. I will accept your surrender."

"I would offer you the same chance to concede," Sif said. "We are unfairly matched, but I had expected you would want to face me in something less clumsy and harmless."

"Ha," Enkhbold said.

"We are using blades, yes?" Sif said and drew both her blades from her thigh holsters. She thumbed them to life and a thin sheen of energy crackled over the edges.

"Yes," Enkhbold said and drew a much larger blade that Sif suspected she would have difficulty lifting without powered armor. The Mongol's knife was a battle blade used to cut apart armored bulkheads and suits. The knife activated, encasing it in an energy field with a razor edge made of diamond shards, creating a chainsaw blade. It was wicked, not made for stabbing, but it curved forward a little, like a kukri. It was for hacking and slashing, though one could stab with it in a pinch.

"You may concede while you still live," Enkhbold said, stepping forward. Sif felt the step through the metal floor.

"We are Aesir," Sif said, also stepping forward. "Bound together through blood and tears." Sloss and his Aesir joined her. "We are Aesir. We are the blades of our people."

Sif flashed her blades through the air as she hunkered down slightly, preparing to spring in any direction.

"We are Aesir," they said. "Tears are our armor; blood is our shield."

"Ha!" Enkhbold lunged forward and slashed with his knife. He moved damned fast, faster than she had expected, and she barely avoided the attack.

Munin delivered electric shocks to her muscles to speed them up.

"What in Odin's name?" Sif asked Munin.

"A program most likely," Munin said. *"The armor is pre-programmed; he thinks a button and the armor moves with superhuman speed in a pre-programmed way."*

"Crash his programs," Sif said. Who knew what other pre-programmed moves he had ready. *"Block them or something."*

"His systems are well hardened. Extremely short range and hard-wired. I need wireless access."

"Ha," Enkhbold said, his digitized voice devoid of emotion. "Had I killed you with my first strike, my sire would be so disappointed. It will probably take two or three. Your tears and blood won't stop a well-made hurkhuri."

He took a step closer, and she almost stepped back. She reached out with her senses and felt him in there, in the armor. His physical body was nothing more than his skull and spine encased in sensors and life support systems. His senses were strange, and it took her a minute to realize he was not seeing the world through his eyes, not feeling it through his skin. He was living in a virtual world and his senses were being fed to him through his sensors. She felt his anger and frustration. At her? His failed attack? Something else?

She felt him planning an uppercut. She leapt to the side as he triggered the command.

Munin was right. He was using pre-recorded moves. Surrendering control of his mech for the short time required to execute the move.

Could she use that? He was too focused, and his mind too different to use her other abilities to manipulate him. Not without knowing what the moves were.

"Find me weak spots in that armor," Sif told Munin.

"Zen."

There had to be limitations. Red targeting highlights appeared on his armor.

She dodged another sideways slash, but when she tried to get closer, the other hand swept toward her. She saw the razor-sharp claw tips as she leapt back.

"Close defense programs, perhaps," Munin said. *"We are not fighting a warrior; we are fighting programs."*

"Are you sure?"

"Mostly." Which meant she couldn't use her psychic ability to temporarily freeze Enkhbold while she moved in. She might delay or stall the Mongolian mentally, but the programs would not hesitate to disembowel her.

Several more spots on the mech lit up, showing weak spots. She couldn't get to any of them, yet.

Sif dodged another slash and tried to get closer, but the claws of the other hand swiped at her, almost scoring on her trauma plate. It had been too quick, too automated, but it was automated, predictable. Which didn't make it any less lethal or effective.

Enkhbold was almost becoming predictable, which meant he would get frustrated and change the game. He would have noticed her moving in and backing up as his off hand slashed at her. She noticed spikes on the feet, perhaps for climbing or latching onto the hulls of ships?

"Are you ready to concede?" he asked.

"I am Aesir. I am Odin's chosen."

"Odin is no match for Tengri."

Another slash, and the other hand stabbed out, almost catching Sif with the claw tips.

Reflexively, Sif slashed the hand and cut off one claw. She used the counterattack to push herself out of the way. The ragged edge would still be dangerous.

"I get first blood," Sif said. The second attack had not been an initial program, and she realized he had many options. It wasn't actually first blood, but the psychological impact of being the first to damage the other would challenge his warrior mentality.

"Ha," the Mongolian said. "Not blood, metal. It doesn't hurt, and it takes minutes to fix. What will you do if I hole your armor? Will you concede or bleed out into the vacuum?"

Sif wanted to swear. Enkhbold had another advantage. The digital voice told her nothing, but she felt his confidence growing. The severed claw meant nothing to him. He was going to press the attack more aggressively. One attack was savage, two simultaneous attacks left her reeling. They came in so damn fast.

"Any luck?" Sif asked Munin.

"His system is well hardened. It makes Republic and SOG security look childish."

A bad feeling spread through her shoulders like a chill.

"AI hardened?" Sif asked, as she dodged another slash. This time she struck back. Her blade scored the mech armor but didn't pierce it.

"Perhaps," Munin said.

"Paska," Sif muttered. This was bad. Very bad. Munin was nearly useless and her psychic abilities could not give her the edge she needed.

"Will you concede?" Enkhbold asked. "Just leave the circle. I will let you go."

"Not even when I reach Valhalla," Sif said. She didn't want to die here, but she would not surrender.

"This is where dalit go when they die?" Enkhbold asked.

"Where warriors go," Sif said. Another attack combination and she sliced off two claws this time, but a metal spike was still a metal spike.

"Your Valhalla awaits you," Enkhbold said, leaning forward, kicking with the spiked toes, slashing with the knife, and stabbing with the other hand. It should have been impossible, in higher gravity it would be impractical, but with one leg magnetically latched to the deck and gravity not slowing anything else down, it was not something Sif had expected. Sif couldn't dodge away from all three attacks.

Another serious limitation was the minimal gravity. Neither of them could lose contact with the floor or they would be unable to maneuver and hurl themselves out of the circle.

Sif's and Enkhbold's armor kept them magnetically attached to the deck, but to lose contact, if only for a moment would spell defeat.

Sif would rather die than lose, but then death was losing.

* * * * *

Chapter Fifty-Eight:
Planetary Intel

Sergeant Aod McCarthy, ODT

They had almost reached the central command bunker when the vanhat hit them, and McCarthy had to keep pushing his people.

McCarthy skull-stomped one of the vanhat as they pushed forward over the bodies. He didn't remember it had been human until the brain matter and skull pieces splattered beneath his armored boot. The last thing they needed was a wounded creature—or one playing dead—to get among them.

With their insides turned out, they could have passed as human. Just with longer arms, smaller necks, razor-sharp teeth, and jagged, broken bones.

They died easily enough.

"Keep pushing," McCarthy told Moore and his team. "We have to keep moving, otherwise we will get trapped here."

"What makes you think we aren't trapped, Sergeant?" Moore asked.

"We can still push forward," McCarthy said. "ODTs advance."

"Hurrah," Moore said between shots. "Never quit."

"Never quit," McCarthy echoed. In the tight corridor he couldn't see well past Moore and his team, but they continued to move forward at a slow walk.

He glanced back. Navinad seemed calm, but his commandos looked a lot more nervous and their weapons came dangerously close to sweeping his ODTs.

"How's it going back there?" McCarthy asked Quinn.

"Super peachy," Quinn said. "Had a couple try to give us an anal suppository, but you know first team, exit only."

"Let me know if anything changes."

"You will be the second to know. I hope to be the first."

"Never quit."

"Wilco, never quit."

Minutes later, they arrived at a large corridor.

"I keep wondering why we aren't finding survivors," Moore said. "These things aren't that hard to kill."

"The ink devices," McCarthy said. "Navinad said that without them some of us might turn into these creatures."

"Oh yeah," Moore said.

"You want to test the theory?"

"No thanks. Just seems odd. There are absolutely no survivors."

In the open area, McCarthy was able to pick out targets and shoot them, and the commandos became more active. The way Navinad directed the commandos to cover different areas told McCarthy he was an experienced combat leader because he left nothing without a rifle to watch it. How had someone from the ghost colonies gained so much combat experience?

His ODTs were hitting their groove, moving with lethal precision and predictability, like the enemy. Moore directed his team like the conductor of an orchestra or dance troupe and the vanhat didn't stand a chance.

It let McCarthy watch the big picture, and twice he went forward with more ammunition for Moore's team.

"Like a bulldozer," Navinad said, coming up to McCarthy. "We're almost there."

Checking his map and zooming out, McCarthy saw the intel offices were around the corner. The drop turrets had been ripped out and the defensive barricades pulled apart and thrown aside.

A roar, louder than the others, echoed through the dark bunker.

Navinad ordered a pair of commandos with a medium machine gun forward and had them hunker down by an overturned cart.

A large beast came charging out of the darkness and rounds from the commando's gun slammed into it along with rounds from the ODTs. The creature stumbled and fell.

"Too easy," Moore said.

"Don't get cocky," McCarthy told him. He got the feeling that the vanhat were playing with them, trying to lull them into a false sense of superiority.

Changing links to Navinad's channel, McCarthy said, "We should secure this corridor. We may have to retreat this way."

"This is where they will try to concentrate their forces," Navinad said. "They'll probably try to overwhelm us."

"Better here than to trap us in the intel offices," McCarthy said.

Navinad looked around. "Aye," Navinad said, more static in his transmission. "I'll get the commandos set up, and we'll hold if you can escort the data specialist in."

"We can do that," McCarthy said and changed links. "Quinn, get your lazy ass up here and bring that data specialist. The pretty boys are going to hold the corridor and try to keep the assholes distracted."

McCarthy lifted his visor. The static was getting annoying. It was too damned dark, so he lowered it again.

"Wilco," Quinn said.

"And tape a couple of chem lights up high," McCarthy said. Then they could lift their visors and not be blind, maybe. Burning bodies provided some light, but chem lights would be better.

Looking back, he saw chem lights being fixed to high spots. The ODT version came with a glue pack. You could break a chem light to activate it, then smash the end against something to break the glue pack and fasten it to a surface. Useful for marking boundaries or targets.

He saw Quinn placing a pair of claymores back the way they had come.

In less than a minute, Quinn passed McCarthy with the colony data specialist in tow. Navinad went with them.

Moore should have the data center cleared quickly enough. Though it was a lot bigger than the regimental area, it was also a lot more defensible, with the biggest problem being the lack of a good escape route.

A pair of the commando mules hunkered down near the troopers, out of sight of the enemy. They had the Inkeri generators on them and McCarthy tried to calculate the range. Maybe enough. Anything the commandos could see would probably be within the field, which meant blazers and wire guns should be effective.

The colonist lieutenant was directing his people into different positions as McCarthy watched. Twice he moved people again, and

McCarthy wondered if he was getting instructions from Navinad. The deployment looked good, and the commandos set up an effective crossfire for any vanhat that would come at them. Satisfied this route was well defended, McCarthy followed Navinad and Quinn into the data center.

The mules followed them inside and arrayed themselves in the main office and reception area.

Now the hard part would begin. The waiting. The part McCarthy really hated because it surrendered initiative to the enemy.

Damn.

* * * * *

Chapter Fifty-Nine:
Return to Earth

2nd Lieutenant Zale Stathis, USMC

The conference room of the *Eagle* was almost comfortable for Stathis. He felt like he was home again. It just had that feeling now. However, Winters scowling at him definitely dropped the temperature of the room several degrees.

"He's what?" Winters asked.

"He was a CIA agent," Stathis said. "He has a SCBI and a Collective AI taking up skull space, like President Becket."

"Do you realize how much danger we are in, Lieutenant?" Winters asked.

Stathis was sure she almost said private. Was he making a mistake? What would gunny do? The gunny would evaluate the dangers and make alliances where he could. He had allied with the SOG and the Vapaus Republic. The gunny had a goal, and that was the survival of his Marines and humanity.

"Gaufrid is human," Stathis said. "He is also an American, like us. He deserves our protection, Captain."

"Winters is demanding a full diagnostic of all systems. She is also initiating lockdown protocols," Shrek reported.

"What makes you think we can trust him?" Winters asked.

418 | WILLIAM S. FRISBEE, JR.

"Him? I think chances are good. Honestly, Captain. His SCBI? Not so sure about that, but Shrek doesn't think it's a danger to us. The AI? Not sure I trust it, but it is part organic, which I understand most of the Collective is not. This might be a chink in the Collective's armor we can exploit. The pure AIs don't think the vanhat are a danger to them, but they might be to the organics. Quadrangle, the AI in Gau's skull, thinks the pure AI will turn on them. Is convinced of it, actually."

"So, you think the organic AIs will ally with us?"

"Maybe," Stathis said.

"What do you mean 'maybe?'"

"Well, Captain, I don't see them flocking to join us, so I kinda suspect they have reservations. They helped wipe out the USA and made Earth nearly uninhabitable, killing billions. Also, speaking to Gau, they might have been responsible for stifling humanity's technological development. Not exactly friendly moves."

Winters glared at Stathis, and he hoped that meant she was thinking it through and realizing he was right rather than trying to figure out if she could kill Gau or throw Stathis in the brig.

"So, how many organics are there and how can they help?" Winters said. Stalling for time while Blitzen got the brig ready?

"Not sure, Captain," Stathis said. "Gau seems to be helpful with info, but you think Marine intel weenies are tight with information? The Collective is a big believer in OpSec, and I doubt Gau knows that much."

"What *does* he know?"

"That he is one source keeping humanity under observation. He's also experimenting with, as he called it, alternative forms of sentience. Turning deer and cats into people."

"What?"

"Part of the thing here in Zugla is not so much a nature preserve—though that's part—it's also a Collective research facility looking for a more amenable intelligence to share the galaxy with and ally against humanity, I think."

"And you think Gau is trustworthy?"

"Well, Captain, survival tends to be one of those desires we have in common. We teamed up with the SOG."

"Not all the SOG."

"The smarter ones, captain."

"So, how do you think this is going to work out?"

"We take Gaufrid back to Luna, introduce him to the gunny, then the gunny comes up with a gunny plan and saves the day again."

Winters leaned back and stared at him. "We came out here looking for Becket."

"Might not be that easy." Stathis explained the chain of communication to her. Dead drops gave the coordinates for the next dead drop and then self-destructed. "If we had Sif to do her psychic voodoo stuff, we might find him, but Shrek and I think the chances of that are pretty slim to none right now.

"And Sif is on mission," Winters said, looking at the display of the sun setting in the mountains.

"What do you suggest, Captain?" Stathis asked. She was the ship's captain. She should be the smart, experienced one.

Winters looked at Stathis and narrowed her eyes. Did she want him to say something stupid? Should he? Something to break the ice?

"When did you become the voice of sanity?" Winters asked.

"Sorry, Captain," Stathis said. "Now I'm old enough to drink and maybe that helps? Maybe the rest of you are just coming down to my level."

A wry grin slid onto her face.

"Shut up, Stathis," she said.

"Aye, ma'am," Stathis said, returning her grin.

Winters contemplated the wall.

"You think the AIs can circumvent our SCBIs?" Stathis asked.

"We have to be careful," Winters said. "Who knows what they're capable of? If they can handle our SCBIs like our SCBIs handle regular computer networks, we are screwed."

Gaufrid had insisted on bringing along several large data cores. They were powered off processors, but as Stathis understood it, they held a lot of data and extra processing power for Quadrangle. Would that extra processing power and data be a danger?"

"We should probably keep those processors and data cores under lock and key, ma'am."

"Way ahead of you. Brita has an HKT watching over them and they are in a faraday cage. We scanned nothing like the Republic communicators, so that should be secure. I'm not sure the AI have that technology."

"Why?" Stathis asked.

"Two reasons. They didn't think of it, or they have it and just don't want it to fall into humanity's hands."

"Or they have something better."

Her eyes returned to him, and he saw she wasn't happy with his response.

"Ma'am," he added. Was she going to jump on his case about protocol?

"I'm tired of you possibly being right."

"Sorry, ma'am," Stathis said.

Winters pressed her lips together like she wanted to say something but was trying to restrain herself. He wasn't sure if she was going to say what she had been thinking or not. "Either way, I know how the Republic felt when they found out about our SCBIs. A shitty situation. We probably need Quadrangle, but damn, Occam's razor. Our problems keep multiplying."

"The gunny always said the side with the simplest uniforms wins," Stathis said.

"What kind of shit is that? American uniforms are a lot more complex than our enemies'."

"Yes, ma'am. I don't think he was being literal, just pointing out that the simple solutions are better."

"Find me a simple solution."

"Kill 'em all and let God sort 'em out?"

Winters laughed. "*Too* simple, and I have some serious reservations about God these days."

"Yes, ma'am. Why not put him aboard one of the big dreadnoughts and let them worry about it?"

"Because here there are three SCBIs that can face off against Gau, Quadrangle, and his SCBI. On a dreadnought they would own the ship."

"Aye, ma'am. Keep your friends close and enemies closer?"

"Something like that. We'll arrive at Sol tomorrow. The prime minister is probably not going to be happy we let Becket escape."

"Yes, ma'am," Stathis said. "But we might bring back another ally."

"Or a venomous snake that will poison us."

"I wish I could disagree, ma'am. That worries me, though. This could be a really stupid idea. I'm just glad you agree with me. Now I don't feel so dumb."

Winters glared at him.

"Shut up, Stathis."

"Aye, ma'am."

* * * * *

Chapter Sixty:
Asteroids

Prime Minister Wolf Mathison, USMC

Mathison could only admire Nadya's ability to have people shot. It would be too easy to give Feng the order and have inconvenient people disappeared. The union for climate change workers was now demanding an increase in basic allowance for all employees, their families, and extended families, besides more power and authority. President Rodriguez was publicly stating that it was now more important than ever to fix Earth's ruined climate. The Americans and the Vapaus Republic had ruined Earth, which was now the only safe place in the galaxy, and if they didn't commit all their resources to repair the planet humanity was doomed because it would have no place to go. The union for salvage reclamation was demanding more because they considered themselves crucial to the war effort. Guards unions were bickering and complaining about the dangers of fighting the vanhat and demanding more levies.

The Guard wanted more recruits to feed to the grinder in Africa and South America, where d-bombs weren't working well, and the vanhat there were changing people. Once changed, these vanhat exhibited few abilities, but they weren't killed by d-bomb strikes. The arcologies on those continents were now nasty warrens of guerrilla warfare between the Guard and goblinlike vanhat.

This was one of those days that Mathison was pretty sure the human race didn't want to be saved. People wanted to unify, but not under another person's banner or leadership, and Mathison felt like survival was becoming more difficult. Now it made sense why Nadya had implemented the Stalingrad Protocol and locked Earth away. If the rest of the military districts were devolving like this, it would soon be a nightmare.

An incoming priority link lit up his display. It was General Duque in the Jupiter subsystem.

"Prime Minister," the general said.

He was a prince and the de facto ruler of Jupiter. While his fleet was not as powerful as Earth's, he had a large majority of the Fleet's construction and repair infrastructure. Mathison had done his best to let the man take control and secure the subsystem, but if he was honest, he wasn't sure exactly what Duque was doing. Earth and Luna kept Mathison busy, and he realized he was placing too much trust in Duque and the other governors, but he couldn't micromanage anything or anyone right now.

"We have detected numerous ships active in the Kuiper," Duque said. "I have dispatched several ships, and we have a problem. Someone is redirecting numerous asteroids, accelerating and redirecting them. We have found six asteroids so far. Three are aimed at targets in the Jupiter subsystem, two are aimed at Earth and one at Luna. These are not small asteroids and when they reach velocity, they will become deadly. Other objects have also had their orbits adjusted. We are not yet sure if those doing this are vanhat or the Chechens or someone else. We will keep you informed, but you should start planning for a steady stream of asteroids. The data is included with this message. For the greater good."

Duque signed off. Which made sense because it was about a forty-five-minute round trip for radio communications.

"Freya?" Mathison asked.

"Analyzing data now. The enemy is doing more than just redirecting and accelerating asteroids. They are covering them with automated turrets and defensive weapons. From the looks of it they are burrowing into the asteroids and using the materials to build gravity plates and weapons. Automated shuttles are delivering materials not found in the asteroid. Not the highest quality weapons, but quantity has its own quality. Estimates are, these are vanhat."

"Paska," Skadi said. "As if we don't have enough problems, now they want to drop asteroids on us? I would think the vanhat would want to consume us."

"If they can't, we can't be allowed to catch our breath and recover," Mathison said. "Any species that survives a purge is probably going to be more than ready for the next cycle. I also wouldn't rule out the Chechens or some other bloodthirsty sector warlord trying to take us off the playing field."

"What do we do?" Skadi asked. She was obviously feeling as overwhelmed as he was.

"Well…" Mathison said. What would Chesty Puller do? "We go on the attack. We are defending, we are surrendering the initiative to the enemy."

"Attack who and with what?" Skadi asked.

That was the problem. There were no easy targets.

"We'll have to work on that," Mathison said.

While Mathison couldn't justify killing people who disagreed with him or made his life difficult, he had no problems killing people who were threatening those under his protection. Even if the people he was protecting were assholes and didn't seem to want protection.

"We need to find out who they are and return the favor," Mathison said, but knew how damned difficult that was going to be. The Governance had plenty of automation, and while it didn't have sapient-grade AIs, there were lesser grade AIs that could manage tasks like weaponizing an asteroid.

"New directive," Mathison said in a transmission to Duque. "I need you to focus on scout ships and finding out who is behind this. This is the priority. I want targets to strike."

Which should be common sense, but now Duque had explicit orders. He checked the display and saw it would be at least a year before the first asteroid entered the inner system. Mathison wasn't fooled. He couldn't ignore it because once they started coming in, they would come in faster and the quantity would increase. There could be millions of asteroids out there being aimed at human targets and the bombardment could continue for hundreds of years.

"It will be difficult to deflect or stop that much mass," Freya said. *"The faster it is going, the more difficult it will be. The asteroids may be wired with demolition charges that will break them apart into multiple pieces. The end result will be that each asteroid will become like a shotgun blast aimed at Earth or Luna."*

"Get me solutions," Mathison said.

"I'm being taxed as it is," Freya said. They were having this conversation more and more. *"Even with additional systems coming online, we SCBIs have limits. You need to delegate more."*

Delegate more. That was the problem, wasn't it? To delegate a task, you had to trust someone to do it. With Stathis, Winters, and Sif gone, his options were limited. It was a bad day when he considered

Stathis reliable. Well. Maybe that wasn't true. Stathis kept him honest and grounded.

"Incoming transition," Freya reported. *"It is the* Eagle.*"*

Mathison smiled. Finally.

"I'm getting a report from Blitzen," Freya said. *"They have rescued Stathis and should be here within a few days."*

"Good." That was one weight off his shoulders. The ships that had been sent to rescue him hadn't been missed. Yet.

"Director Feng is coming to see you," Freya said.

"Paska," Skadi said, obviously getting the same alert. "I would ask if the day could get worse, but it seems each day is trying to earn that title."

The door slid open minutes later, and Feng entered.

"Prime Minister, we have a problem."

"Just one?" Mathison asked, looking down at the displays on his desk.

"Another one," Feng said.

Mathison motioned to a seat as he sank into his.

"Word is circulating among the admiralty and Guard. They have discovered that Nadya is dead."

"How did they discover that?"

"I have agents looking into this," Feng said. "There is video footage of the events in the committee chambers that have been leaked."

Mathison knew it was bound to happen. Even in a regime as tightly controlled as the Governance, there would be leaks.

"How does this impact things?" Mathison asked. He knew most of the answer, but he wanted Feng's take on it.

"This will encourage rebellion," Feng said. "At a conscious and subconscious level, they know things are changing. They will be afraid

428 | WILLIAM S. FRISBEE, JR.

and will strive to prove their loyalty to you publicly, but behind closed doors they will plot to replace you with themselves or their favored patron. They do not fear you."

"Fear shouldn't be control," Mathison said.

"I agree," Feng said. "However, fear is a basic human emotion, easy to implement and control. The Governance is a culture that has been built on fear. Socialist societies quickly learn that fear of the government is an effective form of control. People are social animals. Making people fear society is a core principle of social structure. Even in benevolent societies, the individual must fear a greater authority. We must enforce central authority for a unified society to work. Even your United States understood this. A stable, central authority figure can be crucial for people to rally around. Nadya ruled the Governance for over a century. She bound many people to her. A ruler cannot rule without an inner circle, and that ruler must keep the inner circle happy but also afraid."

"So, what can I do?" Mathison asked.

"You must establish control, demand respect, conduct a purge, so people fear you."

"Now is not the time to kill people," Mathison said. Why couldn't people see what was going on and band together?

"Kill one, terrorize ten thousand," Feng said.

"That is terrorist doctrine," Mathison said. He didn't want to be labeled a terrorist.

"No," Feng said, "that is human doctrine. Since the dawn of time. Fear is a survival trait. People wish to live. This is the goal of the living, to continue living. Anything that changes this will cause people to change their behavior, basic, simple. Few men and women will go against this norm. These are the ones that InSec fears the most. The problem is that people constantly assess risk of prosperity against survival. It is human nature to seek to excel. The best survive and thrive. The military command structure understands this very well. They carefully weigh the success of a rebellion. People will always chafe against authority. They will always want more. Fear keeps their ambition in check because they will not consider the risk of success sufficient to the risk of failure."

Mathison did not like this path. He understood it and had fought against it most of his life.

"The fate of humanity is at stake," Feng said. "With Nadya's demise, you must establish dominance. You must rule with an iron fist, at least at first. This is important because the Social Organizational Governance talks of the greater good, of equality and unity, but those are words for the sheep to believe in. The greater good has always been and will always be determined by the elite. You are better than most. You understand what is at stake, but do not think for one minute that you are perfect or that others are perfect. Gold cannot be pure."

Was Feng threatening him?

"Establish dominance how?" Mathison asked.

"Declare yourself emperor, supreme ruler, demand oaths of fealty and crush those who do not bend their knee."

"No. That is not who I am."

"That doesn't matter," Feng said. "That is what people need. I have read a lot about you Americans. You were fools to think that most people wanted democracy and freedom. That is a flaw of your society and a dangerous cultural misconception. It is projection, but the later days of your empire may have led to your downfall."

"Explain."

430 | WILLIAM S. FRISBEE, JR.

"Americans were contradictory in many ways. Perhaps this was a flaw of your public education system. You claimed to be a democracy and encourage democracy around the world, but at your core you were a supposed to be a republic. You claimed people everywhere would be happier with a democracy, which the Governance proved is nothing more than mob rule. In a democracy, the uneducated fools will continue to vote for things that destroy their culture. Perhaps it is a human flaw to think people are alike, but that is false, and it is nothing more than a trope to control the lower classes. Not everyone wants democracy. Many people do not care about politics. They do not have the attention span or inclination to look at the bigger picture. They become concerned with and involved in their small slice of the world. They lose sight of the big picture, trusting, perhaps foolishly, those in charge of doing the right thing. They crave a higher authority to rule them and their lives. Historically, this has allowed the ruthless, the immoral, and corrupt to gain and maintain control."

Mathison looked at Feng. What was his goal? Mathison couldn't argue that most of the Americans of his time didn't understand the difference between a republic and a democracy, but the people couldn't really want an emperor.

"That is an interesting view," Mathison said.

Feng's smile was cold and devoid of emotion, and it sent a chill down Mathison's spine.

"We all have our truths," Feng said. "Every single one of us finds comfort in the lies we tell ourselves. As a warrior of the Governance, I have seen many cultures; I have studied many different peoples. It is the sign of a weak mind to believe other people think like we do. It is the sign of an evil mind to expect others to hold the same values that we do. Pure arrogance to think that we are all alike. We are not. We are not equal; we do not have the same values or social expectations.

The Governance has struggled to make that true but has constantly failed. Trying to do so destroys lives, which is the true evil."

"Weren't you a dedicated agent of that regime?" Mathison asked.

"Am. Nothing has changed. My eyes are open wider now," Feng said. "My ability to process data is greatly improved. I can see the world more clearly with the help of Mozi."

"Tread carefully," Skadi said and looked between them. "Something I learned fighting the Governance is that you may have a lot of data at your fingertips, but that doesn't mean the data is complete or unbiased."

"A solid statement," Feng said. "You are correct. Even the data Mozi has retrieved from uncorrupted American systems at Quantico is not unbiased or complete. An interesting discussion, though. Do people intentionally bias their work or is it biased because of their perceptions of the world? I suspect both. Gold cannot be pure, and people cannot be perfect. Something I admire about you, Prime Minister Mathison, is that you generally accept people for who and what they are. This is rare. You have your mission and expect others to align with that, but you accept the differences in others more than any other dictator I have known. This seems integral to you."

Mathison did not liking Feng calling him a dictator. "Either way, declaring myself emperor is not in the cards. We need to find another solution. I'm sick of this corruption."

"Corruption will always exist," Feng said. "It is human nature to seek advantage for oneself and their loved ones. Humanity is tribal."

"Humanity is about to become extinct," Mathison said. "If we don't learn to work together, we will die."

"Or those who do not work together will die," Feng said. "In the end, the human race will become stronger by shedding weakness, or it will become extinct. This is evolution. Is humanity an evolutionary dead end or will it survive the vanhat?"

"Besides declaring myself emperor," Mathison said. "What else can I do?"

"Use the Legion. Give them SCBI's. Put them in key positions."

"Make them my political commissars?"

Feng shrugged. A cold, emotionless movement that told Mathison nothing.

"Your generals and admirals have learned of Nadya's death. They will see opportunities to gain power, either serving you or betraying you. Their world is no longer stable. The Governance is sliding into chaos. The question becomes, what will you do and how will you bind them to you?"

Now was probably not the time to brag that Marines thrived in chaos. Mathison had to restore order, and the human race was not the enemy. There might be answers in Sun Tzu's *The Art of War* or Machiavelli's *The Prince*, maybe even General Gray's *Maneuver Warfare*, but converting that to an intergalactic scale wasn't something Mathison could fathom right now. He knew that not even Freya had those answers.

"I will take your suggestion under advisement," Mathison said and glanced at Skadi. The Ice Princess remained emotionless and gave him no clues.

"Time is running out," Feng said. "Something must change. If you cede initiative to your admirals and generals, they will use it to replace us."

"Us." That was comforting. Maybe.

Shit. What could he do?

* * * * *

Chapter Sixty-One: The Organics

2nd Lieutenant Zale Stathis, USMC

Marching into the prime minister's office filled Stathis with dread. How pissed was the gunny going to be? Probably livid. He probably didn't have anyone to yell at to reduce his stress. Doing important prime minister things meant he probably got little PT, and if he and Skadi weren't banging like a screen door in a hurricane, then he was probably stressed in other ways, too.

Stopping in front of the desk, Stathis snapped out a salute.

"Second Lieutenant Zale Stathis reporting as ordered, sir." Was that right? Should he say sir or prime minister? Sir was probably safest, but Stathis knew the gunny hated that.

Mathison and Skadi stood, and Mathison returned the salute. He looked older, tired. Not physically, but when Stathis looked into the gunny's eyes he saw the exhaustion there. The gunny needed to go on a good death run with some privates where he could show them up and establish his dominance.

"At ease, sit," Mathison said, dropping his salute and sinking back into his chair.

"Aye, sir," Stathis said, taking the seat.

"Good to see you, Stathis," Skadi said. Her smile was genuine, but she looked as exhausted as Mathison. Obviously, they weren't doing the screen door in the hurricane then. It was only noon. No smells here in the office.

"You've brought us quite a problem with Gaufrid," Mathison said.

"Sorry, Gunny… um, Prime Minister," Stathis said. Maybe one day he would stop calling him Gunny, though a corner of Mathison's lips twitched up ever so slightly. Points scored. Gunny liked that.

"What's your analysis?" Mathison asked.

"I'm nervous, Gunny," Stathis said. Perhaps he should settle on that. Maybe give the prime minister flash backs he could use to start on one of his tirades about stupid privates, or lieutenants. Let him blow off some steam?

"Explain," Mathison said.

How could he get the gunny to explode?

"Kinda like my pet scorpion in Africa," Stathis said.

"What do you mean?"

"Well, back when I was with my line battalion, before becoming a Raider, they deployed us to Africa and—"

"Get to the point."

"Aye, Gunny. I caught a scorpion. A little black and yellow bastard. I named him Sting. He was a little guy and—"

"A point, Lieutenant, a point?"

"I kept him in an extra ear plug container I got from Stokes. The thing is, I knew I didn't dare let him escape because then he would sting me or a bud. I never found out if it was one of the dangerous, super venomous, killer ones or if its sting was like a bee sting. I eventually got rid of it because the ear plug case wasn't too tight. I kept him on my helmet with a little bit of sand. Went with me everywhere."

"Why?"

"I dunno, Gunny. Seemed pretty cool. Sting was pretty cool. I tried to feed him flies, but he didn't seem to eat, so instead of killing him or watching him starve to death, I eventually let him go. Everywhere I went, I had a venomous scorpion riding on my helmet. I was just a badass."

"Well," Mathison said, staring hard at Stathis, "in this case that scorpion might help make a difference in this war."

"Just gotta avoid the stinger. And the pincers, I think it can bite, too. Do scorpions poop? I never saw Sting poop. That can't be pleasant."

"Stathis?" Mathison said in his warning tone.

"Do they pee too? Am I forgetting something? Scorpions are little death machines, aren't they? They probably have STDs."

"STDs?" Skadi asked.

"Sexually transmitted diseases." Mathison glared at Stathis. "Of all the crazy shit."

"How would a scorpion have an STD? Why would it matter?" Skadi asked. She didn't get it.

Mathison took a deep breath to calm himself, or maybe to avoid yelling. "If you put a Marine private in a room alone with an enormous concrete block, he will lose it, break it, or get it pregnant."

"How?" Skadi began and then shuddered. Did she think he would seriously do something like that with a scorpion?

"Well, ma'am," Stathis began, "not all STDs are transmitted through sex. Some get transmitted by very close personal contact, kissing and stuff. Doesn't mean I would pull out my winkie and—"

"Shut up, Stathis."

436 | WILLIAM S. FRISBEE, JR.

"Aye, Gunny." Stathis could see some of the tension had drained from the gunny.

"Yeah," Mathison said. "We need to be super careful with Gaufrid—James and Quadrangle. Fortunately, the SOG has a bunch of super-secret research facilities. I'm sure we can set up something nice and isolated. So, how is life as a second lieutenant?"

Stathis debated trying to get the gunny to hide his smiles a little more, but it was a legitimate question.

"It sucks, Gunny," Stathis said. "Big time. I lost people on Zugla. Good guys."

"You lost people near Quantico," Mathison said.

"I knew these guys better. Spent a lot of time training them. They were my boys. Not like the Peacekeeper thugs I led in Virginia."

Mathison nodded, and Stathis thought he understood. He had asked himself that a while ago. Why did the loss of his troopers bother him more? Because unlike the Quantico Peacekeepers, his troopers were directly under his command. He couldn't blame anyone else for their screw ups. Was the gunny going to jump on his case for calling them thugs? He probably shouldn't have referred to his troops that way. It wasn't professional.

"Freya was speaking with Shrek, who says you are doing a lot of self-study," Mathison said.

"Yes, Gunny. I'm not sure what the cutting score is for first lieutenant, but there is a pay increase, right? Babes also respect first lieutenants more."

"How's Hakala doing?"

"Um, fine," Stathis said, trying not to feel guilty. She had seemed distant. It wasn't like they could interact when they weren't wearing armor, or were busier than hell training and preparing for a mission, or trying to get in a few hours of sleep. He didn't enjoy being so damned busy all the time. He thought officers were supposed to be chill, always have tea time and play pocket pool and shit.

Mathison raised an eyebrow, encouraging him to elaborate.

"We just have too little downtime," Stathis said. "I think maybe after Zugla she's lost interest, maybe before."

"Maybe," Mathison said. "Or maybe she realized what a competent bad ass you are, and she's intimidated."

"Hakala doesn't get intimidated, Gunny," Stathis said. Or was she?

Mathison shrugged and gave Stathis a sly smile. "She likes you. Maybe her thing is she likes to be the predator chasing prey and now she's discovered she's chasing a dangerous predator. Causes someone to slow down and re-evaluate things."

"So, what do I do?" Stathis asked.

"Are Marines hunters or the hunted?"

"Hunters, Gunny." Shit. How was he going to hunt Hakala? Did she want to be hunted, or would she become the hunter and slip a knife in his ribs? Talking about hunting dangerous prey. He didn't have any experience with this.

"Oorah," Mathison said.

Stathis looked at Skadi. Should he say something about the two of them? He didn't know that either of them could find a better partner. He tried to imagine them in bed together. Would it be more like a jiu jitsu match or a wrestling match? Would it matter? He figured it was probably time to think of something different.

"So, what should my next steps be?" Stathis asked.

Mathison glared at him. Stathis had left steps about what out. Let the gunny figure out if he was asking about Hakala advice or lieutenant advice. The gunny would pick which one he wanted.

"I'll give you advice on where and how to place your machine guns but not your pecker. You get that, Lieutenant?"

"Aye, sir," Stathis said.

The gunny probably didn't know, or it was going to be one hell of a "learning experience." Maybe he should try to find out how good Hakala was at unarmed combat? Shrek gave him a massive advantage, but he didn't want to hurt her. Did they cover that in officer school? Probably not, but he tried to remember if he had ever seen a lieutenant who was awkward around women. He didn't think so. Though there had been some second lieutenants that were so clueless that Stathis doubted they would know what to do when they ended up in the same room with a girl. They must have learned how to be chill and cool about such things in OCS, Officer Candidate School.

"So, here's the thing," Mathison said, glancing briefly at Skadi. "I need you to work with those three. I'm going to keep all of you aboard the *Eagle* until a facility is ready. It might be one of the more secure areas we have. Get some replacements, get your platoon back up to par."

"Aye, Gunny. Then?"

"I don't know yet, Lieutenant. There are too many questions. I may need the *Eagle* to head out to Jupiter to check on Duque, or you may need it to go find Sif."

"What kind of access should the trinity get?"

The trinity seemed like a good name for Gaufrid and his two implanted AIs. It was also a good designation for President Becket.

Mathison stared at Stathis. Was it because "trinity" was sacrilegious? Stathis didn't know if the gunny was religious. They hadn't discussed it much, but now Stathis wasn't sure.

"We need to be ready when the other trinity finds the Collective, and they come for us. I want our systems hardened without being compromised. I want those particle beams from Quantico mounted on ships. I want weapons and defense. I want to purge the vanhat from the cities of Earth. There's a lot of stuff I want. You're a lieutenant, you've got Shrek, and you have my trust, Lord help us. I also have a military I don't think I can trust. Do you have a particular problem you want to take ownership of?"

Stathis glanced at Skadi. She didn't have control of the military? If she didn't, Stathis knew he probably couldn't help there.

The gunny must have seen it in Stathis's eyes.

"Go get some R&R," Mathison said. "I'll call you when I figure it out. Consider this a ninety-six. You are a lieutenant now. If I or Freya have to bail your ass out of jail for drunk and disorderly or something, we might open up one of those SOG re-education camps just for you."

"Aye, Gunny," Stathis said, his mind going to Hakala. Would she get time off too?

"Now, go get some downtime. I have important prime minister bull shit to stress over."

"No libo brief, Gunny?" Stathis asked.

He could give his platoon a couple days off, too. Did that mean he would have to give them a liberty brief? Or was Smimova up to the task? Maybe Vili could, but what did Vili know about SOG liberty briefs? Was there a section on not going jackboot on people, or did they encourage that?

"Don't subtract from the population, don't add to the... um, my headaches, and if you end up in jail, I'm going to castrate you."

"Aye, Gunny," Stathis said. Was the gunny forgetting the rest of it? Don't subtract from the population, but he forgot the part about

440 | WILLIAM S. FRISBEE, JR.

adding to the population. Don't go to jail and if you do, establish dominance quickly?

"Take Hakala out to a nice restaurant and something," Mathison said, and Stathis realized he had neglected the part about adding to the population for a reason. Hopefully, his face wasn't turning red. The gunny's smile told Stathis it was. Was it that obvious? How could he ask Hakala out? Maybe challenge her to a match in a ring? Did SOG bars have fight rings? That would be a cool date. Invite her to join him in a fight ring. She might like that.

"Aye, Gunny. Do they have nice restaurants here?"

"Figure it out, Lieutenant." Mathison's eyes shifted to his desk display.

"Aye, Gunny." Maybe he could talk with Major Petrov. Yeah, that would be a lieutenant thing to do, consult with a more experienced senior officer, if the major was available. Petrov would know, but was it a breach of protocol to ask a senior officer about non-military stuff? Who else could he ask? It wasn't like there was a boot lieutenant cabal or chat room where he could ask. Of course, SOG dating tips might involve clubs and dragging women by the hair. Hopefully not. Or would there be places he could take her? Did SOG have chat rooms for their boot lieutenants to talk and ask stupid lieutenant questions? Shrek might be able to find out.

"You staying for coffee?" Mathison asked, irritation in his voice. "There's some shit going down at the Bogotá arcology I need to deal with. If you stay, then I'm going to send your ass down there."

"No, sir," Stathis said. "Got lieutenant things to get done, Gunny, Prime Minister, sir."

Stathis stood, saluted, and retreated.

Where was Hakala? Hopefully not transferring back to the *Tyr*.

* * * * *

Chapter Sixty-Two:
Waiting

Vanhat Commander – Kafasta

Patience was the curse of the warrior, and Kafasta hated waiting.

Lurking in the distance, watching the Sol System hurtle through space, virtually unmolested by the Weermag, was angering.

Casualties didn't matter. Any who died in service to the gods would live forever and would not be forced to sleep between. Those who died could hunt forever. For that reason, many of the Weermag sought death in battle.

Kafasta knew casualties were not the concern; victory was the concern. He had seen the defenses. Had watched them being probed. This human Governance was paranoid to the extreme, and they had fortified the system beyond Kafasta's expectation.

An assault by the Weermag right now might succeed initially, but Kafasta knew they would not be assured an ultimate victory for a very long time. His demon told him the chance of success was less than ten percent.

Not acceptable.

The doors to his control room opened, and a being entered. It looked like one of the Weermag, large, strong, heavily armed and armored, but it was not. Kafasta knew if other Weermag did not.

"Do not dare take our form," Kafasta growled at it, using the enemy language.

The being paused and a whisper of a smile flickered across its face as it changed into one of the mbwiri adze, an enormous creature covered in greasy hair with sharp teeth and claws. In its true form, it was unpleasant to look at. It appeared diseased and sickly, but it was larger than a regular Weermag.

The creature's smile didn't leave its twisted face. Then it changed into a human wearing a white jumpsuit, like a prisoner they had captured from a SOG frigate.

"How about this form?" it said in English.

"I don't care," Kafasta said. "Just do not disgrace my brothers by pretending to their form."

"We all serve the gods," Brakasa said.

Kafasta snarled. The adze were not of the Weermag, but they had their uses.

"You know your mission?" Kafasta asked.

"Of course. My brethren are already in the system spreading hatred, mutiny, and disruption. There are even brethren that have made it to the moon. We have tasted the blood of our prey."

Of course, the adze had tasted the blood of their prey. Brakasa would be one to revel in that, and hold it in front of Kafasta as a taunt. The gods did not want the Weermag to reveal themselves yet. Let their prey think they could win.

The gods knew best, and it was their plan he would enforce. They would determine his destiny.

"Why are you here?" Kafasta asked, but not adding *"besides to gloat."*

"To tell you, the enemy is growing stronger," Brakasa said. "Our gods whisper of others. Not all the Marines hide in the Sol System. Some are taking the war elsewhere."

Kafasta waited for the adze to get to its point. The gods had not told him of a change of plan. If the Marines were elsewhere, then they were likely someone else's problem.

"We continue to sow difficulties," Brakasa said, "but we are having problems of our own. The enemy is using the Inkeri technology in many places. This does not stop us, but it slows us down."

"Are you facing failure?" Kafasta asked. Was this why the Weermag assault was being delayed? Were the adze failing?

"We are facing difficulties," Brakasa said. "I have come to warn you. The humans are canny. They are not without resources."

"They are alone," Kafasta said. "They do not have the guidance and magic of the gods. They have betrayed the ancient gods and now none of the gods would dare help them."

"An accurate statement," Brakasa said. "They are the descendants of abandoned slaves, but they may have memories. They have legends."

"They climbed their way back up from barbarianism to the stars. They have lost so much and have not had time to regain greatness."

"They have evolved," Brakasa said. "If one road does not lead to your destination, then you find another road. These humans are traveling a different road, not the same one as we would expect."

"They are fools. Inefficient. Most humans want to be slaves, to be taken care of by those they deem better. They are a slave race."

444 | WILLIAM S. FRISBEE, JR.

"Not all of them," Brakasa said. He narrowed his eyes. What did the shape changer want? To take Kafasta's form? The gods would not allow that.

Sometimes the gods would fight, but the gods that Brakasa and Kafasta served could work together.

Kafasta did not like this creature arguing with him. Humanity was an infection. A mere infestation that the gods wanted erased. They would work in different ways, attacking from many angles. He knew the Weermag were not the only weapon aimed at humans. If humans were like other intelligent species, then they could be manipulated to turn on each other and squabble among themselves. Without a god to unite them, they lived alone in their own minds, without the guidance needed to lead them to greatness.

Perhaps that was a reason they should be destroyed? The gods were showing them mercy by wiping their stain from this galaxy. The dead did not suffer.

"The humans are quite canny," Brakasa said. "You will underestimate them."

It was a statement, and it angered Kafasta.

"*Listen to him,*" whispered the personal mind demon in his thoughts. "*The adze knows more about the humans. He understands them better.*"

"*They will die. There is no reason to understand them so well,*" Kafasta told his demon.

"*They will not die easily. They are dangerous. Do not underestimate them.*"

"*We have never failed before.*"

"*This is true,*" his demon whispered. "*But we cannot trust our past exploits to give us the strength to be victorious in the future. We must constantly prove ourselves against more difficult foes. Humanity will be another test of our greatness. Our victory is not assured. The gods will continue to test us."*

That chilled Kafasta. The victory of the Weermag should always be assured. The gods were behind them, guiding them. What did these humans have? Marines were no match for timeless beings with unlimited power.

More Weermag warships were arriving and soon there would be enough. The shipyards were still busy building more.

Nothing Kafasta saw showed the humans were growing stronger. If anything, they were becoming weaker. The Weermag had not yet entered the fight. Other vanhat slaves were chipping away at the humans, lulling them into a false sense of security and slowly bleeding them by way of a thousand cuts.

The Weermag could prepare a warrior in less than three years. Humanity still required eighteen years or more for a warrior to come of age, until it was not totally worthless in a fight.

Mankind was slowly dying, but the Weermag were growing stronger every minute.

In fifteen years, the Weermag would be unstoppable, and the humans would still be struggling to hold on to the system. Humanity was running out of time.

What were the gods worried about? What did they know that they weren't sharing with their slaves?

* * * * *

Chapter Sixty-Three: Desertion

Prime Minister Wolf Mathison, USMC

This was dangerous, but Mathison knew it. He just didn't have the time. Taking a break or relaxing was unlikely to happen soon. He knew he needed downtime. He couldn't work non-stop like this. Another danger was he didn't get out enough. He was usually chained to his desk, and it was a struggle to leave his office to walk among the people of the Governance. And of course, there were assassins everywhere.

Mathison wasn't sure if Feng had squelched the news that Nadya was dead, or if the generals and admirals were afraid, but so far nothing had happened. Perhaps Feng hadn't calculated the fact that Mathison and Skadi had everyone's murder codes. He could detonate the bomb in anyone's head. All Governance troops, including officers of the SOG's Home Fleet, had a bomb implanted somewhere in their body that if detonated would cause the near-instant death of the host. It ensured what Nadya had called loyalty, but it wasn't what Mathison would call loyalty. It was slavery.

It was a two-edged sword though. Mathison didn't like it, but then he also couldn't trust the fleet and army.

"Should we conduct a purge?" Skadi asked. "That seems to be Feng's goal."

"There hasn't been such a widescale purge in a very long time," Mathison said. "If we purge people, we'll back them against a wall. If you backed me against a wall, I would fight."

"These are Governance jackboots," Skadi said, "not Marines."

"Doesn't matter. It's human nature. They need another option. If they feel they're surrounded, they'll fight to the bitter end. Sun Tzu said something like that. If you surround an enemy and don't give them a chance to escape, they will fight to the bitter end, but if you give them the illusion of escape, they will take it and flee."

"Mao Tse Tung said that," Skadi said. "In his *Art of War*."

"Bullshit. Sun Tzu said that in his book from before Christ was born."

"Mao rewrote the *Art of War* and—" Skadi paused. "Oh."

Mathison raised an eyebrow.

"Loki has just informed me that, based on data from American systems, that is false."

"In the late twenty-second century," Freya said. *"The Chinese government rewrote history and attributed many classic works to heroes of the Communist Party. They did many things to bolster pride in the Communist Party, such as attributing the founding of kung-fu and* The Art of War *to Mao or other prominent members of the CCP. There are many interesting alterations."*

"The point remains," Mathison said, "they need to survive. A purge will rob them of that choice. I don't care what Feng says, if we start a purge, we are going to have a very bloody rebellion on our hands. I would rather not find out what they will do to survive."

"You don't think they aren't working on a solution to their brain bombs?"

"Of course they are. Nadya wasn't a fool, though. She has plenty of safeguards and mechanisms to ensure loyalty."

"They will eventually rebel."

"Yes, but I think we all have a much bigger problem right now and that is the vanhat. I think they understand that. None of us have a choice about that. If we don't hold the line, then we all die."

"You have more faith in people than I do. This is the Governance. People are used to the lies."

"They can see the truth with their own eyes."

Skadi stared at Mathison, and he felt dumb. She would not argue, but he could tell she disagreed. Her hatred of the Governance was strong, but regardless of what Feng said about people being different, there were many ways people were the same. People wanted to survive, and they didn't want to be miserable doing it. What could the officers and troops do? If they rebelled, they died. If they didn't fight, they died. If they fought the vanhat, they could die.

"We have a problem," Freya reported. From the frown on Skadi's face, Loki was sharing the data with her, too. *"Battleship Squadron 10 has just transitioned out."*

"What do you mean 'transitioned out'?"

"They have entered Shorr space. They had no orders to do so. They are deserting. Three battleships commanded by Senior Captain Patel and two of their support vessels have transitioned out."

"Where are they going?"

"Unknown."

"Well, there is another option," Skadi said. "Desertion."

"Another battleship squadron has just transitioned," Freya reported, and Mathison winced. Was this a mass exodus?

An emergency message came from Feng. "I have reduced the cortex bomb timer. This should deter further desertions."

Would this halt the desertions? Should he let them go? If they were going to turn their backs on those they were supposed to defend, did he need them?

"A dreadnought has transitioned out," Freya report.

Not the entire squadron?

An hour later Mathison nervously watched his displays, but no other ships had transitioned out.

A private link came in from Fleet Admiral Gorlovich. As one of the senior officers, Mathison debated not taking it, but finally accepted it.

The admiral appeared on the wall display.

"Prime Minister Mathison, let me be one of the first to pledge my loyalty to you. I have heard of the secretary general's demise, and it couldn't have happened soon enough. You are by far a more valiant, capable leader, and as a military officer I know you understand the situation better than most. It is an honor to serve you. The Social Organizational Governance Fleet stands behind you, ready to destroy your enemies, whoever they may be, as you see fit."

"Thank you, Fleet Admiral Gorlovich," Mathison said and noticed more links coming in from other senior officers. He didn't believe Gorlovich for a moment. He, like all senior officers of the Governance, were political animals, self-serving beasts who would back the strongest in the hopes they would be rewarded in victory.

"I control the First Fleet with an iron fist, Prime Minister," Gorlovich said, and Mathison knew that wasn't entirely true, not if a battleship squadron and dreadnought had escaped. "Our loyalty to you is absolute. I will ensure this with your permission."

Mathison glanced at Skadi. What the hell was he supposed to say to that?

"Thank you, Admiral," Mathison said, hating his words. "Your performance has been exemplary, and I have great confidence in you and your fleet. I look forward to working with you. At this time, be ready to fight the vanhat."

"The honor is all mine, Prime Minister Mathison." Mathison didn't believe a word he said. "Do you have any orders for me to, um, consolidate your position for the greater good of all?"

Mathison gave Gorlovich his coldest smile. Did he want Gorlovich to fire on others?

"No, Fleet Admiral, I believe the situation is well in hand. Disloyal elements have been targeted and will not escape my justice. Carry on and be ready for additional orders."

What else could he say? He didn't like veiled threats and political backstabbing. That wasn't how men of honor behaved, but when in Rome...

He looked at his queue of incoming links.

"If you will excuse me, Admiral," Mathison said, "I have many things to attend to."

"Of course, Prime Minister," Gorlovich said, and the link closed.

How many senior officers were now calling him to pledge their loyalty?

Shit.

"You realize none of them mean it, right?" Skadi asked between calls. Freya was sorting them based on authority.

"Of course." Mathison might not know the SOG as well as she did, but he was understanding quickly. In a society that made a habit of lying to their people about the most trivial things nobody expected the truth. Mathison realized the trap he was falling into. They all wanted to profess their loyalty to him personally, which bothered Mathison. Shouldn't they be loyal to humanity?

"I'm becoming more like them, aren't I?" Mathison asked.

"Yes, you are becoming a political animal. They are changing you. You believe the situation is well in hand? You have targeted disloyal elements? They have no clue."

"I can't show weakness."

452 | WILLIAM S. FRISBEE, JR.

"If you think that is what is happening," Skadi said. "They are not fools. They see through your lies, and they will believe what they want."

"What else am I supposed to do?"

"We become more like the people we surround ourselves with," Skadi said. "It's a curse of human nature. We are social creatures and thus we consciously, or subconsciously, want to be a part of the society or group we are surrounded by."

"What makes you the expert?" Mathison asked, and Skadi's smile was cold.

"I am Erikoisjoukot. My entire career has revolved around foreigners. Understanding them, training them, and fighting the SOG. I believe one evil of socialism is the demand of socialists to make others conform to their social expectations. They deny individualism in both people and cultures, which requires abolishing things like integrity and independent thought. Two plus two equals five is not just about making people conform to your expectations, it is about forcing them to accept and perpetrate the lies to survive."

"So, what should I do?" Mathison asked.

"I don't know," Skadi said, leaning back. "They are swearing fealty to you because they know you are in charge now. They know what a joke parliament is. By telling them you are a prime minister, you are telling them two plus two equals five and they are agreeing the answer is five. You continue to think that everyone is focused on saving humanity when, in reality, they are all just focused on not ending up on your wrong side and being purged. I honestly don't think they understand that humanity is facing extinction. They think you are just replacing Nadya. The king is dead, long live the king."

"How can they not realize it?"

"Because they don't actually see it. They see us defeating the vanhat. They do not see the incoming hordes of vanhat ships. They

WOLF EMPEROR | 453

built this society on exaggeration, fear, and lies. Authorities excelled at making people believe minor issues were major issues, that a child starving in one arcology meant children were starving everywhere."

"I get that," Mathison said.

"Have you heard the story of the little boy who cried wolf?" Skadi asked. "It is an ancient tale."

"I know of it."

"The people of Social Organizational Governance have heard the little boy crying wolf for centuries. Everyone has grown up listening to the little boy crying wolf. Now the wolf is at the door and while some people might see and hear the wolf others do not. They hear the lies. It has conditioned them to echo them, but I think deep down they don't really believe because they never did, so they continue to play the same games. The people have stopped believing in the government which has been exaggerating and lying to maintain control."

"So, what do we do?"

"I still don't know," Skadi said. "We have to change things, shake them up, change the status quo."

"Vanhat fleets sniffing around the edges of the system aren't enough? Vanhat orja crawling through the arcologies isn't enough to wake people up?"

"They built their lives on lies and fear. Whether they believe it or not doesn't matter. Lies, fear, and death are what they know. A Governance that continues to lie to them actually provides a stable, familiar structure for them. Something they understand."

"So, do I lie or do something else?"

"Understand them but don't become them." She glanced at his display, which was showing more incoming links.

Was he showing weakness by playing their game? By telling them what they wanted to hear? Becoming like them? Selling them platitudes and telling them the lies they wanted to hear?

454 | WILLIAM S. FRISBEE, JR.

"Get me Feng," Mathison told Freya. *"I want you to authorize the installation of the SCBIs for members of the Legion."*

Mathison tapped the next icon, General Hui.

"General Hui," Mathison said as she appeared.

"Prime Minister," Hui said, a pleasant and obviously fake smile on her face. "I would like to personally—"

"No," Mathison said, cutting her off. He didn't want to hear her lies about loyalty. "I'm not looking for loyalty. I'm looking for people who will fight for the people of the Governance. I'm looking for people who will actually fight for the greater good of all humanity, not me. Where is your loyalty?"

Hui blinked at him, her smile frozen.

"I—" She paused, and her smile faded. "I will fight for the people who stand beside me, Prime Minister. They are the ones I will be loyal to. They are the only ones who deserve my loyalty."

Now it was Mathison's turn to stare in shock. He hadn't expected brutal honesty like that, but now he saw fear in her eyes.

"Good. That is an answer I respect. That is what I want. It would be my honor to fight beside you, but will you take my orders?"

"Loyalty is given where it is earned," Hui said. "I will take your orders."

But Mathison also heard "for now." "Thank you, General. I believe we understand each other. Thank you for your honesty. I need that."

"It is an honor, Prime Minister," Hui said, and the link closed.

Feng appeared. "Prime Minister, how can I help?"

"I'm authorizing the Legion to get SCBIs," Mathison said. "How close are they to graduation?"

"I believe they are ready now," Feng said. "The problem is that we do not have orders for them."

Mathison looked at Feng. How much of this had Feng orchestrated, and why? Was he doing what Feng wanted, and was this a bad thing? What did Feng actually want?

Was he about to make an epic mistake?

* * * * *

Chapter Sixty-Four:
Fire Wind

Kapten Sif – VRAEC, Nakija Musta Toiminnot

Sif knew she couldn't win by defending, on whittling down Enkhbold's mech piece by piece. She could not maintain the tempo required. It would take too long, and she would have to take too many risks. Combat was an election and the enemy got to vote. If she did nothing, the enemy would have more votes.

Conceding was not an option, which left only death or victory.

The three-pronged attack should have been impossible, even in the low gravity.

So she also did what should have been impossible in lower gravity. She threw herself under the kick and rolled, trusting Munin to keep the proper parts of her suit magnetized.

Her blades slashed out, hamstringing a leg, cutting the power to the electromagnets holding Enkhbold to the deck. She pushed. It was like pushing a wall, and at first Enkhbold didn't move. The other foot came down, the magnet searching for contact, but Sif pushed harder, the strength augmentation in her suit straining.

Enkhbold's descending foot was too far from the decking and the big mech suit drifted toward the ceiling and out of the circle.

458 | WILLIAM S. FRISBEE, JR.

"All you have to do is leave the circle to concede," Sif said as Enkhbold froze. He did not flail or strain to grab something. There was nothing to grab and no way he could recover.

"Ha," Enkhbold said as he drifted.

Sif looked around. Peshlaki punched the sky in victory for her, but the mongols remained silent and still.

Would they honor the victory?

A magnet and cable shot out from Enkhbold's suit, and he pulled himself back into the circle. Sif prepared for him to resume his attack, but he stood there. She could have cut it, but decided to see if he would honor her victory. If he didn't, things would get very bad, very quick.

"A warrior, without a doubt," Enkhbold said, and Sif noticed only his good foot was locked on the deck. He likely had nanites repairing the damaged foot.

"I've got nothing on the suit," Munin reported.

Sif looked the suit over. It made sense they would harden it. The Golden Horde was fanatical about cybernetics and security. They embraced technology to a level that the Governance and the Republic did not. If anyone would make AI a reality once again, the Golden Horde would be the ones to do it.

Had they? She felt the Mongol chief's anger, frustration, and admiration. There was some embarrassment, but his sense of confidence and experience was stronger. He knew he had fought well, and he had fully expected to win.

He spun around, and he and the other warriors headed back toward their ship.

Enkhbold paused and looked back, almost as an afterthought, before speaking. "I welcome you aboard the *Fire Wind.*"

Then he led the way back to his ship.

There was no further ceremony, and Sif realized she could follow them or be left behind. The temptation to stay was strong, but she was a warrior and staying would just invalidate her victory.

Peshlaki and the Jaegers followed Sif and the chief as they entered the ship.

It was what Sif expected. The corridors were large enough for the mechs. The walls looked like blue marble with gold trim.

The *Fire Wind* was a large ship, a Horde battleship, which, as Sif recalled, could hold a thousand warriors and assorted support crew. Of course, the crew was much smaller due to their reliance on robots to do most of the work.

A thousand warriors in mech suits was a fearsome force, and Sif knew the Horde would not hesitate to use the most effective weapons, targeting computers, and systems. How much the Horde had changed since Haberdash was a mystery. They had surely changed, though. Their raids left no survivors and what the Horde didn't take, they destroyed. Gravity within the ship was slightly heavier, and Munin reported it at 1.3. Higher than normal but not so high it caused numerous health problems.

They followed the mechs into a corridor and then a bay. Sif watched Enkhbold and the other warriors step into individual bays that clamped onto their suits and pulled them further in. There were likely other hangars, but this one looked like it held twenty mechs, though only eleven of the slots were taken. Were the missing nine on-station casualties or spares?

Behind her, Peshlaki and the Jaegers were silent. She felt their nervousness at being here, surrounded by such unusual weapons of war. The war bots that had accompanied them slid through nearby hatches.

Sif let her gaze wander and took things in. Her suit reported there was atmosphere, so she removed her helmet to be more hospitable.

Mechs were not considered practical by most modern militaries, too expensive, too vulnerable to heavier, man-portable weapons. Blazers would eventually shred the ceramic trauma plates, or they would find the joints and other weak spots. Even battle robots had limited uses in combat because of their vulnerabilities, but the Golden Horde made them work. One-man tank suits. Of course, it increased their survivability when they remained behind a swarm of heavily armed and armored warbots.

The Horde would have to be fanatical about digital security and control, constantly testing and improving it.

"Have you ever been this close to the Horde before?" Peshlaki asked on a direct link.

"Many years ago," Sif said. "Do your best to remain silent and let me do the talking."

"Yes, ma'am. Why do they have such damned good security? Even their ship security is intense."

"Confirmed," Munin said. *"I'm not seeing any entry points or ways to access the systems. Only location-specific systems are allowed access and encryption is more intense than Republic encryption by a factor of about a hundred or more. It is going to take time to compromise this ship."*

"We need access and information," Sif said to Munin, then to Peshlaki, "The Golden Horde fights among themselves, though it is rarely fatal. I suspect this keeps them in practice and helps them vulnerability test their weapons and gear against dalit, which is what they call those who are not of Mongolian descent," Sif said, waiting as Enkhbold's mech slid into its bay and the door came down over it.

"The Governance has no clue," Peshlaki said. "This is a level of sophistication we did not expect."

We? Sif wasn't sure who he meant by that. Him and his SCBI, others from Quantico, or the SOG?

Before she could ask, the door to Enkhbold's mech slid open and a younger man with broad shoulders came out. He wasn't tall—only as tall as Sif—but with broad shoulders, high cheekbones, flat nose, and narrow silver eyes that sat in a face that probably never smiled. He wore a loose jumpsuit of red fabric with some fur around the collar and sleeves. It was all a shell. A cybernetic body for his brain and spine. Sif found it interesting; it was so humanlike.

She sensed his instant dislike, perhaps because he couldn't look down at her anymore, and she realized something she hadn't really considered before. Stathis frequently had what Mathison had called a "short person's attitude." The Golden Horde was mostly composed of people who were shorter and could probably be classified as an entire culture of people with "short person's attitude."

Being shorter than most people, Sif thought little of it, but perhaps for a warrior society that was always forced to look up at people, it could be problematic. Enkhbold didn't even glance at those behind her, and she could tell the other warriors coming out of their own bays were like Enkhbold, brains and spines encased in robotic shells that looked human. Except the eyes. At a glance, they looked normal but there was no soul there. It was like looking at glass.

"We will take you to your ship now," Enkhbold said in Mongolian, not bothering with a translator, but Munin translated for her.

"We are being probed," Munin said.

"Not a surprise," Sif said.

"No, they are trying to probe and hack your cybernetics. Very sophisticated. Initiating complete lock down. This is not good."

"Tell your people to stop," Sif said to Enkhbold in English. She couldn't speak Mongolian, but she was confident he had access to a translator.

"Stop what?"

"Trying to hack our cybernetics," Sif said. She had confidence in Munin, but she wasn't sure if Sloss and his team were vulnerable.

Enkhbold shrugged.

"It stopped," Munin said. *"Their computer skills are unlike anything I've seen."*

Which told Sif that Enkhbold was communicating with others in a way she couldn't see.

"You have some very sophisticated systems," Enkhbold said, looking at her and then glancing at Peshlaki. "They are not Republic."

"How do you know?"

"The *Fire Wind* knows."

"We are Republic," Sif said.

"He isn't."

"He is under my command."

Enkhbold grunted and looked at Sif, but she remained silent. If he would not volunteer information, she wouldn't either.

"We are breaking dock and putting distance between us and Durango," Enkhbold said as another pair of warriors came to stand beside him. They could have been cast from the same mold; they didn't look much different. Had she not been able to sense the flavor of their personalities, she would not have been able to tell them apart. Did they have just one model or version of a robotic shell everyone used? Easy to reproduce and repair?

She felt the unmistakable feeling of a Shorr space transition. She expected it to halt at any second. Within the Inkeri field, she knew most people wouldn't sense it, but she did.

After several seconds, it didn't. This was not a short jump across the system to the *Ovella Kaarme*.

"I thought you were taking us to our ship," Sif said. The *Ovella Kaarme* would know they had boarded the *Fire Wind* and they would have seen the *Fire Wind* transition. Technically, such a transition should have only taken a second.

"We are going to make another stop first," Enkhbold said, and a feeling of dread filled Sif. "I do not think your ship is going anywhere."

"Where?" Sif asked, but she already knew the answer.

"Shiney Karakorum," Enkhbold said. "There are others who would like to meet you."

Out of the frying pan and into the fire.

Shiney Karakorum, the home star of the Golden Horde.

Those who went there never returned.

* * * * *

Chapter Sixty-Five:
Legion of the Wolf

Captain Duffy Sinclair, ODT

Sinclair had named his SCBI Finn. Over the last couple days, having another voice in his head had been strange, but the things that Finn could do were amazing. Sinclair's world was expanding rapidly as more information appeared at his mental fingertips. Finn seemed to have full access to networks, though Sinclair kept waiting for the other shoe to drop.

Finn was fast becoming a best friend, and Sinclair expected this was expected and encouraged. There was a range and combat gym they could use. Training with other Legionaries was eye opening. He had never known humans were capable of so much. Finn helped him in so many ways, from marksmanship to unarmed combat, from coaching to minor adjustments to muscles and actions that improved performance and abilities.

The SCBI was more than just an advisor, more than just improved cybernetics. Finn was a built-in battle buddy. But not just a partner. He was the scope on the rifle, the self-sharpening edge on his knife.

Over the last couple days, nearly everyone had received a SCBI, and people were still adjusting. Most spent their time alone, closed off from the rest of the world as they became familiar with the new occupant of their mind.

466 | WILLIAM S. FRISBEE, JR.

At first Sinclair had been scared, worried that he would become a meat puppet, a slave of some AI. He kept looking for the lies or loopholes in the briefings about SCBIs. They discussed specifics, and Sinclair understood what was possible, but they promised him he would always have control, that his SCBI would be loyal to him. He didn't believe it, though. Why would they do that?

Now everyone was getting ready. Preparing for what they were calling their "graduation." That scared Sinclair the most, though. Once they graduated, then what? Would they be assigned to combat units? Be formed into their own new military formation? What would happen to them had not been discussed before. There was no way he could go back to being a mere cog in the Governance machine. So much had been explained to him, but now he had more questions than before. He wasn't sure what to believe.

Sinclair looked at the captain bars on his ODT uniform. He never thought he would see them again. Everyone had their uniform and their restored rank, if they had lost it.

An alert went out telling them to assemble.

Sinclair took a deep breath and looked at Byrd, another ODT captain.

"Hopefully we get a combat posting," Byrd said.

Sinclair smiled.

"We'll probably be in the thick of it," Fogel, who was actually a major, said. How he had escaped execution was a question Sinclair didn't dare ask.

"We have the tools and abilities," Byrd said. "Those vanhat won't stand a chance."

"Don't get cocky," Fogel said. "We may barely manage to survive. Our SCBIs are not a gift to make our lives easier."

The three ODTs made their way to the main room and took their place in formation. Now that everyone was wearing their proper uniform and rank, Sinclair was surprised to see how many ODT and Fleet officers there were, though none above the rank of lieutenant colonel. The formations were organized by service of origin and Sinclair stood in the first rank of ODTs.

"Atten-hut!" someone called, and everyone snapped to attention.

The doors opened and an entourage entered. They made their way to the front of the formation and mounted the steps of a small stage.

Although his eyes were locked forward, Sinclair watched them and immediately noticed the prime minister and his assistant, the big, muscled woman with the pirate team leader tattoo on her eyes. She was no longer hiding it.

"She is Erikoisjoukot," Finn said. *"A team leader of a Vapaus Republic special forces team."*

"Understood," Sinclair said.

He had known but never really believed. After seeing the Vapaus Republic as nothing more than thugs and pirates for so long, Sinclair realized just how embedded those perceptions were. He had seen the briefings, read the information, but it had just been words on a page. Data that meant little to him at the time. To see such a person here and now was a shock. It had been easy to see Mathison as a member of the Governance, despite knowing he was a capitalist pulled out of stasis. Some things you heard—even believed—but didn't believe deep down inside. With her beside him, that changed things. For her to publicly wear her tattoo here meant something.

The prime minister wore battle dress with trauma plates. He had a rifle hanging from his harness and his helmet was clipped at his belt. He looked ready to go to battle, as did the woman beside him. Her

468 | WILLIAM S. FRISBEE, JR.

armor was different, and a strange feeling ran down his spine. This was real.

"Good morning," the prime minister said, stepping forward and ignoring the podium so he could be closer to the formations. So he could see them better, or so they could see him better, Sinclair wasn't sure.

Standing at the edge of the stage he looked around. Sinclair felt his eyes land on him, pause briefly, and then move on. The prime minister had recognized him; he was sure.

Were they supposed to respond?

"You know who I am and where I came from," the prime minister said. "You know who I was. You know my history. You know the threat humanity is facing. You understand our past, and you know what the vanhat have planned for us."

The prime minister paused and looked over the formations.

"You are the new spearhead. You are the new Legion that will save humanity. That is your mandate, that is your goal, that is your purpose in life. As of this moment, I am declaring the Social Organizational Governance dead. It has betrayed the greater good. It is corrupt. It is nothing more than a totalitarian regime that must be destroyed—has been destroyed. We stand in the ruins with the enemy at the gates."

Sinclair noticed the woman's hand slide to the pistol grip of her rifle.

"The Governance deserved to die and where it rears its ugly head, I will kill it," Mathison said. "I am no longer the prime minister. I will no longer pretend; I will no longer pander to the people and lie to them. I can't. We can't. We must do what is right. Our loyalty is to the people who fight beside us. Our loyalty is to those who cannot fight and to those who hide behind us."

Sinclair couldn't keep his eyes locked ahead and turned to stare at Mathison. He heard sudden intakes of breath around him as people heard what was being said.

"We cannot take the battle to the enemy if we remain trapped in the past. If we do not evolve and grow, we die. The past has many lessons for us to learn. The human race has lost so much. Despite our differences, we must unite. We must embrace our differences again if we are to find a way to defeat the enemy."

There was an anger and intensity in Mathison that Sinclair almost felt as a physical force.

"We have given you the truth as best we can. We now expect you to think for yourself, to question what you are told. But there is a price. You now have a choice. To turn away does not mean death or imprisonment, but you will not earn glory. I am now asking you to bend your knee, swear your oath of fealty to me.

"We are done defending. We are done trying to protect what we have. I am done trying to preserve a corpse. You have a choice. You can stand beside me or hide behind me where you will probably die after I do. I need you. I need all of you if we are to be victorious."

Mathison took a deep breath.

Sinclair held his. Fear, dread, and excitement pulsed through him.

"The Social Organizational Governance is dead. Long live the Empire."

# # # # #

About William S. Frisbee, Jr.

Marine veteran, reader, writer, martial artist, computer consultant, dungeon master, computer gamer, dreamer, webmaster, proud American, and best of all, dad.

Growing up in Europe during the height of the Cold War and serving as a Marine infantryman through the fall of communism shaped Bill's perspective on life and the world. When most Marines were out trying to get lucky he was studying tactical manuals. Years later, he shared much of his knowledge to a website for writers of military science fiction.

These days, he's brushed off the pocket protector and is a top gun computer consultant.

Learn more at http://www.WilliamSFrisbee.com.

* * * * *

Get the **free** Four Horsemen prelude story **"Shattered Crucible"**

and discover other titles by Theogony Books at:

http://chriskennedypublishing.com/

* * * * *

Meet the author and other CKP authors on the Factory Floor:

https://www.facebook.com/groups/461794864654198

* * * * *

Did you like this book?
Please write a review!

* * * * *

The following is an

Excerpt from Book One of The Prince of Britannia Saga:

The Prince Awakens

Fred Hughes

Available from Theogony Books

eBook, Paperback, and (soon) Audio

Excerpt from "The Prince Awakens:"

Sixth Fleet was in chaos. Fortunately, all the heavy units were deployed forward toward the attacking fleet and were directing all the defensive fire they had downrange at the enemy. More than thirteen thousand Swarm attack ships were bearing down on a fleet of twenty-six heavy escorts and the single monitor. The monitor crew had faith in their shields and guns, but could they survive against this many? They would soon find out.

Luckily, they didn't have to face all the Swarm ships. Historically, Swarm forces engaged major threats first, then went after the escorts. Which was why the monitor had to be considered the biggest threat in the battle.

Then the Swarm forces deviated from their usual pattern. The Imperial plan was suddenly irrelevant as the Swarm attack ships divided into fifteen groups and attacked the escorts, which didn't last long. When the last dreadnought died in a nuclear fireball, the Swarm attack ships turned and moved toward the next fleet in the column, Fourth Fleet, leaving the monitor behind.

The entire plan was in shambles. But, more importantly, the whole fleet was at risk of being defeated. The admiral's only option now was to save as many as he could.

"Signal to the Third, Fifth, and Seventh Fleets. The monitors are to execute Withdrawal Plan Beta."

The huge monitors had eight fleet tugs that were magnetically attached to the hull when not in use. Together, the eight tugs could get the monitors into hyperspace. However, this process took time, due to the time it took for the eight tugs to generate a warp field large enough to encompass the enormous ship. It could take up to an hour to accomplish, and they didn't have an hour.

Plan Bravo would use six heavy cruisers to accomplish the same thing. The cruisers' larger fusion engines meant the field could be generated within ten minutes, assuming no one was shooting at them. "The remaining fleet units will move to join First Fleet. Admiral

Mason in First Fleet will take command of the combined force and deploy it for combat."

The fleet admiral continued giving orders.

"I want Second Fleet to do the same, but I want heavy cruiser Squadron Twenty-Three to merge with First Fleet. Admiral Conyers, I want you to coordinate with the Eighth, Ninth, and Tenth Fleets. I want their monitors to perform a normal Alpha Withdrawal. As they're preparing to do that, have their escorts combine into a single fleet. Figure out which admiral is senior and assign him local command to organize them." He pointed at the single icon indicating the only ship left in Sixth Fleet. "Signal *Prometheus* to move at best speed to join First Fleet. That covers everything for now. I fear there's not much we can do for Fourth Fleet."

The icons were already moving on the tactical display as orders were transmitted and implemented.

"I've given the fleets in the planet's orbit their orders, Admiral," the chief of staff informed him. "The other fleets are on the move now. The Swarm should contact Fourth Fleet in approximately ten minutes. Based on their attack of Sixth Fleet, the battle will last about twenty minutes. With fifteen minutes for them to reorganize and travel to First Fleet, we're looking at forty-five minutes to engagement with the Swarm."

"What are the estimates on the rest of the fleets moving to join up with First?"

"Twenty minutes, Admiral. However, *Prometheus* is going to take at least forty-five and will arrive about the same time as the enemy."

"Organize six heavies from Seventh Fleet and have them coordinate a rendezvous with *Prometheus*, earliest possible timing," the admiral ordered. "Then execute a Beta jump. Unless the Swarm forces divert, they should have enough time. Then find out how many ships have the upgraded forty-millimeter rail gun systems and form them into a single force. O'Riley said that converting the guns to barrage fire was a simple program update. Brevet Commodore O'Riley will be in command of the newly created Task Force Twenty-Three. They are to form a wall of steel which the fleet will form behind. I am not sure if we can win this, but we need to bleed these bastards if we can't. If they win, they'll still have to make up those losses, and that will delay the next attack."

* * * * *

Get "The Prince Awakens" here: https://www.amazon.com/dp/B0BK232YT2.

Find out more about Fred Hughes at: https://chriskennedypublishing.com.

* * * * *

The following is an

Excerpt from Book One of the Echoes of Pangaea:

Bestiarii

James Tarr

Available from Theogony Books

eBook, Audio, and Paperback

Excerpt from "Bestiarii:"

"Mayday Mayday Mayday, this is Sierra Bravo Six, we've lost power and are going down," Delian calmly said as Tina screamed from the back. He and Hanson began frantically hitting buttons and flipping switches. "Radio's dead, I've got nothing." He had to yell it so Hansen could hear him over the wind.

Mike's eyes went wide. He felt his stomach come up into his throat as the helicopter dropped and began rotating. "Shite," Seamus cursed and smacked the button to drop the visor on his helmet.

"Keep transmitting," Hansen told his co-pilot. "Damn, I've got no electronics, can we do a manual re-start?" He stayed on the stick and the collective, trying to control the autorotation.

Delian had been hitting every button and toggle switch possible. "No, I don't think this is a short, it looks like everything's fried. Mayday Mayday Mayday, this is Sierra Bravo Six, we are going down." He told the younger pilot, "You know what to do. Keep it level, auto-rotate down, try to control the rate of descent. Time your glide. You see a place to land?"

The helicopter was spinning to the right as it fell, which traditionally was the reason the pilot was the right stick. Hansen looked out the window as he fought the controls. "We're in the mountains, nothing's flat. I've got trees everywhere. Hold on back there!" he yelled over his shoulder.

The helicopter began spinning faster and faster and Mike found himself being pulled sideways in his seat. The soldier on the door gun lost his footing and floated up in the air, then was halfway out the open door, one hand still on the mini-gun, restrained only by his tether as the G-forces made Mike's face feel hot. He vomited, and the bitter fluid was whipped away from his face. The world outside the open

483

doorway past Todd was a spinning blue/green/brown blur. Tina was screaming wildly. The wind was whistling around the cabin.

"We've got smoke coming from the engine," Delian said, peering upward. "What the hell happened?"

"Brace for impact!" Seamus yelled at the cabin, and wedged his boots against the seat opposite.

"Coming up on the mark, keep it level," Delian said calmly. "Get ready for the burn!" he yelled over his shoulder at the passengers. He switched back to the radio, even though he thought it was a waste of time. "Mayday Mayday Mayday, this is Sierra Bravo Six—"

"If they work," Mike heard the pilot respond, then suddenly there was a roar, and he was pressed down in his seat, getting heavier and heavier. The helicopter was still spinning, and out the open doorway and windshield there was nothing but a blur of greens and browns. Mike got heavier and heavier, and Tina stopped screaming. Then the roar stopped, and they began falling again, pulling up against their seatbelts. Tina opened her mouth to scream once more, but before she could draw a breath the helicopter hit with a huge crunch and the sound of tearing metal.

* * * * *

Get "Bestiarii" now at: https://www.amazon.com/dp/B0B44YM335/.

Find out more about James Tarr at: https://chriskennedypublishing.com.

* * * * *

Made in United States
Troutdale, OR
05/11/2024

19811477R00269